★

THE

MAP

of

TRUE

PLACES

★

ALSO BY BRUNONIA BARRY

The Lace Reader

THE

MAP

of

TRUE

PLACES

BRUNONIA BARRY

WILLIAM MORROW
An Imprint of HarperCollins*Publishers*

Grateful acknowledgment is made for permission to reprint excerpts from the following:

"The Harp of Aengus" by W. B. Yeats, reprinted with the permission of Scribner, a Division of Simon & Schuster, Inc., from *The Collected Works of W. B. Yeats, Volume I: The Poems, Revised,* edited by Richard J. Finneran. Copyright © 1924 by The Macmillan Company; copyright renewed © 1952 by Bertha Georgie Yeats. All rights reserved.

"Leda and the Swan" by W. B. Yeats, reprinted with the permission of Scribner, a Division of Simon & Schuster, Inc., from *The Collected Works of W. B. Yeats, Volume I: The Poems, Revised,* edited by Richard J. Finneran. Copyright © 1928 by The Macmillan Company; copyright renewed © 1956 by Georgie Yeats. All rights reserved.

"Stolen Child" by W. B. Yeats, reprinted with the permission of Scribner, a Division of Simon & Schuster, Inc., from *The Collected Works of W. B. Yeats, Volume I: The Poems, Revised*, edited by Richard J. Finneran. Copyright © New York: Scribner, 1997. All rights reserved.

HarperCollins books may be purchased for educational, business, or sales promotional use. For information please write: Special Markets Department, HarperCollins Publishers, 10 East 53rd Street, New York, NY 10022.

FIRST EDITION

Designed by Jamie Lynn Kerner

Library of Congress Cataloging-in-Publication Data has been applied for.

ISBN 978-0-06-162478-0

10 11 12 13 14   ov/rrd   10 9 8 7 6 5 4 3 2 1

For my parents, June and Jack. I miss you every day.
And, as always, for Gary.

It is not down in any map; true places never are.

—HERMAN MELVILLE

PROLOGUE

I N THE YEARS WHEN her middle name was Trouble, Zee had a
habit of stealing boats. Her father never suspected her of any wrong-
doing. He let her run free in those early days after her mother's death.
He was busy being a pirate reenactor, an odd leap for a man who'd been
a literary scholar all his life. But those were desperate times, and they
were both weary from constantly carrying their loss, unable to put it
down except in those brief moments when they could throw themselves
into something beyond the reach of their memories.

In her fantasy world, the one where she could forgive herself for
what happened that year, Zee liked to think that her father, Finch,
would have been proud of her skills as a thief. In her wildest dreams,
she pictured him joining her adventure, a huge leap for the professor,
but not for the pirate he was quickly becoming.

She had a preference for speedboats. Anything that could do over
thirty knots was fair game. There was little security back then, and
most of the keys (if there were any) were hidden somewhere on the
boats themselves, usually in the most obvious place imaginable.

The game was simple. She would pick a boat that looked fast and
sleek, give herself exactly five minutes to break in and get the engine
started, and head out of the harbor toward the ocean. Once she passed
the confines of Salem, she would open up the engine and point the bow

straight out toward Baker's Island. Later that night she would return the stolen boat.

There was only one rule. She could never return a boat to the same mooring from which she had stolen it. It was a good rule, not just because it presented an additional challenge but also because it was practical. If she put the boat back on the same mooring, she would be much more likely to get caught. Everyone knows that the last thing any good thief should do is revisit the scene of the crime.

Usually Zee would abandon the boat at one of the public wharves that lined Salem's waterfront. Often it was the one at the Willows, the first wharf you came to when you entered the harbor. But when the cops started looking for her, she began to leave the boats in other, less obvious places. Sometimes she would jump someone else's mooring. Or she would leave a boat in one of the slips at Derby Wharf, which made it easy to get away, since she lived so close.

Only one time did she mess up and misjudge the fuel level. She was all the way up by Singing Beach in Manchester when the engine died. At first she didn't believe she had run out of gas. But when she checked the fuel again, her mistake was clear. Fighting the panic that was beginning to overtake her, she tried to come up with a plan. She could easily swim to shore, but if she did, the boat would either drift out to sea or smash against the rocks. For the first time, she was afraid of getting caught. In a strange way, she was grateful that there were no other boats around, no one she could signal for help. Not knowing what else to do, she let the boat drift.

She looked up at the moonless sky, the stars brighter than she had ever seen them, their reflections dissolving in the water around her like an effervescent medicine that seemed to dissolve her panic as well. Here, floating along with the current, staring up at the heavens, she knew that everything would be all right.

When she looked back down at the horizon to get her bearings, she found she had drifted toward shore. A dark outline of something appeared in her peripheral vision, and, when she turned to face it, a wharf came into focus and, on the hill beyond it, a darkened house. She grabbed an oar and began to steer the boat in toward shore, catching the onsweep of tide that propelled it broadside toward the wharf. She grabbed the bowline and jumped, slipping and twisting her ankle a little but keeping the boat from colliding with the wharf. She tied up, securing bow and stern, and scrambled over the rocks to the beach. Then she made her way up the road toward the train station, limping a bit from her aching ankle but not really too bad, all things considered.

Zee wanted to take the train back to Salem, but it was past midnight, and the trains had stopped running. She thought about sleeping on the beach. It was a warm night. It would have been safe. But she didn't want to concern her father, who had enough to worry about these days. And she didn't want to be anywhere in the vicinity of Manchester when they found the stolen boat.

So she ended up hitchhiking back to Salem. Not a smart thing to do, she thought as she walked to the Chevy Nova that had stopped about fifty feet ahead of her and was frantically backing up.

It was a woman who picked her up, probably mid-forties, slightly overweight, with long hair and blue eyes that glowed with the light of passing cars. At first the woman said she was only going as far as Beverly. But then she changed her mind and decided to take Zee all the way home, because if she didn't she was afraid that Zee would start hitchhiking again and might be picked up by a murderer or a rapist.

As they rode down Route 127, the woman told Zee every horror story she had ever heard about hitchhiking and then made Zee give her word never to do it again. Zee promised, just to shut her up.

"That's what all the kids say, but they do it anyway," the woman said.

Zee wanted to tell her that she never hitched, that she wasn't the victim type, and that she had only thumbed a ride tonight to cover a crime she'd committed—grand theft boato. But she didn't know what other cautionary tales such a confession might unleash, so she kept her mouth shut.

As she was getting out of the car, Zee turned back to the woman. Instead of saying thank you, she said, in a voice that was straight out of a Saturday-morning cartoon show she'd watched when she was a little girl, "Will you be my mommy?"

She had meant it as a joke. But the woman broke down. She just started crying and wouldn't stop.

Zee told the woman that she was kidding. She had her own mother, she said, even though it wasn't true, not anymore.

Nothing she could say would stop the woman's tears, and so finally she said what she should have said all along: "Thank you for the ride."

Of course Zee hadn't given the woman her real address—she didn't want her getting any ideas, like maybe going into the house and having a word with Finch. She had planned to hide in the shadows until the woman drove away and then cut through the neighboring yards to get home. But in the end she just walked straight down the road. The woman was crying too hard to notice where Zee went or how she got there.

TEN YEARS LATER, AS ZEE was training to become a psycho-therapist (having outgrown the middle name Trouble), she saw the woman again in one of the panic groups run by her mentor, Dr. Liz Mattei. The woman didn't remember her, but Zee would have known her anywhere—those same translucent blue eyes, still teary. The woman had lost a child, a teenager and a runaway, she said. Her daughter had been diagnosed as bipolar, like Zee's mother, Maureen, but had refused to keep taking lithium because it made her fat. She'd been last seen hitchhiking on Route 95, heading south, holding a hand-lettered sign that read NEW YORK.

It was the winter of 2001 and ten years since the woman had lost her daughter. The Twin Towers had recently come down. The panic group had grown in size, but its original members had become oddly more calm and helpful to each other, as if their free-floating anxiety had finally taken form, and the rest of the country had begun to feel the kind of terror they'd felt every day for years. For the first time Zee could remember, people in the group actually looked at each other. And when the woman talked about her daughter, as she had every week they'd been meeting, the group finally heard her.

The world can change, just like that! the woman said.

In the blink of an eye, someone answered.

Tissues were passed. And the group cried together for the first time, crying for the girl and for her inevitable loss of innocence and, of course, for their own.

BIPOLAR DISORDER HAD RECENTLY BECOME a catchall diagnosis. While it had once been believed that the condition occurred after the onset of puberty (as it had with this woman's daughter), now children were being diagnosed as early as three years of age. Zee didn't know what she thought about that. As with many things lately, she was of two minds about it. She hadn't realized her joke until Mattei pointed it out, thinking it was intentional. No, Zee had told her. She was serious. Certainly it was a disease that needed treatment. Untreated bipolar disorder seldom led to anything but devastation. But medicating too early seemed wrong, something more in line with insurance and drug-company agendas than with the kind of help Zee had trained for years to provide.

The world-famous Dr. Mattei had long since abandoned her panic group, leaving them for Zee or one of the other psychologists to over-see. Mattei had moved on to her latest bestselling-book idea, which pro-posed the theory that the daughter will always live out the unfulfilled dreams of the mother. Even if she doesn't know what those dreams are, even if those dreams have never been expressed, this will happen, ac-cording to Mattei, with alarming regularity. It wasn't a new idea. But it was Mattei's theory that this was more *likely* to happen if those dreams were never expressed, in much the same way that *those who cannot re-member the past are condemned to repeat it.*

Zee had often wondered about the woman with the translucent eyes who came back to the panic group only once after that evening. She wondered about her unfulfilled dreams, expressed or unexpressed, and she wondered if there was something that the daughter was acting out for her mother as she herself had stood on Route 95 and accepted a ride from a stranger heading south.

Zee was glad that the woman had left the group before Mattei had brought up her latest theory. The mother blamed herself enough for her daughter's disappearance, wondering every day if she might have changed the course of events if only she'd given her daughter that one elusive thing she'd failed to provide—something tangible and even or-dinary, perhaps, like that red dress in Filene's window. Or the week away at Girl Scout camp that her daughter had begged for years ago.

No one understood the concept of "if only" better than Zee. She lived it every day, though she didn't have to search to find the elusive thing. She thought she knew what her mother had wanted that day so many years ago, what might have helped lift her out of her depression. It was a book of Yeats's poetry given to Maureen by Finch on their wed-ding day, and it was one of her mother's treasures. Zee's "if only" had worked in reverse. *If only* she hadn't gotten her mother what she wanted that day, *if only* she hadn't left her alone, Zee might have been able to save her.

PART 1:

May 2008

METHOD OF KEEPING A SHIP'S RECKONING . . .

A ship's reckoning is that account, by which it can be known at any time where the ship is, and on what course or courses she must steer to gain her port.

NATHANIEL BOWDITCH: *The American Practical Navigator*

LILLY BRAEDON WAS LATE.

Mattei poked her head through Zee's door. "It's so damned hot out there," she said. "Oh, God, you're not in session, are you?"

"I'm supposed to be," Zee said, looking at the clock. It was three-fifteen.

Mattei was re-dressing as she spoke, kicking off running shoes and pulling on her suit jacket. She walked five miles along the Charles River every afternoon, weather notwithstanding. When she was overbooked, which was a good deal of the time, she had been known to conduct her sessions while strolling along the river, calling it a walking meditation, telling patients it would be easier to open up if they didn't feel her prying eyes on them. A week after she started conducting sessions that way, every shrink in Boston was out walking with patients.

"God, not that agoraphobic again." It was another of Mattei's jokes. Fifty percent of their patients had some degree of agoraphobia, a phenomenon that made attendance poor at best and had lately prompted Mattei to start charging time and a half for missed appointments, though Zee seldom required her patients to comply with this new rule.

Mattei was trying harder than usual to make her laugh today, meaning that Zee must be frowning again. Zee's natural expression seemed to be the type of frown that inspired joke telling, often from total strangers, who always felt compelled to make her feel better somehow. Just this morning an older gentleman who had neglected to pick up his dog's poop in Louisburg Square had walked over to her and ordered her to smile.

She stared at him.

"Things can't be all that bad," he said.

If he hadn't been older than her father, Zee would have told him to get lost, that this was her natural expression, and that a man who didn't pick up his dog's excrement shouldn't be allowed to roam free. But instead she managed a vague smirk.

"So seriously, which patient?" Mattei was waiting for an answer.

"Lilly Braedon."

"Mrs. Perfect," she said. "Oh, no, I forgot, that's you."

"Not yet," Zee said a little too quickly.

"Aha!" Mattei said. "Simple, simple. Case closed. That will be three hundred and fifty dollars."

"Funny," Zee said as Mattei gathered up her running shoes and left the room.

It was Lilly Braedon's husband who had originally sought help at Dr. Mattei's clinic. People came from all over the world to be treated by her. Harvard trained, with a stint at Johns Hopkins, Mattei was a psychiatrist who had great credentials. She'd written the definitive article on bipolar disorder with panic for the *American Journal of Psychiatry*. She had also worked closely with a team of genetic researchers who had uncovered a correlation between the disease and the eighteenth chromosome, a substantial and groundbreaking discovery.

But then Mattei's career took a turn. She became fascinated by a more popular approach to psychiatry. The book she wrote during her tenth year in practice, a folksy self-help book entitled *Safe at Home,* lifted her to celebrity status. The book was inspired by a Red Sox second-stringer she had successfully treated for panic. Her practical solutions to his terror were based on biofeedback, desensitization, and sense memory.

"The world is a terrifying place," Mattei explained first to a local newscaster and later to Oprah. "And here is what you can do to stop being afraid." The book was filled with sensory tricks, tips almost too simple to inspire much credibility: carry a worry stone, smell lavender, breathe deeply. The companion CD featured guided meditations, some with music, some including nature sounds or poetry. It even quoted the old Irish prayer (the one that basically tells you not to worry about a damned thing because the worst thing that can happen is that you'll go to hell, but that's where all your friends will be anyway, so it's pointless to fret). Though Mattei herself was a loose fusion of French, Italian, and Japanese ancestry, with not a bit of Irish blood, for some reason she loved everything about the Irish. It might have been a Boston thing. She loved James Joyce and even swore she had read and understood *Finnegans Wake,* which Zee seriously doubted. That Mattei loved Guinness and U2, Zee did not doubt. Zee and her fiancé, Michael, had spent last St. Paddy's Day at a bar in Southie with Mattei and her partner, Rhonda, and Mattei had held her own, drinking with the best of Boston's Irish. And just a month ago, Mattei had come back from one of her therapy walks sporting a pair of pink Armani sunglasses that looked very similar to a pair Zee had once seen Bono wear.

Mattei had done the usual book-tour circuit. But it was when she landed on *Oprah* that things went wild. There was a growing sense of panic in this country, Mattei explained to Oprah. It was everywhere. Since 9/11, certainly. And the economy? Terrifying. "Do you know the number one fear of women?" she had asked. "Becoming homeless," she said. She went on to explain that the number one fear of the general population is public speaking. Many people say they'd rather die than get up in front of a group to give a presentation. After she reeled off such statistics, Mattei turned and spoke directly to the camera. "What are you really afraid of?" she asked America. It became a challenge that echoed through the popular culture. She closed the show with a paraphrased quote from Albert Einstein. *The only real question you have to ask yourself is whether or not the universe is a friendly place,* she explained, then went on to translate into terms anyone could understand. *Once you've decided that,* Mattei said, *you can pretty much determine what your future will hold.*

Her book hit the top of the *New York Times* Best Seller list and stayed there for sixty-two weeks. As Mattei's fame grew, her patient list expanded exponentially, and she brought in interns to mentor, though her real work was still with bipolars.

"Did you know that eighty percent of poets are bipolar?" Mattei asked Zee one morning.

"My mother wasn't a poet. She wrote children's books," Zee said.

"Nevertheless . . ." Mattei replied.

"Nevertheless" was probably the best thing Zee had ever learned from Mattei. It was a word, certainly, but much more than a word, it was a concept. "Nevertheless" was what you said when you were not going to budge, whether expressing an opinion or an intention. It was a statement, not a question, and the only word in the English language to which it was pointless to respond. If you wanted to end a conversation or an argument, "nevertheless" was your word.

Zee often thought that what had happened with her mother was another reason Mattei had hired her. Maureen's case history might well be considered good material for a new book. But Mattei had never approached her about it. When Zee mentioned her theory one day, Mattei told her that she was mistaken, that she had actually hired Zee because of her red hair.

Theory and research were still Mattei's passion, and though she had a thriving practice, she also had that elusive second book to write and her new mother-daughter theory to document. So most of Zee's patients were Mattei's overflow. Her "sloppy seconds" is what Michael called them, though he was clearly unaware of the perverse meaning of his slang. He'd meant it to be amusing rather than pornographic. The truth was, anything Mattei did was okay with Michael. They had been friends since med school. When Mattei suggested that Michael meet Zee, telling him she thought she'd found the perfect girl for him, he was only too happy to oblige.

Soon after that, Zee had found herself out on a blind date with Michael.

Upon Mattei's recommendation, he had taken her to Radius. He had ordered for both of them, some Kurobuta pork and a two-hundred-dollar Barolo. By the time they finished the bottle, Zee found herself saying yes to a weekend with him on the Vineyard. They had moved in together shortly afterward. Not unlike the job Mattei had given her, the relationship just sort of happened.

What followed still seemed to Zee more like posthypnotic suggestion than real life. Not only had Michael easily agreed that Zee was the perfect girl for him, he'd never even seemed to question it. And exactly one year after their first date, a period of time most probably deemed respectable by Mattei, Michael had proposed.

Zee had been grateful when Mattei chose to hire her. She had just received her master's and was working on her Ph.D. when Mattei invited her to join her practice, giving her some group sessions to moderate and mentoring her as she went. By the time she'd earned the title of doctor, Zee had ended up in a corner office with a view of the Charles and a patient list that would have taken her years to develop on her own.

The phrase "case closed" was one of Mattei's biggest jokes. Though patients almost always got better under her care, they were never *cured*.

There was no such thing as case closed. Not in modern American society anyway, Mattei insisted. Not in a country that planted the most fertile ground for both mania and the resultant depressive episodes, the country that had invented the corporate marketing machine that left people never feeling good enough unless they were overextending their credit, buying that next big fix. Not that Mattei minded the corporate marketing machine. That machine had made her rich. But there was definitely no such thing as case closed. Case closed was decidedly un-American.

WHEN LILLY BRAEDON CAME ALONG, Mattei quickly handed her off to Zee.

In the past year, Lilly had developed the most crippling case of panic disorder. She'd been to local doctors, who had ruled out all probable physical explanations: thyroid, anemia, lupus, et cetera. Then, after watching an episode of *The View,* something he swore he'd never done before, her husband, who in his own words "loved Lilly more than life itself" (a quote that resonated on a very problematic level with both Zee and Mattei), went to the Spirit of '76 Bookstore in Marblehead to purchase Mattei's book, only to find that they were sold out. He immediately ordered two copies, one for himself and another for his ailing wife.

But Lilly was too troubled to read. The only time she left the house in those days was in the late afternoon, when the shadows were longer and the bright summer light (another irrational fear) was dimmer. In the late afternoon, her husband said, Lilly often took long walks through the twisted streets of Marblehead and up through the graves of Old Burial Hill, to a precipice high above Marblehead Harbor, where she sometimes stayed until after sunset.

"So technically she isn't agoraphobic," Mattei said to the husband when she finished her initial patient analysis of Lilly. "She does leave the house."

"Only for her walks," her husband said. "She says she does it to calm herself down."

"Interesting," Mattei said.

But Zee could tell she didn't mean it. The reason Zee was in attendance at Lilly's session was that Mattei had already decided she was handing her off. Mattei wasn't interested in Lilly Braedon.

But Zee was very interested. From the first time she met her new patient, Zee suspected that there was much more to the story than Lilly was telling.

Every Tuesday, Zee had her own therapy session with Mattei. Mostly they talked about her patients, or at least the ones who required meds, which was most of them. If patients with panic attacks weren't on meds these days, you could be pretty sure there was a reason. Perhaps they were in some kind of twelve-step program, usually for alcohol or drugs, or else they had the kind of paranoia that kept them from taking any medication at all.

This morning Zee had gone through "the usual suspects," as Mattei called her list of patients. This one had improved, that one was self-medicating with bourbon and sleeping pills. Another one had taken herself off all meds and was beginning to show signs of a manic episode. When they got to Lilly, Zee told Mattei she had nothing to report.

"Unsatisfactory," Mattei said. Normally Mattei didn't seem to care one bit about Lilly Braedon. But something Zee had said at their last meeting had piqued her interest for a change and prompted a question. When Zee reported that nothing had changed, Mattei wasn't having any of it.

"Does that mean that Lilly is in a normal phase?" Mattei was referring to Lilly's bipolar disorder, which had been their diagnosis. Bipolar disorder was something Zee understood only too well. It was what her mother had been diagnosed with years ago, except that in those days it had been called manic depression, which Zee had always thought a better description. In most cases the disorder was characterized by severe mood swings followed by periods of relative normalcy.

"I wouldn't say normal," Zee said.

"Any more trouble with the Marblehead police?"

"Not lately," Zee said.

"Well, that's something."

AT 3:35, LILLY STILL HADN'T arrived. Zee walked to the window. Across Storrow Drive a homeless woman sat on one of the benches, but there was no one walking along the Charles River. It was too hot and humid for movement of any kind. Traffic was snarled, the drivers honking and agitated, trying to get onto roads heading north. The "cardboard bridge," as Zee called the Craigie, looked like a bad fourth-grade art project. Years of soot had collected in the wrong areas for shading, and today's haze made it look even flatter and more one-dimensional and fake than it had ever looked before.

AT 3:45, ZEE DIALED LILLY'S number. It was a 631 exchange, Marblehead. It used to be NE 1, Lilly had told her when she'd scribbled down her phone number for the records. "NE for Neptune—you know, Neptune, the Roman god of the sea?"

Zee thought back to her school days. Neptune—or Poseidon, his Greek equivalent, god of the sea and consort of Amphitrite, which had been Zee's mother's middle name. Though Maureen Doherty was a decidedly Irish name, Zee's grandmother had given all three of her children the middle names of Greek gods and goddesses. Thus Zee's mother was Maureen Amphitrite Doherty. Uncle Mickey's middle name was Zeus, and Uncle Liam, who had died back in Ireland before Zee was born, was Antaeus, a clear foreshadowing of the mythmaking violence in his future. Zee remembered Maureen teasing Uncle Mickey about his middle name. "Well, what mother doesn't think her son is a god?" Mickey had answered. *Indeed,* Zee thought.

Zee willed herself back to the present. Lately her mind had been wandering. Not just with Lilly, but with all of her patients. They seemed to tell the same stories over and over until her job became more like detective work than therapy. The key wasn't in the stories themselves, at least not the ones they told and retold. Rather it was in the variations of their stories, the small details that changed with each telling. Those details were often the keys to whatever deeper issues lay hidden beneath the surface. What wasn't the patient telling the truth about?

"Everybody lies," was another of Mattei's favorite expressions.

And so as the weeks passed, Zee listened to Lilly, to the variations in the stories she told over and over. But on the day that Lilly had mentioned Neptune, the story she told was one that Zee had never before heard.

"Back in the day," Lilly was saying, "before the phones in Marblehead had dials, way back when the operators used to ask 'Number, please' in a nasal four syllables, you would have to say 'Neptune 1' for the Marblehead exchange." Lilly was far too young ever to have remembered phones without dials and operators who connected you, but for some reason she seemed to find this bit of trivia very significant.

"Does Neptune have a special meaning for you?" Zee asked.

Lilly's face contorted. "I've always been afraid of Neptune," she said. "Neptune is a vengeful god."

AT 5:20, ZEE DIALED HER wedding planner. "I'm very sorry, but I'm going to have to cancel again, my five-o'clock is late," she said, relieved that she'd gotten the machine instead of the person—who, she had to admit, scared the hell out of her.

Zee felt a bit giddy, the way she'd felt as a kid when there was a snow day. Michael wouldn't be home from Washington until the last shuttle. Having come up with the winter image, Zee decided to treat this unanticipated block of freedom as a snow day. Never mind that it was ninety-six degrees outside. The evening stretched ahead of her. She could do anything she wanted with it. Zee couldn't remember the last time she'd had an open evening. Between her work schedule and the wedding plans, there'd been little time for anything else lately. She hadn't even seen her father in the last few months, and she felt guilty about it, though she knew he understood.

The wedding date was not until the late fall, but it seemed as if there was at least one major wedding item a day on her to-do list. Zee hated the process. Tonight they were supposed to be sampling sushi at O Ya, and three kinds of sake. Not a bad evening, all things considered. But Michael wasn't going to make it back in time, and she couldn't deal with the wedding planner alone. The problem wasn't the planner, who was arguably the best in Boston. The problem was that Zee couldn't make a decision, couldn't make herself choose anything from the myriad of options the wedding planner offered.

Her excuse had been a lie—well, more of a twist, really. Lilly was her three-o'clock, not her five, and whether she showed up or not would make little difference to tonight's plans.

★ 2 ★

THOUGH IT WAS AN easy walk to their house on Beacon Hill, Zee hailed a cab. She wasn't Mattei. She didn't like to sweat. Out on the streets, exhaust and steam merged, creating a heat mirage that made the buildings across the river look as if they were beginning to melt. Both inbound and outbound traffic were completely knotted. A truck that had found its way onto Storrow Drive had knocked down one of the overhead crosswalks, and now there was no movement in any direction. Zee directed the taxi driver away from the traffic and up the hill.

It was chilly inside the cab. Mahler played on some weaker station, interrupted by intermittent static from the driver's iPhone as it checked for e-mails. A king-size bottle of hand sanitizer had spilled onto the front seat and was spreading its alcohol scent, unnoticed by the driver. Zee's mind moved to old spy movies, chloroform on a handkerchief, a hand over the mouth, and waking up in some dark place. She cracked the window and tried not to breathe, or anyway not to breathe too deeply.

She thought of Mattei's sense exercises. *Close off two of your senses and switch them.* Smell and what? Hearing? No, touch was better. Zee ran her fingers along the door handle and the fake leather seat. *Shut off the offending senses, choose the ones you can manage.*

When they finally reached the house, Zee tipped the cabbie and walked around back, climbing the outside stairway to the deck, letting herself in through the kitchen door. The room was freezing, which fit well with her snow-day theme.

She had been happy for the heat a few minutes ago, and now she was happy for the cold. Zee seemed to need these extremes more and more lately, something she didn't want to think about because it reminded her too much of her mother. She removed her shoes but didn't take a pair of slippers from the bin that Michael provided for guests. Her hot feet left moist footprints on the cool, dark wood floor. With each step forward, the footprints she left behind slowly disappeared.

She was vaguely hungry. She opened the fridge. There were some leftovers from the party they'd had last weekend, some imported prosciutto and a ton of cheese. They'd invited several people over. Mostly people Michael worked with and some of Mattei's friends, too, including Rhonda, whom Zee really liked. Mattei and Rhonda were planning a wedding, too, now that such things were legal in Massachusetts. Rhonda wanted to talk about all the details: her flowers (all peonies tied tightly in a nosegay, but with spiraling stems that remained visible), her music (jazz-pop fusion). Their wedding was to be in August, the day before Labor Day, which fell on September 1 this year. That Rhonda so clearly knew what she wanted didn't bother Zee all that much. Rhonda had probably always known what she wanted, Zee thought, the way most girls know that kind of thing, straight or gay. Listening to Rhonda, Zee had wished for the first time that she were one of those girls who knew what she wanted. She'd been one of those girls once, but it seemed so long ago that she could barely remember how it felt.

July was fast approaching and, with it, the official beginning of summer parties. She thought back to last year's Fourth of July. While Michael and Mattei had made the rounds, passing hors d'oeuvres and making small talk, Zee and Rhonda sat on the deck and watched the fireworks. The condo Zee shared with Michael had one of the best views in Boston, the perfect place to see the light show, though you couldn't hear the Pops from here—you'd have to be on the esplanade for that. So Michael had turned on the radio, creating a sound track that was a second off from the visual, each beat later than the flash.

Michael had seemed so happy then, walking around refilling everyone's glass with another good Barolo he'd found at auction. Last weekend he had served all French wines, some second-*cru* houses. Michael had a good collection, all reds.

Zee reached into the vegetable bin and pulled out a half bottle of Kendall-Jackson chardonnay that she'd hidden the night of the party, not in the wine fridge but in with the lettuces, which was somewhere Michael would never look. He hated salads, the only things she ever made as a main course. She created elaborate salads with homemade dressings, vinaigrettes, and infusions. She made oatmeal, too, for winter breakfasts, steel-cut stuff that took forty minutes to cook, and cowboy coffee with an egg, which was something Michael actually did like, though he didn't much like her method of letting the pot boil over onto the stove before she dumped the cup of cold water in to clear it. Michael said he expected that the boiling-over bit worked better with a campfire, and couldn't she just grab the pot before it bubbled up and went all over everything? The answer was no, she couldn't seem to, though she always cleaned up her messes afterward.

Zee filled a coffee mug with the K-J and started to recork the bottle. Then, seeing how little was left, she dumped the rest of the wine into the mug. She carefully placed the bottle into the trash compactor, then flipped the switch, waiting for the pop and the smash. The bag was almost full, so she removed it and took it out to the deck, walking all the way back down the stairs in her bare feet, placing the compacted bottle into the bottom of the garbage bin, not with the recyclables, as she would have preferred, but with the regular trash, so that there would be no evidence of the bottle. It wasn't that Michael minded her drinking, but he definitely minded her drinking an oaky California chardonnay.

She walked back up the stairs and ran a bath, letting the water get as hot as she could stand. She went to her closet and grabbed her winter bathrobe, a worn terry-cloth thing she'd stolen from some spa Michael had taken her to when they first met, which she'd later felt guilty about and sent a check to the hotel to cover its cost. If this was going to be a snow day, then let it be a snow day, she thought. It certainly was cold enough in this house to imagine snow on the roof.

She filled the tub as high as she could and slid into the water. She took one gulp of the wine, then another, then finished the cup. When the falling feeling hit her, the slackening of muscles, a momentary release that came and went fast, she glided under the water, letting it into her ears, her mouth. She pushed her legs wide and let the heat fill her. As her head finally began to quiet, she forgot about Lilly, and the intimidating wedding planner, and Finch, and finally about Michael and the gnawing feeling of guilt she felt most of the time now when she thought about the wedding and everything she was supposed to be getting done.

ZEE DIDN'T REALIZE THAT SHE had fallen asleep until she saw Michael standing above her in the bathroom. How long had it been? The water had gone cold, the sky outside was dark.

She stood up and grabbed a towel.

"I didn't hear you come in," she said, wrapping herself in the terry-cloth robe.

He just stood there watching her, his expression difficult to read. She could tell he had something to say, something important from the look of things, but she wasn't ready to talk.

"Give me a minute, will you?" Zee said, and Michael turned and walked out of the bathroom.

She went to the bedroom and grabbed a pair of socks, so her feet wouldn't leave more prints on the wood floors. She put on a sweatshirt and jeans.

She found him in the kitchen. He was eating a piece of salmon. She recognized the O Ya box.

"What's all this?" she asked him.

"I've been calling you. You didn't answer either phone."

"Sorry," she said. "Sorry" seemed to be the word that started most of her sentences these days.

"The wedding planner quit," Michael said. "But she's charging us six thousand dollars for her time." He held out the tray to her. "I figure these are worth about half a grand apiece."

She shook her head. She wasn't hungry. She felt a little sick.

"For that price she should have sent the sake, too," he said.

She walked over and hugged him, holding on for longer than she wanted. He didn't return the embrace. "I'm sorry," she said. "I'll pick up the expense."

"It's not about the expense," he said. She could see him considering before he continued. "I have to ask you an important question," he finally said.

"What question?"

"Do you *not* want to get married?"

His question caught her off guard. "Why would you even ask me that?"

"Come on, Zee."

A long silence followed. The truth was, she didn't know. She didn't know if she didn't want to get married at all, or if she just hated the process. The big wedding was clearly something he wanted. She could count only about five people she would even invite.

"Maybe I just don't like the wedding planner." She knew that much was true, though it was all she seemed to know. She felt suddenly foolish for the snow day and guilty that she'd made him feel bad.

"Well, you've solved that problem, I'd say."

"Oh, come on," she said. She reached into the box they'd sent over and pulled out a piece of sushi. She would take a bite, and then she would tell Michael how much she liked it and that she thought they'd found the perfect food for the wedding. "It's really good," she said. "Great, actually." She didn't have to lie.

The phone rang. Zee didn't move to answer it.

She could follow his thought process. Michael was a game theorist and as famous as Mattei in his own right. He was paid to predict what groups of people would do. As a result, Michael always seemed to know what she would do before she did it, even when (as was so often the case these days) she had no idea herself.

Don't answer the phone, she thought.

She didn't say it. It would have been stupid. And it would have been futile. As she stood there with him, she felt as if she were the one who was the game theorist. She knew exactly what he would do.

Michael picked up the phone on the fifth ring. "Yes?" he said into the receiver. Zee could tell that it was Mattei. Then, so she continued to feel his earlier reprimand, he went on, "No, evidently Zee does *not* answer her cell." He listened to Mattei for a moment, and then, at her direction, he walked over to the TV and flipped it on. "What channel?" he asked. Then he handed the phone to Zee.

Zee kept her eyes on the television as Michael changed the channels, settling on the local news, Channel Five.

"What's going on?" Zee said to Mattei.

On the screen several cars were pulled over on the top level of the Tobin Bridge. An SUV with its driver's door opened sat next to the leftmost guardrail. Police were trying to contain the crowds who were leaning over the side, pointing. The TV camera panned across the blackening water, but aside from a few pleasure boats nothing seemed unusual. The camera cut back to the newscaster, a blonde in a blue top.

Pointing the microphone at the toll collector, she asked, "Did you know she was going to jump when she pulled over?"

The toll taker shook her head. "I thought she was opening the door because she had dropped her money."

Another eyewitness leaned into the microphone, vying for camera time. "She didn't jump, she dove."

The newscaster held the microphone out to a man who stood off to the side, staring over the railing. "I am told that you witnessed the whole thing," she said to him.

He didn't say anything but just stared at the newscaster.

Zee recognized shock when she saw it and hoped one of the medical personnel would treat him for it.

The woman poked the microphone closer. "What did you see?"

As if suddenly realizing where he was, the man pulled himself together. With a look of disgust and anger, he pushed the microphone away. "Stop," he said.

Zee felt dizzy. She held on to the couch arm to steady herself. A faint beeping sound was still audible from the SUV's driver's-side door, near where the key had been left in the ignition. It was weak and failing, but no one had thought to put a stop to it.

Zee recognized the car.

"Her husband left a message on the service," Mattei said to Zee.

Michael stared at Zee, still not understanding what was happening. "Who was it?" he finally asked.

"My three-o'clock," Zee said.

★ *3* ★

ZEE TOOK THE TUNNEL to the North Shore instead of the
bridge. The old Volvo she'd gotten in grad school barely passed
inspection every year, and though she seldom drove in town, she couldn't
seem to give it up. The alignment was so bad that she had to keep both
hands firmly on the wheel to stay in her lane as she drove.

Zee hated tunnels—the darkness, the damp, the dripping from
overhead, where she imagined the weight of water already pushing
through the cracks, finding any weak spot and working its way through.
She wasn't alone. Since the Big Dig tunnel ceiling collapse a couple of
years back, most Bostonians were skittish about tunnels.

"Water always seeks its own level," Zee said aloud, though she was
alone in the car and the sound of her own voice seemed wrong. The
thought was wrong, too. It only made her more tense. *Think of something else,* she told herself. She wished she had taken the bridge. At the
same time, she wondered if she would ever be able to take the bridge
again.

Both Mattei and Michael had told Zee not to go to Lilly's funeral.

"Why would you do that?" Mattei asked.

"Because she was my patient," Zee said. "Because I'm a human
being."

"I hope you don't have any delusions that the family will welcome you," Mattei said.

"I'm going," Zee said.

ZEE HAD PLANNED TO STOP to see her father before the funeral, but she was running late. These days she didn't drive enough to know how bad the traffic would be this time of day. The Big Dig might officially be over, but traffic was still a mess. She had planned to go directly to Salem and surprise Finch with a visit. She was worried about him. Lately she had only seen him in Boston when he came in for his doctor's appointments. He seemed frail and weak. And she couldn't help but feel that he was hiding something from her. So today she planned to drop in unannounced to see for herself. But it was too late to go to Salem now. She'd have to see Finch after Lilly's funeral.

She altered her route, electing to take the coast road directly to Marblehead, winding along the golden crescent of beach that stretches from Lynn through Swampscott to the town line. At the last minute, she decided to take a shorter route through downtown Lynn, not counting on road construction. It was summer. Road crews were everywhere, the required extra-shift cops sleepily directing traffic.

Zee hadn't been on this road for a long time. Mostly the streets were as she remembered them. Roast-beef and pizza places lined every block. Popping up next to them were bodegas, nail salons, and the occasional package store. The businesses were essentially the same. But the ethnicity had changed. Small groceries sat next to each other, their signs in Spanish, Korean, Arabic, Russian. Lynn had always had a diverse population. These days there were more than forty languages spoken in the Lynn schools. Zee forgot who had told her that. Probably it had been her Uncle Mickey.

Her mother's people, including Uncle Mickey, were from Lynn, though they were originally Derry Irish. They had come over from Ireland to become factory workers at a company on Eastern Avenue that made shoe boxes.

They were all IRA, or at least the two brothers had been, Uncle Mickey and his brother Liam, who died in an explosion in Ireland. Zee remembered her mother telling her that their emigration had been sudden. Maureen's reluctance to say more about it left Zee wondering about the details. It was out of character for Maureen to hold back any details when she was telling a story. Whatever it was that had happened, the family had no longer been safe in Ireland. They'd had to leave the country overnight, taking only what they could carry.

Maureen had told her all this in such a matter-of-fact tone that Zee had never quite believed the story.

"Make no mistake," her mother had said many times. "We are, every one of us, capable of murder. Given the right circumstances, it is within each of us to take a life."

Zee never knew whether by "every one of us" her mother had meant all of humanity or simply all of the Doherty clan. She had often thought about asking that question, but she never did. In the end she decided she really didn't want to know.

Their house had been on Eastern Avenue, near the factory but farther down the street, closer to the beach. Zee doubted if she could find the place now. It was so long ago that her grandmother had died. Her mother died only a few years later, just after Zee turned thirteen. Besides Zee, Mickey was the only Doherty left.

The factory where they'd once worked had long since closed. A sign on the front of the building read KING'S BEACH APARTMENTS. It was directly across from Monte's Restaurant, where she used to go for pizza with her father and Uncle Mickey in their pirate days.

When her grandmother died, Uncle Mickey had moved to Salem. He wanted to be closer to his sister, he said. Mickey could pilot a boat with the best of skippers, but he had never learned to drive a car. Though it was only a town away, Lynn was too far from what was left of his family, he said. And he didn't like riding the bus. Though Maureen had killed herself just a few years after he made the move to Salem, Mickey stayed on. He had grown to love the Witch City. He was both a born entrepreneur and a natural salesman. He had a bit of the old clichéd blarney in him as well. When Salem reinvented itself, Mickey was right there to take advantage of the opportunity. He now ran a witch shop on Pickering Wharf, several haunted houses, and a pirate museum. He had done well. People in Salem fondly referred to Mickey Doherty as "The Pirate King."

Lynn, Lynn, City of Sin. Zee recited the old poem in her head. A sign on a Salvation Army building read CITY OF HIM. People were always trying to find a new image for Lynn. Zee liked it the way it was. It seemed to her a real place where real people led real lives.

She could smell Lynn Beach from here, fetid and heavy. At the Swampscott town line, she noticed a little shop with a woman in the window seated at a sewing machine. Outside the store hung a sign, hand-lettered, with penmanship that slanted downward as it progressed: MALE/FEMALE ALTERATIONS.

City of Sin. There was a reason she felt so right here, Zee thought. As sins go, Zee had committed her share. She felt guilty about a lot of things, not the least of which was the question that Lilly had asked shortly before her death. Lilly's question reminded Zee so much of Maureen that she hadn't shared it with Mattei. It was the thing that in retrospect should have tipped her off about Lilly, but instead it hit her in a much more personal way, as if someone had punched her in the stomach.

The last time she'd seen Lilly Braedon, Zee had been trying so hard to rationalize the risky behavior Lilly had been engaging in that she found herself unprepared for the question. Just as the session was ending and Lilly was walking out the door, she turned back to Zee and asked, "Don't you believe at all in true love?"

4

WHEN LILLY'S HUSBAND HAD first brought her to Mattei, Lilly had been heavily dosed on Klonopin. Her anxiety had become so debilitating that the internist her husband had been taking her to had first prescribed Xanax and then, when that failed, increasing doses of the branded clonazepam. Lilly could barely speak. She couldn't drive. The pupils of her eyes looked like tiny pinpoints. But she was no longer anxious. She was zombie calm.

It turned out that Lilly hadn't driven for the better part of a year, which had been inconvenient at best with a husband and two young children to care for. Instead of taking the kids to the yacht club to swim, Lilly had started walking them down to Gashouse Beach, which she said she preferred. But the kids missed their friends and the swimming lessons they had signed up for, and Lilly had such a bad feeling about the ocean—a terror that it would take her children, that the surf would send a rogue wave or that some remnants of red tide would seep through their skin to infect them—that she didn't even let them wade in the water at the beach. Instead they were allowed only to sit on the rocky shore, playing in what little sand they could find, building castles, and slathered with so much 45 SPF that the blowing sand began to coat their pale bodies, making them look like sugar cookies.

By August, Lilly's husband had taken pity on her and hired a nanny. That was when the real trouble started.

Lilly willingly surrendered her SUV to the nanny, happy to be free of it, preferring to walk around town. She had Peapod deliver groceries. And then she paced.

At first she confined her pacing to the house. She went up and down stairs. She circled from the foyer to the kitchen, through the sunporch to the dining room and library. She climbed all three flights of stairs, avoiding the basement but pacing the rough, unfinished floor of the attic, feet tapping a rhythmic heel-toe, heel-toe. She slept little, pacing the house at night until the nanny complained that she thought the old place might be haunted, because she could hear someone walking above her ceiling.

The next day, when the nanny took the children to their lessons, Lilly's feet took her outside, through the labyrinth of Marblehead streets, past the fading window boxes where the vinca and blue scaevola struggled against the August drought. On the day when the drought finally broke, she ducked into the Spirit of '76 Bookstore to get out of the rain, but the place was too quiet for her and she imagined that everyone could hear the squishing sound her sneakers made as she walked on the carpet, so she went back outside. But it was pouring, thundering and very windy. She stood under the awning and watched as a black plastic garbage can caught wind and rolled down the two-lane street, hitting a standing group of planters like a bowling ball, leaving a seven-ten split. She stayed under the awning until she noticed people looking at her, and then she crossed the street and entered the Rip Tide, someplace she'd never been to in her life.

It was three-thirty. The construction workers who weren't already finished for the day were finally called off the job because of the rain, and the bar was filling up. Lilly walked to the far end and took one of the high stools, one she could wind her feet around to still their movement.

"What can I get you?" the bartender asked.

Lilly didn't drink. She had no idea.

"Do you have any kind of food?" she asked the man. She was aware that she was the only woman in the place. She could feel all eyes on her.

"They have great steak tips," a man two stools down offered.

"Lunch is over. The kitchen doesn't open until five," the bartender said.

"Oh, come on, the lady looks like she could use a good steak."

She knew they were looking at her, but she had no idea how she must appear. Wet-T-shirt contest was the first thing she thought, but she was too skinny for wet tees to matter much. Her collarbones felt sharp and jutting.

The bartender muttered and went to the back to cook. "You owe me one," he said, not to Lilly but to the man who'd procured the steak tips for her.

The man dragged his bar stool over to hers.

His name was Adam, he told her. He lived above one of the shops on Pleasant Street, just a few houses down on the left. He did finish carpentry for a local contractor, the same one her husband had recently hired to do some work on their house.

Lilly ate the steak tips. She ate the salad that came with them, too. She even ate the garnish, something pickled and sour, though she couldn't name what it was.

SHE HAD GONE TO HIS house, she later told Zee, because he'd offered her a dry T-shirt and a ride home.

They'd done it that first afternoon, she said, not in the bedroom but right there on the green couch in the corner, the wind whipping the aluminum sign against the side of the building, hailstones the size of golf balls crashing hard against the windows, denting the cars in the bank parking lot across the street.

"I felt safe for the first time in years," Lilly told Zee.

Zee thought Lilly's description sounded anything but safe, yet she knew it was an important statement. "What about it made you feel safe?"

"The couch, for one thing. It was this deep-cushioned thing, kind of a dark green velvet. Like a forest or something."

"Forest green?"

"Yes, and the light from the window."

"You said it was stormy."

"It was. Maybe it wasn't the light—it was the sound of the hail against the window. It was also what was outside. The car sounds and the shops. The bookstore and a ballet school. You could hear the music from the school, and I was picturing the little girls doing their barre exercises."

"Even in the storm, you could hear so well?" Zee asked.

"Yes," Lilly said. "I could hear the music. It was as if real life was happening right outside the window—all around us, really—and we were part of it somehow. I've never felt that way before. Safe and warm," she said.

He had given her a ride home in his red truck. She made him drop her off down the hill from where she lived, near Grace Oliver Beach, by the little house that had once been a penny-candy store. "Can I see you again?" he asked, taking her hand. He was so sweet that he made her want to cry. She told him no. He told her he thought he loved her.

They made love every afternoon all summer, sometimes at his place, sometimes in the truck if they could find a secluded spot to park. She was always home by five. Lilly thought it was important that Zee know this.

"I'm always home in time to cook dinner," she explained.

What Lilly actually cooked were huge guilt feasts. The more she fooled around, the better she cooked. She pureed vegetables, adding odd flavorings like strawberry and peanut butter, anything the kids would actually eat. She went organic at the farmers' market. She even dug up the backyard at midnight to put in a vegetable garden. She never finished it, which caused a huge issue with their landscape designer. The Guatemalan yard workers seemed to have less of a problem with it. They just mowed around the pit as if they believed that it really would become something beautiful one day, and they never filled it in as their boss had suggested. One of them even found a packet of seeds in the shed and planted a few rows of what looked at first like carrots but later revealed itself to be yarrow.

As the days grew shorter, Lilly sank into a depression that rivaled those of the great poets. She stopped walking. She fired her nanny. Dishes piled up in the sink. One of the children got lice, and she didn't even know it until the school nurse sent home a note and a bottle of Pronto shampoo.

How did that make you feel? Zee never even had to ask the standard shrink question. She already knew the answer. Lilly felt all the most destructive emotions out there—fear, judgment, inadequacy—as if there were some secret to parenting that she'd never been taught.

"Look," Mattei had told Lilly's husband when he'd dragged her in to see the famous doctor in what amounted to his last hope for his wife. "Most places they give you a pill, they send you on your way. I'm not going to do that." Zee could see the look of relief in his eyes as Mattei explained the process. First they would wean Lilly off all her meds, and then they would be able to see just what they were dealing with. In the meantime Lilly would be given a complete physical and all the standard tests, checking thyroid and estrogen levels, and even a dexamethasone-suppression test to rule out Cushing's, though both Mattei and Zee were already pretty sure what the diagnosis would turn out to be.

"We already had a physical," the husband said, confused by some of the terms Mattei was using but clear on this one. He gestured to the folder he had presented her with earlier.

"I want you to have it at Mass General," Mattei said.

They agreed. Then Mattei asked Lilly one more question, one she asked all of her patients.

"Where were you when you had your first panic attack?"

There was a long silence. The husband, who usually answered every question for his wife, looked baffled.

Everyone waited for Lilly to speak. Finally, after the silence was so awkward that the husband was getting nervous, he started to make suggestions to Lilly. *In church, maybe? Or at the market? Maybe at the beach with the kids?*

"Let your wife answer the question," Mattei said.

"I don't know where I was," Lilly said. Her voice was flat.

"That's bullshit," Mattei said privately to Zee after the session ended. "Everybody knows."

★ *5* ★

THE PARKING LOT ACROSS from the Old North Church in Marblehead was already full, so one of the funeral directors waved Zee down a side street where there were more spaces. When she turned the corner, she caught a flash of ocean so bright her eyes throbbed with it.

The pallbearers were unloading the coffin as she climbed the steep granite steps. She hurried ahead, into the wide expanse of church, taking a seat in the back row. An old woman moved aside to make room for her, dragging her cane across the wooden bench with a scraping sound.

There were photos of Lilly everywhere.

Zee had to swallow hard to keep from crying. She hadn't cried yet; up until now all she had felt was shock. And guilt. She recognized Lilly's children from photos. They sat in the front pew, the little girl unaware and chatting; the boy, who was reputedly so spirited, sat apart from his father and sister, staring straight ahead at the plain white wall. Zee couldn't take her eyes off the boy. His stoicism stole her heart. She almost expected him to salute the coffin like the famous photos of John-John Kennedy, though she knew it would not happen.

★ ★ ★

MATTEI HAD PRESCRIBED LITHIUM TO Lilly at their third session. She diagnosed Lilly with bipolar 2 disorder, probably with a chromosomal element, she said, and definitely with panic. Mattei treated Lilly alongside Zee for the first two months, until she was certain the medication was working. So often during manic periods, patients were tempted to discontinue their medication. It was very important to monitor both the meds and the dosage. When Mattei was certain that the drugs were properly dosed and were being taken, she turned the case over to Zee.

It had taken Lilly several months to start talking. But when she finally did, it was like opening the floodgates at Salem Harbor after a nor'easter. She didn't stop. Her childhood had been ideal, she said when Zee asked. There was no abuse of any kind and no history of alcoholism. Her mother and father had a wonderful relationship. And Lilly loved her husband. Maybe not more than life itself, the way he said he loved her, but she did love him. She spent the next three sessions talking about how and why this was true.

"I WAS HAVING SEX." LILLY hadn't answered Mattei's question until her sixth month of treatment with Zee. So it took a moment for Zee to understand the implications. "When I had my first panic attack . . . I was having sex with Adam."

It was before Lilly had told her the story of Adam. At first Zee thought that she meant her husband. But her husband's name was William, not Adam. Lilly watched for Zee's reaction. She expected to be judged. But Zee didn't flinch.

"Tell me about Adam," was all she said.

IT WAS ABOUT THIS TIME that Zee stopped sharing all of Lilly's stories with Mattei. Her case discussions, which had always been so detailed, began to have their sharper edges rounded over, so that they would more easily merge into the general. There were more discussions about the symptoms, the phases and progression of disease, than about the details of each case. For her part, Mattei thought this was a good step, that Zee was gaining confidence as a therapist. Sensing that she could handle the caseload, Mattei began to send more patients Zee's way.

BY JUNE IT WAS APPARENT either that Lilly had stopped taking her medication altogether or that the dosage Mattei had prescribed was insufficient. Lilly was in the middle of one of the most clearly manic periods Zee had ever witnessed.

Lilly's feet were moving again. She never slept. She spent huge sums of money. Her food bills alone for the elaborate guilt feasts she was cooking for her family were running about $750 a week—for two adults and two children, both of whom were picky eaters. Lilly no longer remembered why she'd ever needed a nanny in the first place. She could easily handle two young children. And her trysts with Adam were getting more and more daring. With no nanny on board, Lilly had taken to sneaking Adam into her house in the late afternoons, claiming that the place needed some repair work, first on the playroom shutters and later on a crooked piece of crown molding in the living room that had bothered her for years.

Lilly and Adam had sex on every horizontal surface in the house. Hearing their cries of passion one afternoon and thinking that someone was hurting the children, a neighbor called the police. As the cruiser pulled up in front of the house, Adam went out the back door of the basement, hurrying across the yard by Black Joe's Pond and down Gingerbread Hill, pulling on his work clothes as he ran. The police were waiting for him at the bottom of the hill, where his red truck was almost always parked these days. He knew them all, had gone to high school with a couple of them.

"Everyone knows what you're up to," one of the cops told him. "Why don't you try to keep a lower profile?"

There were some stifled smiles, maybe even a pat on the back from the cop he knew.

"They don't exactly disapprove," Adam had said to Lilly when she freaked out about the cops. "One of us? Messing with some rich guy's wife?"

It was the first time Lilly had felt uneasy about what she was doing and the first time she felt bad for her husband. Sweet William, who had never done anything to deserve this. For the first time during her long affair with Adam, Lilly felt shame. And the minute the shame cloud descended, things began to fall apart.

At Zee's direction Mattei wrote a script and added a sedative to take the edge off and a light sleeping pill to keep Lilly's feet from wandering. When Lilly complained of weight gain from the lithium, they switched her to an antiseizure medication.

It was difficult to say when Mattei started to become suspicious. "Tell me what's going on," she asked Zee directly. "I don't mean with the symptoms, I mean in her life."

"She's been having an affair," Zee confessed, feeling her face redden.

"And you didn't tell me this because . . . ?"

"Doctor-patient confidentiality." Zee knew that this was a hot button with Mattei, who claimed to have enormous respect for doctor-patient confidentiality.

"What's the real reason?" Mattei said.

"That *is* the real reason," Zee insisted.

"Is the affair still going on?"

"Yes," Zee said.

"What else is she doing?"

"What do you mean, what else?"

"Is she drinking, is she doing drugs? What other kinds of risky behavior is our so-called Mrs. Perfect indulging in?"

There was some triumph in Mattei's voice as she asked. She'd begun calling Lilly "Mrs. Perfect" ever since William's initial goddess-like description of her. No one was that perfect, Mattei had told him with Lilly right there. Perfect was a huge burden for any woman.

"Just the affair." Zee was aware that her stomach was churning. She wished she hadn't said anything. Her face felt hot and red. She wanted to throw up. In all the cases she'd treated so far, nothing like this had ever happened to her. It was as if she had just confessed to the infidelity herself.

"Maybe you should take back this case," she said.

Mattei seemed to think about it for a while before making her decision. "No," she said. "I don't have time to take on another patient. And you're not getting out of this that easily."

Zee sat quietly as she waited for Mattei to mull over their plan of action. She thought about getting up and walking out of the office and never looking back. It had become her fantasy lately. Not yet five years into her practice, and she was already having burned-out escape fantasies. Not a good sign.

"We're upping her meds," Mattei said, reaching for her pad. She slid a prescription across the desk.

As the new dosage of antiseizure medication started to work, Lilly seemed to come back to mid-range. During the next several sessions and into the early fall, she drove herself to Boston and spoke in her sessions with Zee the way a more normal patient might have. She talked about going back to college, or at least taking a class or two. She talked about the competitive process of getting her son into their private school of choice.

She had stopped seeing Adam, she told Zee. It had been very difficult for her. The medicine hadn't changed the fact that she thought she was in love with him. She said she believed that Adam was the great love of her life, her soul mate. But she was trying hard to do the right thing. For her children. And for the man who used to be referred to simply as "my husband" and who had now taken on the permanent moniker of "Sweet William."

It seemed to work. Right up until Halloween weekend, when (as she later put it herself) "all hell broke loose."

First Lilly's cat had disappeared. She'd looked everywhere, hanging posters all over town, calling all the neighbors. The children were upset, especially her daughter, who'd planned to carry the black cat she had named Reynaldo with her as part of her witch costume. But by Halloween night there was still no sign of the cat, and so her daughter had refused to wear the costume Lilly had made for her and refused to go trick-or-treating until Lilly took her downtown to buy another one.

It had been raining intermittently on Halloween, so instead of paper bags Lilly had given them pillowcases in which to collect their candy, but her daughter was still little, and her pillowcase hung too low and dragged along the sidewalk as they went house to house. The kids had wanted to trick-or-treat alone, insisting that they were only going to the neighbors' homes, that they wouldn't leave Gingerbread Hill. But Lilly wouldn't hear of it. Terrible things happened to children all the time: razor blades in apples, kidnapping. No town was immune, not even Marblehead. She had always taken them trick-or-treating, and she wanted to go along. She even had a costume picked out for herself—or half a costume, at least. She still had on her jeans, but from the waist up she was Snow White, or a rather Disneyfied version of the famous beauty. She wore a black wig with a red bow, a half-length pink cape, and a blue shirt with puffy sleeves. In her hand she carried an apple.

She was actually excited about going. But at the sight of Lilly dressed up and ready to walk with them, her daughter started to cry. "I'm not a baby!" she insisted. And so Lilly walked behind them, staying in the shadows, watching while they knocked on the doors of her neighbors, and eventually eating the apple she carried house to house, dropping the core into a neighbor's compost pile.

When they got home, it was past their usual bedtime, though

William was still at work. She had hoped to keep the children up long enough for him to see their costumes, but tomorrow was a school day. They had their baths. She tucked them in. As she started down the stairs, she heard a noise from the basement. She decided it was the wind, slapping the French windows they'd recently had put in. It had happened before. The house had a walk-out basement, which they'd had remodeled a few years back. But the new windows were faulty; they often didn't close properly. She'd already had two of them repaired by Adam. She'd been meaning to speak with him about fixing this final one, but she hadn't gotten around to it before she stopped seeing him.

William returned home later that night, but Lilly wasn't there. The children were asleep. At midnight he called the police and reported her missing. They told him he'd have to wait forty-eight hours before they got involved. Though they didn't share their information with him, the police had a pretty good idea where she might be.

Lilly didn't come home until two days later. When she did, she was sullen and down-cycling. She wouldn't eat. She had several bruises. No matter how many times she was asked, she would never say where she'd been or what had happened.

After the emergency room took care of her injuries, Zee had Lilly admitted to a Boston psychiatric hospital on an involuntary seventy-two-hour hold.

Lilly's three-day stay turned into three weeks. Zee went by every other day. One weekend, when Lilly wasn't expecting her, Zee showed up. Lilly was in the lounge, a book in front of her. Instead of reading, she was staring out the window.

Zee paused to watch. Lilly was looking at a red construction truck, idling outside in the parking lot. Zee recognized it immediately. She had walked out of the office one day after Lilly's session in time to see her getting into that same truck. Adam clearly knew who Zee was, and the look he gave her as she walked by that day had sent a shiver up her spine.

"You have to get away from him," Zee said to Lilly.

Lilly didn't answer.

By offering advice Zee knew she had crossed a line with Lilly. A therapist is never supposed to tell a patient what to do. But it was a line Zee felt she had to cross.

Zee left Lilly and called security.

WILLIAM DIDN'T KNOW WHAT HAD happened while Lilly was away. He could tell from the police reaction that they were not as worried as he was. "People walk out on marriages all the time," they said.

He had convinced himself that it had been a kidnapping, from which his wife had narrowly escaped. He waited until Zee had been seeing Lilly at the hospital for almost two weeks before he couldn't stand it anymore and came by the office.

He demanded to know what had happened to Lilly. "I know she told you," he said.

"She didn't, actually," Zee said. "But even if she had, I couldn't tell you."

"I'm the one who brought her to you. I'm the one paying the bills," he said.

"Lilly has to be able to trust me," Zee said calmly. "Doctor-patient confidentiality."

It was the only time she had seen William angry. "What the hell am I paying you for?" he demanded.

The sound of his raised voice brought Zee to her feet. Mattei got to the door in time to see him hurl a glass paperweight across the room, shattering it against the far wall.

"Do you need some help in here?" Mattei asked Zee.

William looked confused and embarrassed. "I was just leaving," he said.

"Let me see you to the door," Mattei said.

"I'm sorry," he mumbled to Zee.

Mattei held the door for him, shooting Zee a look as they left.

TWO DAYS BEFORE LILLY WAS scheduled to be released, both Zee and Mattei were called to the hospital. Lilly's hospital psychiatrist sat across from a social worker named Emily, whom Zee recognized from the Department of Social Services.

"What's going on?" Zee asked.

"We're here because of Lilly's physical injuries," Emily said.

"What physical injuries?" Zee asked.

"The ones she initially presented with," the social worker said.

"Lilly refuses to talk about them," the staff psychiatrist said.

"She told me she fell," Zee said. "On Halloween night."

"That's what's on her admission records," the psychiatrist said. "'Suffered a fall on Halloween night due to slippery rocks.'" She looked at the others. "It *was* raining pretty hard on Halloween."

"The bruises aren't consistent with a fall," Emily said. "They seem more like a beating."

"You think she was beaten?" Zee asked.

"This is routine procedure," Emily said. "Especially when the woman doesn't give an explanation consistent with her injuries."

"Lilly is scheduled to be released in two days," the psychiatrist said. "She's stable, her medications are properly dosed, and she's showing no signs of depression."

"I would respectfully disagree on that last point," Zee said. "I think she seems depressed. She's normally much more communicative."

The psychiatrist paused to consider. "There *is* one point that makes me agree with you, Dr. Finch."

"Only one?" Zee was getting annoyed. "What's that?"

"Lilly does not want to go home."

"Which plays into our suspicions of spousal abuse," the social worker said.

"It's not William," Zee said.

"But if she's afraid to go home . . ." the social worker said.

"She doesn't feel safe at home." Zee turned to Mattei. "If she was abused in any way, it's Adam."

"Who's Adam?" Emily asked.

"Lilly was having an affair with him several months ago. He was here the other day."

"Maybe the husband found out about the affair," Emily suggested. "Maybe that's what made him violent."

"It's not William," Zee said again. "He's not the type."

Emily looked to Mattei for verification.

"I think Zee's right," Mattei said. "But I can't say for certain that it wasn't William."

Zee shot her a look.

"I would have agreed with you until the other day," Mattei said.

"What happened the other day?"

"There was an incident. We had to escort him from the office."

"I think we have to cover all bases," the psychiatrist said.

"What we really need is a formal complaint," Emily said. "No matter which one it is."

"You can try," Zee said. "But I can tell you right now, she'll never give it to you. She doesn't want William to know about her affair. And she's afraid of Adam."

NOT ONLY DID LILLY REFUSE to file a complaint, but when she was released from the hospital, she decided she wanted to see another therapist. "One closer to home," William told Zee.

The internist who had initially prescribed the Klonopin set her up with an old-school Freudian analyst who worked out of Salem Hospital. She had agreed to meet with him five days a week and to start analysis.

"You're kidding me," Mattei said.

But Zee was clearly upset. "We have to stop them," Zee said. "She shouldn't be starting over again. That's not the right kind of therapy for her. And she won't tell the new therapist the truth until it's too late. . . . We have to do something," Zee said to Mattei.

"There's nothing you can do," Mattei said. "She's not your patient anymore."

IT HAD BEEN A TOUGH winter for Zee. She'd begun to dream about Lilly, and in her dreams the images of Lilly and Zee's mother, Maureen, had become confused. They were still separate people, but in the dream she was unable to tell them apart and kept having to ask which one she was talking to.

"This is good," Mattei said when Zee detailed the dream in her next session.

"Really? How so?" Zee asked.

"Let's talk about the real reason you became a therapist."

"It wasn't the unfulfilled dream of my mother, I can tell you that much."

"Wasn't it?"

"Oh, please," Zee said.

"What was the unfulfilled dream of your mother?"

"We both know what it was."

"Why don't you tell me again?" Mattei said.

"The Great Love. It's what she wanted from my father—and what she never got."

"So already there's a similarity to Lilly."

"And just about every other woman in America," Zee said.

"True enough. Your mother was onto something when she started writing fairy tales about The Great Love."

"Something that evidently killed her," Zee said.

"Which?" Mattei said.

"Was it the fairy tale that killed her? Or The Great Love?"

"Aren't they pretty much the same thing?"

"You tell me," Mattei said.

When Zee didn't take the bait, Mattei asked a different question. "What's the other dream of the fairy tale?"

"Besides true love?"

"What are both your mother and Lilly looking for?" Mattei asked.

"My mother's not looking for anything. My mother's dead." Zee was growing tired of this line of questioning.

"Bear with me for a moment," Mattei said.

Zee folded her arms across her chest.

"What did your mother want from you then, and what does Lilly want now?"

"I don't know," Zee said.

"Think about it."

ZEE THOUGHT ABOUT MATTEI'S QUESTION, and she thought about Lilly Braedon many times during the next few months.

It was William who finally contacted Zee. He was desperate. "She's not doing well," he sobbed into the phone. "I don't know what to do." He told Zee that Lilly had stopped the therapy within the first month. Convinced that the doctor was coming on to her, she had refused to step back into his office. "I don't know," William said. "She's such a beautiful woman. Men can't help throwing themselves at her. I tend to believe her." He tried to compose himself before going on. "She won't even get out of bed."

Whose bed? Zee wanted to ask. But she didn't. Instead she agreed to go to the house to meet with Lilly, and with that, Zee crossed another line.

THE HOUSE WAS A MESS. It hadn't been cleaned for weeks, William told her. Finally, in frustration, he had hired a maid service, three women from Brazil who didn't speak much English, which he decided was a good thing, because he was afraid of what Lilly might say to them if she started talking. But instead of speaking even a word of hello, Lilly had taken to locking herself in her bedroom and crying the whole time they tried to clean—huge, wrenching sobs that finally upset the maids so much that they quit. "What was she crying about?" he'd asked the women, but they didn't know. Gesturing, they managed to communicate to him that Lilly had been talking on the phone with someone.

William thought that maybe the phone calls had been to Zee.

Zee didn't tell him what she already knew, that the phone calls were to Adam.

"You didn't break up with Adam, did you?" Zee asked Lilly at her first return session.

"I couldn't," Lilly said. Then she started to cry.

LILLY BECAME ZEE'S PATIENT ONCE more. And once again her meds were adjusted. Soon she was driving herself into Boston on a regular basis. She seemed better. Spring was turning to summer again, and Lilly's spirits were lifting.

They didn't talk about Adam anymore. Lilly wouldn't, and there were clearly boundary issues that Zee had violated; she didn't want to risk making things worse. For now it was important not to drive Lilly away again. It was enough that she was here and that she seemed to be improving. It was Lilly who finally brought up Adam.

It was about six months later, in one of her sessions. "We think we're free," she said, "but we're not. We're the product of every association we've ever made, and sometimes of ones we inherited from people we never even knew."

"That's very profound," Zee said.

"So you agree?"

"It doesn't matter whether I agree or disagree. What matters is what you think."

"I just told you what I think."

"So you did," Zee said.

Lilly made a face.

"What?" Zee said.

"Did you ever want to get out of something but you didn't know how?"

"What is it you want to get out of?"

"Just about everything right about now," Lilly said.

"Why don't you tell me the specifics, and I'll see if I can help you work through it," Zee suggested.

"My marriage, for one," Lilly said.

"Why do you want to get out of your marriage?"

"I feel as if William set up this elaborate trap for me and made it look all pretty, and I just fell into it," Lilly said.

"And now you want to free yourself from the trap?"

"Yes." Lilly looked at Zee. "You don't approve."

"It doesn't matter whether I approve."

"But you don't."

"I didn't say that. People get divorces. No judgment," Zee said.

"So you're saying it's okay?"

"Do *you* think it's okay?"

"I have two children," Lilly said.

"Yes, you do."

"I feel like I'm dying," Lilly said.

"Let's explore that," Zee said.

Lilly said nothing.

"In what way do you feel like you're dying?" Zee asked.

"Not dying. Trapped. I can't leave because of the children. And I can't stay."

"I understand feeling as if you can't leave. Why do you feel you can't stay?" Zee said.

"It's not safe," she said.

"Are we talking about Adam?"

"It's not Adam. Adam is wonderful," Lilly said.

"Are you telling me you *want* to be with Adam?" Zee asked.

Lilly looked confused for a moment. "No, I never said that."

"Why do you feel unsafe?" Zee asked again.

"I don't want to talk about this anymore," she said. "I'm sorry I brought it up."

"I'm glad you brought it up. If you feel unsafe in any way, I need to know about it," Zee said.

"I told him what you said. That I should get away from him."

"We're talking about Adam now," Zee said.

Lilly hesitated for a second. "Yes. Adam."

"Adam whom you just described as wonderful."

"I'm so confused." Lilly started to cry.

"It's okay," Zee said.

Lilly clearly looked frightened.

"And what did Adam say when you told him that?" Zee asked.

"He said that you were a bitch and someone should teach you to mind your own business," Lilly said. "Those were his exact words."

It took Zee by surprise. She sat for a moment trying to figure out how to put what she needed to say next. Finally she leaned forward. "There is no need for you to be afraid of this man," Zee said. "There are things you can do."

"Like what?"

"Like a restraining order, for one thing," Zee said. "If he's harassing you, we can go get a court order making him stay away from you."

"Then William would find out," Lilly said.

"Probably," Zee said.

"I can't do that," Lilly said. She couldn't stay seated but got up and stood nervously by her chair.

"Did Adam threaten you in any way?"

"I don't want to talk about this anymore."

"Did he threaten your children?" Zee asked.

"No. I didn't say he threatened anyone. You're putting words into my mouth."

"So he *didn't* threaten you," Zee said.

"No," Lilly said.

Zee could tell she was lying.

"Isn't your safety and the safety of your children more important than keeping this secret?"

"I'm so stupid." She was crying in earnest now. "I can't believe I ever started up with him."

"You're anything but stupid," Zee said. "You made a mistake."

"One I can't recover from," Lilly said.

"I think you can," Zee said.

"With a restraining order?" Lilly asked.

"As a start," Zee said.

"Do you know how many women are killed every year who've gotten restraining orders?"

Zee had to admit she had no idea. But it was interesting to think that Lilly had been looking into it.

"A lot," Lilly said.

★　★　★

ZEE WENT TO MATTEI AS soon as the session was over.

Mattei called a detective she knew in Marblehead, a woman she'd been on some panel with a few years back, who agreed to look into things.

"Can you do it discreetly?" Mattei asked. "We already have confidentiality issues with the husband."

"Do you have a last name for Adam?" Mattei asked, turning to her.

Zee shook her head. "But he drives a red truck. A Ford. With the name of a construction company on the side."

"Do you know the name of the company?" Mattei asked.

"No," Zee said. "I think it's an Italian name." Zee thought for a moment. "It starts with a *C*?"

A FEW HOURS LATER, MATTEI came into Zee's office.

"We might be lucky," she said. "This Adam guy seems to have left town."

"Really?"

"The truck belongs to a local company. Cassella Construction, I think it was. They said that Adam drove the truck once in a while. He hasn't been around lately. He got into some kind of fight with the foreman, and he took off. They said he's a good worker. They were actually hoping he'll come back to work," Mattei said.

"That doesn't mean he left town."

"The police stopped by his house. None of the neighbors has seen him for several weeks."

"Are you sure Lilly was telling you the truth?" Mattei asked. "The only reason I ask is something the detective said."

"What was that?"

"She told me that this wasn't the first time there'd been trouble involving Lilly Braedon," Mattei said.

"What is that supposed to mean?"

"Evidently the Marblehead police have gotten calls about her before. Not just with this Adam but with other men as well."

Zee sat staring. "Men? As in plural?"

"Classic bipolar if you think about it. Sex with multiple partners certainly qualifies as risky behavior."

Zee thought about it for a moment. "It doesn't mean that one of them isn't stalking her," Zee said.

"No," Mattei said. "It doesn't."

Zee looked shaken.

"The police will keep an eye out for Adam," Mattei said.

"Which won't help a bit if she takes off with him again," Zee countered.

"Well, at least we now know it wasn't William," Mattei said.

Zee shot her a look but said nothing.

6

THE FUNERAL SERVICE WENT on for far too long. Zee was aware that many people spoke, though she could not keep her mind on their words. Her eyes scanned the crowd.

Sweet William sat silent and obviously drugged in the first pew.

Zee realized that both Mattei and Michael had been right about her coming here today, if for different reasons. Mattei thought it was unprofessional and strongly advised against it. Michael hadn't advised her at all; he simply put forward a question: *What good could come of it?*

She wondered just that as she sat here. The family certainly wouldn't want to see her. Years later, as they looked back on this day, they might be glad she'd paid her respects. But today it would only serve as a harsh reminder that she hadn't been able to save Lilly.

There was another reason Zee had come, though she hadn't admit-ted it to either Michael or Mattei. She needed to see for herself whether or not Adam showed up. If he did, it would mean one thing. If he stayed away, it would mean something else entirely. By all rights he shouldn't come anywhere near them today. But if he had been stalking Lilly, as Zee still believed he had, he probably wouldn't be able to stay away.

Even if she was right, though, there wasn't much to be done about it. Lilly had jumped off the Tobin Bridge and into the Mystic. It was suicide, not foul play.

It turned out that Adam didn't come to the funeral. But, to Zee's surprise, two of the eyewitnesses showed up. Not the woman who had been so competitive for camera time, as Zee might have expected. It was the other woman, the toll taker, who came. And the man in the blue van, the one who'd been so reluctant to talk with the newscaster, was there as well.

WHEN THE ORGAN SIGNALED THE end of the service, the funeral director gave the sign to the pallbearers to lift the coffin, and the congregation filed out behind, family first and then, row by row, the other congregants.

As the family passed, Zee was careful not to catch William's eye. Whatever he might feel when he saw her, she didn't want to make it any worse.

As the crowd moved out into the bright sunlight, Zee followed them to her car. She didn't see the red truck until it was directly in front of her. It was pulled over illegally, half blocking the street. Adam watched the pallbearers and the family. When she looked up, his eyes met hers. He looked at her coldly. Then he put the truck in gear and pulled out, tires screeching, leaving about twenty feet of rubber.

Shakily, Zee let herself into her car. Stuck in the middle of the funeral procession, she moved with it through old town and around Peach's Point to West Shore Drive and Waterside Cemetery.

She wanted to pull out of the procession, to head directly to the police station and tell them what she'd seen. But she and Mattei had already talked it through. Lilly's death was a suicide. The police were not likely to open any kind of investigation. And if they did, and the story of Lilly's affair with Adam came out, it would only hurt the family more than they'd already been hurt.

"Let it go," Mattei had told her.

When the other cars turned right, into the cemetery, Zee went straight, following the signs on West Shore Drive that aimed her toward Salem. She had waited too long already. She needed to see Finch.

BOTH OF THE OLD MAN'S knees had stiffened to the point that movement had become nearly impossible. Even his arms would not move, and so he stood near the window looking out at Maule's Well, or at the re-creation of it now on his cousin's property. After *The House of the Seven Gables* became well known, his cousin had grown obsessed with re-creating the building as befitted the story. No, not his cousin— his mind was playing tricks on him again. It was not his cousin but someone else entirely. The strands of his memory were breaking. Often now he would struggle to make his way from one room to another only to find when he arrived at his destination that he had no idea why he had come. Names escaped him. Even the simplest of language eluded him now, as if his words, yet unformed, had been stolen by the salt air and blown out to sea.

He looked out over Turner Street at the old house. It had changed so much over the years that it was difficult to picture its reconstruction. At first it had been simple, just a few low-ceilinged rooms. As fortunes grew, the house had been added to, so that eventually there were the full seven gables of his famous book. But Federalist fashion had dictated simplicity, and so gables had been removed, then added back again when his book had made the house so popular. It was amusing, truly, that this woman, whose name he could not even remember, had under- taken to display the house to the public, and more amusing indeed that the public wanted to see it, seemed willing to pay money in fact to see not just the house with its secret room but other things that had never existed in the house before his fictional account, things like Hepzibah's Cent-Shop and Maule's Well.

He was not certain how he felt about any of it. He was a shy man by nature and did not appreciate the accolades afforded to him. Still, he loved the house more than any dwelling before or since, and he felt a deep responsibility to watch over the property. It seemed his only job now. His hands could no longer hold the pen. And his words were gone. But he was aware (because his writing had made it so) that the gabled house, however cursed it might be, belonged, always and forever, not to the family who originally built it, or to his cousin, or to the woman whose name he could not remember, but to the characters he had created in his story, to Hepzibah and Clifford and Phoebe.

Somewhere in the distance, he could hear a phone ringing. He was not well today. It was not simply his knees. His head was foggy, more foggy than usual. And his hands had a rigidity he could not soften. He had taken something for it. A visitor, one he had at first thought to be his beloved Hepzibah, had given it to him. He was going to die soon. He could feel it. Slow and steady, death seemed to crawl over him. He could sense the rigor mortis already, in his knees. He was leaning against the wall, looking out across the street at his famous house, and he could not move. He had turned to stone, and all he could do was wait for the medicine or for some force of nature to release him.

Where were the ones he had so loved in life? Where was Sophia? Dead, he thought, though he could not remember her passing. He thought then about Melville, and the tears started to fall. Melville wasn't dead. Couldn't be. Then an anger rose up in him, an almost murderous rage.

He stood here now, a statue, a formation of cold granite that trapped just a trace of life inside its chill. The statue could see and feel and want. What he wanted now—wanted desperately, it seemed—was to see the gardens across the street where, in his famous story, the old rooster he had named Chanticleer and his two aging hen wives had been able to come up with only one last diminutive egg, which, rather than ensuring the rooster's aristocratic line, had been served for breakfast. He had found the words amusing when he'd first written them. But today he mourned Chanticleer and the hens and their loss of lineage. But of course it wasn't real, had been real only in his imagination and on the page. And there was a wall between them now, a very real wall that his vision could not penetrate. Standing here today, he could not see his beloved gardens, though he could still manage to see the ocean beyond.

He wanted to cry out for Hepzibah, though he knew she wasn't real, and she seemed to him now two different people, the wizened old woman he had created, the one the actual shop was modeled on, and someone as young and beautiful as he might have once imagined her. And he was filled with love for this last Hepzibah, who was really in his mind more like his character of Phoebe might have been, Phoebe who had come into their lives and changed everything and brought the light back to the old house and love to it as well. He started to cry and was aware that he was crying for what once had been, and for what had passed.

More than anything now, he wanted to see his Hepzibah, and he willed her to him with a force so strong that his knees released their grip and his throat loosened. Slowly, almost imperceptibly at first, he could feel the stone cracking to release him. He moved first a hand and then an arm. Then, carefully, he took a step away from the wall and toward the window.

When he was able, he began his daily work. His strength growing, he raised his shutter and opened the cent shop. It was not Hepzibah's shop, the one he had created in the book; it was not even a bad rendering of it. But it was the best an old man could do.

The customers bought what he put out. One by one they came, shyly at first like the little boy in his story, but then more boldly.

ZEE COULDN'T FIND A PARKING place on Turner Street. Tour buses lined the lot at the House of the Seven Gables, and the tourists

who came in their own cars parked on the sidewalk, ignoring the RESI-
DENTS ONLY sign in favor of a ten-dollar ticket they would never pay.

She finally parked on the small patch of green where Finch kept
his bird feeders. As she got out of the car, she noticed a tourist walking
away with an antique ship's model, which seemed to fly through Finch's
first-floor window and into his hands.

Her first thought was that Finch was being robbed. Then she noticed the tourist's bags hanging from the guy's arm, a small child at his
side. As she got closer, she spotted the hand-lettered sign in the top of
the window: HEPZIBAH'S CENT-SHOP. And underneath it a smaller sign,
also hand-lettered: EVERYTHING MUST GO.

Finch's hair stood up in white tufts. His voice was hoarse. He didn't
recognize her until she stood directly in front of him, and when he did,
he immediately started to cry.

The tourists moved back, out of the way.

"Dad," she said. "What's going on here?"

"Hepzibah," he said. "My Zee." He reached out for her, gripping
her hand as hard as he could. "I willed it so," he said, and then turned
to his audience, his faith in life itself renewed. "I willed it so!" he cried.

PART 2:

June 2008

*The ancient method of Dead Reckoning or
deduced reckoning is often unreliable. Winds,
tides, and storms can easily push the ship off
course. Every mistake is compounded, alter-
ing her passage in critical ways, often with
tragic results. For this reason, sailors eventually turned to celestial navigation. The stars
are a constant. The earth spins, but the stars
remain fixed in the heavens. Even the stormi-
est sky eventually will clear to reveal them.*

★ *7* ★

FINCH PRACTICED TOUCHING HIS thumb to his middle finger as rapidly and accurately as he could. He had succeeded fairly well with his right hand but was slower and clumsier with his left.

"There's usually one side that's weaker than the other," the doctor said, taking notes.

"I'm aware of that," Zee said. They'd been through the routine at least a dozen times. "We're here about his medication."

"Unfortunate," he said. "But we did know that this one might not work. This particular medication came with warnings. It causes hallucinations in some people."

"And clearly he's one of those people. He thought he was Nathaniel Hawthorne."

The doctor's eyebrows raised. "Creative. Of course, considering his background . . ."

Zee fired him a look.

"Often men believe they're working for the CIA, some covert-ops kind of thing. Women's hallucinations often tend to be more sexual in nature," he said, grinning at her.

Zee ignored his remark.

Neurologists have a rather warped sense of humor, Mattei had told her more than once.

"We'll take him off it."

"I've already done that," she said. When she hadn't been able to reach the doctor by phone, she had checked the *PDR* and had called a friend of Michael's who was also a neurologist. There was no danger from sudden withdrawal, no weaning period.

"Don't talk about me as if I'm not here," Finch said. His voice, once loud enough to be heard unmiked in lecture halls of a hundred or more students, was now barely audible.

"Sorry, Dad," she said.

"The hallucinations are not usually unpleasant. They're generally more alarming for the family than for the patient."

"Nevertheless," she said, ending any possibility of continuing the meds. It seemed astounding to Zee when she thought of the side effects some doctors expected their patients to contend with. Any television ad for pharmaceuticals these days came with a list of contraindications so long it sometimes seemed amazing to Zee that people would dare to take so much as an aspirin.

The doctor stood up. "Can you walk for me, Professor Finch?"

Finch stood shakily. Her first impulse was to help him, but she willed her hands to stay at her sides.

With great effort Finch shuffled fifteen feet across the doctor's office. Zee could tell how difficult his effort was only by his breathing. His face was masked, a classic sign of Parkinson's.

Once a reserved New England Yankee, Finch had become more emotional with the progression of his disease. But his emotion showed neither on his face nor in any vocal inflection. It was a more subtle energy that told Zee how frustrating and impossible this short walk had become for her father.

She had often wondered at the fact that Finch didn't have the shaking so common to Parkinson's. Ten years into the disease, he had only recently developed any kind of resting tremor, and even that was so slight that anyone who was not looking for it would never notice.

Curiously, none of these symptoms had been the first signs of Finch's illness. The first cause for concern had happened in a restaurant in Boston, the night Finch had taken them all out to dinner to celebrate the release of his new book based on Melville's letters to Hawthorne. The book was aptly titled: *An Intervening Hedge,* after a review that Melville once wrote for one of Hawthorne's books.

Finch had been working on the book for the better part of ten years. The fact that he had finished it at all was cause enough for celebration; the fact that someone had actually published it represented job security. Finch didn't need to work. His family had left him money. But teaching was something he loved, and teaching Hawthorne and the American Romantic writers was his greatest joy in life.

Finch presented a copy to both Zee and Melville, the name of the man for whom Finch had left Zee's mother. That's what Zee often told people who asked, though neither statement was very accurate. Actually, Finch never left Maureen, though he had met Melville for the first time during one of Maureen's extended hospitalizations. And Melville's name was really Charles Thompson. Melville was a nickname Finch had given him, one that stuck.

Zee opened her book to the title page, which he had inscribed to her. *To my sweet Hepzibah,* he had written in a hand that was much diminished from the one she remembered. *A million thank-yous.* Zee was contemplating just what those thank-yous might be for when she caught the dedication that was printed on the following page: FROM HAWTHORNE TO MELVILLE WITH UNDYING AFFECTION.

Zee had always had mixed feelings about the book, which hinted at a more intimate relationship between Hawthorne and Melville than had previously been suspected. Though even Finch admitted that the men of the times had been far more accustomed to intimacy than those of today, often writing detailed letters of their affection for each other and even sharing beds, the fact that Finch had tried to prove that there was something deeper there bothered Zee more than she liked to admit.

In espousing this theory, it seemed to Zee that Finch was attempting some strange form of justification for his own life choices, justification that was, in Zee's opinion, both far-fetched and unnecessary.

That Finch and Melville were the real thing, Zee had never doubted. Not only were they clearly in love, but because they were so happy and devoted to each other, they had provided for Zee the kind of stability that Finch and Maureen never could. So despite any damage their love might have caused to the family, Zee would always be grateful for that stability.

But the relationship between Hawthorne and Sophia was a legendary love story, the kind Maureen had always wished she could find for herself. The fact that it was a true story, and one her mother had loved so much, made it sacred for Zee. Although her father was one of the country's preeminent Hawthorne scholars and, as such, had more intimate knowledge of Hawthorne than Zee would ever have, that didn't make it any easier for Zee to handle. From the time she was little, Finch's love of Hawthorne had made the writer's life almost as real to her as her own, but until recently she had never heard Finch's theory about Hawthorne and Melville. Maybe it was some kind of misplaced loyalty to her mother, or the desperate hope that The Great Love really did exist, but Zee hated the idea that Finch was messing with the story of Hawthorne and Sophia.

She felt her face getting hot. She could see Melville watching her. Not wanting to ruin the evening, she excused herself from the table. "I forgot to feed the meter," she said, standing too quickly, almost knocking over her glass of wine. "I'll be right back."

She walked out the front door and onto the street. The truth was, she had parked in the lot and not at a meter. She walked halfway down the block before she stopped.

It was Melville finally, and not Finch, who caught up with her. She could feel him standing behind her on the corner. He didn't speak, but she could sense his presence. At last she turned around.

"I'm sorry," he said.

She just stared at him.

"I had no idea he was going to write that dedication."

"Right," she said. She realized as she looked at him that it was probably true. She had noticed the expression on his face when he opened the book, the quick glance that passed between them. Finch loved him. That was the truth of it. They loved each other.

"Hawthorne adored his wife," she said to him. "There are volumes dedicated to that fact."

"I don't think anyone is disputing that," Melville said.

"His whole book is disputing that."

"I've read it," Melville said. "It isn't."

They stood together on the sidewalk. People walked around them.

"It's possible to truly love more than one person in this life," Melville said. "Believe me, I know."

She regarded him strangely. It was the first time she'd ever heard Melville say anything so revealing about his past.

She had no idea what to say.

"This night means so much to him," Melville said.

He wasn't telling her how to feel; he was just telling her what was true.

She felt stupid standing here, like a kid who had just thrown a tantrum. It surprised her. "I don't know why that got to me."

"I think it's fairly obvious," Melville said.

"You know that I believe you two belong together."

"Of course," Melville said.

"It's just the way he does things sometimes. It brought everything back."

"I know," Melville said, putting his hand on her shoulder. "Come on inside with me."

They walked back together. Finch was sitting alone at the table, looking confused. She kissed his cheek.

"I'm sorry," she said. "My car was about to be ticketed. Lucky for me Melville had quarters."

Finch looked so relieved that Zee almost cried. The book sat on the table where she had left it. She picked it up and turned it over, reading the blurbs on the back. A picture of a younger-looking Finch stared out at her from the jacket cover. He was standing in front of the House of the Seven Gables. "To those hedges," she said, raising her glass.

She could see Melville's amusement at her toast. As much as she resented him sometimes, Melville was one of the only people in the world who truly got her.

They ordered dinner and drank several glasses of wine.

Since the celebration was in Finch's honor, Melville had planned to pick up the tab. But Finch wouldn't hear of it and insisted on paying. The bill came to $150, but Finch laid down $240 in cash, unusual for him, as a frugal Yankee. Melville reached over and retrieved three twenties. "I think these bills were stuck together," he said, handing them back to Finch. "Damned ATMs."

Finch looked surprised and then slightly embarrassed. He stuffed the returned bills into his pocket.

Zee could see that he was genuinely confused.

"WHAT'S THE MATTER WITH MY father?" she called to ask Melville the next morning. She was moving between classes, and the reception on her cell phone kept cutting in and out.

"He had a lot of wine," Melville said.

"He always has a lot of wine."

"Maybe the bills really did get stuck together."

"Right," Zee said.

At Melville's insistence Finch had already made an appointment with his primary-care physician. Zee said she would prefer for him to see a neurologist in Boston.

She felt relief for about sixty seconds when the neurologist said it wasn't Alzheimer's.

"It's Parkinson's," the doctor told them.

NOW, ALMOST TEN YEARS LATER, it took Finch more than a minute to shuffle to the other side of the doctor's office.

"Good," the neurologist said. "Though you really should be using your walker. Any falls since your last visit?"

"No," Finch said.

"What about freezing?"

"No," Finch said. "No freezing."

The doctor pulled out a piece of graph paper and once again drew the wavy curves he'd drawn for them at every appointment they'd been to for the last ten years. He drew a straight line through the middle, the ideal spot indicating normal dopamine levels, the one that meant the meds were working. The waves seemed larger and farther apart in this new drawing, the periods of normalcy much shorter.

"The idea is to try to keep him in the middle," the doctor said.

She knew well what the idea was. At the high point of the wave, there was too much dopamine and Finch's limbs and head moved on their own, a slow, loopy movement that made him look almost as if he were swimming. At the low point on the wave, Finch was rigid and anxious. All he wanted to do then was to pace, but his stiffness made any movement almost impossible, and he was likely to fall.

"It's a pity he didn't respond to the time-release when we tried that," the doctor said. "And the agonists clearly aren't working for him. As you were informed, they do cause hallucinations in some patients." He turned to Finch. "We can't have you living as Nathaniel Hawthorne forever, now, can we, Professor?"

Finch looked helplessly at Zee.

"So what's our next step?" she asked.

"There really isn't a next step, other than upping the levels of dopamine."

He took Finch's hand and looked at it, then placed it lightly in Finch's lap and watched for signs of tremor. "The surgery only seems to help with the tremor, and you really don't have much of that, lucky for you."

Zee had a difficult time finding anything lucky about the disease that was slowly killing her father.

"We'll keep the timing of his Sinemet the same. But with an extra half pill added here"—he pointed to the chart—"and here."

"So basically he still gets a dose every three hours," Zee repeated, to be certain she was correct. "Though two of those doses will increase."

"That's right," the doctor said. "Every three hours except when he's asleep. There's no need to give him a pill if he's sleeping."

"He nods off all the time. If I don't wake him to give him his pills, he'll only get one every six hours."

"Wake him during the day, but don't give him anything at night," he instructed. "You have any trouble sleeping at night, Professor Finch?"

"Some," Finch said.

The doctor reached for his prescription pad and wrote a prescription for trazodone. "This is to help you sleep," he said to Finch. To Zee he said, "It should help with the sundowning as well, which should stop his wandering. And give him his first dose of Sinemet about an hour before he rises. He'll want to move, but he'll be too stiff. We see some nasty falls in the mornings."

Zee looked at Finch.

"Your daughter will have to keep a close eye on you in the morning," the doctor kidded.

She wanted to tell the doctor that she didn't live with her father, that it was Melville he should be telling all this to, but Melville hadn't come home last night, and she had no idea where he was. When she had asked Finch where he was, all he would say was that Melville was gone.

The doctor started to the door and turned back. "Do you have ramps and grab bars?"

"He has one grab bar," she said. "In the shower."

"I'm going to send over an occupational therapist to check the house. The OT can tell you what you're missing."

The doctor extended his hand for Finch to shake. "Nice to see you again, Professor," he said too loudly, as if he were talking to a deaf person and not someone with what Zee had just now come to realize was advanced Parkinson's. She wasn't certain how Finch and Melville had kept that fact from her.

"I'm sorry the meds didn't work out," the doctor said. "Not so bad to be Nathaniel Hawthorne for a day or two, though, all things considered."

Finch didn't smile back. He took Zee's arm as they left the office together.

"You lied to the doctor about the freezing thing," Zee said. "I've seen you freeze." She remembered the last time Finch had come to Boston for one of his checkups. As they were leaving the restaurant, he'd frozen on his way out the front door. He couldn't move forward and he couldn't move back. They had all stood helplessly waiting for the freeze to break, freeing Finch to step out the door.

"Not for a while," he lied. "I haven't frozen once since the last time he asked me that damned question."

8

FRIDAY-AFTERNOON TRAFFIC NORTH FROM Boston was brutally slow. Zee dialed the house again from her cell, hoping that Melville would answer. She was really starting to worry about him.

"Did he go to see his family?" she asked. Melville had family somewhere in Maine, a sister and two nieces. They weren't close, but he'd been known to make occasional visits.

"No," Finch said.

"Well, where the heck is he?" Zee was frustrated. She had asked Finch where Melville was at least ten times and was tiring of his one-syllable answers.

Melville had seldom left Finch's side for the better part of twenty years now, a fact that Zee found difficult to comprehend in these times of trial marriages and soaring divorce rates. The two had become a couple long before her mother's suicide, though Zee had been too young to realize it at the time. When they'd first gotten together, Zee had believed her father when he told her that the reason they spent so much time with each other was that Melville was his best friend. It wasn't a lie, it just wasn't the whole truth.

Zee's mother was the one who told her about Finch's preference for men. As with many of the inappropriate things Maureen had told her during her manic episodes, Zee would only understand the full impact of the statement in retrospect. At the time the professor had begun to hang out with Mickey and his pirate-reenactor buddies on weekends and during school vacations, and Zee supposed that was what her mother had meant by a preference. Zee was very aware of how much partying they all did together. The pirates drank and they sang, and Finch, who was usually almost prim in his New England reserve, drank and sang with them. Sometimes she would hear him singing as he made his way into the house late at night, the clichéd songs of the gutter drunk that she recognized from the old movies she watched with her mother. Finch was the singing, tippling, happy drunk of 1930s comedies. His joy at such times, especially as it contrasted with Maureen's growing depression, made Zee believe she understood why her father preferred the company of men. Men drank and sang and had fun. Her only wish at those times was that *she* could be one of them.

Maureen, being Maureen, eventually told Zee intimate details of Finch's predilection for men. Much later, when Zee was old enough to have a reference point for such things, she began to understand what her mother had meant and why she had told the stories with such anger. Finch's misrepresentation of himself to Maureen had become the major betrayal of her mother's life.

In Zee's mind, Maureen's unfulfilled dream had always been to experience what she referred to as "The Great Love." It was what she wanted most in life and what she had sworn to have from Finch when they first met and when they spent the early days of their marriage on Baker's Island. She often spoke longingly of the night he had recited aloud to her—not the dark lines of Hawthorne but Yeats. On their wedding night, he had presented her a copy of the book the poem had come from, and that book became one of the treasures of her life. She kept it locked on Baker's Island in the room where she'd spent her wedding night and which had since become her writing studio. That she no longer found such passion in her everyday life with Finch was her cross to bear. Being Irish and Catholic, Maureen Finch was all too familiar with the idea of burden, and hers had become an increasingly loveless marriage within the confines of a religion that vehemently discouraged her escape.

After it became clear to her that Finch had turned to men, a time Maureen referred to as "The Betrayal," Maureen had holed up in her cottage on Baker's Island and had begun to write the story she'd never been able to finish, which she had entitled "The Once." Finch marked this as the first sign of her impending insanity, though when Zee thought about it now, it was more likely a very bad case of postpartum depression, and one from which Maureen had never fully recovered.

It had been a difficult pregnancy and an even more difficult labor and delivery. The fact that Maureen hadn't bonded with the child she'd borne him was no great worry to Finch—he had bonded well enough for both of them. The birth of his beloved Hepzibah was the single factor that kept him in his marriage, for, not being a Catholic himself, he was more inclined to believe that the mistake he'd made with such a hasty marriage might be easily remedied.

The days leading up to Maureen Finch's death had been so terrible that Zee and her father had never talked about them. Zee *had* talked with Mattei about them many times during her sessions, but never with Finch. In retrospect she wondered how many of those days Finch actually remembered, his drinking having progressed, on many occasions, to the blackout stage.

What Zee remembered only too well was a late night, not long before Maureen's death, when Finch, drunk and dressed in his pirate garb, stood in the kitchen and recited Hawthorne in a voice loud enough to fill one of his lecture halls: "'No man, for any considerable period, can wear one face to himself and another to the multitude, without finally getting bewildered as to which may be true.'" At the time Zee had believed that he was talking about being a pirate. Now, of course, she knew better.

Whether Finch remembered the day of the suicide or not, Zee would never forget his face. Coming home from his revelry, singing up the alleyway, he was instantly sobered by the sound of Maureen's screams. He rushed into the house and up the stairway to find Maureen bent backward, spine arched in backbend until her head was almost resting on the floor. Her arms stuck straight outward parallel to the floor as if she were performing a gymnastic feat of great difficulty. He stood in the doorway staring, then watched as his wife collapsed. It was such a bizarre and frightening sight that Zee thought of demonic possession and even of the Salem Witch Trials of 1692.

Zee stood helpless and distanced, praying that the 911 ambulance she had called would arrive in time. She did not dare touch her mother's body. A moment before, her touch had started her mother's third convulsion—she was certain of it. Zee and Finch stood back, staring in horror, completely helpless as they watched Maureen die.

Ironically, it had been the wail of the approaching ambulance that had sent Maureen into her final convulsion.

FOR THE NEXT TWO YEARS, until the day Melville came back for good, Finch had dedicated himself to the process of totally anesthetizing himself, leaving Zee stealing boats and otherwise fending for herself.

They didn't talk about Maureen's death, not directly anyway. One night almost a year later, Finch turned to Zee and invoked another quote from Hawthorne, speaking of "'That pit of blackness that lies beneath us, everywhere. The firmest substance of human happiness is but a thin crust spread over it, with just reality enough to bear up the illusive stage-scenery amid which we tread. It needs no earthquake to open the chasm.'"

Finch was clearly distraught. Family life, strange though it might have been with Maureen, was nonexistent now. So when Melville came back and moved into the house to stay, with him came a certain peace that Zee had not previously known. Finch stopped spending all his leisure time with Mickey and the pirates. And he slowed his drinking to a pace that was quite respectable for a seacoast town in New England—that is to say, more than moderate but not too extreme. He didn't sing anymore, but Zee could see that Finch was truly happy.

One day in Zee's freshman year of high school, she came home and announced, "My friend Sarah Anne says that our home is not a normal place."

Finch thought about it for a long moment before he spoke. This time, instead of quoting Hawthorne, he quoted Herman Melville: *"It is not down in any map; true places never are."*

Zee recognized the quote immediately. Though Finch usually quoted Hawthorne, he had schooled his daughter well in all the American Romantic writers. *Moby-Dick* was her all-time-favorite book.

Zee had to admit that, for the first time she could remember, there was a semblance of family in the old house on Turner Street. And though it might seem an odd situation to the outside world, it was far more normal than anything Zee had yet experienced in her young life.

FOR HIS PART, FINCH SEEMED rather to enjoy shocking people with his new status, a fact that ultimately turned Mickey against him. Taking it up a notch, Finch often introduced his new partner to people he'd known his entire life, telling them that Melville was not only his live-in lover but an ecoterrorist as well. Actually, Melville was a journalist. Before he met Finch, Melville had been investigating a Greenpeace splinter group that was trying to interfere with minke whaling off the coast of Iceland. The nickname Finch gave him stuck. Everyone in town now called him Melville.

He wasn't a bad guy. In some ways Melville was easier to be around than Finch. Her only real objection was that Finch always let Melville run interference for him. Melville handled everything that Finch found difficult in life, which was a lot. And although Finch was happily letting the rest of Salem know of his relationship with Melville, he had never really talked to his daughter about it. It had been Melville, finally, who explained the kind of love that he and Finch had for each other, though by the time he got around to talking to her about it, she had pretty much figured things out for herself.

Finch and Melville had started seeing each other during her mother's final and longest hospitalization. The way Melville explained it, Finch had led him to believe that Maureen was probably never going to get out of the hospital. Zee always wondered about that. It was the opposite of what Finch had told Zee on their Saturday trips to see her mother. Every Saturday, on the way to the hospital, Finch assured his daughter that Maureen would be coming home soon and that they shouldn't give up hope.

Still, she believed Melville when he told her that he'd been misled by Finch. It seemed important to Melville that she know this, desperately important somehow that she not think he was a man who would intentionally break up a family. Surprisingly, she believed him. Zee knew all about The Betrayal, though she was certain that Finch didn't know she knew. Maureen was a talker, particularly when she was in one of her manic periods. Over the years she had told Zee much more than was appropriate to tell a daughter about her father. And Zee could do nothing with the information her mother had given her. Maureen had sworn her to secrecy. So Zee became aware, as Maureen had intended, that her father was sometimes less than honest and forthcoming when it came to getting what he wanted. She didn't fault him for it. Zee knew better than anyone how difficult Maureen's illness had become. But she noted it.

When Maureen had finally come home from the hospital, it was Melville who had disappeared, accepting a writing assignment that took him first to California and later as far away as the Aleutian Islands. He didn't return to Salem until two years later. By that time Maureen was dead, Finch was spending his summer vacation drinking with the pirates, and Zee was out stealing boats.

Finch immediately sobered up, quit pirating, and moved Melville into the house.

Months later, when Zee was caught stealing a cuddy-cabin boat, it wasn't Finch who came to post bail but Melville. It was also Melville who accompanied her to court and Melville who made certain that her juvenile records were sealed.

And when she was required to go to therapy in Boston, it was Melville who drove her. Finch, who had no idea she was stealing boats to get herself out to Baker's Island and the house her mother had left her, not only was disgusted by her behavior but accused her of being just like her mother.

"You don't understand," she heard him say to Melville. "This illness runs in families. She's showing the same kinds of signs, doing the same kinds of dangerous things. She's skipping school. She's stealing boats. I can't have it," he said. "I'll send her away to school before I will deal with this again."

And so Melville took her to a therapist and waited for her in the waiting room. The therapist found no signs of manic depression. While it was clear that Zee was acting out, the therapist thought it was a cry for help, or at least for attention from her father.

If the therapist was correct and it *was* a cry for help, it had been Melville, and not Finch, who answered it.

"He's threatening to sell your mother's house on Baker's Island," Melville told her on the way home from her session with the psychiatrist.

"He can't do that," Zee said.

"He can. You're a minor, and Finch has been paying upkeep and taxes."

Zee panicked. The house was the last thing she had of her mother's. "I'll get a job," she said.

"It wouldn't be enough."

"I'll quit school and get a job."

"If you quit school, he will sell the house immediately. Don't even think about quitting school."

"What am I supposed to do? He can't sell my house."

"If I were you," Melville said, "I think I would learn to behave."

It was simple advice, and she heeded it. From that day on, Zee didn't steal another boat. She didn't skip school again. And, to the best of her ability, she tried to learn to please her father and do what was expected of her.

THE RIDE BACK FROM BOSTON had taken forever. Finch was weary, and so was Zee. She turned the car onto Turner Street, stopping to let a group of day-campers, who had just come from the Gables tour, get back onto their yellow school bus. After they passed, Zee pulled the car into the driveway next to Melville's boat. Dusty, the cat next door, who had become the mascot for the House of the Seven Gables, was sunning himself on the bench in the stern. He looked up, yawned, then stretched and settled back into a more comfortable sleeping position.

The old lobster boat was wrapped in white plastic that had begun, over the years, to flake and tear. A screen door that was cut into the wrapping over the stern showed through to the boat's interior ribs, revealing the vital internal organs: the galley, the bunk beds, the head. A yellow slicker she recognized as Melville's was still slung over the brass cleat near the captain's chair. The old boat gave the impression of a sugared Easter egg, the old-fashioned kind that contained a whole world inside.

Seeing the boat, Zee was prompted to ask one more time after Melville.

"What do you mean, gone?" she asked when Finch repeated the word for probably the fourteenth time.

"Gone, disappeared, poof!" he said, making an upward sweep with his hand.

In a way she wished, hoped, he had not altogether given up speaking as Hawthorne. At least Hawthorne would have answered her question with a recitation that might have yielded more meaning.

This time she changed her question. Instead of asking where Melville had gone, she asked, "Well, when do you think he will be back?"

"Never," Finch said.

SHE SHOULD HAVE LET HIM off at the kitchen door, she thought. It would have been a much easier walk. Because they used the front door, there was a long and cluttered hall that Finch had to negotiate. She grasped his arm to guide him down the hall to the kitchen, but he shook her off. He could do it himself, he told her.

It took several minutes for Finch to travel the long hall from the front door to the kitchen of the old house. She followed his stiff-legged shuffle the length of the hall. The ceilings were low in this house. The wide pine floors sloped on the diagonal. A child's marble dropped in the living room would end up in the kitchen, which made walking difficult enough. But the piles of newspapers Finch had collected over the years seemed to grow precariously out of the floor every few feet. They were waist-high in some places, and they seemed to sway when she walked by them like Disney rocks that were about to tumble. And then there were Finch's books, piled on every surface: the mantels, the desk, the raffia awning-striped wing chair in his den. She was reminded of a pinball machine as she watched Finch navigate unsteadily through the room. His walker stood in the kitchen fireplace. Still wrapped in plastic, it was the same yellowing white as Melville's boat.

After she helped Finch inside, Zee went around the side of the house and began to collect the assorted things that he had placed outside the window of the cent shop he'd created: two pairs of shoes, fishing gear, several lightbulbs of varying wattage, and a set of binoculars. Slowly she began to realize that most of the items Finch had been selling actually belonged to Melville. The hand-lettered sign he'd hung on the window, the one saying that EVERYTHING MUST GO, began to take on a new meaning.

Some people throw people's belongings to the curb. Finch, ever the practical Yankee, had opened Hepzibah's Cent-Shop and tried to make a profit.

"Don't bring that stuff back in here," Finch said when he saw her coming through the door with a pile of Melville's shirts.

"What the hell happened between you two?" Zee asked.

"None of your business," he answered.

She put the shirts and the rest of what she could gather on Melville's boat, forgetting Dusty was there and almost tripping herself in a last-minute effort not to step on his tail. "You'd better be getting on home," she said when the old cat looked up at her. "It's going to rain."

By dinnertime Finch seemed almost his normal self again. She wondered how much of this was the meds. Though he was considerably better than he had been, she knew that the drugs were still in his system. The doctor had told her they wouldn't totally clear out of his bloodstream for another forty-eight hours.

"Let me make you something for dinner," she offered.

"No, look, I've got it right here," he said.

He opened the fridge to reveal a row of labeled sandwiches. She noticed the script on the labels, cursive and feminine, decidedly not Melville's. *Peanut Butter, Tuna, Deviled Ham*—dates scribbled under the titles. Finch took out the deviled ham, pointing to the others and telling her to help herself.

He couldn't swallow very well anymore. She remembered Melville's telling her that. Melville had also told her that bowel movements were becoming increasingly difficult for Finch, peristalsis slowing with the disease. She remembered he was supposed to eat prunes. She looked around for some, searched in cabinets and in the fridge. Then she wondered if they had settled on some medication instead.

She needed to ask Melville these questions. Even if he was gone, as Finch insisted, she still needed to talk to him.

"What do you want to drink?" she asked.

"Milk," he said.

He wasn't supposed to drink milk with his pills. He knew that. She poured him a glass of ginger ale instead. She chose a tuna sandwich for herself.

They ate in silence. She could see the difficulty he was having swallowing his food. It made her sad. But at least he was eating. Melville had long ago replaced Finch's favorite Wonder bread with whole wheat. Two Oreo cookies had been placed on the side of each plate, Saran Wrap tight over the top. Finch had always loved Oreos.

She slid the two cookies on her plate across the table to him. He smiled at her. Standing up slowly, he shuffled toward the fridge.

"What do you want?" Zee asked. "I'll get it for you."

"I told you," he said. "Milk."

"You can't have milk with your pills," she said. "Milk interferes with dopamine absorption." She was there when the doctor had told him that.

Finch acted as if he had no such recollection. But Zee could tell by his smirk that he was lying. This was his form of cheating. Oreos with milk.

"I took my pills half an hour ago," he said.

"Twenty minutes," Zee corrected.

He rolled his head back and forth to demonstrate the ease of movement. He was acting, exaggerating the range, imitating the looping head of the dopamine at its peak. "See, it's working already," he said. He was right, of course. If it weren't working at least a little bit, he would be too stiff to fake any movement. As if to punctuate, he touched his thumb to his middle finger over and over, the way they made him do in the doctor's office.

"Suit yourself," Zee said. But he knew she didn't mean it.

He ate the cookies and sipped at the milk. The fun had gone out of it for him, though. He left half a glass on the table when he got up and made his way into the den.

By 7:00 P.M. he was asleep in his chair, heavily dosed with Sinemet, his head flopping forward. A long string of saliva dripped out of his open mouth and onto his pressed shirt. He wouldn't wake up again until it was almost time for the next pill. Then he would be agitated, looking for something, anything, to take away the tension his brain was creating. He might open his cent shop again for the tourists, though they had cleared out by now. Most likely he would try to walk, the worst thing he could do.

It turned out that Finch had been right. The medicine was working. The flattened midpoint of normalcy the doctor always drew on the wave graph had happened exactly when Finch said it had happened, when they were in the kitchen eating the Oreos. She realized that now. She should never have complained about the milk.

9

S TRANGELY, IT WAS MICHAEL and not her father who finally let her know where Melville was.

"He's been leaving you messages on the home phone," Michael said.

"Why didn't you tell me before?"

"You're in Salem. I figured you knew."

She could tell that Michael was angry. She'd been feeling guilty
about it all week, but now she was angry, too. He'd been traveling again,
and he hadn't called. She'd been leaving messages on the home phone as
well as his cell. She'd also been texting.

"So how was the funeral?"

"Okay," she said.

"Did it turn out as you expected?"

"I don't know what I *expected*," she said. "But no."

A long pause, then from Zee, "Could we please get back to Melville?"

"I told you all I know."

"He didn't say anything else? Just that he had moved out?"

"That and the phone number," he said.

She wanted to call immediately.

"How's Finch?" he asked.

"Not good," she said.

She could hear his tone soften as they talked about her father. The two men had always gotten on well together. In many ways they were a lot alike. "You want me to come out there?"

"Not right now," she said, a little too quickly.

"Jesus," he said.

"That didn't sound the way I meant it."

"You sure about that?"

"Let me call Melville and see what's going on. I'll call you right back," she said. "Then we can decide whether or not you should come out."

"Don't do me any favors," he said. "I already had plans for the weekend—*we* had plans, actually."

More wedding stuff, she thought. "I can't talk about any of that right now," she said.

"Nothing to talk about. Just a statement of fact."

"I'll call you back," she said, hanging up.

She dialed the number Melville had left for her.

He picked up on the first ring. "Oh, thank God," he said. "You're in Salem."

"Yeah, I am. Where the hell are *you*?"

"Finch kicked me out," he said.

"Excuse me?"

"He's very angry at me."

"I can see that," Zee said. "What did you do to him?"

"I don't know." He paused for a long moment. "Actually, I do know. But it doesn't make much sense. It was something that happened a long time ago, something I thought we had worked out."

"Evidently not," she said. "He was selling all your things through the window when I got here."

"Please tell me you're kidding."

"I'm not," Zee said. "He has re-created Hepzibah's Cent-Shop in the front room. He was selling all your belongings."

Melville couldn't help but laugh.

"It's not funny," she said.

"No, but it's creative," he said. "Forgive me, it's the only time I've even smiled all week."

"I rescued some of your shirts," she said.

"For that I am eternally grateful."

"The doctor thinks it's the new meds," she offered. "They were causing hallucinations. We took him off them."

"What's he doing instead?"

"More Sinemet. One every three hours with two half doses added in twice a day."

Melville was quiet.

"Are you still there?" Zee asked.

"Yeah." After another long moment, Melville changed the subject. "I hired a home health aide," he said. "Her name is Jessina. She doesn't work on Fridays, but she'll be in tomorrow."

"I don't understand how you've been keeping all this from me," Zee said. "Or why."

Melville sighed. "Finch didn't want to worry you."

She thought back to the effort it must have taken them both to keep things from her. "Any other secrets?"

"You should come over here. We need to figure things out," he said.

"Where is 'here'?"

"I'm house-sitting," he said. "Friend of a friend. Over by the Athenaeum. Come by tomorrow after Jessina gets there."

She wrote down the address. After she hung up, she went to the bedroom to check on Finch. He was sleeping soundly. She walked back to the kitchen and dialed Michael.

It rang three times before it went to voice mail.

* * *

Zee took out her anger on the kitchen. She cleaned. She
scrubbed down stove and counters. She polished the toaster until it
shined. As she pulled the canisters away from the wall and began to
clean behind them, she found several items meant for decorating cakes:
red and blue sugar, some bottles of food coloring, and some spices, including an old amber bottle—all stuff obviously left over from some
baking project of Melville's. She opened the amber bottle and looked
inside at the tiny silver balls, the kind you might find on a fancy cake
or maybe Christmas cookies—dragées, she thought they were called.
They were probably too old to keep, but she didn't want to throw anything out without asking, so she put all the bottles back in the cabinet
with the other baking things.

Melville was a great cook, but he had never been great at cleaning
or organizing. As she put the cake decorations away, she started reor-
ganizing the cabinets, putting like with like, the canned goods in one
cabinet, the spices in another. Her anger was fading, but the energy of
adrenaline was not, and so she moved from cabinet to cabinet, wiping
down the surfaces as she went, arranging the labels. She became aware
that she was being a bit obsessive when she actually considered alpha-
betizing everything.

When she got to the third cabinet, she was surprised. Hidden behind
the boxes of cereal, she found all the wine that Michael had given Finch,
every birthday and Christmas for the last four years, all second-growth
vintages, really good wines from Michael's own collection. They weren't
stored on their sides but stood upright, a sure way to ruin the corks. Horrified, she pulled them out and set them on the counter.

Before his diagnosis of Parkinson's, from his pirate days on, Finch's
alcohol consumption had been increasing steadily. He had developed
a real fondness for wine. From a medical standpoint, this now made

sense to Zee, though she'd never seen the phenomenon described in any of the medical journals she'd begun to read on a regular basis. Alcohol releases dopamine, the one chemical that Parkinson's patients need.

Finch hardly drank at all now, not since he was put on dopamine, and Melville didn't drink much either. She had tried to tell Michael that, but Finch was always so effusive in his thanks that Michael wouldn't listen to her.

This was such a waste, though. She looked for the wine rack she had given them and found it under the sink. There was space enough for twelve bottles to be stored horizontally, but there were thirteen bottles here. She put the rack on the counter, moving the canisters down to make room. She had to look hard to find the corkscrew, which she finally located in the laundry room. She opened the thirteenth bottle and poured herself a glass. She was still angry with Michael for not answering his phone, but she was grateful, tonight, for his impeccable taste in wine.

S LEEPING IN A NEW place had always given Zee nightmares. Not that her childhood room was a new place. But it was certainly a strange place.

"The Museum of the Perfect Childhood" was how Finch referred to the room that Maureen Finch had created for her daughter.

Zee's room was reminiscent of the fairy tales Maureen was so fond of writing: white canopy bed with pink roses hand-painted on the headboard, ballerinas in different poses on the wallpaper, a dressing table with mouth-blown perfume atomizer bottles, though Zee, who hated any kind of scent, had never filled them up. The silver brush-and-mirror set placed on the diagonal bore her initials in the classic signet H. **F.** T.

Zee had never actually found out her middle name. During her teenage years, Finch and Melville had joked that the T. stood for "trouble." *Trouble is her middle name,* Finch was fond of saying. Sometimes, if he was in a particularly playful mood, he would sing her the song "Trouble" from the soundtrack of *The Music Man,* but then he would catch himself, saying that a dignified man of his age and persuasion should never be caught singing a show tune, that it was just too much of a cliché.

The fact was that even Finch had never had any idea what Zee's middle name was. Hepzibah was the name he had chosen for his daughter, the derivation obvious to anyone who knew him as a Hawthorne scholar. Maureen was given the honor of choosing the middle name, and she had chosen T. Whenever anyone asked Maureen what the T. stood for, she always replied that it simply stood for the letter T. "It is what it is," she was fond of saying.

Zee had always believed that one day Maureen would tell her what her real middle name was, but now of course it was too late. When Maureen died, everything was frozen in place, from Zee's middle initial to the childhood room her mother had spent so much time decorating for what she clearly hoped would be the most perfect of little girls, her little princess.

That Zee was neither perfect nor a princess was evident elsewhere in the room. There were whole segments of wall where she had taken her Crayolas and colored in the ballerinas—head to toe to tutu. She'd had the measles at the time and therefore couldn't be punished for her crime. Maureen, who didn't believe in inoculation, had insisted that Zee stay in a dimly lit room for days with nothing to do. To entertain herself Zee moved systematically around the perimeter of her little world, decorating only as high as she could reach and choosing the colors she most preferred—Electric Lime and Fuzzy Wuzzy.

The colorful ballerinas were creative enough but fatally flawed, Maureen always said, though when Zee asked what she meant, her mother could never articulate a response. Instead Maureen had waist-high wainscoting put up around the room covering the flawed dancers. She painted it white and had rosebuds stenciled along the chair rail to match the bed. Just a trace of Zee's artwork remained now, the occasional wild scribble looping upward past the wainscoting, then disappearing back down again.

There were other signs as well, through the years that followed, that Zee was not the princess type. Scuba gear dangled off the ballet bar, from a job she'd gotten untangling mooring and lobster lines from the propellers of the tourists' boats that so often became caught in them. Those jobs paid forty dollars a pop, better than she could make waitressing, for a task that usually took less than twenty minutes. If she wore her bikini, she often got paid even more, but usually the men hung around and tried to help, which just made things take longer.

Regarding the room now, Zee thought that it did seem she was sleeping in a strange place, or rather the place of a stranger. The room had so little connection to her now that she found herself imagining what the girl who lived here might have been like. What did she want? What were her dreams? In some faraway part of herself, Zee seemed to know. But she couldn't get to the answer.

ZEE HAD FINISHED TWO-THIRDS OF the bottle of wine before she crawled into bed. She was so tired that she didn't even bother to change her clothes, just removed her jeans and slept in the T-shirt she'd been wearing. She had a lot on her mind: Finch, Lilly, Michael. She wasn't angry at Michael anymore; she was simply exhausted, both emotionally and physically. She fell asleep in less than five minutes.

SHE AWAKENED FROM A DEEP sleep to feel another presence in the room. She was not alone. She sat up quickly, her heart pounding.

He was standing over her now, and the scent of him was familiar. And then a voice, one she recognized, barely above a whisper.

"Please help me," Finch said.

As her eyes focused, Zee recognized her father. He stood still as marble, frozen in place, unable to break free.

FINCH HAD TWO MORE freezing episodes the following morning. It was Jessina, and not the neurologist, who finally taught them "Up and Over."

Jessina and her son, Danny, lived in the Point, an area of Salem just off Lafayette Street that had a large Dominican population. She'd been a nurse back in the Dominican Republic and was taking night classes at Salem State, trying to complete her RN certification. Days she worked part-time in a nursing home and part-time as a private home health aide, initially for a woman who had died from complications of Parkinson's six months before and now for Finch.

Jessina was addicted to the Lifetime Channel and to Swedish Fish candies, both facts that for some reason Finch seemed to find hilariously funny. For such a tiny woman, she had a huge presence. Zee marveled at the way she took over a house simply by entering it, speaking to Finch in a poetic stream of consciousness that included her native Spanish, Dorchester English, and an affectionate baby talk that she had developed to soothe her patients.

If Finch had minded the way the neurologist talked down to him, he didn't seem to mind the baby talk from Jessina. It was clear that he genuinely liked her. They had developed a routine in the last few months. Breakfast cereal hand-fed, then a shower, then television—something that Finch had seldom, if ever, enjoyed.

"If you step up and over, you can break the freeze." Jessina demonstrated the exaggerated step the next time Finch froze in place.

He looked at her strangely.

"Come on, you know this!" she encouraged. She turned to Zee. "It's a different part of the brain that is used to climb."

She helped Finch to lift his leg in an exaggerated fashion, Zee reached out to steady him. And it worked. The step freed him, and Finch continued his shuffle toward the bathroom.

"Thank you," Zee said to Jessina.

She shrugged. "I taught him that trick a while back. He just forgot. Can you pick up some Depends while you're out?" Jessina asked her.

Zee was shocked. "He wears Depends?"

"If you want to get the store brand without the elastic, it will save you money. I can just put them on inside his underpants."

Finch grimaced. He didn't mind the baby talk, but he clearly didn't like this discussion.

"I'm sorry, Papi," Jessina said, and squeezed his hand.

Zee could hear her singing a song to Finch through the closed bathroom door:

> Los pollitos dicen pío, pío, pío
> Cuando tienen hambre, cuando tienen frío.
> La gallina busca el maíz y el trigo.
> Les da la comida y les presta abrigo.
> Bajo sus dos alas acurrucaditos
> Hasta el otro día duermen los pollitos.

She wondered how Jessina would have reacted—did react, perhaps—when she heard Finch as Hawthorne. The thought of the Hawthorne monologues being answered in this lilting baby talk seemed surreal. Perhaps Jessina hadn't even noticed the difference in Finch's speech pattern. Perhaps she thought he'd simply been more talkative than usual.

ZEE COULDN'T FIND A SUITCASE, just a canvas bag from L.L. Bean that was on Melville's boat. She went through the things she had rescued from the cent shop, packing the items she thought would be most important to Melville: two pairs of jeans, several dress shirts, a collection of ship's bells. It was odd being on the boat again, and even odder that it hadn't been in the water for so many years. When she was a teenager, Melville had allowed her to use this boat as a refuge when thoughts of Maureen had come back to her, and she couldn't sleep. Melville's mooring was directly off the Gables, and many nights she had walked down in her nightshirt and bare feet and rowed out in the skiff, sleeping on the deck and looking up at the stars, the movement of water the only thing that could lull her into a dreamless sleep.

Melville had always loved the boat even more than she did, and she wondered that he hadn't put it in the water for so long. But Finch hated boats, and caring for Finch had taken so much time that she thought Melville probably had to let it go.

MELVILLE WAS LIVING OVER NEAR Federal Street in a condo he'd been taking care of for someone at the Athenaeum, the historic membership library where he'd been working for the last several years. His official job title was sexton, though Zee had for years called him "the sextant," not in an attempt to be clever and name him after a navigational instrument but because she kept getting the words mixed up. Still, the job description had little to do with either sexton or sextant. A sexton was a caretaker, a position for which there had been budget approval at the time Melville was hired. What Melville actually did these days at the Athenaeum was more archivist than caretaker. Day to day he researched and documented the donated and acquired collections that included such historically significant items as the original Massachusetts Bay Charter.

Melville's new place was on the second floor of one of the converted Federal mansions in the McIntyre District. The doorways had the traditional carved-wood friezes. The stairway wound three floors skyward in a hanging spiral. Though Zee thought it was a shame to chop up any of these old houses, this conversion had been done well.

Melville opened the door and hugged her. "Thanks for coming," he said.

She handed the bag to him. "You're lucky," she said. "He hadn't gotten around to selling this stuff yet."

Melville looked terrible. His sandy hair hadn't been washed, and he hadn't shaved for days. He wore a dirty lime green Salem tee with a logo that read LIFE'S A WITCH AND THEN YOU FLY. He was a big man, muscular from working the boats and from years spent in the merchant marine before he became a writer and an archivist. "I know," he said when he noticed the way she was looking at him. "I avoid mirrors."

The second-floor condo was windowed, sunny, and historically perfect, with the same green-over-gray shade of verdigris that had been used in the sitting room of the House of the Seven Gables. She recognized antiques from the 1850s China Trade. The one suitcase Melville had brought with him sat opened by the door, the unfolded pile of grab-and-go that he'd hastily stuffed into it spilling out onto the floor in contrast to the perfect room. The chairs had the light, spindly legs of expensive antiques, and Zee couldn't imagine Melville daring to actually sit on them.

"Nice place," she said. She looked around for a place to sit, but this was more museum than living room, with feminine touches but altogether too perfect in its execution. It was definitely a gay man's house, Zee concluded, probably someone who dealt in antiques. Her mind jumped to the reasons for the split with Finch.

"I'm *just* taking care of the place," Melville said, reading her. He'd always been able to read her.

"You want coffee?" he asked, pointing toward the kitchen.

"Please," she said.

The kitchen was obviously where Melville was spending most of his time. He gathered up the copies of the *Boston Globe* and the Salem papers and old *National Geographic*s that covered the farm table. Several coffee cups in various stages of abandonment sat on the table and on countertops, one with a fuzzy white-and-green skin growing across the top.

"I've got to wash some of these," he said, taking them to the sink.

"Nice light," she said. The kitchen windows looked out on the North River. It was perfect New England painter's light. Zee caught a glimpse of the dog park that ran alongside the river below. At least ten dogs were off leash, barking and chasing a tennis ball some kid had thrown.

Melville rinsed the cups and the old enameled cowboy coffeepot, a twin to the one she had in Boston, which Melville had given her the year she went away to college because he knew she wouldn't make it a day without his coffee.

The Starbucks bag was empty. He rifled through the cabinets and found some Bustelo. "Pretty strong stuff," he said.

"I can take it if you can," she said.

He opened the fridge and reached inside, pulling out an egg, holding it up to her as a magician might, then making it disappear. It was a trick he'd developed to amuse her after her mother died. He presented the egg to her once more, from behind her head this time, and she took it, smiling.

He smiled back, then the misery overtook him again.

"Are you okay?" she couldn't help asking.

"Do I look okay?"

It was the saddest she'd ever seen him.

"How is Finch today?" he asked.

"I don't know," she said. "Pretty much the same, I guess."

Like Zee, Melville was hoping it was the medication that had made Finch behave so irrationally after so many years. "This is awful," he said.

He brought the old enameled pot to the table, along with a wooden spoon. He watched while Zee threw the egg into the pot, shell and all, heaving it as hard as she could, smashing it against the bottom of the pot. It was part of their ritual. When she was finished, he handed her the wooden spoon, and she stirred the egg, shell, and grounds into a paste.

She smiled, remembering the many times she'd made Melville's cowboy coffee for people, first at school and later for Michael's friends. Part of the shock value of making the coffee was the looks of disgust it brought to her friends' faces to see her make it, then their looks of delight if she could get them to actually taste the stuff, which they all admitted was some of the best coffee they'd ever had.

The first time he made it for her, Zee accused him of teasing her. She was eleven and already had a caffeine habit from years of drinking it with Finch's pirate friends.

"You shouldn't be drinking coffee at your age," Melville had said to her. "But if you insist on continuing such an unhealthy habit, you should at least have some protein along with it." She watched as he threw a whole egg, shell and all, into the grounds, then added water and told her to mix it into a paste. She still thought he was kidding when he put the coffee on the stove and waited for it to boil, then dumped a cup of very cold water into the mix. He strained it into a cup and presented it to her.

"Gross," she said, looking at the mixture in the strainer.

"Try it," he said, and waited.

"No way."

He shrugged. "You don't know what you're missing," he said, pouring himself a cup and sitting down across from her at the table. He sipped his coffee as he read the paper.

Zee watched him drink almost a full cup before she took a sip.

"Not bad, huh?" He grinned.

"Not too bad." It was the best coffee she'd ever had.

"The egg takes away the bitterness, and the shells make it clear." He took her cup and dumped three-quarters of it into the sink. Then he took what was left and added milk, filling the cup.

"I drink it black," she said.

"Not anymore, you don't. When you're sixteen, you can switch back if you want to. For now it's café au lait," he said. "Mostly lait."

Today Melville watched as Zee stirred the grounds the way she had as a child, biting her lower lip, trying to make sure it was right. Finally she glanced up and handed him the pot. She couldn't read his look. "What?" she asked.

"Nothing," he answered, taking the pot back to the sink, filling it with cold water to the spout line. Then he put the pot on the stove and turned the gas burner to high.

Some part of Melville had always foreseen this ending, the impossibility of the relationship with Finch. Bad beginnings don't lead to perfect endings. How could they?

When he came back from sea that last time, he'd gotten himself a job at the Peabody Essex Museum. Just cataloging and doing a bit of writing, descriptions of their collections, the same thing he did for the

Athenaeum now. The Peabody Essex had a huge maritime collection, much of it undocumented. It would be a long time before the museum opened, and they had little room for everything they'd acquired, so it sat in boxes and crates, with the directors of the museum not even realizing in many cases what treasures they had. Melville had been among those whose job it had been to figure it out.

He was grateful for the position, and even more so for the relative obscurity of it, and for the fact that he was back on dry land. For the last several years, he'd been running from something that he knew was absolutely wrong for him, something that had both intrigued and scared the hell out of him at the same time. He didn't come back to Salem until he was certain that its hold on him had loosened.

The impossible affair was something that happened when he'd been working for a magazine, writing an article on whaling off the coast of Massachusetts and on the Greenpeace splinter group that was trying to stop it. They had met when he took his boat up to Gloucester to do an interview. On the return trip, the boat had engine trouble, so Melville stopped at one of the local islands to use a phone. He'd ended up staying the night.

The next day he'd booked himself onto one of the swordfish boats heading out from Gloucester, one he'd heard was looking for crew, thinking he'd do an article on it for a local magazine. Then, later, he signed on to a longer run from Portsmouth up to Nova Scotia, a trip that lasted past Labor Day. He slept with every man he could in every port. It was a stupid thing to do, a dangerous thing, and unlike him, really. And when it didn't erase the night he was trying to forget, he found himself back on the island, but the houses were all closed up for the winter. Grateful, he booked himself onto a merchant marine ship headed out to the Middle East, thinking he'd write a book about the experience. He liked the life enough that he'd made three runs with them, and on the third the ship had an encounter with some pirates in the Strait of Malacca just off Sumatra. The pirates sprayed the ship with fire from several HK MP5 submachine guns that were probably stolen from the Malaysian army. Their attempt to take over the ship had failed—the cheap, low-mass bullets were no match for the thick steel plates of the ship—but several pieces of shrapnel had lodged in the muscles of Melville's left forearm, impairing his grip and ending any thoughts he might have had of pursuing a career as a mariner.

When he got back to Salem, he'd found the job at the museum and rented the room on Essex Street. He went to the free clinic and got himself tested and counted himself luckier than he had any right to be.

He had met Finch through Mickey Doherty. Along with some of the other pirate reenactors, they were trying to raise money to reconstruct the *Friendship,* a 171-foot East Indiaman that had sailed out of Salem Harbor hundreds of years ago when Salem had been the wealthiest city in the New World. Melville liked the idea of raising money for the tall ship but hated pirates and told Mickey so. "We're not that kind of pirates," Mickey said good-naturedly. "We're the old-fashioned kind."

"The kind with parrots on the shoulders?" Melville asked.

"Not parrots." Finch grinned at Melville. "Monkeys."

"One monkey," Mickey said, insulted. "And only because I won him in a poker game."

In those days, before Mickey Doherty had become the Pirate King of Salem, the unofficial mayor of commerce, he had taken his pirating quite seriously. He considered the mention of parrots an affront. If anyone, upon seeing him in costume, made the regrettable mistake of uttering an *"ARGHH"* in his presence, that unfortunate soul would most likely find himself at the connecting end of Mickey's fist.

The monkey, however, was another matter entirely. Though he would deny it if asked, Mickey had a genuine love of the monkey he had named Liam, after his dead younger brother, but that most of his friends now referred to as Mini Mick.

Melville told Mickey he would have to think about it.

Finch smiled at him. A flash of recognition passed between them. For the first time in months, Melville felt like himself.

MELVILLE MET FINCH FOR THE second time at the museum. Finch was doing research for his book on Melville's letters to Hawthorne. Most of them were held by family or had been documented in previous work, but Finch was also interested in the museum's journal of the *Acushnet,* a ship that Herman Melville had served on and then deserted in the Marquesas.

Finch was older. And brilliant. They hit it off immediately.

Over the next several months, they worked late nights at the museum.

Melville met Finch's daughter.

One night Finch told Melville the story about Hawthorne's wife, Sophia. Melville was familiar with the tales of Hawthorne and Sophia. Theirs was one of the great romances of the literary world. But it was not their love story that Finch talked about that night.

Sophia had always had problems with her nerves, as well as terrible debilitating headaches that had plagued her most of her life. As a child she'd been quite sickly. One medical theory that was popular at the time, and one Finch had just heard about, involved mercury and teething. Every generation has its remedy for a particular malady, and every generation has something they blame for disease of any kind. These days it might be pollution or chemical sensitivity or even vaccination. In the days of Sophia's youth, it had been teething. Teething was blamed for everything from paralysis to insanity to consumption. The belief was that the sooner one could complete the teething process (which was undeniably fraught with torment for the child), the better. Disease could be avoided only if the teeth poked through the gums in a timely fashion.

For this reason parents would often cut the gums of their children with implements as unsanitary and as imprecise as kitchen knives. Then they would apply mercury to the open wounds.

"Mercury?" Melville said to Finch. "You've got to be kidding."

"Not at all," Finch answered. "Mercury was used as late as 1960 in this country as an antiseptic. Are you old enough to remember Mercurochrome?"

Melville did remember Mercurochrome, though it was a vague memory, an old bottle with a fraying red-orange label.

"A lot of poisons were used to treat infection in the old days," he said.

He went on to say that there was a new theory that Sophia's headaches and her somewhat erratic personality were probably the result of mercury poisoning.

Melville couldn't remember how Finch had segued from Sophia's personality to Maureen's, but he did remember that it had been masterly. Before Melville knew it, Finch was talking about his wife, her own mercurial personality, and the illness that had kept her hospitalized indefinitely.

"My wife is manic-depressive," Finch had said. "She has been in and out of hospitals for as long as I can remember."

"That must be difficult," Melville said.

"It is difficult, most particularly for my daughter. This last time has been very difficult for all of us. This time I'm afraid she won't be coming home."

"I'm so sorry," Melville said.

Finch looked at him so pitifully that Melville's response was automatic. Though they were standing in the middle of the East India Hall, Melville reached out and hugged him. They stood for a long time, the sound of passing footsteps echoing in the halls around them as Finch cried quietly on Melville's shoulder.

To say they started seeing each other would be wrong. It was more as if they kept seeing each other. Research turned to late dinners of take-out in Melville's room on Essex Street, and when Finch expressed concern about leaving Zee for so long, Melville had his boat moved from its mooring down by Congress Street to one just off Turner Street. They began to meet on the boat, after Zee was in bed. Since her mother had been hospitalized, Zee often had nightmares, and the boat was close enough, sound carrying well over water, to hear her if she cried out.

"The first time we met, I thought you were straight," Finch said to him one night.

"No you didn't." Melville called him on his lie.

"Bi, then. I thought you were bi."

"I was," Melville said. It wasn't a lie. He'd once considered himself bisexual, but that had been a long time ago. "And may I point out that you are the one who is married."

The weight of it hit them both.

"I'm a good deal older than you," Finch said, "and from an entirely different generation." Regret showed on his face. Then guilt. Neither of them brought up the subject again.

On Saturdays, Finch and Zee visited the hospital. On Saturday nights Melville would cook for them. They ate together at the kitchen table, Zee often quieter after the visits with her mother. Sometimes on Sunday, Melville would take Zee out in the harbor and they would fish for stripers, which they would clean and cook outside. Sometimes she would help him work on his boat.

Melville liked Zee. She was a good kid, if somewhat stressed and worried about her mother. Sometimes she would talk about it, saying she didn't understand how her mother could be so unhappy. And she would talk sometimes about the other side of the disease as well, telling him some of the outrageous and amusing things her mother did. But he could see that it scared her. He could also see that for a long time Zee had been her mother's caregiver, trying to keep her from hospitalization as the inevitable depressions set in. Zee didn't have a lot of friends, just one or two from school. She hadn't had much time to be a kid.

And though he felt guilty about his feelings, Melville found himself happier than he'd ever been. He felt bad about the situation, worse for Zee than for Finch. But he let his mind linger on the possibilities: that Finch's wife might stay hospitalized forever, as Finch had predicted, that they could live as a family, that they could go on like this indefinitely. And he was guilty that the thought made him happy. But there it was.

And then, one Saturday in August, Maureen Finch was released. It was a surprise to Melville, although he found out later that Finch had known just before it happened but couldn't figure out how to tell him. What he'd said instead was not to make dinner that night and that he thought they might be late getting back and would probably stop somewhere to eat along the way.

It was the first thing Melville had ever blamed Finch for, and it was a shock. When they pulled into the driveway and he watched as Zee helped her mother out of the car, he had a second shock. Maureen Finch looked up at him. Their eyes met and held.

Zee turned to see what her mother was looking at and spotted Melville. She started to speak to him, but something in her mother's eyes stopped her.

Looking guilty, Finch helped Maureen into the house.

MELVILLE'S PHONE WAS RINGING OFF the hook by the time he got back to his room. He knew it was Finch. But he didn't pick up. Instead he packed his things and, for the second time in his life, he ran, first to California and then up to the Aleutian Islands, where he stayed for the next two years.

★　★　★

THE STOVE BURNER SIZZLED AS the coffee boiled over the rim, pulling Melville's consciousness back to the present. He jumped up and grabbed the pot by the handle, moving it off the burner.

"I'm glad you do that, too," Zee said. "Michael thinks it's only me."

He poured a mug of cold water into the pot.

"How is Michael?" he asked. "God, I hope this doesn't mess up the wedding plans."

"I seem to be doing that all by myself," she said.

He looked at her, choosing his words. "I thought Michael was the one who was making all the plans."

"What gave you that idea?"

"I don't know. It just always seemed to me as if the whole thing was his idea."

"The marriage?" she asked.

"Everything, from you moving in with him to getting married. It always seemed more like his plan than yours," he said.

"Well, it wasn't," she said.

"I'm glad to hear that," he said.

"And what difference does it make whose idea it was?"

"You tell me," he said.

She could feel her face growing red.

"Don't get me wrong, I like Michael," he said. "It's just been a long time since I've seen you being you."

"You know what?" she said, coming back at him.

He looked at her. "I'm sorry."

"I came here to talk about your problem, not mine," she said.

She saw him decide not to comment.

"Unfortunate choice of words," she said.

"At least an interesting one," he said. But he didn't pursue it, and she was grateful.

When the coffee had settled, Melville strained it and poured each of them a cup. He brought the mugs over to the table, taking a seat across from her. He hadn't been to the store, so there was no milk or sugar. He'd been meaning to go for days, he said, but he hadn't gotten around to it. "Good thing we both drink our coffee black."

"So what happened between you two?" she asked. "Why in the world would Finch throw you out?"

"It's complicated," he said.

She didn't fill the silence. It was a trick she'd learned as a therapist. If you don't talk, the patient will. But it didn't work on Melville, or at least not the way she had hoped. He was better at this than she was. And he'd always been comfortable with silence.

"You met Jessina," he said, changing the subject.

"I did," she said.

"She's quite a character." He tried to smile. "She's good with him, though."

"Were you unfaithful?" She was thinking about the apartment again.

"Why would you even ask me that?"

She could tell he was insulted. The truth was, on some level she had been expecting it. He was so much younger than Finch, and the disease was so terrible. She realized she would forgive him for it if it had happened. But it wasn't something you could say.

"I have never been unfaithful to your father," he said as if wounded.

"I'm sorry," she said.

"It was something that happened a long time ago," he said. "Before you were even born."

"You didn't even know Finch before I was born," she said.

"Exactly," he said.

"I don't understand," she said.

"I don't understand either."

"Maybe it was the drugs," she said.

He nodded. It was what he'd been hoping. If it wasn't the drugs, it meant that Finch had entered a crossover stage, something that often happened in patients with advanced Parkinson's, where they began to exhibit the signs of Alzheimer's. He didn't want to think about that.

"Maybe it will go away, when the drugs get out of his system, and you can come back."

"Let's hope so," he said.

Just then an ungodly howl started from the back of the house, echoing up the stairway and shaking the walls.

"What the heck was that?"

Whatever it was howled again. Zee thought it must be one of the fright tours Salem was so famous for, or maybe one of Mickey's popular attractions.

Melville went to the back door and opened it. Then he returned and sat down and sipped his coffee as if nothing unusual was happening.

It sounded as if a body were being dragged up the stairs. A moment later a very winded basset hound entered the room. He took one look at Zee and howled again.

"Zee, meet my roommate, Bowditch. Bowditch, this is Zee."

The dog walked over, laid his chin on her jeaned leg, and gave her the most sincere look she'd ever seen.

"He's begging. Bowditch loves coffee, but it's not good for him."

She couldn't help laughing. She patted his head, and the dog did a sliding kerplunk at her feet.

"I'm dog-sitting, too," he said.

"I think I just figured that out," she said, still laughing.

MELVILLE AND ZEE BOTH DRANK their coffee black, and they both loved dogs. It was one of the many things they had in common: dogs, the ocean, Myrna Loy movies. They both had a love of dark chocolate and a virulent hatred of lima beans, which Finch adored and asked Melville to cook all the time. Finch preferred cats to dogs, especially Dusty, the cat at the Gables. And he didn't share Melville's passion for the ocean. Melville and Zee would go out together sometimes, on his day off. He would take her up the coast, sometimes as far as the Isles of Shoals off the coast of New Hampshire.

Coming back one moonless night, Melville stopped the boat to look at the sky. Stargazing had once been his hobby, especially in the long months at sea when he was in the merchant marine. He owned a telescope, and he often set it up on their deck at home, finding specific stars and planets, showing Zee and Finch. "I always wanted to learn to navigate by the stars," he told them one night. "But I'm afraid it's a lost art."

The only place Melville refused to take her on their outings together was the house on Baker's Island, which had been left to her by Maureen. Both he and Finch refused to go there, but Melville would sometimes drop her off on the island on his way out to fish and then pick her up again at the end of the day.

Finch didn't understand why she would want to go. He wanted to sell the place, especially if it made Zee sad. He refused to pay the taxes on it. But Melville got it. It was Melville, finally, who kept the taxes paid and hired someone to maintain the old place, keeping it shuttered but in good shape in case she might want it someday when she grew up and had a family of her own. "New life chases away old ghosts," he once told her.

SHE STAYED AT MELVILLE'S FOR an hour and a half. "I have to go," she said at last. "I have to pick up some groceries. And some Depends."

"Walgreens has the best prices," Melville said.

"How long has he been incontinent?" she asked.

He shrugged. "For a while."

"You sure you want to come back?" she said.

"Don't even kid," he said.

"Let's maybe give it a couple of days," she said. "Wait until the medicine completely clears out of his system."

On her way out the door, Zee walked past Melville's suitcase. Something akin to an electric shock ran down her spine. She stood stunned and staring. When she could move again, she bent over and picked up the book of Yeats poems. It was right there in the top of his suitcase, its spine jutting out from under a green cable-knit sweater. She was surprised she hadn't seen it before. "Where did you get this?" She stared at him.

"It's mine," he said, gently but quickly sliding the book out of her hands.

"It belonged to my mother." It was the book Zee had gone to get from the island the day Maureen killed herself. She would recognize it anywhere. The book was white, but it had a purple mark down the front cover where one of Zee's crayons had melted. Zee pointed to the stain. "It's the book that Finch gave her on her wedding day."

Melville looked surprised.

"Where did you get this?"

"From Finch," he said, his surprised look slowly morphing into a wounded one.

She stood looking at him for a long time, the impact of his statement sinking in. The anger that she had once felt for Finch, that she thought she was finished with a long time ago, surfaced in her once again.

"I don't believe this," she said.

★ *12* ★

MAUREEN AMPHITRITE DOHERTY FINCH was a writer of fairy tales, not simple happily-ever-after stories that lulled children to sleep but much darker tales with wildly implausible happy endings, usually involving rescue from incredible odds. Very seldom were those rescues performed by handsome princes. Maureen often declared that she was allergic to princes, by way of being Celtic and Irish and fresh off the boat. She wasn't fresh off any boat that Zee knew of. She'd come to America just after she had turned sixteen, after her brother Liam was killed, and there were no boats involved in their crossing. They had all traveled to Boston by plane. But there was no arguing with Maureen when she was telling a story.

Being Finch's daughter as well as her mother's, and more governed by logic than her maternal heritage might suggest, Zee had always tried to point out that there were Celtic princes Maureen could have written about, like Efflam and Treveur, as well as great warrior kings to choose from, like Cormac or Cadwallon. Zee suggested the latter two because she knew that her mother had always had an affinity for great warriors. But Maureen would simply reply that the Irish valued poets more than kings and princes.

Zee listened to the stories. The fact was, in those days she had loved listening to her mother's voice. And during Maureen's manic phases, when the urge to talk became something that seemed to take her over, Zee had become smart enough to realize that letting Maureen's monologues continue uninterrupted would sometimes prevent the more drastic acting-out that she became prone to at such times. Occasionally her mother would stop, upset by something she'd just revealed, and Zee, who'd heard the same stories over and over again for years, would pitch Maureen ahead into her monologues, avoiding the parts that upset her, like an old vinyl record with a scratch that launches it midway into the next song.

Even in those manic times, Maureen was a much better storyteller than she was a writer, and the stories Zee loved were not the fairy tales at all but the real stories about growing up and meeting Finch.

MAUREEN TOLD ZEE THAT SHE and Finch met at Nahant Beach, the long stretch that connected what were once islands to the mainland and more particularly to Lynn, where the family lived now, in a house owned by Maureen's new stepfather.

Maureen had just turned nineteen and was celebrating with her friends, three girls from the shoe-box factory where she worked as an elevator operator. The other girls worked on the machine line, but Maureen, being more beautiful than most, had been plucked from the line and trained to run one of the two elevators that took the executives to their seventh-floor offices. She was good at her job, if not enamored of it. She didn't like being inside, in a moving box inside a much larger box, she said. She was accustomed to much harder work than this— suited to it, actually. Still, she knew the privilege of being chosen, and if she would have preferred the line, she simply had to listen to her friends, who daily offered to trade places with her, to appreciate what a lucky girl she was.

Her shift ended at three. Every afternoon, winter or summer, she walked Lynn Beach, not on the esplanade as most walkers preferred but far below it, on the sand itself. She loved the ocean. Living so close to water made the move from Ireland bearable, though she would have preferred staying there, moving south from Derry to a town in the Republic, maybe, to Ballybunion, where they had traveled once as a family, while her father was still alive and before they lost Liam, and everything changed so terribly, and the Dohertys moved to America and another coastline that, while wildly different and strange, was at least in the end a part of the same ocean.

The day Maureen met Finch was exactly five years to the day that she had stood with her brothers on the cliffs at Ballybunion. It was the first day of summer, and though there were no cliffs in this new world, there was a beautiful beach. Although the water was cold, one could actually swim here, in the protected crescent of bay that stretched toward Nahant. The Irish beaches that Maureen knew, with their wild tides and rough waters, had always been too dangerous for swimming.

On the day she met Finch, Maureen had not been swimming, though two of her girlfriends had. The waters were still too cold. It would take until July for Maureen to go into the water.

She noticed him immediately. He was wearing linen pants and a light cotton shirt, dressed more for a garden party than the beach. He had photo equipment with him, an old eight-by-ten plate camera on a worn wooden tripod. It was very old-fashioned, as was he. "Elegant," is what her girlfriends called Finch. He had a Gatsby-era quality more suitable to the twenties than the seventies, but lovely just the same, maybe all the more so for its strangeness.

He had noticed all of them. But it was Maureen he approached.

"May I take your photograph?" he asked.

Her girlfriends smiled.

Maureen stared.

"I beg your pardon," he started again, "but I wonder if you'd allow me the privilege of taking your portrait."

The girls started to giggle.

"Are you a photographer?" she asked, because she wasn't sure what else to say.

"Alas, no," he said.

The girls fell into gales of laughter. "'Alas'?" one of them repeated.

Finch's face turned red.

"Why?" Maureen asked, realizing she was making it worse.

"You can take my picture," the girl called Kitty said. "You can take my picture anytime."

"Why would you want my photograph?" Maureen asked again, ignoring her friend.

"Because you are by far the most beautiful girl I have ever seen."

Having brothers, she was not used to such flattery, and she was certain that he was making fun of her.

Convinced she had just been insulted, she turned away from him, but, as she did, she caught an expression on his face that broke her heart. He looked so stricken.

"You should go," she said, not meeting his eyes.

But the look had caught her friends, particularly Kitty. "You should pose for him," Kitty said. "Maybe he could make you a model or something."

Maureen ignored her friend. Kitty was a silly girl who had no place giving advice to anyone. Maureen became aware that Finch was still standing in front of her. She could feel his eyes on her. He hadn't moved.

"Oh, for pity's sake, Maureen," her other friend said after it became apparent that Finch wasn't going anywhere. "Let him take your damned picture."

Maureen confessed to Zee that she had allowed Finch to lure her beyond the shore to where the tall beach reeds and the wild roses grew.

He told her the light was better there, and the photo would gain a certain texture.

At this point in her rendition of their love story, Maureen would always turn to Zee and say, "You, my darling, will never be talked into such a thing by any boy. Going off into solitary places with a boy you do not know is the kind of unfortunate choice that leads to rape and murder."

It was the only part of her story that ever rendered Zee speechless. She found herself unable to breathe until Maureen continued, laughing.

"Of course, we didn't know then, did we, how absolutely harmless Finch was in that area." Sometimes she would choke as she said it. Sometimes she would laugh.

Finch was older than Maureen—thirty-five, maybe, she said—and had always seemed to be from another era. Later, when she saw the way he had grown up, she would understand. There was a bit of the outsider about him—he always held himself a bit apart—which was something she understood well. In a time when the world was changing fast, they both seemed to belong to some other time and place.

When Finch won her heart, she said—and he did so quickly—it was not with his photographs but with poetry. Not Hawthorne, she said, but Yeats. Yeats spoke to her soul in the same way that Hawthorne spoke to his, and he had guessed this about her. He knew her soul, she said.

The night she finally knew she loved him, Maureen told Zee, they were out on Nahant, by the old coast guard station. An early hurricane was predicted, and already the winds were whipping around them and waves crashing white and foamy on the rocks below. Finch stood in profile, far too close to the edge, and recited "The Harp of Aengus," his words delivered back to her on the wind.

> *Edain came out of Midhir's hill, and lay*
> *Beside young Aengus in his tower of glass,*

Where time is drowned in odour-laden winds
And Druid moons, and murmuring of boughs,
And sleepy boughs, and boughs where apples made
Of opal and ruby and pale chrysolite
Awake unsleeping fires; and wove seven strings,
Sweet with all music, out of his long hair,
Because her hands had been made wild by love.
When Midhir's wife had changed her to a fly,
He made a harp with Druid apple-wood
That she among her winds might know he wept;
And from that hour he has watched over none
But faithful lovers.

Maureen and Finch married at City Hall in Salem, with Mickey as best man and Maureen's mother conspicuously absent. Not only was Finch not a Catholic, but as far as Catherine Heaney (she had quickly remarried and left behind the name of Doherty in favor of the name of her well-to-do Irish-American husband) could determine, he wasn't much of anything. A service that was not in the church was a slap in the face. Never mind that he had agreed to raise the children Catholic, a civil ceremony was tantamount to mortal sin. At the very least, they should have been married at the rectory, and by a priest. *No good can come of it,* she declared, and stayed away.

Maureen told Zee she had spent a week's wages on the outfit she was married in, a pastel suit perfect for the trip to Niagara Falls the couple had planned. But on the day of the wedding, Maureen refused to go on their planned honeymoon and begged Finch to take her instead to the cottage on Baker's Island, a place owned by her wealthy stepfather that had once belonged to his first wife. A generous man who was embarrassed by Catherine's treatment of her daughter, he had presented the cottage to the couple as a wedding gift. And though Finch hated being on the ocean and was seasick for the ferry ride from Manchester, he canceled their trip northwest and took his new bride to honeymoon on Baker's Island.

Her two-week vacation came and went, and when Maureen didn't return to the factory, they replaced her with another of the young Irish girls, and life in the elevator went on without her.

Days and nights blended. Finch and Maureen lived by the sun and the tides. Food was delivered by boat, though Maureen insisted that they lived on love and never ate a bite. Pies made from wild blueberries were left on their doorstep by neighbors whose families had summered on the island for generations. The couple never came ashore until October 12, when the ferries and shuttles stopped running and Baker's connection with the mainland was severed.

Every time Maureen told Zee the story, the honeymooners stayed longer and longer on their island. "We made love by starlight," she often told her daughter. "We lay naked in the roses."

When they got back to Salem, Maureen went on to say, she had changed from a girl to a woman. She was happy and contented. But when they settled in the house on Chestnut Street with its staff of native Irish, Maureen was mostly stunned. In the time they had courted, Maureen had no idea where Finch lived. She knew that his parents were no longer alive, and, being a proper Irish girl, she hadn't thought it right to visit him unchaperoned. So she had never seen the old mansion with the twelve bedrooms and the staff kitchen in the basement and a cook named Brigid (of all things) Doherty, a slap in the face to both Maureen and the middle-aged servant who looked at the new lady of the house with immediate disdain.

The furniture in the house reminded her of the best that she had seen in Ireland, nothing like she'd ever been accustomed to growing up. It illustrated their class difference to her in a way that she hadn't noticed when Finch was courting her. How had this happened? Only here in the New World would a wealthy gentleman such as Finch have anything to do with the likes of her. This kind of match would never have happened in the old country. Best that his family was dead, she heard Brigid say. If they had been alive, they would have stopped such a union before it ever started.

Maureen was miserable. Though the house was only a few blocks inland, she missed the smell of the ocean and the pull of the tides. She began to have bouts of insomnia and periods of panic where she almost believed that Brigid was trying to poison her, to punish her for overstepping her bounds. She pushed back against these thoughts, and the reasoning of logic prevailed. She found that she could talk herself out of such thinking. Still, she ate little at all, and nothing prepared by the Irish cook. Maureen grew thinner and weaker as the months wore on.

If Finch noticed the change in Maureen, he never said so. Smitten as he seemed, he spent the winter photographing her and the rest of the time either teaching his classes on Hawthorne and the American Romantic writers or in his darkroom. And during that time Maureen started writing.

When she found the house on Turner Street, Maureen said, she convinced Finch, who would do anything in those days to make her happy, to purchase the old building and move there, getting rid of the mausoleum on Chestnut Street and firing the staff. He did it to please her, but the fact was that it pleased him, too. The house she had found was only a few houses removed from the ocean, which surely made Maureen happy, and it was almost directly across the street from Hawthorne's famous House of the Seven Gables. Since Finch had recently been awarded a grant to study Hawthorne's journals as well as his letters from Melville, he could think of no better place to be.

Maureen thrived in the new house. She and Finch were happy for a time, she said. But the winter after they moved in, things went sour. Finch traveled to New York to participate in a guest lecture series on America's Romantic writers at Columbia, and when he returned, Maureen's mood was glum.

She began her fairy-tale collection that winter, a dark assortment that was, in Zee's opinion, far more Brothers Grimm than Disney. "A fate worse than death" was one of Maureen's favorite phrases. In her spare time, she began delving into the history of the house, which was so familiar to her that the only explanation she could offer was that she had lived in it in a past life and that it had lured her back. The house had a story to tell, she was certain of it.

Hearing her alarming theory, Finch might have convinced her to move again, except that he'd fallen in love with the house. He had friends at the Gables; he was very fond of their gardens. He loved everything about the place, including the re-creations of both Hepzibah's Cent-Shop and Maule's Well that they had added to the property to match Hawthorne's story. And the fact that the settlement had recently relocated the house in which Hawthorne was born to the same seaside property as the Gables was an added bonus. All things Hawthorne were now within fifty feet of his front door.

That summer Finch had been offered a teaching post at Amherst at their summer theater, where they would be performing *The Scarlet Letter*. The college production included a newly created dramatic reading from the young Hawthorne himself, which they had invited Finch to compose. He was excited by the prospect of a summer of Hawthorne, immersed as usual in his hero's life, but away from the classroom and in western Massachusetts, very close to the place Hawthorne had spent so many of his later years.

But, as she admitted to Zee, it wasn't a good time for Maureen. As she found herself becoming more and more obsessed with the house and its history, she began to hear it talking to her and would sometimes answer directly in the middle of a conversation about something else.

And though he had planned to take her with him to Amherst, Finch found himself not telling Maureen about his offer. He couldn't bring her along, not in her current condition, and he was starting to fantasize about escape. He did love her, that was true, but for him it had always been in the way one loves a beautiful painting or Bernini's sculpture of Daphne and Apollo. It was love of the feminine ideal, and not based in everyday life. In their daily life, he was beginning to see how troubled she was. Finch had always wanted children. It hadn't happened, and he was growing distant, unable to be near her now, sleeping separately in the downstairs guest room.

But then spring hit and, with it, the lengthening days and bright sunshine. Maureen's mood brightened as well. She began to gather the things they would need at the island cottage: blankets for warmth, seeds for planting summer corn and tomatoes. Knowing his dream of having children, Maureen went to Finch's bed at night. She brewed him tea and whispered to him in the dark about the beautiful and brilliant children they would have. They made love. But when Finch began to relax and told her of the summer appointment he had accepted without her knowledge, Maureen refused to go. It was a betrayal, she said. Moving that far from the sea would surely kill her.

And so, Maureen told Zee, Finch went to Amherst, and she went to Baker's Island. But halfway through the summer, she realized that she was pregnant. She left the island and made her way to Amherst, announcing her impending motherhood in front of the entire cast, one of whom looked stricken, a student playing the young Hawthorne, a beautiful boy who, when in costume, achieved the haunted beauty of Hawthorne himself.

"I should have seen it then," she often confessed to Zee. "I should have seen what was coming."

BUT SHE DIDN'T SEE IT for a while, and neither did Finch. The pregnancy itself agreed with Maureen. She had never been as happy, she said. And Finch's joy was so great that she rode her mania throughout the months of her pregnancy, not descending into sadness with the winter light, and almost to summer before the postpartum depression hit her so hard that she had to be hospitalized.

Maureen was diagnosed as manic-depressive. These days she would have been labeled as bipolar 1, with full-on hallucinations. Maureen heard voices, she saw spirits.

After her diagnosis Finch took over as caregiver, and when Maureen came home, he treated her as one might treat a priceless statue, fussing over her but not getting too close, fearing that the slightest touch might break her.

Maureen came home from the hospital only to remove herself the following summer to the island, where she accepted no visitors, not even Finch. She begged to be left alone, and Finch obliged, partly because he didn't know what else to do and partly because Maureen had left Zee behind, and it was all he could manage to care for his new daughter.

In the two months that followed, Finch could do little but have neighbors check on Maureen's safety and make sure she had food. She threw herself into her writing and produced several more fairy tales.

When she returned in September, Finch asked no questions. He was so happy to have his family restored and to have Maureen excited both about her new career and (at long last) about her new child that it never occurred to him that what he'd been witnessing for the last several years was the onset of Maureen's mental illness, or so he had often told Zee.

Over the next several years, Finch tried his best to get Maureen the help she needed, but treatment was of an era, and though she tried the medications of the time, each new one left her hazy and sluggish and more depressed than the last. Eventually she rejected them all in favor of the wildly manic episodes that fueled her creative energy even as they left her family devastated and exhausted.

One big thing that evolved out of Maureen's untreated illness was a strange and inappropriate mother-daughter relationship that only got more disturbing as Zee grew older. Sometimes unable to attach to her child, at other times Maureen treated Zee as a best friend, confiding much more than a mother should ever relate to a young daughter, outrageous facts and stories that were more embarrassing than helpful: the far-too-early uncensored facts of life from periods to promiscuity, and even sex tricks and methods of seduction to use on boys, details that no normal mother would ever share with a daughter and that Zee had no business knowing. Such confidences assured two things: that Zee would seldom bring a friend into the house and that, at some point much too early in her childhood, Zee and Maureen would switch roles, with Zee becoming the mother figure and Maureen reverting to adolescence.

Maureen had three more breakdowns that required hospitalization during Zee's childhood. The first two were short stays, less than a month in duration. And the last one was the long one, when Melville came into their lives.

★ *13* ★

Today Zee was thinking about Finch's affair with Melville, the relationship that had ultimately put an end to the substance of their marriage if not the form.

She was still angry about the Yeats book she'd seen this morning at Melville's house. The long months of darkness leading up to Maureen's death had been something she had tried for years to forget. Seeing the book brought it all back to her, that and Lilly's suicide.

She wasn't angry at Melville—she was angry at Finch. How dare he give Melville the same book he'd once given to her mother! Sometimes she thought she hardly knew Finch. She knew he had ultimately won Maureen with Yeats. That much her mother had told her. Perhaps that was the way he won all of his conquests, she thought.

She wondered about the boy at Amherst, the one who played the young Hawthorne. Had he been given a volume of Yeats as well? Perhaps Finch had purchased many copies and made it part of his romantic ritual. The thought made her angrier. But it didn't make much sense. Zee knew in her heart that there weren't several copies of Yeats that Finch had doled out to potential partners; there was only the one copy. The book she had seen protruding from Melville's suitcase was the same book Finch had given to Maureen. It had sat for years on top of the bed at Baker's Island in a room that was no longer used as a bedroom but as Maureen's writing room.

Desperate to lift her mother's spirits, she had gone to Baker's Island that last day to get the book of Yeats for Maureen. Zee's original idea had been to take Maureen out there for the day, and she had even borrowed Uncle Mickey's dory to get them there, but Maureen refused to go, saying she was sick and opting to stay upstairs in her bed. Frustrated, Zee went by herself. If she could only get the book to her mother, something Maureen had wished for aloud on many occasions, maybe it would do the trick.

It was something she had always blamed herself for. Had she not gone to the island that day, or had she gotten back earlier, she might have saved her mother's life. As it was, Zee got back sooner than her mother had expected, soon enough to watch her agony but not soon enough to save her.

Zee often talked about her guilt in her sessions with Mattei. But while her mentor would always listen to her rehashing the story, she would not let her take the blame for her mother's suicide.

"Clinging to this idea makes you responsible," Mattei said. "You make yourself guilty and then ruin your own life because you're too afraid to be happy when your mother was not so lucky. It's the easy way out, and it keeps you from having a good life. Frankly, it's beneath you."

Zee had been angry and guilty for years. Though she blamed herself, she also blamed her father and Melville, and in good part she blamed her mother, too. It was that anger and blame that she was working on these days with Mattei. When asked to be more specific about her anger as well as her other feelings about her family, Zee was not able. In a family that had erased the boundaries between parent and child, she had never known exactly where she fit in. She knew that it was this undirected anger and the resultant guilt that had propelled her headlong into a career that she was beginning to doubt she was suited for, especially in light of what had just happened with Lilly Braedon.

Since Lilly died, Zee found that her anger had quickly begun to focus on more specific recipients. She was angry at Michael, though she had no real reason for this except that he so clearly knew what he wanted in all areas of his life, while she couldn't seem to make as simple a choice as whether or not to serve sushi at the wedding. And when she saw the book in Melville's suitcase, all the unresolved anger she felt for her father came flooding back.

"Girls marry their fathers" was another favorite psychological cliché that Mattei was fond of quoting. Michael and Finch were in many ways very similar. Zee wondered how much of her reluctance to make her wedding plans was somehow related to her unexpressed and poorly directed anger toward her father. But just as it was difficult to be angry with Maureen, who had unquestionably been ill, it was almost impossible to be angry at Finch when she looked at him now. She wanted to scream at him. How dare he give Melville the book her mother had treasured? How could he be that cold? But when she looked at Finch now, she didn't feel anger, she felt sad. In a very real sense, the man she was angry at no longer existed. Any anger she felt for Finch, she now directed at the disease that was consuming him.

She needed to talk to Mattei, and to Michael. But she couldn't go back to Boston. Not yet. Not until Melville returned or they figured out some other means of caring for her father.

On Sunday afternoon Zee left another message for Michael. Then, tired of waiting for him to call back, and getting antsy sitting around the house, she asked Finch if he wanted to take a ride.

"Where to?" he asked.

"Up Route 127," she said.

He looked doubtful.

"We can turn back anytime you like, if you get tired," she said.

He still wasn't sure.

"I'll buy you ice cream," she offered.

"Done deal," he said.

They drove up through Prides Crossing, and then on through Manchester-by-the-Sea. When they passed Singing Beach, Finch wanted to stop. They tried walking in the sand, but it was too difficult for him, so they returned to their car and sat with the windows rolled down. She remembered the night she got stuck here, remembered Finch in those pirate days. It was hard to reconcile that man with the one who sat next to her now. She felt many emotions when she looked at him today, the largest of which was empathy. She realized to her surprise that this Finch was easier for her to understand; his vulnerability sparked something in her, perhaps some misplaced maternal instinct she'd been unaware she had.

ZEE HAD NEVER WANTED CHILDREN, a fact that Michael knew and didn't seem worried about, but one that Mattei had found troublesome for a number of reasons.

"Why aren't you worried?" Zee asked Michael just after he proposed.

"Because you'll get over it," he said, confident.

"You don't think it's possible that I might never want them?" She had been frustrated by his lack of concern. "I know you want to be a father."

"When the time is right," he said.

Zee doubted seriously if the time would ever be right. Though Michael refused to talk about it, she and Mattei spent the next four sessions discussing children. At the end of the month, Zee was confused but unchanged.

"What do you want instead?" Mattei had asked her.

"I want a life," Zee said.

"What kind of life?" Mattei had asked.

Zee had once known exactly what kind of life she wanted. Now she drew a complete blank.

THEY DROVE AS FAR AS Hammond Castle before they turned back. Zee bought Finch a coffee ice cream in a cup at Captain Dusty's on their way back through Manchester, and she drove out to the point where there was a clear view of Baker's Island.

"We should sell that house," Finch said, frowning.

"No," she said too quickly, realizing only now that it was the one place that was really hers, though she hadn't been there for years. It had been left first to Maureen and then to Zee with Finch as trustee. "It has some good memories," she said. "Even for you."

"I never set foot on that godforsaken island," he said.

She knew better. But she also knew enough not to argue with a man who in her opinion was beginning to show signs of dementia. Finch's temper had quickened. She had no idea what was going to set him off these days. If his quick and apparently permanent dismissal of Melville for some old grievance was any indication, Zee thought it better not to risk any such confrontation.

She realized suddenly that she had forgotten to give him his three-o'clock meds, then cursed herself for not giving them to him before the ice cream. She got some bottles of water from the ice-cream shop and went back for a paper cup when she realized that Finch could no longer coordinate the use of a straw.

"I have to go to the bathroom," he said after a few minutes.

He was too stiff to navigate, so they parked in the handicapped spot, hoping not to get a ticket. Realizing he wasn't going to make it alone, she steered him toward the ladies' room. If he noticed, he didn't say so.

The door to the stall didn't lock, and she held it closed for him. Several women came in and out.

"Do you need help?" she asked Finch.

"No," he said.

She stayed, leaning against the door for what seemed a long time. After several more minutes, she let the door open slightly and peered into the stall. Finch sat, pants around his ankles, looking as if he were about to cry. The diaper he'd been wearing was now half on, half off and hanging into the toilet.

Oh, God, she should have been helping him.

"I'm sorry," he said.

"It's okay," she answered. She gathered up the soiled diaper and stuffed it into the box marked FEMININE HYGIENE. She wiped him clean and helped him pull up his pants. "We'll get you a shower when we get home," she said.

He nodded.

When they exited the stall, Zee noticed a grandmother standing at the row of sinks with her grandchild, watching while the girl washed her hands. Zee walked Finch to the sink next to them and helped him with the soap dispenser.

"There's an old man in the ladies' room," the little girl said to her grandmother.

Finch's face flushed.

The grandmother gave Zee an apologetic look.

"Men are supposed to use the men's room," the little girl said to him.

"Be quiet, now," the grandmother said.

"But they are."

"Hush," the grandmother said, trying to distract the girl.

"But they are!"

Zee had never wanted to slap a child before, but she wanted to now.

Instead she took Finch's arm and walked him outside. As she let him into the car, she was trying hard not to cry. Things were hard enough for her father without her falling apart.

FINCH FELL ASLEEP IN THE car on the way back to the house. He refused dinner, saying he just wanted to go to bed. She felt bad about doing it, because he said he was too cold, but she made him shower first, not washing him completely, just using the sprayer to wash his lower region. It was the first time she ever remembered seeing her father completely naked. His skin hung in folds, no fat on his frame, his muscles rapidly disappearing. He was wasting away.

"I'm sorry," she said as she toweled him off.

They walked together to the bed. Zee tucked him in and kissed his cheek.

He smiled up at her. "'Life is made up of marble and mud,'" he said, quoting Hawthorne.

"Sleep well," she said.

THERE WERE NO MESSAGES FROM Michael. He hadn't called her back. She knew he was angry with her, not only about the wedding planner but about the fact that she'd told him not to come. She guessed that she was being punished.

She opened another bottle of wine and drank more than half of it before she was finally calm enough to sleep.

ON MONDAY MORNING SHE CALLED one of the other psychologists and asked her to cover her patients. Then she called Mattei and left a message on her voice mail.

"Hi. It's Zee. I've forgotten, maybe you're at the clinic this morning.

I wanted to talk to you live. I'm in Salem with my father. He's not doing well. He and Melville broke up, which no one bothered to tell me, and, long story short, Finch was having some kind of reaction to his meds, a really bad reaction with full-on hallucinations." She paused, realizing she was saying more than was necessary. "Call me when you can. I need to take some time off. I already asked Michelle Berman to cover my patients for the next week, or to cancel them, which she said she was fine with." A long pause. "I need to stay. At least until I can sort out what's going on here." She struggled for more words. "Just call me, okay?"

At one o'clock Mattei called back.

"What's going on, Zee?"

"Did you listen to my message?"

"I did. How's Finch?"

"Not good," she said, her eyes filling up again as she heard her words.

"I figured something was wrong. Otherwise you would have been here. Michael is not being his normal, social self."

Only as Mattei spoke did Zee realize why Michael had been so angry when she spoke with him on Friday night. It wasn't wedding planning that they had scheduled for last weekend. They had planned a long weekend in Chatham with friends of Michael's and Mattei's from medical school. Everyone was taking Monday off. It had been in the works for months.

Damn, she thought. "Is Michael there?" she asked too urgently.

"Rhonda and I are on our way back to the house. They're all at the nineteenth hole."

"Will you ask him to call me?"

"I will," Mattei said. "We miss you." She was temporarily distracted by another conversation. Zee tried to recognize the voice but couldn't. "Listen, take as much time as you need with your father," Mattei said. "Just keep me posted, okay?"

Zee hung up. She'd been angry at Michael for being angry at her, first about the wedding plans and then for not understanding her need to be here with her father. When he said they had weekend plans, she'd thought he meant more wedding planning. He had a right to be angry about that, or at least annoyed. But in light of what Finch was going through, it seemed rather cold. Now she understood. This weekend meant a lot to Michael. The fact that she had completely forgotten it was unforgivable.

She called his cell and left a message. "I'm so sorry," she said. "I've been so confused by this whole thing, first Lilly and then Finch. I completely forgot about this weekend."

WHEN MICHAEL DIDN'T CALL BACK, her mind started in on her. She thought about what a bad fiancée she was. So bad he'd actually had to ask her if she really wanted to get married. A question she had never answered as it turned out. After that thought churned for a while, she started to think about Lilly. Bad fiancée, bad shrink. Two for two. She should have seen Lilly's suicide coming, but she hadn't. She'd seen danger all right, but she hadn't seen suicide. She hadn't been able to predict it any more than she'd been able to predict Maureen's. Let's see: bad fiancée, bad shrink, bad daughter, the Triple Crown.

There were similarities here between Lilly and Maureen, things that went beyond the obvious diagnosis of bipolar disorder and the suicide. There was something else, but she couldn't put her finger on what it was. The real similarity, of course, was a personal one, and one that Mattei had pointed out when she began to treat Lilly.

"Lilly Braedon isn't Maureen Finch," Mattei said.

"I know that," Zee said.

"Yes, and I'm going to keep reminding you."

As it turned out, Mattei should have reminded her more often. Not long into Lilly's treatment, Zee began to see Maureen. In one of their sessions, Lilly had declared, "I should never have had children," and Zee, without realizing, had nodded her agreement, something she had quickly covered. As time went on, Lilly became more and more important to Zee; it became increasingly important to help Lilly work out her relationship with her kids, important ultimately to save her. Still, when Zee should have seen the signs, she saw nothing. Even now, though she had seen the newscast and heard the eyewitness accounts, Zee was having trouble believing that Lilly's death was suicide.

"Denial is a funny thing," Mattei had said to her the next day.

"Not that funny, actually," Zee answered.

THAT MAUREEN'S DEATH HAD BEEN a suicide was something Zee had never questioned. The image of Maureen's last hour was so permanently etched in Zee's memory that for years she had trouble seeing anything else about her mother except the brutal way she'd killed herself. It took five years of therapy as a teenager and another two with the famous Mattei for her to be able to see the more everyday images of Maureen and not just that last horrible day. Zee knew that the fact that these images were now merging with her images of Lilly was cause for concern. She knew it would take some serious therapy to untangle them, but she was not ready to begin the process. Not yet. She understood that at least part of the grief she was feeling at Lilly's death was a delayed reaction, something she should have felt and didn't when her mother died. When Maureen died, all Zee felt was disbelief.

That night, after Finch was asleep, Zee slipped the key out of his desk and unlocked the door to the room on the second floor, the room that had once been the master bedroom. After Finch had moved permanently downstairs, this had become her mother's room. It was the room where Zee had heard most of Maureen's stories. It was also the room where Maureen had died.

Zee didn't linger. Instead she looked around to find what she'd come for, the half-finished story her mother had been working on for so long and had never been able to complete. As soon as she found it, she switched off the light and took the loose handwritten pages back downstairs, locking the door behind her. She didn't put the key back in Finch's desk but in the kitchen drawer, where she could access it more easily. Then she poured the rest of the bottle of last night's wine into a glass, glanced out the kitchen window at the dark water of the harbor and the even darker and starless night sky. She closed the windows in the kitchen against the rain that was on the way, took a seat at the kitchen table, and began to read.

THE ONCE—BY MAUREEN AMPHITRITE DOHERTY FINCH

Once upon a time, Salem was a great world trading port. Hundreds of her ships sailed out of these waters, and there were thousands here who made their living from the sea. There were pepper millionaires and those whose ships made the far runs to China and Sumatra and other ports, trading the lowly New England cod, magically turning it into other treasures, first into molasses from the West Indies and later into such luxuries as French brandy, salt from Cádiz, Valencia oranges, and wine from Madeira.

Arlis Browne was an ambitious young seaman who had worked himself up the ladder in the whaling fleet of Nantucket. He had once been, if not exactly handsome, then clearly striking in a rough-and-tumble kind of way, and he had caught the eye of many a young girl in Nantucket. For the most part, the islanders did their best to keep their daughters away from him, for they could see that under his flashing white teeth lurked a sharper set of canines. But when Arlis Browne turned his gaze in the direction of a local merchant's daughter, the man was so happy to have a suitor for his only child (who was not a beauty and had no other prospects) that he did not look closely at the seaman, and most certainly never checked his teeth.

The merchant died less than a year later, leaving his daughter and all his worldly goods to Arlis. A few months after that, the daughter died, some say under mysterious circumstances. Arlis sold the house and the shop and left Nantucket before any fingers could point in his direction. He had heard about Salem's pepper millionaires, for many of the whalers were leaving the whaling fleet to make their fortunes on the wealthy merchant vessels that sailed from that famous port. With his newfound money, Arlis Browne intended to purchase his own ship and to turn his meager fortune into a grand one.

But Arlis Browne had no idea of the kind of riches he was to encounter in Salem. The merchant vessels were much larger and fancier than the ships he was accustomed to, and they were owned mostly by the old shipping families: the Crowninshields, the Derbys, and the Peabodys, or by the new partnerships and trading companies established by their heirs.

Salem's was an aristocracy of wealth and power controlled by a handful of families for their own enrichment. So when Arlis Browne approached the shipowners with his meager offer of purchase, he was nearly laughed out of town, a slight that didn't sit well with the prideful seaman and one he would not soon forget.

Having nowhere near the fortune needed to purchase a ship, Arlis Browne turned to the thing he knew second best: supplying the goods and services that sailors needed when they were in port.

Thus the disappointed seaman bought himself a decent if not grand house on Turner Street near one of the more than ninety wharfs that lined the bustling Salem waterfront. The house that Arlis Browne bought was not nearly as grand as the one he had sold in Nantucket, and its acquisition left him in a lower social position than the one he had abandoned, a fact that embittered him profoundly. Still, he was resourceful, and more determined than ever to succeed.

Through his harsh travels, Arlis Browne had lost some of the striking appearance that had heretofore attracted the ladies of Nantucket. In the more worldly port of Salem, his weathered face did not turn many heads. Nevertheless, he wasn't discouraged. He knew well what he was entitled to, and he was determined to get it in any way he could. One day soon he would have power, and he would have money, and when he had enough of both, he would also have the prettiest girl in Salem as his own.

Arlis Browne hired a housekeeper, a Haitian woman, once a slave, who had been picked up in port by one of the Salem captains after her husband was freed from slavery by the British and then impressed into service in the British navy, leaving the woman alone and defenseless. She had become the captain's mistress while on board ship, and when he grew tired of her, she was used by some of the crew as well, with the promise of release once she reached the city of Salem.

With his new housekeeper in charge, a woman who had developed the crusty, no-nonsense edge of the damaged survivor, Arlis Browne set about making money by renting rooms to sailors, providing beds and enough hard liquor that his Turner Street address became the most popular rooming house in all the port. Still ruthlessly opportunistic, he booked onto one of the ships owned by the very people who had laughed at his offer of purchase, embarking on journeys that often lasted more than a year. Coming back to port only long enough to bank his money and return to sea. Over time, he amassed a considerable fortune.

Arlis Browne's fifth trip as first mate was a long and difficult voyage, first to Sumatra, then on to Java. When the ship arrived in Salem once again, the captain was gone and First Mate Arlis Browne had taken over the ship. No one ever knew what happened to the captain. There had been a brief inquiry into the matter, but the fact was that the ship came back with such enormous bounty, its best haul in history, that its owner quickly let his ledger sheet override his suspicions. And since jobs on a merchant ship were lucrative and hard to come by, sailors were unlikely to stick their necks out as witnesses, least of all for a dead man. With no one coming forward, the inquiry was brought to a swift close, the missing captain listed as lost at sea. The very next day, the ship's owner hired Arlis Browne permanently as his new captain.

Having secured the position as captain, Arlis turned his attention from commerce to courtship. And just as he had in business, Arlis Browne schemed, plotted, and eventually succeeded.

Her name was Zylphia. She was a girl he'd met in town, not higher in station than he—he had learned his lesson about that—but achingly beautiful, with titian hair that sparkled red in the sunlight. She was so beautiful that her father had received many offers of marriage for the girl but had held off, hoping to snare one of the merchant-ship owners and thus secure his own fortune. But he'd been waiting for quite a while, and all the merchant owners who would pay for such a beauty were already married off to the daughters of the other prominent shipping families. And so when the offer came from Captain Browne, Zylphia's father accepted it gladly. She was nearly nineteen, with no other prospects in sight. This was the best that could be done. No dowry needed to be offered—in fact, the reverse was true. Her beauty commanded a price in itself, the securing of the father's future and enough money for him to retire.

Upon the announcement of his betrothal, the captain quickly kicked the sailors out of his rooming house, keeping only the housekeeper, who had become his eyes and ears in town. Then he set about renovating the house to make it suitable for his new bride. He even added a widow's walk to the very top of the roof, so that Zylphia could search for his ship on the horizon as she waited patiently and longingly for his return.

After the wedding Zylphia's father took his payment and moved inland, to more country parts, where he could live for a long time on his small fortune. His daughter never saw him again.

Zylphia was not a happy bride. She had loved her father and believed with all her heart that he loved her, too. But never for one moment had she loved the captain, whose canines she saw immediately, though it was clear to everyone how taken he was with her. He didn't want her out of his sight, not for a minute, and when he was on land, she was required to be at his side at all times. He brought her wonderful luxuries from his travels: an ivory fan from Shanghai, silks from Calicut, and sugar from the Caribbean.

Everyone in Salem loved Zylphia. The townspeople were always happier in her presence, the way people are often happier in the reflected light of great beauty. Simply to gaze upon her lifted one's spirits. And gaze upon her they did. But they were careful never to speak to her. The captain required that when his wife speak at all, she speak only to him.

Arlis Browne sorely wanted Zylphia with him when he sailed, but it was well known that it was bad luck to have a woman on board, bad luck for many reasons, not the least of which was the large number of men. And he knew that he did not have the complete loyalty of his crew.

For his part, Arlis Browne had begun to resent the voyages. He was becoming a rich man now and still wanted to own a ship of his own. Yet any time spent away from his young wife filled him with jealousy and fear. *What does she do in the long days when I am away?* he wondered.

Every time he set out to sea, Arlis Browne gave strict instructions to the housekeeper to accompany his bride everywhere she went or, better yet, to see to her every need and make sure she went nowhere at all.

And so the girl became a prisoner in her own home.

Night and day she could be seen on the widow's walk. Everyone talked about it, assuming that she was gazing out to sea, looking for her husband. *What a great love they have!* everyone said. *What a wonderful thing to have such longing for your husband!*

But, alas, it wasn't love at all. It was a terrifying panic. She knew she was trapped. The more she watched for his ship on the horizon, the more frightened she became.

Then one night a young sailor happened by. He had been at sea on the East Indiaman *Friendship,* which had just docked and was undergoing repairs. The sailor had not been back in the port of Salem for a few years but had stayed at the captain's rooming house once before and, not having heard of the change, went back there to seek lodging. He knocked on the door, but there was no answer, for the housekeeper, having nothing much better to do, had recently taken to the drink and had as a result become a very heavy sleeper.

Frustrated by the lack of response from within, the young sailor pounded harder on the door. When finally he awakened the housekeeper, she was angry. She yelled at him to go away and leave her in peace. The sailor quickly apologized for the disturbance and went to sleep in the gardens of the gabled house across the street. He intended to awaken at first light and be gone before anyone was the wiser. He soon fell into an exhausted sleep.

But the moonlight was bright, and the sailor was awakened by its luminous glow. As he looked heavenward, he saw a vision, a beautiful girl on the neighboring widow's walk. He told himself that this was surely a dream, for he had never before seen such beauty. Then, just as he was dismissing the vision as impossible, Zylphia turned to face him. Their eyes met. There was such a look of sadness on her face, and such longing, that he found himself weeping, though he hadn't wept since he was a small child.

The sailor came back the next night, and the next, and every night she appeared to him, and every night she looked at him with the same longing. After many nights he realized that her sadness had vanished and that only the longing remained. And from the way her eyes gazed into his, he understood that the longing she felt was for him.

He realized then what he had to do. He had no fear of heights as some of the men did. In a storm he would be the first to climb the rigging and unfasten the sails. He was first in the crow's nest to search for foreign land. And so he easily climbed to the lady who longed for him, making his way carefully up the side of the old house, using only the wisteria and ivy vines as foothold. When he reached the widow's walk, she took his hand. He knew her immediately. He felt as if he had always known her.

They made love on the widow's walk under the moon and the stars. He thought they would die in each other's arms. Such perfection could happen only once in life, and he found himself wishing not to live past this moment. He wished with all his heart for a chill winter wind to blow from the east and freeze them together forever in place.

But the winds were those of summer, and not winds at all but gentle breezes. And every night, after the housekeeper had drunk herself to stupor, the young lovers met on the widow's walk. He knew that he was risking his life for her. He knew he was risking hers as well, for surely one night they would be caught or at least spotted high up above the world by some passing ship or even by a neighboring family who happened by.

He had known with their first kiss that this was to be no happily-ever-after tale. He could taste the bitter with the sweet. But even as he knew their fate, he was powerless not to play his part. He could do nothing else.

When the captain returned from sea, he was quick to hear the stories. He had his spies everywhere, and there are always people who love to be the first to tell a person bad news. The town gossips never thought about the consequences, as gossips never do. If they had known that he would take his revenge on Zylphia, whom they loved deeply, they might not have been so impulsive in their tale telling. They might have stuffed stones into their mouths to keep from speaking, or sewn their lips shut with flaxen thread. But, alas, it was too late. The dreadful damage was done.

He immediately dismissed the housekeeper, calling her a useless drunkard and casting her into the street. Then he went upstairs to take vengeance on his betraying wife.

Yet when he saw her beauty, he could not bring himself to hurt her. Instead he fell down on his knees and begged her to love him. But she could not, and her innocent eyes were too unwily to hide what it would have been in her best interest to disguise. Enraged by her refusal, he chained her to the wall of the bedroom below the widow's walk, and there he sat with her, brooding and scheming.

Evening came and went. And then another.

Each night the sailor climbed to the widow's walk, and each night Zylphia was not there. With no food or water, she failed to thrive. And as she grew weaker, the captain, who was fueled best by jealousy and bile, grew stronger.

On the third day, the sailor did not return. He began to doubt that she had ever loved him. He began to doubt that true love existed at all. And his mind began to play tricks on him. Who was he to think he deserved such love? She was the wife of a captain—how could she love him?

"You see?" the captain said to her when the sailor did not appear again. "He does not love you enough. He does not love you as I do."

The captain grabbed an ax and began to chop the widow's walk from the house. When he was finished and his anger exhausted, he unlocked the chains and kissed the cuts and bruises on her wrists while he cried with despair at what he knew would leave scars and spoil her perfection. "Tell me you love me," he said to her as he carried her to the bed. "Tell me you love me and I will forgive you all."

But the girl could not. She could not lie.

Now bad times were coming to Salem. The British had placed a trade embargo on all American ships, hoping to stop their lucrative trade with France, with whom Britain was at war. Since Salem's profound wealth was almost completely dependent on trade with foreign ports, the city had been severely damaged by the embargo, and the only ships sailing out of port these days were the newly commissioned privateers, which the British ships stood waiting just off the Atlantic coast to intercept.

Like so many others, the captain's ship was at the wharf, with no sail date on the calendar. And though he did not want to leave his wife again, he had begun to hatch a plan that would end his troubles. But the plan involved going to sea. So when he was approached by Leander Cobb about a new venture, he was more than eager to hear the man's proposition.

The *Maleous* was an old slave-trading ship that was as evil-looking as its name implied. After five years in dry dock, the ship still held the stench of death and decay.

Though there had been slave traders in Salem as in Boston, the Salem ships had long ago given up the practice. Most of the old slave ships had been destroyed, some set afire and cheered as they burned, but the *Maleous* was different. It was a huge vessel, and there had been plans to convert it to a merchant vessel, but that had never been done, many considering it cursed. For years it had sat empty and neglected at the far end of Cobb's Wharf.

Old Leander Cobb was a practical man, who owned many ships. Not wanting to risk his other vessels in such dangerous times, he had begun to have the *Maleous* restored, removing the rough wooden sleeping decks where slaves had been forced to lie on their sides so that they occupied less than three square feet of space as cargo.

Aided by the embargo, which had stolen the livelihood of many a sailor, Cobb was fairly certain he could muster a crew for the *Maleous,* cursed or not. But there was only one captain whom he would consider for the job, and only one likely to take it. Cobb knew that Arlis Browne would come at a price. And with all trade suspended and his fortunes dwindling, Leander Cobb was more than willing to pay that price.

Cobb offered Browne more shares of the ship than he had ever earned as a captain, an amount large enough to ensure him voting rights with the promise that he could purchase the *Maleous* as soon as the embargo was lifted and Cobb was able to go back to sailing his full fleet. Arlis Browne would finally get his ship. Browne easily agreed. It not only fit his lofty idea of himself as a ship's owner, but it suited the new and more devious plan that he had hatched for the young sailor who'd stolen the heart of Zylphia.

Cobb had been right—the captain had little trouble getting his crew back together. Most of the sailors had already spent all or most of the money they'd earned during their last voyage. Broke and debauched, the men were eager to go back to sea and had scant prospect of sailing if not with Captain Browne.

Hard times engendered more loyalty to their captain than was previously seen, and so when Browne asked their help with the young sailor, no one was able to refuse his request, its being a condition of their new employment on the *Maleous,* one of the only ships likely to sail from Salem anytime soon.

What the captain was asking was not unheard of. He was not asking for murder or even revenge on the young sailor. All he asked was that his crew get the sailor drunk and press him into service on the *Maleous* in much the same way that the British navy was pressing sailors into service on their ships every day.

It was not difficult to get the young sailor drunk. He'd been drinking every night in an effort to forget his true love, whom he now believed to be deceitful and false. A simple lie did the rest of the trick. The crew of the *Maleous* told the young sailor that they were taking him back to the *Friendship,* which had been repaired and was preparing to sail. It was in fact just what the sailor had been praying for. He went along easily and far too drunk to notice, on that starless night, that it was the *Maleous* they were boarding and not the *Friendship.*

Early the next day, with the seaman still asleep, the *Maleous* sailed out of Salem Harbor. Zylphia was left on her own, with no housekeeper. Of course the captain was also gone, and for now that was enough. Propelled by love, she searched ceaselessly for the sailor, but to no avail. Those who knew the truth of what had happened were too afraid of Arlis Browne to tell her the story. They looked away. Someone who'd seen the seaman that last night said he had sailed on the *Friendship,* but the *Friendship* had not yet sailed, and the seaman was not on board. She began to despair.

True love speaks from the heart, so the town could not stay mute forever. A sailor who took pity on the lovers told her what he'd heard, that the captain had taken her lover on board the *Maleous* and that the young seaman was not likely to return alive.

Zylphia screamed in horror. She sobbed. She begged God to save her sailor, she begged the townspeople to do something, anything—but what could they do? The ship was on the high seas, en route to Sumatra and Madagascar, and would not return for over a year. She should go on with her life, they advised her. She should go home and live the life of a captain's wife, as was fitting to her station. She should forget her seaman and the notion of true love. There was nothing to be done but that.

With no other choice, the girl went back to the captain's house. When she was there, she grew strong again and waited for her sailor to return. For she never lost her faith in true love, and she knew, somewhere deep inside, that he was still alive. She would know if he wasn't. The world would stop if he was no longer part of it, she was certain of that.

One day Zylphia saw a beggar on the wharf. She recognized the brown skin, the familiar hunch of shoulder. It was the housekeeper. Though she had once known the woman as her captor, Zylphia was kind, with a forgiving heart. She knew well what a woman alone was sometimes forced to do. She took the beggar back to her house, for the former servant was as alone in the world as she was, with nothing and no one to save her. The housekeeper who had been cast out was welcomed back to the house on Turner Street. Zylphia nursed her back to health.

Together they opened a cent shop and sold goods through the window to the townspeople. The housekeeper instructed Zylphia in the ways of the islands. Long ago, back in her native land, she had been a practitioner of the healing arts. She taught Zylphia to formulate poultices using bread, milk, and herbs. They brewed cough syrup by boiling bark and bethroot. In the year they had spent together, the old woman and the captain's wife became not just friends but sisters. The townspeople came to the shop for medicines, for cures for everything from boils to pneumonia. Zylphia learned that a poison used to kill the huge rats that came off the ships could also be used in minute amounts to cure respiratory ailments.

And when the mast of the *Maleous* was one day sighted on the far horizon, Zylphia knew what she must do. She paid the housekeeper all the money she had in her accounts and said a tearful good-bye to the woman with whom she had grown so close. Then she waited for the ship to reach the wharf.

But the *Maleous* did not head directly into the harbor. Instead she stopped, as ships did in those days, on the Miseries to drop off her sick sailors, for there had been an outbreak of yellow fever and many of the crew were ill and dying of it. Falsely fearing contagion, the port of Salem would not allow the ship and its bounty to unload at the wharves with sick sailors on board. So Captain Browne discharged the ship's ill and dying on the Miseries, neighboring islands aptly named for the sailors who were left to die within sight of the homes they were struggling desperately to reach.

Now, try as he might, the captain had not been able

to kill his wife's young lover in the long year they had been at sea.

With each day he feared their return to Salem and the loss of his young wife, whom he had begun to dream of feverishly every night as they got closer and closer to home. He began to pray that the sailor would die before they reached Salem. And as even our darkest prayers are sometimes answered, the unfortunate sailor contracted yellow fever. And so the captain left him on the Miseries, to die with the others before the waning of the moon.

The captain returned to port, and his wife was waiting on the wharf as the ship landed. His heart leaped at the sight of her. Was it possible? Did she finally love him? But it wasn't to be. When she looked at him, her eyes held nothing but hate. Her gaze moved beyond him, scanning the crowd for her true love. His rage was murderous, and he shouted aloud without any thought to listening ears. "An entire year gone and not even a tender look for me?"

And though it would have been in her best interest to do so, she could not feign even the slightest warmth for the man who had taken her true love from her. She could not lie.

During his long months at sea, the captain had almost been able to convince himself that she would love him one day, but now he feared it would never be.

He rushed toward her, grabbing her roughly by the arm and pulling her down the street. "Your lover is dead," he told her coldly. "He died of the yellow fever, crying out in pain and suffering. And he never cried your name, but the name of the South Sea maiden he got the fever from."

"You killed him," she said, not believing his story about the maiden but desperately fearing that her true love might be dead.

"Don't you hear me, girl?" he said, digging his fingers into her arm. "I told you he was dead. Infected, as all men are, by a faithless woman." Then he dragged her back to the house while the townspeople watched in horror.

He beat her until she cried out. But without her sailor, Zylphia had no will to live. She did not try to stop him. When he finally struck her with his closed fist, she fell to the floor, motionless and mute.

For the first time, the captain feared he might lose her, not to the sailor but to death. He cradled her in his arms, begging her to come back to him and vowing to nurse her back to health.

He carried her downstairs, to a room with cooler air and a view of the ocean. In the days to come, he cooked for her. But she would not eat. He bought fresh fruit and sugar, which he knew she had loved, but still she would take nothing. On the third day, the housekeeper appeared at the door, with a pig roast and apples and some soup made of mutton and celery.

"It is no use," the captain said. "She is beyond nourishment and will take no food."

"Let me see her," the old woman suggested. "For it is her choice to live or to die."

Desperate for her help, and knowing about the

Haitian woman's healing powers, the captain let the old woman into Zylphia's sickroom.

"Leave us," she said, and the captain obliged.

The old woman sat on the edge of the bed. "Your true love lives," she whispered, and at those words Zylphia opened her eyes.

The captain was so grateful to the housekeeper that he offered to take her back with full wages, but she refused, saying she would stay only long enough to prepare their meal. When the food was ready and the table set, she returned to Zylphia and whispered softly in her true friend's ear, "Make your peace now with your husband. Eat your evening meal at his table. Take what nourishment you can, for you will need your strength. But do not drink the porter. Not one drop."

The housekeeper helped Zylphia to the table. Then she left the house.

The captain was so happy to see his wife alive that he ate a hearty meal and then drank heavily of the porter, filling himself with ideas of what he would buy his wife now that she had chosen to live.

When the convulsions began, his arms standing straight out by his sides, she sat wide-eyed and disbelieving. His head arched back until it almost touched the floor behind him. She stared as his body stiffened, then collapsed. She had no strength to move.

By the second round of convulsions, the housekeeper was at the door carrying clothes needed for travel and medicine to heal the sailor of his fever. "Come quickly," she said.

Released from her nightmare, Zylphia followed the

housekeeper out the door and down to the stolen dory. "Your true love is alive on the Miseries," the housekeeper said. "Hurry on now, and do not look back."

Zylphia, weak only moments before, now found the strength it took to row.

As she left the mouth of the harbor, she passed the *Friendship,* just hoisting sail and making ready to head out to sea. She passed one of the smaller fishing boats coming into port. She looked at neither but kept her eyes focused straight ahead, never taking them off the island where her true love waited. . . .

★ 15 ★

MAUREEN'S MANUSCRIPT OF "THE ONCE" had never been completed. Though she wrote dozens of drafts with varied endings, she had never been able to finish the fairy tale. Maureen had re-created the legend as far as historical documentation would allow, but she had no idea where to go from there.

What she did know about the story was that the chief clerk at Derby Wharf had reported the missing dory to the Salem authorities. It was found days later and returned by a ship heading into port after dropping off sick sailors on the Miseries. Its thole pins (or oarlocks) were worn down and ruined from the long row. No sign of either Zylphia Browne or her young lover was ever seen again.

Maureen's own belief in The Great Love would dictate a happy ending, but she could not seem to find the happily-ever-after for the fairy tale she was writing. The reason was simple. Partway into the story, Maureen had decided that the only suitable escape for the star-crossed lovers was aboard the *Friendship,* not the re-creation of the tall ship that sat at Derby Wharf these days, the one the tourists lined up to see, but the ship that had sailed out of Salem during the early 1800s.

Maureen had done significant research and had discovered that the young sailor of her story had originally been part of the *Friendship*'s crew. But the problem was that, on the very voyage in which the *Friend-ship* might have been instrumental in carrying the star-crossed lovers to their happily-ever-after, the ship was captured by the British in the re-cently declared War of 1812. There was certainly no record of the young woman, who would most probably have tried to disguise herself as a man or, barring that, as a cabin boy, in order to safely make this voyage with a predominantly male crew. A woman's passage as anything but a captain's wife was not only considered unlucky but dangerous for her as well. Yet when Maureen searched the records of the *Friendship,* she was unable to find any mention of either the young man who had sailed earlier aboard the ship or, had he decided to travel under a different identity, of any new names on the ship's register.

That the young woman, Zylphia Browne, had escaped her home and her abusive husband was a matter of public record. Whether or not she had poisoned her husband was speculation. The captain, who was known for his brutality, had many enemies. It was well docu-mented that he had been poisoned with a substance that was most likely brought back on one of his own ships and that his death was as painful as the beatings he'd been known to inflict not only on his crew but on his servants and his wife.

Even Maureen had to admit that there'd been little real evidence about Zylphia Browne's escape. There was some documentation by an eyewitness who had seen someone rowing the stolen dory in the direc-tion of the Miseries. The witness knew it to be Zylphia, he said, only by the red hair that escaped from under the brim of a boy's cap. The dory was later discovered on the Miseries, oarlocks worn down to bare wood. But no sign of the young lovers was ever found.

Maureen never questioned the idea that the lovers escaped. Her belief in The Great Love would allow for no other possibility. But try as she might, she could never find the happily-ever-after ending that she so needed to complete the story. Though most of her stories were fictional, and though her original intention was to create the happily-ever-after, she found herself obsessed by her search for the truth. In the writing of the story, she had developed a strong bond with Zylphia Browne. She knew the woman well, she said. She told Zee that it almost felt as if she were walking around in Zylphia's skin.

Zee had known for a while that her mother had begun to believe that the story was her own. And so when Maureen announced one day that she was certain she'd been Zylphia Browne in a prior lifetime, Zee wasn't as alarmed as she should have been.

Looking back on a tragedy, there is often a moment one can point to when everything changes and begins to move more quickly toward its inevitable climax. As Zee looked back, she realized that the moment for Maureen had been the day she began to talk about reincarnation. For while she had initially believed that Maureen was talking about who she had convinced herself she'd been in her last life, Zee realized only later that she was also talking about who she was most certain to become in her next.

"People reincarnate in groups," she told Zee in those last days. "So do not despair, for we will most certainly see each other again in another place and time."

★ *16* ★

ON TUESDAY MORNING THE occupational therapist showed up. Jessina was there, hand-feeding Finch. Oatmeal spilled down the front of his shirt.

"Can't he feed himself?" the OT asked.

"He can," Jessina said.

"Then he should be doing it."

"He likes it when I feed him this way, don't you, Papi?"

Finch managed a weak smile.

The OT addressed Finch directly. "It's important that you do this yourself. You have to keep up your skills."

She walked through the house taking notes, more like a Realtor than a medical professional. She pointed out two more spots in the bathroom that needed grab bars, one more in the shower next to the one that Melville had put in earlier and another one next to the toilet. "You should raise the seat in here," she said. "Try Hutchinson's on Highland Ave." She also suggested a hospital bed. "They can be rented," she said. "His insurance will probably cover it." Zee followed her back to the hall. "You'll need a railing in this hallway," she said. She looked at the tilt of the floor, the slope of old pine.

"Do you know of anybody who can install one?" Zee asked.

She shook her head. "I don't. But a local carpenter can probably do it for you.

"And get rid of these newspapers," she said. "Falls are inevitable with Parkinson's, but this is an accident waiting to happen."

The OT wrote out her report, leaving a copy for Zee. She said good-bye to Finch, who ignored her. Zee walked her down the long hallway to the front door.

"He really should be in a nursing home," the OT said.

It shocked Zee to hear it. "I was thinking maybe assisted living of some sort." There was a nice place in Back Bay not far at all from where she lived. But even that was only in case of emergency, meaning if Melville didn't come back and she couldn't figure out anything else.

"He wouldn't qualify for assisted living," the OT said matter-of-factly. "He's incontinent, and he needs to have his meds administered. A few years ago, maybe, but not now."

Zee barely heard the rest of the instructions. All she wanted was for the OT to leave.

"Make sure he showers every day. And gets dressed. I forgot to ask you about skin breakdown."

"I haven't noticed any," Zee said.

"Pay attention to his skin," she said. "There's always a danger of skin breakdown with incontinence. And skin breakdown can kill them. That and falls." She gestured toward the newspapers again.

"I'll take care of those," Zee said.

SHE WORKED ALL AFTERNOON ON the piles of papers. When Jessina was making dinner, Zee decided to walk down to the wharf to pick up some more recycling bags.

"Can you stay a little longer tonight?"

"Sure," Jessina answered. "What else do I have to do?"

"I can't tell if you're serious or if you're being sarcastic," Zee said.

"I am never sarcastic," Jessina said.

"Again," Zee said, "I can't tell."

Jessina laughed. "Go. Take your time. I can give him his pills and get him to bed if you like."

Technically, Jessina wasn't supposed to give Finch his pills. But with her nurse's training, she was certainly capable. Zee left the seven-o'clock dose on the table.

"Thanks," she said, then added, "don't let him have milk with them."

ZEE WALKED DOWN DERBY STREET toward the wharf. This was a street of American firsts: first candy shop, first brick house. The street was named after America's first millionaire, Elias Hasket Derby, a man known locally as "King Derby," who had been made famous by the lucrative shipping trade that came into this port. Zee remembered her Uncle Mickey telling her something about the first elephant in America as well. It had come in on one of the Salem ships. For some reason she thought the elephant had a drinking problem and laughed to herself, dismissing the thought as a trick of memory. But then she remembered the story. Running low on water, the crew had fed porter to the elephant. By the time the ship arrived in Salem, the elephant had developed a strong taste for the stuff. That much of the story was true. Uncle Mickey's embellished version included 1800s AA meetings and elephant detox.

She thought about Mickey and decided to stop by. There was no love lost between Mickey and Finch, not since Maureen had died and Melville had come into Finch's life. But Zee hadn't yet said hello to her uncle. She knew she should tell him what was going on, and she figured he might know someone who could install the rails and grab bars Finch needed. If anyone was connected in the city of Salem, it was Mickey Doherty.

Zee ducked into Ye Olde Pepper Companie to buy Finch some Gibralters. The Salem confection was the first commercial candy in America and might have been responsible for some of the success of the Salem ships, which stocked the candy as ballast on their outbound voyages. They were hard candies with a shelf life longer than the life span of any human, and it is said that the captains bribed the customs officials in the far ports with Gibralters to get more favorable trading rights. "The original strangers with candy," is what Finch called the Salem ships.

Finch loved Gibralters, and he loved Black Jacks as well, so she bought both for him. She helped herself to one of the Black Jacks, smelling the sweet molasses as she opened the bag.

She walked past the Custom House with its gold roof, where Nathaniel Hawthorne had worked his day job before his writing made him famous. Then she crossed the street to Derby and Pickering wharves.

There were only a few wharves left in Salem now. In the shipping days, there had been almost a hundred, along with all the businesses that went along with the shipping trade: coopers, boatwrights, stables with wagons for transportation, and shipyards.

In those days there were many rivers that emptied into the sea here. New Derby Street, where it connected to Lafayette and Salem's Route 114, would have been mostly underwater, with the North River running down the other side of town. It was possible back then to get around Salem almost completely by boat. Even the Point, where Jessina and many of the Dominican and Haitian population lived now, had once been bordered on three sides by water. The street noise from the wharves and the resulting trade eventually became loud enough to send the shipping millionaires uptown, either to the Common or to Chestnut Street, depending on their politics.

Now there were only a few of the old wharves left down here—Derby Wharf, where the *Friendship* was docked, and Pickering, where Mickey's store and Ann Chase's witch shop were.

These days Derby Street was an endless array of tourist traps. Costumed pirates and monsters handed out flyers for haunted houses and wax-museum tours. Though the main attraction was still the witches, any unrelated but marginally frightening side business was fair game. The real witches, who didn't exist at all in Salem back in 1692, thrived here in great numbers now.

A number of shops and tours belonged to Uncle Mickey, whom the locals referred to as the "Pirate King." Mickey had seen the tide turning in Salem way back in the seventies and was entrepreneurial enough to take great advantage of it. For the most part, the witches kept a lower profile, selling their wares for cash but practicing their religion quietly, as if they were never quite certain that their new elevated status would last in a city that sported images of witches riding broomsticks on the doors of their police cars while at the same time it launched a campaign to "Ditch the Witch" in favor of Salem's less famous but in many's opinion more significant maritime history.

But for now that campaign had not taken hold, nor had the ordinance that someone had proposed to limit the number of haunted houses per city block, a proposal that Mickey had vehemently opposed, owning so many of them himself.

Zee started her search for Mickey in one of his many haunted houses. Summer hires from Salem State College worked the counter as they munched on Wendy's takeout. Their fake scars looked disturbingly real alongside their piercings and tattoos from the Purple Scorpion down the street. Screams echoed from behind the hanging curtain, followed by demonic laughter that Zee recognized as Mickey's recorded voice. Cackling and trying to frighten one another, a group of tourists exited through the gift shop.

"Oh, my good God, what *was* that!" A woman in her sixties giggled nervously and tried to catch her breath.

A man with a crying child was less impressed. "That is extremely frightening," the man said. The kid, who wouldn't let go of his father's hand, seemed equally frightened by the teenagers behind the counter. "You ought to have an age limit. Post a sign or something," the father said. As he stepped down into the brighter lobby, the kid tripped, the father dangling him by the arm until he righted himself.

"Wimps," the tattooed girl said under her breath.

"It says right on the door." A kid sporting a Frankenstein half-head extension with bolts glued to his neck pointed to a sign: THE SCARIEST HAUNTED HOUSE IN SALEM. Frankenstein reached for one of the girl's french fries, and she slapped his hand.

"Is Mickey here?" Zee asked. She didn't know any of these kids. Mickey had a new crop every summer.

"He's at the other store," Frankenstein said.

"No he isn't. He said he was going to the *Friendship,*" the girl said.

"One or the other," Frankenstein said.

Zee thanked them and exited as a large group of tourists crowded through the door. They all wore red T-shirts saying DON'T MAKE ME CALL MY FLYING MONKEYS! Zee navigated her way through the crowd, crossing the street in front of their silver tour bus, heading for Pickering Wharf.

She could see the masts of the *Friendship* in the distance, but she figured she'd stop at Mickey's shop first. Then she saw her Auntie Ann.

Ann Chase stood in the doorway of her store, the Shop of Shadows. Its name was a reference to the *Book of Shadows,* a well-known journal used by real witches to record spells, rituals, and philosophy, plus recipes for herbal potions and teas. Ann was in costume today, her black robes rustling in the early-evening breeze. "Hello, Hepzibah," she called when she spotted Zee. "I heard you were home."

"Hi, Auntie." Zee smiled and walked over. Ann was not Zee's real aunt, but she'd been Maureen's best friend. Zee had called her Auntie for as long as she could remember.

They hugged each other.

"So great to see you," Ann said, looking at her. "It's been a while."

Zee thought back. It had been over a year. When she came home to visit, she always stopped by the shop to see Ann, but the last time she'd been here, Ann's shop had been closed, and there was a sign on it saying that Ann had flown south for the winter along with the other snowbirds.

"How was Florida?" Zee asked.

"Warmer than here," Ann answered, laughing. Then, more seriously, she asked, "How's Finch doing?"

"Not great."

"I heard he broke up with Melville."

"Word travels fast," Zee said. Salem was more small city than small town, but people still had a way of knowing one another's business. "Does Mickey know?" Zee asked.

"He's the one who told me."

On some level Mickey would be glad. It was no secret that Mickey blamed Melville for his sister's death. Though Ann had loved Maureen, she held no such grudges. Everyone who knew Zee's mother well also knew how sick she was. Mickey had always been in denial about her illness, and finding someone to blame was easier for him than looking at the whole truth.

Zee believed that her Uncle Mickey had always been in love with Ann Chase. For Ann's part, she seemed uninterested and barely tolerated his constant flirting. Every once in a while, she would get annoyed, especially when his rival but bogus witch shop advertised something that she found personally offensive, like the time his aura machine broke and he made coupons sending a bus full of tourists from Cleveland over to Ann's shop advertising that Ann Chase, one of Salem's most famous witches, would tell their fortunes by reading the bumps on their heads for half her normal price.

"Group rates!" he said when she yelled at him. "I don't know what you're complaining about—I sent you forty-five brand-new customers."

Mostly, though, Ann and Mickey got along well. To their credit, most of the witch and horror shops in Salem got along. The only exception had been a recent issue about a psychic street fair that came to Salem every October. Almost everyone agreed it was a good thing, but some of the witches, particularly those who paid rent all year long down on Essex Street, where the fair was held, resented the itinerant psychics who came in to make a quick buck during the peak tourist season, then left town. The witches said they were afraid some of the traveling psychics might bilk tourists out of too much money or give them bad advice, thereby sullying the reputation of the year-round fortune-telling community.

For this reason the town had recently begun to require all practicing psychics to be licensed if they wanted to tell fortunes in Salem. Though Zee had wondered exactly how one goes about licensing a psychic (Salem, in the end, had adopted San Francisco's policies, which included a fee of twenty-five to fifty dollars and a record of permanent address along with a valid Social Security number), she nevertheless thought it was a good idea. She remembered a horrible incident that she and her mother had had with a psychic named Arcana not long before Maureen committed suicide.

AS SHE WAS WRITING "THE ONCE," Maureen had become convinced that she was not only the writer of one of the great love stories in history but that she was its heroine as well. She began to believe she was the reincarnation of its main character, Zylphia Browne. So absorbed was she in the story that she'd started searching for someone who could confirm her belief.

First Maureen went to her friend Ann, asking for a past-life reading. But Ann, whose New Age belief systems had only recently led her to Wicca and not yet to reincarnation, said she didn't do such things. The only things Ann read in those days were the bumps on your head and a few astrological charts, and even those were a recent addition to her repertoire of New Age razzle-dazzle.

"Why do you want a reading?" Ann asked. She had of late begun to worry about Maureen, whose behavior had been growing more and more erratic in recent months, causing her to neglect both her home and her child in favor of this fairy tale she couldn't finish. Though it was based on a true story, like many true stories it was left uncompleted, and Maureen had taken it upon herself to supply the happily-ever-after ending the story needed. But she'd been agonizing over the tale for several years, and it had become Ann's opinion that not only was Maureen never going to finish the story but that in all probability the story might just finish Maureen.

"I think I was Zylphia," she told Ann one day when they were at the shop. Zee had been busy flipping through the pages of the book entitled *100 Easy Spells for the Young Witch*.

"Excuse me?" Ann said.

"I think I was the main character in my story," Maureen said. "In another life, I mean."

At this point Zee looked up. Her eyes met Ann's.

"What makes you think that?" Ann asked as calmly as she could.

"Don't patronize me," Maureen said.

"I'm not."

"And don't be *careful* with me either. I hate it when people are careful with me."

"I'm not being careful with you. I just asked you where you got this rather unusual idea," Ann said.

"Isn't it obvious?" Maureen said. "I live in her house, I have the same bad marriage."

"Not exactly the same, I hope." The husband in the story had beaten and tortured his wife and essentially held her prisoner.

"You know what I mean," Maureen said.

Zee was pretending to be absorbed in her book. But they both knew she was listening, so they lowered their voices, which only made the girl listen more intently.

"It isn't just that I live in her house, it's everything else," Maureen said. "I dream about her all the time. I know the torture her husband put her through. I even know how she killed him, or how the house-keeper did."

Maureen had spent the better part of last summer trying to figure out how Arlis Browne died. It was murder, no doubt, but historic rec-ords were sketchy about who had poisoned him. Maureen had deter-mined (for the sake of her story) that it was the Haitian housekeeper and not Zylphia who had administered the poison. Though she was determined to stick to the facts in her storytelling, she needed a sympa-thetic heroine, she said.

"Strychnine," Maureen said.

"They didn't have strychnine in the early 1800s," Ann said. "It wasn't even introduced until the 1840s."

"Yes, but they had the nux vomica plant, which is where strychnine comes from." Maureen smiled at her discovery. "It grows in India or Southeast Asia, and it is quite possible that it could have come in on one of the Salem ships."

Zee had put down her book and was now clearly listening to the conversation.

"You can buy the stuff at a garage sale," Maureen said. "Do you know they used it as late as the sixties in small amounts as a medicine? This incredibly toxic substance, and they were feeding it to us."

Ann wanted to say that they were *still* using it, that you could walk into the homeopathic section of any health food store and find nux vomica, which was still widely used, though the amounts were minute. But she decided against telling Maureen.

"Let's change the subject," she said, indicating Zee's interest. Not only did Ann not want to talk about such subjects in front of a twelve-year-old, but she hesitated to talk with Maureen about such things at all. The previous year Maureen had taken Ann's advanced herbal class for the sole purpose of learning how to poison someone, which hadn't helped either the class or Ann's reputation in Salem. Ann was studying to be a Wiccan high priestess and wanted to make sure her respectability was sacrosanct. In those days witches were not yet commonplace in Salem. Ann had been one of the first. Though Ann knew a lot about many substances and their effects, both good and ill, she didn't think it wise to share any information that could potentially hurt anyone.

Ann tried to avoid talking to Maureen about her story. She didn't like the idea of Maureen fictionalizing the tale, filling in its historic blanks. Some stories should remain unfinished, Ann told her friend. But Maureen didn't listen. She was too obsessed by the plight of the young wife and by trying so hard to prove her happily-ever-after. The only real evidence of any ending to the story was the husband's poisoned body and the worn oarlocks or thole pins in the abandoned boat. How the young lovers had escaped Great Misery Island, if they had indeed escaped at all, was anyone's guess. It was a dark story, and one that Ann believed should be left alone, especially by someone as impressionable as Maureen Finch.

Ann told her again that she didn't do past-life readings and didn't know anyone around here who did. "I think you'd have to go out to California for that kind of thing," she said.

"As if I can do that," Maureen said.

★ ★ ★

MAUREEN'S OBSESSION CONTINUED LONG INTO that last summer. She tried the First Spiritualist Church, where she'd had some luck before, but they were mediums, not past-life regressionists. She read a book about Edgar Cayce, who believed strongly in reincarnation. She read many books about Buddhism, hoping to unlock the secrets to samsara or the process of rebirth. But she still couldn't find anyone to help her.

Late that July she finally found a psychic down by the Willows who said she did past-life readings for a fee and booked an appointment for Maureen before she had a chance to change her mind.

Zee was immediately suspicious. She seemed to remember some kind of scandal a year or so back, where a psychic who lived down by the old amusement park had pretended she had a talent for talking to the dead and conned a senior citizen out of two Social Security checks before the old woman's children had gone to the police. Zee didn't know if this was the same psychic, but she wasn't taking any chances. Though she knew that there was no talking Maureen out of anything once she decided to do it, Zee wasn't about to let her go alone.

They parked the car over by the arcade and walked around back to a three-decker house with peeling paint and a second-floor sign that read WORLD-FAMOUS ARCANA, PSYCHIC TO THE STARS.

Their feet echoed up the two flights of stairs. A bare lightbulb cast a weak halo around itself on the upper landing making it appear, as they approached, as if it were an aura around Maureen's head.

Arcana threw open the door just before they reached it, as though she had psychically sensed their presence. The gesture was overly dramatic and clearly for effect. Anyone with two ears could have heard them coming, but Zee could tell that Maureen bought it.

"Who are *you*?" Arcana demanded of Zee. Her feet were unshod, and she was wearing a caftan with a towel around her head, as if she had just washed her hair and couldn't be bothered to dry it.

"I'm her daughter," Zee said.

"It'll cost you extra if you both want a reading."

"She doesn't want a reading," Maureen said. "She just came to keep me company."

The psychic grumbled and lit a cigarette. She gestured them to a card table covered with a plastic cloth. Zee noticed the posters on the walls, photos of Indian mystics, all wearing turbans. Maybe she *hadn't* just washed her hair, Zee thought—maybe this was a bad attempt at a turban.

It wasn't difficult for Zee to see that the psychic hated Maureen on sight. She demanded the money up front, which Maureen was glad to provide, but Maureen was nervous and couldn't find where she'd put her wallet. Flustered, she sent Zee back to the car to look for it.

Zee looked under the seats and in the glove compartment but found nothing. Then she knelt down by the driver's door and looked under the car, but all she found was an empty Almond Joy wrapper and one dirty child-size cotton sock. When she came back, Maureen was tense but finally located her wallet in her jacket pocket. The psychic rolled her eyes but took the money—and ten dollars extra because Maureen had brought Zee along. "I'm not used to working in front of an audience," she said.

"You have done past-life readings before," Maureen said.

"Of course," Arcana said. "I do them all the time."

Zee could tell that it was a lie, but the look on Maureen's face was so hopeful that Zee took a seat on the couch and was quiet as the psychic had instructed.

Though the table was flimsy and the decorations looked fake, the psychic had some high-tech tools. On the floor under the table were two switches: a dimmer and a dial that controlled the sound system.

"I demand silence," Arcana announced with the authority of a sanctimonious second-grade teacher.

Zee wondered at the declaration, since no one had uttered a word.

With her bare, simian feet, the psychic flipped the two switches, grabbing them each with her toes and turning the dials expertly. First the music came up, a cross between Indian mystic and theremin music from a bad fifties sci-fi film. With the other foot, her toes dialed the lights down until Maureen and Zee were left in near darkness. The only source of illumination was the neon sign for the midway across the street.

Maureen was anxious. "Am I supposed to do anything?"

"Not yet."

For the next four or five minutes, the psychic did breathing exercises. Deep breaths in through the nose and out through the mouth, making a great show of her hyperventilation.

When she spoke again, her voice had dropped an octave.

"Hello, this is ARCANA," she said. "What is your question?"

Zee tried to keep from laughing.

"I don't have a question. I'm here to find out about my past lives," Maureen said softly.

"What is your *question*?" Arcana's voice boomed.

Maureen looked at Zee. "I guess my question is whether I was Zylphia Browne in a past life."

It wasn't going at all as Maureen had told Zee it would. Somehow she'd gotten the idea, or had read somewhere, that she would be the one going into the trance. In the book she had read on past-life regressions, the therapist would put the seeker into a trance and then record the outcome. When the seeker woke up, she would be able to listen to what she'd said under hypnosis. Or, barring that, another approach would be that Arcana might go into a trance herself, the way Edgar Cayce did, and just start relating her impressions. Maureen seemed surprised that she would have to ask a question herself.

Zee was trying hard not to laugh.

The psychic said nothing. But Zee could feel her annoyance through her supposed trance. She couldn't tell for sure that Arcana was faking it, but she would have bet she was. Zee was aware that the psychic was watching her. In another minute, if she couldn't stop giggling, she was pretty certain that Arcana would kick her out.

"What is your question?" Arcana boomed.

"She told you. She wants to know if she was Zylphia Browne in another life," Zee finally said.

"Silence!" Arcana hissed.

Maureen shot Zee a warning look. Maureen's voice shook as she once again formed the question. "Was I Zylphia Browne in a prior life?"

Everyone in Salem knew the story of Zylphia Browne, who had killed her husband and then disappeared, never to be seen again.

"The *MUR-der-ess?*" Arcana bellowed, stressing the first of the separated syllables and arching her eyebrows like Gloria Swanson in *Sunset Boulevard*.

It was wrong to classify Zylphia as a murderess; rather she was a victim of severe abuse who happened to escape. Even Zee believed that much.

It didn't take a psychic to figure out the answer Maureen wanted to hear. It also didn't take a psychic to know how much this woman didn't like Maureen. Maureen was a beautiful woman with a childlike presence that could seem ingenuous if you didn't know her and which often had the effect of enraging women who had to make their own way in the world and weren't having an easy time of it. Arcana seemed instinctively to know that her answer could do some damage to Maureen. And she seemed fully prepared to do it.

"Mirror, mirror, on the wall," she said to herself. The growl of a Harley from the street below drowned her words.

"Excuse me?" Maureen strained to hear her. Even Zee sat forward in her seat.

"You are not Zylphia Browne," Arcana said in a voice that neither of them could miss. "But your daughter is."

Maureen stared at her, uncomprehending at first.

Arcana poked an accusing finger out from under her caftan and pointed at Zee. "Your daughter is the young Zylphia Browne come back to life."

Maureen stared in disbelief.

Arcana seemed to know immediately what she had won. The look of devastation on Maureen's face was unforgettable.

And though she didn't buy it for a minute, a chill ran down Zee's spine.

As they descended the stairs and through the midway to the car, Zee could see that Maureen was in shock. They got into the car and sat in silence.

"You know that she was playing you, don't you?" Zee said.

"What are you talking about?"

"She didn't like us from the moment we walked in."

Instead of having the desired effect, it had the opposite.

"You didn't have to be so rude!" Maureen said. "You didn't have to laugh!"

"I'm sorry," Zee said.

Maureen's hands were shaking as she turned the key in the ignition. She flooded the engine several times before the car finally started. Zee fought the urge to tell her mother that she wasn't doing it right. She'd already said far too much.

★　★　★

ON HIS WAY BETWEEN SHOPS, Mickey had spotted Zee talking to Ann in front of her store. He walked over to join them. "What?" he said. "You're stopping to see her before you say hello to me?"

When Zee looked at Uncle Mickey's eyes, it was like looking into Maureen's. It had always been disconcerting. Uncle Mickey had the same deep blue Irish eyes that his sister had had, though the look in his had always been much more playful.

He lifted her up and spun her around. "How's the little bride-to-be?" he said.

"Good. Fine," she said. "A little dizzy, actually."

He laughed and put her down, winking at Ann. "How's Finch?"

"I think you know," she said.

"I've been meaning to get over to see him," Mickey lied.

He'd been saying the same thing for years. Zee didn't challenge him.

"I need a carpenter," she said. "One who can put in some railings. I thought you might know someone."

"Sure," he said. "I know a couple of people who could probably do that for you."

He thought about it for a moment, then they said good-bye to Ann, and he walked her over to the next wharf, where the *Friendship* was moored.

At 171 feet, the tall ship was impressive. It had always seemed an odd coincidence to Zee, with so many ships having sailed out of Salem in the age of sail, that the *Friendship* of Maureen's book was the same historic vessel the city had later chosen to re-create. There had been no real connection between the *Friendship* and Maureen's book, no record that she had ever been used for the young lovers' escape. As it turned out, the very voyage that Maureen had chosen, the only one that would have accurately fit with history, had been the *Friendship*'s final one. On that final voyage, the East Indiaman had been captured by the British, and its entire crew had been taken prisoner. Maureen's choice of vessels had rendered her desired happy ending impossible.

When they got to the rigging shed, Mickey put two fingers to his mouth and gave a loud whistle.

Zee spotted the man Mickey was whistling at, perched high in the rigging of the *Friendship*'s forward mast.

When the man didn't turn, he whistled again. Then yelled, "Hey, Hawk, come down here a minute, will you?"

The man started down the web of rope. At first glance Zee thought he had fallen, his descent was so rapid. It was only when he got closer that she saw the way his arms and legs moved in rhythmic coordination. Like a dancer. Or a spider.

He walked over to where they stood. He looked very familiar. She had seen him before.

"What's up?" He glanced from Mickey to Zee and back again.

"This is my niece, Zee. She needs someone to do some carpentry work."

"I'm not a carpenter," he said. "I'm a rigger."

"Rigger, carpenter, navigator—this guy can guide a ship home just by looking at the stars."

"That's a slight exaggeration," Hawk said.

"Seriously, he's a jack-of-all-trades," Mickey said to Zee.

"And master of none," Hawk said, laughing.

"And he's modest, too," Mickey said, slapping him hard on the back.

"Thanks a lot," Hawk said, and Mickey laughed. Hawk turned to Zee. "What do you need done?"

"Just railings," Zee said. "And some more grab bars in the bathroom.

"It's for my dad," she added.

"I guess I can do railings." He looked at Zee for a long moment. "I know you," he said. His eyes did a body scan, and he clearly liked what he saw. He squinted at her face, analyzing. "Where do I know you from?"

"She's engaged," Mickey said, lifting her hand to show him the ring, not realizing he'd already seen it. "And she's a shrink. Meaning she's far too smart to fall for a tired old line like that one."

"A shrink, huh?" Hawk said. He grinned and shrugged. But he kept looking at her, as if he were still trying to figure out where he'd seen her before.

She knew immediately where she'd seen him, though she didn't want to say so. It had been just a few days ago, at Lilly Braedon's funeral. And before that on the bridge as she watched the television the night Lilly jumped. He was one of the eyewitnesses, the one in the blue van who hadn't wanted to talk to the reporter.

"When can you do the railing?" Zee asked.

"I don't know. Maybe tonight or tomorrow night. Are you in a hurry?"

"It's not urgent, but it is important." She wrote down the address and handed it to him.

"I'll get there my first free night," he said.

"Hey, Hawk, we need you up here!" one of the guys yelled from the rigging.

"I've gotta get back."

"Thanks," she said.

He nodded and smiled.

Zee and Mickey watched him walk back to the ship.

"His name is really Hawk?" she said to Mickey.

"It's a nickname. Short for Mohawk, someone told me. That's his boat," Mickey said, pointing to an old lobster boat tied up at one of the slips. Instead of displaying a name on the stern the way most of the boats did, this one featured a painted image of a hawk in flight. "I hear he's the best worker on the ship. Don't know if he has any Native American blood, but he sure can climb."

Zee felt her dizzy spell return as she watched him climb back up the rigging. She put out her hand, grabbing Mickey's arm for support.

"I know," Mickey said. "I can't even watch him." He turned to her. "How much time do you have?"

She looked at her watch. "About an hour."

"Come on. I'll buy you a drink," he said, steering her toward Capt.'s, a waterfront restaurant and bar on the wharf directly across from the *Friendship*.

★ *17* ★

MELVILLE STOPPED AT THE post office to pick up his mail. Then he walked over to Steve's Quality Market to get some of the prime beef he knew Finch liked. Finch could no longer chew very well, and he had trouble swallowing. But the butcher at Steve's would grind the beef for him, and then Zee could scramble it with mushrooms and some garlic and oregano. It wasn't much, but at least it wouldn't be sandwiches. He hoped that Zee was giving Finch his vitamins. He'd have to remind her.

For the first time in weeks, Melville felt hopeful. Maybe it was a side effect of the new drug that had made Finch behave so erratically, he thought. That would explain everything. Why else would something that had almost killed their relationship once before have come back so suddenly, as if the whole thing had happened not more than thirty years ago but just in the last few weeks? Melville hoped it could be explained away by the new drug that Finch was taking, the one that was said to cause hallucinations in some people. It would be great if Finch's rage were mere hallucination. Melville would move back in, and he would never mention the fight they'd had. They would go on as usual, as if the whole thing had never happened.

Finch had been off the drug for several days. It should have cleared out of his system by now. But if Melville were honest with himself, he'd have to admit that the whole thing had started before the new drug. It had begun a few months ago with an offhand remark about Maureen. Before he knew it, they were fighting about everything, from the dripping kitchen faucet to the piles of newspapers in the hall.

The subject of Maureen had come up many times lately. And just as Finch always did when he didn't know how to say something, he had quoted Hawthorne: "A woman's chastity consists, like an onion, of a series of coats."

"What is that supposed to mean?"

"It means what it means."

"If you have something to say, I'd appreciate your saying it straight out," Melville replied. He didn't like talking about Maureen. His guilt on that matter had almost done them in. He put a hand on Finch's shoulder. "Tell me what this is about."

"I don't know," Finch had said, suddenly realizing how confused he was.

Melville leaned over, taking Finch's face in his hands. "'This relationship has to succeed, not in spite of what happened with Maureen but because of it.'" He looked at Finch. "Those are your words," Melville said.

"I know." Finch was crying.

"You know how much I love you," Melville said.

"Perhaps you had better keep reminding me," Finch said.

He was losing Finch to this damned disease. It was a fact he seldom faced directly, yet there it was. He knew the inevitability of demise, but they had been together for so many years, happily together. Even after the Parkinson's, they had been happy. He knew that the illness would rob him of Finch eventually. He'd found himself looking away when the shaking began, not wanting to see it. Luckily, shaking had not become a major part of Finch's case, though there were many other elements of the disease that had taken their toll. He had to remove himself sometimes so that Finch wouldn't see him cry.

He had read all the books, knew that there'd be a time when there was some crossover. If he were to look at things honestly, he would have to admit that it had already happened. Parkinson's patients, if they lived long enough with the disease, often got what was called the "Alzheimer's crossover" and started to show signs of dementia. When Finch had initially presented with a bit of dementia, Melville remembered how relieved they were to find out it was only Parkinson's. Only. That was a joke. To say something was only Parkinson's was like saying that Hurricane Katrina was only in New Orleans for a day. Parkinson's was one of the cruelest diseases out there. If you lived long enough with it, if something else didn't get you first, you'd end up in the fetal position in a bed in some institution, sometimes for years. Melville often wondered—often hoped, in fact—that he would have the strength it took to help Finch end things if it came to that. He knew Finch's wishes, and he also knew that Finch had been saving pills for years against the inevitable.

But things were changing, and they were changing fast, with a look, an offhand remark, or a sarcastic tone of voice that he'd never heard Finch use before.

The night he kicked Melville out, Finch threw the volume of Yeats at him, hitting him in the head, leaving a bruise. Melville hadn't seen the book for so many years—he and Finch had put it away after Maureen's suicide, in a place where Zee would never find it.

"Get out!" Finch had screamed. "And don't come back!"

Melville called a doctor he knew in Boston, a neurologist friend of a friend, and someone he'd had coffee with a few years back.

"Dementia is funny," the doctor said. "Sometimes it's worse when it starts. There's so much anger involved. The patient is trying to hide his symptoms yet is clearly terrified. But then there's a second stage, when things start to settle down. And usually that gets better for everyone for a while. I call it the honeymoon period. Of course there will also be a time when he may not even know you at all," the doctor said. "But, hopefully, that won't happen for a long time."

THE PLAN THAT MELVILLE AND Zee had come up with today had been logical enough. He would drop by, ostensibly to pick up some of his belongings. Then they would see how things went. If Finch's anger had been a product of the drugs, maybe he would have forgotten it by now. Melville would move back in and take care of Finch until the end. And if it were something else, some new progression of the disease, then they'd figure out what to do next.

It felt odd to knock on the door. He didn't think he'd ever done that before. When he had first become involved with Finch, when Maureen was in the hospital, he'd almost never come into this house. He and Finch had always met elsewhere, usually somewhere in town. And later, after he'd moved his boat up here, when he thought Maureen wasn't coming home, Finch had started leaving the door unlatched for him and he'd slipped into the house as quietly as possible late at night, so as not to wake Zee. In those first years, they had been very careful.

ZEE ANSWERED THE DOOR. "HE'S asleep in his chair," she said. Melville checked his watch. "Three-fifteen." Finch's pill was due at four. He should have timed this better.

She was bundling papers in the hallway, her hands blackened, an old bandanna from Finch's pirate days around her head.

"I'd been meaning to do that," he said, remembering how Finch had talked him out of it every time Melville started to clear the newspapers. Finch had claimed he was going to read them all, though he couldn't read anymore, hadn't been able to for quite some time.

Finch was a bit of a hoarder by nature. Such was his respect for the written word that he could never bear to part with any printed material. Even the ad circulars from the weekend papers had to be kept for at least a month, with Melville sometimes sneaking them out of the house and down the street to throw them away, so that Finch, finding them missing, wouldn't raid the trash and bring them back inside.

"Does your father know you're doing that?" Melville asked Zee.

"He knows," she said. "He doesn't like it, but he knows."

Melville helped her get the recycling bags to the curb. They were lucky—tomorrow was trash day, and in his current state Finch was unlikely to try to reclaim them.

They sat in the kitchen making small talk, waiting for Finch to wake up. She didn't mention the Yeats book, and neither did he, though he wanted to. Part of him wanted her to have it. But years ago he'd made a promise to Finch, and Melville always kept his promises.

Zee checked her watch. It was almost four. "It's nearly time for his next pill," she said. "He should be waking up soon."

As if on cue, she heard the sound of Finch's walker.

"You got him to use his walker?"

"Yup," she said.

"I'm very impressed."

Neither of them spoke as they waited while Finch negotiated the long hallway.

Melville willed his heart to slow down. He couldn't stay seated.

"I hired a carpenter to put some railings in the hall," she said, sensing his nervousness, trying to calm him.

"Good idea."

He took a breath and held it. He stared at the floor. When the walker paused at the kitchen threshold, Melville looked up at Finch.

Their eyes locked.

"Hello, Finch," Melville said.

Finch stood still and stiff, his expression masked and unreadable.

"I brought you some sirloin," Melville said. "I put it in the fridge."

Finch lowered himself into his chair. Falling the last few inches, he winced. When he finally spoke, it was not to Melville but to Zee.

"I want him out of here," he said quietly. It was almost time for his next pill, so his voice was gone. The sound scratched as if tearing his throat. But his words were unmistakable.

★ *18* ★

Z EE TOOK THE PHONE into the den. She'd been talking to Melville for the last half hour, trying her best to calm him down. By the time she hung up, Jessina had put Finch to bed and had left Zee a note.

"Get some sleep," she said to Melville after they'd talked in circles for the third time. "We'll figure things out tomorrow."

The television was still on, but muted. Zee sat on the couch, flipped the remote, finding Turner Classics: *Jane Eyre* with Joan Fontaine and Orson Welles. She didn't turn up the sound but just sat staring at the screen. "Who is Grace Poole?" she said to the television set. It was a game they had invented, she and Melville and Finch, a kind of *Jeopardy!* for the literary set. Something Finch had tried on his lit classes. *Who is Grace Poole?* was the answer. The question was one she had written herself: *She takes care of Rochester's crazy wife in the attic.* No one had talked about the parallel to her mother when the question was asked. She thought now about the way her question should have been worded: *She takes care of Rochester's crazy wife.* There was never any mention of an attic in Brontë's book, and, in the film, it was more like a tower room than an attic. She had always gotten it wrong. It was Maureen and not Mr. Rochester's crazy wife who lived in the attic. And though both Finch and Melville had challenged wrong answers all the time and must certainly have noticed the error of her question, they had never challenged Zee on this one.

Zee fell asleep to the sound of foghorns. She dreamed of the stars and of the *Friendship,* not the reproduction that was at the wharves today but the old one that Maureen had tried to write about. Then she dreamed about Bernini's sculpture of Neptune and Triton as it had once been described to her by Maureen. Or maybe it was Lilly. . . . No, it was Maureen.

★ *19* ★

THE DAY MAUREEN KILLED herself, Zee had borrowed Mickey's dory and gone to Baker's Island to get the Yeats book in an effort to cheer her mother.

Maureen's mood seemed better that day. Certainly she was kinder to Zee, whom she had been ignoring ever since the visit to Arcana's psychic studio. The last few months had reminded Zee of the Snow White fairy tale, not just because of Arcana and an image she kept having of her holding out a poisoned apple, but because her mother, who had once loved Zee so much, had grown cold ever since the pronouncement of the psychic, as if the very existence of Zee were keeping her from her fairy-tale ending.

That was the way it was between them for the rest of the summer. Maureen stopped writing "The Once"—in fact, she stopped writing altogether. Mostly she just stared out at the water or sat upstairs in her room. She hardly ate and rarely if ever slept.

So on her way to the island to get the book, Zee was encouraged. Her mother's mood seemed lighter, and though Zee hadn't been able to talk her into coming along, Maureen had sounded almost interested when Zee told her what she was planning to do.

"You've always loved that book," Zee said hopefully.

"Thank you for doing this," Maureen said, and actually got out of bed and came down to the kitchen to see Zee off.

"I love you," Maureen said to her.

It seemed an odd thing to say, because of how bad things had been between them since the episode with the psychic. But Maureen was smiling when she said it, another encouraging sign, or so Zee thought at the time.

In retrospect, Zee knew that such behavior was a common occurrence in suicide cases. The victim would often feel much better once the decision to end things had finally been made. The uplift in spirits often left family members that much more shocked when the suicide happened. "She seemed so much better," they would declare.

Though Lilly had been Zee's first suicide since she'd become a psychologist, she had heard stories from other therapists, including Mattei. A vast and rapid improvement in a depressed mood can be cause for alarm. In bipolar patients it is often the signal of impending mania. In suicidal patients it often means that they've made that final decision and, upon making it, feel an almost exhilarating sense of relief. But Zee had no such knowledge when Maureen died. Though to most people who met her, she seemed older, Zee had only recently turned thirteen.

Baker's Island wasn't as close by as some of the other Salem islands were; it was actually closer to Manchester than to Salem. When Zee finally got there, it was after three. She tied up the dory and hurried up the ramp.

Zee walked past the spot where the residents parked their wheelbarrows, the only vehicles used to carry things to and from the old cottages, and then she headed toward the cottage, greeting people as she passed, grown-ups and children she'd known since she was little, whose families had summered here for generations. She wanted to stop and chat with them, but she couldn't. Not today.

She let herself into the cottage with the key that Maureen always left in the window box. The front room was dark and shuttered. Maureen hadn't been here once all summer, a clue that only in hindsight Zee realized should have been cause for alarm. Every summer since Zee was a baby, Maureen had used the cottage as her writing space.

This year the house had not been opened. As Zee entered the doorway, she watched a mouse dart and hide; she couldn't see where it went. The cottage was tiny, only two rooms, the large front room with a small soapstone sink and hand pump and an old-fashioned icebox. A round table sat in the middle of the floor. If the house had been on the mainland, its decoration might have been right out of the Shabby Chic or Maine Cottage catalogs, but here one recognized it as the accumulation of hand-me-downs or discarded items from other places that had been collected over a number of summers: an old rubber bathing cap hanging on a hook, its chin piece cracked and splintered, a straw sun hat from the 1920s that had once had a silk flower on top but that now had only a small hole where that flower had once been attached.

Zee pulled open the four French windows over the sink, then pushed out the shutters beyond. Bright light flooded the room. A nursery web spider took shelter in a crack between the rafters.

Zee had always loved this place. When Maureen planned to stay overnight, she usually brought Zee along, her only requirement being that Zee learn to amuse herself, so that Maureen could write undisturbed. That was fine by Zee, who spent as much time outside as she could. On rainy days she would sit on the rug and draw pictures or play solitaire while her mother worked on her stories. Sometimes Zee read the old Nancy Drew mysteries that had been left there by her stepgrandfather's first wife when she was a child.

The rug was rolled up in a corner. It bulged slightly in the center, something she hadn't noticed before. Either it had been improperly stored or something had been rolled up with it. Her cards, maybe? A box of crayons?

The door to the bedroom was closed. Zee hesitated before it. For as long as she could remember, she'd been forbidden to enter what had once been the bedroom. Though there was a double brass bed in the corner, they did not sleep in the room when they stayed here. Maureen slept instead on the couch and Zee in a sleeping bag on a huge canvas air mattress on the floor next to her mother.

Zee opened the door and stood looking at what had once been her parents' marriage bed. The brass was greening where a leak in the roof had caused a slow drip. She could see the sheets on the bed, never changed, and she could make out the faded green chenille bedspread, which smelled musty from the leak.

On that last day of Maureen's life, Zee stood again in the bedroom on Baker's Island. But something was wrong with the picture. It wasn't just that the roof was leaking or that the green chenille bedspread was mildewed from the moisture. It was something else. As she looked at the pillow, she realized that the Yeats book was not there. The one thing her mother wanted, the one thing she had come here to get, was missing.

Zee tore the house apart looking for the book. She looked behind and under the bed. She looked in the icebox and in all the drawers. She even looked outside, around the whole perimeter of the house. Finally she spotted the rug and again noted the bulge in the center of it.

She rolled out the rug, and with it something went tumbling. The force of the rolling threw whatever it was across the room. Hopeful, she took a step to retrieve it, and she saw the mouse. It was the same mouse that had scurried across the floor earlier, and with it was a tiny mouse, presumably its baby. Their eyes were wild. The mice were frozen in place. Zee realized that in rolling out the rug she had destroyed their home. Beside the baby mouse, as if in haute décor, was the silk flower the mice had gnawed from the old straw hat and the ball from her game of jacks that had rolled under the bed so long ago. Next to it was the book.

★   ★   ★

STRYCHNINE WAS THE POISON MAUREEN had researched for her story, the one she'd had the housekeeper use on the captain. It was also the poison Maureen ended up using on herself.

There were many easier poisons available, a few she had learned about from Ann and others as nearby as her garden. Maureen had considered and rejected them all. Strychnine is a poison that travels up the spinal cord and heightens the intensity of the convulsions it causes. It is a terrible way to die. Any emergency worker who has ever seen strychnine poisoning would be unlikely to forget it. The seizures are often brought on within ten minutes of ingestion and are triggered by stimulation of any kind—from fear of death to bright light to the sound of a distant car passing on the road. Theoretically, it is possible to survive strychnine poisoning, if one could keep the poisoning victim absolutely calm and quiet for twenty-four hours or so, until the poison clears out the system. But it almost never happens. A noise, or even the softest touch, will set off seizures that flex the back until the head and feet touch the floor, the body creating an almost perfect arch. After each seizure the victim will collapse in a heap, gathering the energy to seize again. After five or six seizures, the body's energy is drained, and the victim dies of respiratory failure or exhaustion.

MAUREEN PLANNED HER DEATH CAREFULLY, if not well. Finch was on summer vacation from teaching and was carousing with his pirate friends, who were participating in a two-day encampment at Winter Island. And with Zee gone for several hours, Maureen had taken advantage of the opportunity.

The note she left behind was hidden in a place where only Finch would find it. At the bottom of the note, she finished with the verses that matched the book her daughter was just that moment bringing back to her.

> *Come away, O human child!*
> *To the waters and the wild.*
> *With a faery, hand in hand.*
> *For the world's more full of weeping than you can understand.*

Less than fifteen minutes after Maureen took the poison, Zee came home with the book. She slammed the screen door in the kitchen before she bounded up the stairs. It was the sound of the slamming door that sent Maureen into her first seizure.

When Zee woke up, she was still on the couch. The sky had cleared, and the moon was rising over the harbor. It was huge and yellow, and she hadn't seen one like it for a long time. As she sat up and got her bearings, she realized that it wasn't the moonlight that had woken her but the sound of someone pounding on the door.

Finch was already in bed, and Jessina was gone for the night.

At first she thought it might be Hawk. He'd said he might come by tonight to do the railings. But when she looked at the clock, she saw that it was after eleven. Confused and still sleepy, she made her way to the door.

It was Michael.

"I got your message," he said. "I'm sorry, too."

Though they were both exhausted, neither Michael nor Zee slept much that night. Zee's childhood bed was an old-fashioned double, and it dipped in the middle like a hammock, which was fine for Zee alone but not great for two people. And Finch was sundowning again.

In the short time she'd been here, Zee had noticed that Finch seemed to become disoriented as the day slipped into evening, often leading him to get very agitated by normal activities like washing or dressing for bed. A normal occurrence in some patients with dementia, it was called "sundowning." He often seemed fearful at such times, and he often wandered, which is what he'd been doing that first night he stood at Zee's bed before the freezing episode began. Sundowning was something Zee knew about, but it was more common to Alzheimer's patients than those with Parkinson's.

When he was sundowning, Finch often didn't want to take medication. It took her until 4:00 A.M. to convince him to take some trazodone, and by 7:00, when he was due to have his first dose of Sinemet, Finch was fast asleep.

"I'm sorry," Michael said to her again after witnessing Finch's deteriorating condition. "I thought you were just being dramatic."

It was the same phrase that William had used to describe Lilly when he'd first brought her to see Mattei. It was an interesting choice of words, and one that Zee might have called Michael on if they both hadn't been so tired. She bristled but decided it wasn't worth an argument.

"I hate to say it, but I agree with the occupational therapist," he said. "Finch definitely needs to be in a nursing home."

"He would rather die than be in a nursing home."

LATER THAT MORNING, CLEARLY FEELING guilty, Michael helped Zee clean out more papers. She was making a pile of Melville's belongings, things she would get to him or things he could come sort through one day when Finch was out of the house.

They talked little as they worked.

At six o'clock they sent out for Chinese, and they ate it in the kitchen with Finch and Jessina, who was making jokes about the chopsticks, threatening to feed Finch with them instead of the fork she was using.

"Let him feed himself," Zee reminded her. Everyone was quiet as they watched Finch try to manipulate the fork.

After dinner she opened a bottle of twenty-year-old port that Michael had given Finch for his sixty-fifth birthday.

"He still has this?" Michael was amazed.

"He still has most of them," she said, showing him. "Melville opens one every so often, but Finch doesn't drink anymore."

"Man," Michael said.

"I told you that a long time ago," she said.

He looked at her as if her last statement couldn't possibly be true. Then, trying to cover, he searched the cabinets until he found a proper glass for the port.

ZEE HAD TOLD MICHAEL MORE than once that Finch had stopped drinking, but Michael could never seem to remember it and continued giving him expensive bottles of alcohol on birthdays and holidays. There were other things he'd forgotten as well, things she was pretty sure she'd told him that he didn't remember. She told herself his job was stressful. And the added stress of the wedding plans she hadn't been making only made things worse.

It hadn't always been like this. At least she didn't think it had. In the beginning of their relationship, they'd talked about things. Or maybe it had been Michael who did most of the talking. He'd always been so clear about what he wanted. And the fact that he'd wanted her was flattering. Michael could have anyone. And though it angered her lately, Zee had originally liked his certainty. There was something attractive and almost seductive about knowing where your life was going. It was new for Zee.

But somewhere along the line, she had stopped talking to Michael. Maybe it was because he was no longer listening, or maybe she'd never really talked to him that much. She had certainly never told him *her* dreams. But that was largely because she didn't know what they were. Beyond completing grad school and getting her license to practice, she hadn't really allowed herself to dream much at all. She knew that this was a product of childhood, of living with Maureen's illness and not ever being able to make plans. But the fact was, from the moment they met, Michael had always just assumed that he knew Zee. He had never asked her what she wanted out of life. Which was probably a good thing. Though she might have known when she was twelve, these days she had to admit that she had no idea.

Tonight Michael was drinking too much. He had finished the bottle of port and had found and opened a Côtes du Rhône. As he drank, his face reddened, and she could feel the tension building.

He reached to pour another glass and caught the lazy Susan with his sleeve, setting it spinning, sending the salt and pepper shakers and Finch's prescriptions flying.

She started to reach for them.

"I'll get them," he said angrily.

She waited while he retrieved the bottle of Sinemet and the salt shaker.

"This is a dangerous drug," he said. "I don't understand how anyone could be stupid enough to leave it on the table."

Zee said nothing. She knew he was trying to start a fight.

"Stupid," he said again. He got up and walked to the bathroom and put it in the medicine cabinet. "Someone should have done that a long time ago," he said as he sat back down at the table.

Zee said nothing for a moment. Then, instead of engaging him, she asked a direct question. "When did we get so angry with each other?"

"You may be angry. I'm not," he said.

"Please," she said. "I've never seen you so angry."

"I was angry this weekend," he admitted. "But you explained and apologized, and I totally understand what happened."

"You were angry the night Lilly jumped off the bridge."

"That wasn't anger, that was frustration."

"Semantics," she said.

"I had to pay the wedding planner six thousand dollars."

"I'll pay the wedding planner," she said. "I told you that."

"That's not the point."

"I hated the wedding planner. She was bossy and intimidating, and I didn't like her taste."

"You liked the sushi."

"Of course I liked the sushi. Everyone in Boston likes O Ya sushi. I didn't need a six-thousand-dollar wedding planner to tell me I liked O Ya's sushi. Which, by the way, we never would have served to over a hundred people. I don't even think O Ya caters."

"So we've established that you didn't like the wedding planner."

"Did you?"

"Not really," he admitted. Then he thought about it. "Actually, I couldn't stand her." As soon as he said it, he started to laugh.

"Then why the hell did you hire her?" Zee smiled back at him.

"It's what you do. You fall in love, you propose, you hire a wedding planner."

"Simple, simple, case closed," she said, quoting Mattei.

"For most people," he said.

"Evidently not for my people," she said.

"True enough," he said.

His glass was empty, and he filled it again. He started to fill hers, but she put her hand over the top. "I've had enough," she said.

"So what do we do now?" he asked.

"I don't have any idea," she said.

"Do you want to postpone the wedding?" he asked. "I mean, in light of what's going on with your father."

"We probably should," she said.

"But you still want to get married," he said.

"I never said I didn't," she said. "You were the one who said that."

"Okay," he said.

"Okay what?"

"Okay, we can postpone," he said.

She wanted to say something else, something definitive. She knew she should, that he was waiting for something more from her, but nothing came. She was exhausted. "I'm going to bed," she said. "Are you coming?"

"No," he said. "I think I'll stay up for a while."

She could hear him pouring himself another glass as she walked down the long hall to the bedroom.

LATE THAT NIGHT MICHAEL FINALLY crawled into bed next to her, rolling them both into the sagging center of the old mattress. Zee awakened to the smell of good wine turned sour on breath. Michael was kissing her.

Instinctively, before she was awake enough to catch herself, she turned her head away.

"I'm sorry," she said when she saw the hurt look on his face and realized what she had done.

She knew he was angry, but he was also very drunk. And she was too exhausted to talk about it now.

She picked up her pillow and went to the den to sleep, leaving him the bed.

By the time she woke up the next morning, Michael was gone. The note on the table was short but clear.

Dear Zee,

You were right. I am angry. I've had enough.

ZEE CRIED MOST OF the day on Wednesday. More than a
few of the tears were relief; because it was over now, she had no
big decisions to make. Some of the tears were for the last three wasted
years of her life. Some were for Finch, some for Maureen and The Great
Love, and some were for Lilly Braedon.

She listened to her thoughts roll around her achy brain. Her sinuses
were swollen from crying, she didn't dare look in the mirror. She went
into the bathroom, ran cold water in the sink, and splashed it onto her
face.

Outside, she heard the sound of Finch's walker. Jessina was in the
kitchen making breakfast. Zee dried her hands. She noticed the engagement ring on her left hand, wondered what she should do with it.
Should she send it back to him? Should she even call him? She didn't
want to, realizing on one level how relieved she was not to have to call
and, at the same time, understanding that she would have to get in touch
with him eventually to pick up her things. Eventually, but not now.

WHEN SHE COULDN'T STAND BEING in the house any longer,
she decided to take a ride, driving Lafayette Street into Marblehead,

then taking a left onto West Shore Drive. There was something she'd
been meaning to do, and now was the time. She stopped at the Garden
Center and picked out a grave planter basket, with geraniums, trailing
petunias, and dracaena spikes. Then she kept going until she reached
Waterside Cemetery.

She pulled the Volvo down the narrow, tree-lined lane and up to
the office, where she parked and walked inside.

"Hi," she said to the woman sitting at the desk. "I hate to bother
you, but do you think you could direct me to Lilly Braedon's grave?"

Cathy took in Zee's blotchy face. Normally she might have had to
look up the location of a grave site, but Lilly Braedon's headstone had
been installed only yesterday, and Cathy had seen Lilly's husband and
kids come by to visit it as she was leaving last night. So sad, she thought,
wondering what would have caused the young mother to make the leap
from the Tobin Bridge into the Mystic River. She felt particularly sorry
for the kids.

Cathy walked Zee to the door and pointed up the hill. "It's right up
there next to the pavilion," she said. "Under that big oak tree."

"Thanks so much," Zee said.

Zee left her car by the office and carried the flower basket up the
hill, stopping at one of the faucets to water it. When she reached the top
of the hill, she took in the view. From here she could see all of Salem,
from the Willows to the Gables, to Shetland Park and the old mill
buildings with their peaked rooflines that looked like a row of white
tents. Beyond Shetland was the district called the Point, with the tene-
ment houses where the mill workers had once lived—the Irish, the Ital-
ians, the French Canadians. The mills were long gone, but the housing
remained. These days it was mostly Dominicans. Jessina and her son,
Danny, lived in the Point.

Zee found Lilly's gravestone. It was simple granite, a matte gray.
On it just Lilly's name, her date of birth, and the day she died. Zee

found herself doing the math. Lilly was thirty-four, only two years older than Zee and the same age as Maureen had been when she committed suicide, but Lilly had seemed younger than Zee ever remembered her mother being. Certainly more naive, she thought, though it was odd to make that judgment, Maureen's era would have almost certainly dictated a lesser sophistication than Lilly's. Looking back on it now, Zee realized that it was the filter of a child's vision that had clouded her perception. If she saw them next to each other, most likely they would have seemed the same. In many ways, of course, they already did seem the same, at least in Zee's mind's eye. It was barely possible to keep them separate while Lilly lived, but now their images were blending more and more.

Zee placed the basket on the flat base of Lilly's grave. She hadn't thought past doing it, but now she thought she ought to say a few words or, barring that, at least a silent prayer or something, but nothing came to her.

She tried her best to clear her head, to think about Lilly, but when she looked at the gravestone, she just wanted to cry again, which would have been appropriate except that she didn't think she could stand to cry anymore. Her head ached so much from crying that she willed herself not to. Instead she walked up to the pavilion and sat looking out over the harbor toward Salem.

The House of the Seven Gables was partially visible from here. She tried to identify Finch's house, but it was blocked by the boatyard across the street. The light from the Salem Harbor power plant blinked on and off, and for some reason, standing here, she thought for a moment of Gatsby standing and looking out at Daisy's pier, though that light was green and not white, and lower to the ground and not on top of some coal-fired smokestack that people in both towns were trying their best to get rid of.

Zee fell asleep watching the harbor. It surprised her, first that she could sleep in the daytime—she had never been one to take naps—and second that she could sleep out in the open in a public place. The added confusion of an interrupted dream cycle meant that for a few seconds after she woke up, she had absolutely no idea where she was.

It had been the sound of an engine that had awakened her. A red truck was moving along the narrow lanes, driving first up one side of the hill and then down the other, taking each parallel street slowly, finally stopping and backing up when it came to Lilly's grave. Adam didn't turn off the engine before he got out of the truck. It idled and sputtered, creating a sound track that in retrospect would make what Zee saw him do seem more like a film than real life.

Adam walked over and stood for a long time in front of the grave. He looked at the headstone and then at the basket of flowers. Then he looked around to see if anyone was watching him. He picked up the flower basket Zee had just laid on the grave and heaved it. She watched as it arced in slow motion up and over the gravestones, finally landing on the pavement, where it smashed and scattered. Then Adam got into his truck and took off.

Zee was so shaken that she didn't move for a while. She didn't walk into the office and report the incident. Instead she got into her car and drove back to Salem. When she stopped for a red light, she dialed Mattei's number and left a message.

"I know you told me to let it go, but I just saw something that made me think that Lilly Braedon's death really wasn't suicide. I need to talk to you."

★　*22*　★

FOUR HOURS LATER MATTEI sat across the kitchen table from Zee. She'd had a hell of a time finding a parking place and ended up leaving her car way down on Congress Street at a four-story public garage, where she still had to wait almost twenty minutes for a space.

Zee had left her two phone messages that day, the first while she was still at the house, requesting a leave of absence so that she could take care of Finch, and the second two hours later, declaring that she didn't think Lilly's death was a suicide.

MATTEI HADN'T BOTHERED TO CALL Zee back. Instead she had gotten into her car and driven to Salem.

"I KNOW WHAT I SAW," Zee insisted as they sat across the table from each other.

"I'm not disputing that," Mattei said.

"He smashed the flower basket," Zee said. "He's dangerous."

"We don't know if he's dangerous. He certainly seems angry."

"We know he threatened her."

"Yes," Mattei said.

"You didn't believe it before," Zee said.

"I never said I didn't believe it. It was the Marblehead police who were skeptical. And Lilly wasn't exactly reliable. Or cooperative, for that matter."

"She wasn't suicidal," Zee said.

"She jumped off a bridge."

"What if he drove her to it?"

"What if he did?" Mattei asked.

"Shouldn't we tell someone?"

"Tell them what?" Mattei asked.

Zee looked frustrated.

"Let's think it through," Mattei said. "There's absolutely nothing anyone can do. You can't arrest a person for driving someone to suicide. If you could, the jails would be full of husbands, wives, relatives, and employers. Isn't it always somebody else's fault?"

"Even so . . ." Zee said.

"She was bipolar," Mattei said.

"I'm well aware of that," Zee said.

"Well, you know from personal experience that this is how things sometimes end."

"You mean my mother," Zee said.

"Yes," Mattei said.

"My mother was BP1. And unmedicated."

"Medication doesn't always work. Case in point, Lilly Braedon."

"I would have known if Lilly was suicidal," Zee said. Before Mattei had a chance to respond, she added, "I was thirteen when my mother died. And if it happened now, with my training, I would have seen the signs."

Mattei was silent.

"And there's something else," Zee said.

"What's that?"

"*You* didn't think she was suicidal either," Zee said.

"Now you're telling me what *I* thought?"

"You wouldn't have given her to me to treat if you thought so," Zee said. "Admit it. She was as much part of my treatment as I was of hers."

"Interesting theory," Mattei said.

"You knew she reminded me of my mother. You thought I could treat her and make it turn out differently. Hell, that's what I thought."

"As in, 'They all lived happily ever after'?"

"As in, 'Work out some issues.'" Zee was clearly getting agitated. Her hands were shaking. She clasped them together, trying to steady them.

"Take a breath," Mattei said.

Zee looked frustrated. But she obeyed. She took a deep breath and held it as long as she could. Then she slowly exhaled.

"Are you okay?"

Zee nodded.

"This is all very predictable. You just lost a patient. One who was important to you. You broke off your engagement. Your father is very ill. I don't want you to underestimate any of this," Mattei said.

"I'm not," Zee said. "I'm well aware of the effect all this is having on me. I just think that we should tell someone about Adam."

"'We' already have."

"Then we should tell them again."

"Again, let's think it through," Mattei said, more forcefully this time. "Think of the family. Do you really want to put them through more than they've already suffered? Lilly was having an affair with Adam. And from what the police told us, there were other men she was involved with as well. Is this really something you want to pursue?"

Zee remained silent. Mattei was right.

"If it's any consolation," Mattei said, "you were right. I didn't see it coming."

There was a sound at the kitchen door. Someone was on the deck. Jessina let herself in with her key, then looked at them.

"I'm sorry," she said. "Do you want me to come back later?"

"No, you're fine. Jessina, this is my friend Mattei. Mattei, this is Jessina. She takes care of Finch."

"Nice to meet you," Mattei said, extending a hand.

"I was going to make cookies for him," Jessina said, holding out a bag of flour she'd brought.

"Jessina is a great baker," Zee said.

"From scratch, not a mix?" Mattei asked.

"I never use a mix," Jessina said.

"Very impressive," Mattei said.

ZEE AND MATTEI MOVED OUTSIDE to the deck off the kitchen. From here there was a great view of the harbor, only partially blocked by the boatyard to their left. The house straddled two streets, Turner and Hardy. It was long and narrow, with an entrance on either end.

"This is a really old house, isn't it?" Mattei said, looking back at the twelve-over-twelve windows, the central chimney.

"Except for the deck," Zee said. "And the widow's walk."

Mattei looked up. "I don't see a widow's walk."

"Just the remains of one. See, up there? That flat part on top of the roof?" She pointed. "This house was purchased by a sea captain back in the late 1700s. Eventually he added the widow's walk, then reportedly chopped it down in a fit of jealous rage."

Mattei walked over to the historic sign posted on the side of the house: HOME OF ARLIS BROWNE, SEA CAPTAIN. "Wasn't that the captain in your mother's story?" Mattei asked.

"The very same."

"Nice guy," she said.

"Yeah, right," Zee said.

A double-decker tour bus pulled out of the Gables' parking lot and got itself stuck trying to make the right onto Turner Street. It backed up, then went forward, and then finally all the way back into the parking lot, where it did an exaggerated U-turn and exited the wrong way onto Derby Street, leaning precariously as it emerged, sending tourists scattering.

"There are a heck of a lot of tourists in this city," Mattei said.

"Boston has tourists," Zee said.

"Not dressed in witches' hats, we don't."

They sat in silence for a few minutes, gazing out at the harbor. The sun was bright and playing on the water, making it look as if the light were emerging from the water itself, a million random bubbles of silver popping to the surface and then disappearing.

"What's that over there?" Mattei pointed across the harbor.

"That's Marblehead," Zee said.

"Ah, the infamous Marblehead."

Jessina brought out some lemonade and two glasses, placed them on the table without saying a word, and then turned to go back inside.

"You didn't have to do that," Zee said. "But thanks."

Jessina smiled, closing the door carefully so it wouldn't slam.

"She seems great," Mattei said.

"She's a treasure. Melville hired her. She was a nurse in the Dominican Republic. She's raising a son by herself and trying to finish a nursing degree at Salem State. All that with English as a second language."

"I'm in awe," Mattei said. "Aren't you?"

"Every day," Zee said.

Mattei sat and considered for a moment before speaking. "So I take it Melville's not coming back."

"He tried. Finch kicked him out again."

"Why?"

"I have no idea. I know they had some kind of disagreement, but Melville said it was an old argument that had been settled a long time ago."

"Evidently not," Mattei said.

"That's exactly what I said," Zee said.

"So that leaves you as caregiver."

"Pretty much," Zee said. "At least until I can figure something else out."

Mattei looked at her.

"I want to do this," Zee said.

"That's very noble." Mattei paused. "But caregiving is very difficult."

"I have Jessina," Zee said.

"Even so."

"It's been okay," Zee said.

"And you've been doing this for what? A week?"

"Nevertheless," Zee said. It was meant to end the conversation, and Mattei knew it.

"Just promise me one thing."

"What's that?"

"Promise me you're not just hiding out here."

Zee thought about it. "I'm not," she said.

"Okay," Mattei said. "Take a leave of absence. But I don't want to lose you. You're too good a therapist."

"Recent evidence to the contrary."

"Stop it," Mattei said.

★ ★ ★

MATTEI LEFT ZEE WITH THE name of a caregiver-support group at Salem Hospital and a prescription for sleeping pills.

"I don't need the pills," Zee lied.

"You told me you weren't sleeping," Mattei said. "It doesn't hurt to fill the prescription. If you don't need them, don't take them."

"Thanks," Zee said.

Zee thought about it before bringing up the next subject. "There's one thing we haven't talked about," Zee said.

"Really? What is that?"

"I'm assuming you talked to Michael."

"We've spoken, yes."

"Just tell me one thing," Zee asked. "Is he okay?"

Mattei thought carefully before she spoke. "He'll be fine. Given the right amount of time and enough red wine."

Zee nodded. She didn't want to know any more.

★ 23 ★

HAVING FORGOTTEN THAT HE'D agreed to teach the class tonight, Hawk had planned to go to Zee's after work to install the railing.

As part of his employment contract for the summer, he was to co-teach a celestial-navigation course sponsored by the National Park Service. Though most of the *Friendship*'s navigation was done by GPS, Hawk was the only member of the crew who was proficient in celestial skills, and the captain wanted each of the ship's journeys logged as if it were still the early 1800s, when all navigation was done by the stars.

This would have been fine with Hawk, except that many of the classes, which were taught at the Visitors' Center and not at sea, conflicted with his duties on the ship. When he had agreed to teach, he'd assumed that the classes would be held on the *Friendship* as she sailed, allowing the students to learn to take the twilight sights. What he didn't know at the time was that the *Friendship* rarely sailed at all, and when she did, she sometimes carried a few VIPs, but almost never any regular passengers. Though she was coast guard–certified to sail, as a general rule the *Friendship* stayed in port except when she served as Essex County's or the National Park Service's flagship for maritime festivals up and down the coast. Most days she sat at the wharf while large groups of tourists boarded and disembarked.

Recently an application had been made to the coast guard to commission the ship, which, if accepted, would allow the *Friendship* to take passengers out to sea and provide students and any other groups with a firsthand experience of Salem's sailing history, something they were unlikely to understand any other way. But commissioning was a slow process. Hawk was able to bring the class aboard the moored ship to practice noon sights and learn to determine latitude, but he hadn't been able to take them out to sea. For the most part, this summer's celestial-navigation course had been confined to the classroom, something Hawk found appalling, and he didn't hesitate to say so.

He was no less vocal the night of the first class when the other instructor, a man who had been teaching the course for the last five years, espoused the theory that sun sights alone were sufficient for navigation and that he had made several trips across the Atlantic taking nothing but sun sights.

"What other instruments did you have?" Hawk sounded doubtful.

"Well, we didn't have GPS, I can tell you that much," his co-teacher huffed.

Hawk's co-teacher was an older gentleman named Briggs, a seasoned veteran with good credentials, who had once crossed the Atlantic solo from Plymouth, England, to the United States in a sixty-five-foot multihull. Hawk thought the guy was lucky to have made it. He didn't criticize Briggs in front of the class, but he later expressed a strong opinion that the class should be taught using more than one navigational technique. Sun sights were certainly a part of celestial navigation, but so were moon, planet, and star sights, and Hawk could not conceive of teaching a course without all of them.

"They will learn to use a sextant," Briggs said. "And for this beginning class, sun sights are quite satisfactory."

In an odd twist, this year's class consisted entirely of women. The other crew members kidded Hawk because the online brochure for the class had featured photographs of both instructors, and they were certain that this was the reason for the exclusively female enrollment.

"He looks like a young George Clooney," one of the crew said, referring to Hawk's photo.

"Shut up," Hawk said.

After the first class, Hawk wanted to quit. Not only did he think an inside class was ridiculous, but the conflicts in his schedule left the *Friendship* shorthanded. And there was another reason. For the most part, the class full of women was fine with him, but there was a small group of them, known well to the other instructor, that the crew had nicknamed the "Yacht Club Cougars." Three of them attended the first class. By the second, the group had expanded to seven. It wasn't that he had anything against them, though they were a little cliquish and very outspoken, which tended to keep the other, less outgoing women from asking many questions. But their attempts at humor were fairly bawdy and were usually directed at Hawk, which might have amused him had it not made Briggs envious and argumentative. After one particularly disagreeable class, Hawk decided to talk to his boss. Contract aside, this class didn't need two instructors, and the two men clearly didn't like each other. Hawk would volunteer to quit.

But the other instructor beat him to it. "I can't work with him," Hawk overheard Briggs tell their boss. "You're going to have to choose one or the other of us, and let me remind you that not only do I have seniority, but my family has donated quite a bit of money to this project over the years."

Hawk quit the class. But a few weeks later, his boss came back to him. They'd had some complaints from the enrollees, who agreed strongly with Hawk's assessment that the class should be taught at least in part on the water.

"Great idea," Hawk said, happy that the students would finally get their money's worth. "But why are you telling me?"

"We have an issue," his boss said.

"Yeah? What's that?" Hawk said.

"Over the years Briggs seems to have developed a problem with seasickness."

"You're kidding." Hawk couldn't help but smile.

"We were hoping we could convince you to take them out in your boat. It would only be for one class," he said. "And we do have a contract."

Hawk was well aware that they hadn't docked his pay when he'd stopped teaching the class. "Okay," he said. "Which class are we talking about?"

"The one on twilight sights," he said. "We've titled it Rocking the Sextant. The sign-up sheet is already full."

"I'll bet," Hawk said. Behind his boss, some of the crew were snickering. "You wouldn't have had anything to do with that title, would you?" he asked one of them.

"Not guilty," his friend Josh said. "But if you're looking for crew to help out with the Cougars, I'm sure you'll get some volunteers."

"Funny," he said.

"So you'll do it?" his boss asked.

"Do I have a choice?"

"Not without a pay cut."

HAWK ARRANGED TO TAKE THE class out in his boat, a 1941 Sim Davis lobster boat, a forty-footer with the winch and gear removed, which Hawk had spent last summer restoring and was now living on just a few slips down from the *Friendship*.

THERE ARE TWO TIMES A day when it is best to take sights: dawn and dusk. Twilight sights are taken just before the horizon disappears into either darkness or light, in those few minutes when the planets and locator stars are still visible. It's a moment in time, and it takes practice. For the beginner especially, it would be important to get to a spot where Hawk knew that the stars would be visible along the horizon. Which meant they had to get away from shore.

They left an hour before sunset in order to make it to open ocean. It was a relatively calm evening, and his boat was sturdy, so they wouldn't have to deal with much chop. This was both good and bad. The sextant was a durable instrument meant to take vertical angles from a moving ship. One of the reasons for going out was that the students would get used to the movement of the boat and accustomed to taking readings in any conditions.

The women arrived early, with picnic gear and bottles of wine.

"I hope you also brought your notebooks and sextants," he said when he saw the bottles sticking from their L.L. Bean canvas bags.

They headed out, passing the tiny lighthouse on Winter Island, then the Salem Willows Park with its long wharf lined with men fishing for stripers. When Hawk passed the confines of Salem Harbor, he gunned the engine, heading between the Miseries and Children's Island and as straight out to sea as was possible in the sheltered waters that ran between Salem and Cape Ann.

"Where are we going?" one of the Cougars finally asked.

"We have to get past land by twilight," he said. They sat quietly in the stern. He finally stopped the boat at a spot he knew well, where the chop wasn't too bad. Behind them, fading into the distance, was the entire North Shore, and to the south the vague outline of the Boston skyline. But straight ahead, if you didn't look back, was a clear horizon line.

"It's a bit rough out here," another student said.

"Not at all," Hawk replied.

"What if we're in the middle of a shipping lane?"

"Sometimes a shipping lane is a perfect place to be," he said, laughing.

They all looked around nervously.

"Relax," he said. "We're not in a shipping lane."

"Phew."

"But can anyone tell me when a shipping lane might be a place you'd want to be?"

They all looked at each other.

Finally, one of the shyer women spoke up. "If you get in trouble and need to be rescued," she said. "A shipping lane would be a good place to get to. Like if you're breaking down or something."

"Are we breaking down?" Another woman asked, horrified.

"Relax, ladies, we're not in a shipping lane, and we're not breaking down. But I'm glad to see someone has been reading the book."

One of the women had pulled out a bottle of wine and was looking for a corkscrew.

"I didn't know this was a party," Hawk said.

"I generally like to have a little wine before I rock my sextant," the woman said.

The other women giggled, and Hawk hoped he wasn't blushing.

"You ladies are relentless," he said.

"We prefer to think of ourselves as focused," one of them said.

"I think you'll focus better without the wine," he said.

"You're not very playful." The woman sounded disappointed.

"Work now, play later," Hawk said, taking the bottle and putting it back in the bag.

They got out their notebooks and their plastic sextants, things Hawk hated but had to admit were adequate for this class. He kept one of them himself as a backup, though if he had to, he could get a reading without a sextant at all. Watches were another matter. In order to get an accurate reading, you had to track Greenwich Mean Time to the second. If you spent enough time on the water, you planned for all possible worst-case scenarios. He knew at least three sailors who had horror stories about failed GPS devices. Some were ocean legend, but he knew that at least a few of them were true.

Tonight the ladies were all wearing quartz wristwatches, something you didn't see much in these days of cell phones. Hawk turned on the shortwave and tuned in to WWV to sync with Greenwich Mean Time. He listened to the tick and the tones until the time was announced, and he looked on as the women checked their watches. So far they seemed to know what they were doing. A good sign, he thought.

Only one of the women hadn't brought a watch, and he quietly handed her his. He had at least two more of them in the cabin—more worst-case-scenario planning. It was possible to figure Greenwich Mean Time by taking moon sights, but it was difficult and not nearly as accurate, and he didn't like to do it except in an extreme emergency. He wasn't going to even bring up moon sights tonight. He didn't want to confuse them. Let them master using the sextant first.

"OKAY," HE SAID. "FIND A spot you're comfortable with and set up your sextants."

He watched as the women positioned themselves in the stern, setting up their instruments and consulting their almanacs.

"Have you all done your calculations? Do you know what stars you're looking for?"

They couldn't have tracked their present location in preparation for tonight, but they were close enough to where they started that the locator stars should be the same. He walked around, checking their calculations. They looked pretty accurate.

"Now what?" a woman said.

"Now we wait."

Hawk went below and checked the time. He had hoped to be back in time to do Zee's railing tonight.

"May I please use the head?" one of the women asked him.

Hawk pointed her to the bow of the boat.

When she came out, she spotted the brass sextant in the mahogany case that sat open on the table.

"That's a beautiful sextant," she said. "Is it an antique?"

"It was my grandfather's," he said.

"May I try it?"

"Sorry," he said. "There's an aluminum one over there, if you want to give that one a try, but this one's off-limits."

He handed the other sextant to her, and she went back on deck looking as if she had just won a prize.

"Hey, where'd you get that?" one of the other women asked.

"Jealous?" She laughed and set up the aluminum sextant in the stern.

Hawk came out on deck and checked the sunset. In the distance the landscape of Boston glimmered red and purple.

Seeing the trace of Boston skyline, Hawk's mind jumped to Lilly Braedon and her fall into those same waters. Though it hadn't happened that way at all, in his mind's eye her fall was in slow motion, the cell phone falling with her as it dropped out of her hand. It seemed such a surreal sight that his mind played it in slow motion frame by frame until she disappeared into the shining sapphire of the water below, slow, dreamlike, impossible to believe even in memory.

Quickly he turned away from the image and in the opposite direction, toward the horizon line. The sun had set about ten minutes ago. It was twilight.

"Check your watches," he said. "It's time."

The chatter that had been a low part of the sound level stopped.

"Tonight we're looking to fix our position on at least two of the three stars you have chosen. With any luck we will be able to see all three. They should be low on the horizon. This won't be like the sights you took from the *Friendship*. There's a lot more motion out here. You will want to rock the sextants back and forth, watching the arc, and keep adjusting until the star you sight is sitting directly on the horizon line.

"Don't worry," he said. "These instruments are built for chop. It's actually easier to get a reading on a moving ship than from a fixed position."

He walked back and forth, helping the women position their instruments. "Don't be fooled by the planets. We're looking for stars. Planets look more like disks—they don't twinkle."

It took a while, but they all seemed to get it. When they began to take their readings, the group grew even quieter. The shyest of them gasped. Hawk leaned over and took a quick look at her sight, then smiled at her.

"Nice, huh?" he said.

"Beautiful." She seemed amazed.

He had done this thousands of times, but it never failed to fill him with awe. There was a moment when you spotted that first star, a pinpoint of light just where (if you had done your calculations correctly) it was supposed to be in the sky. He'd heard it described as a religious experience. He wasn't sure about that. But when you spotted that first star or when the stars crossed exactly where they were supposed to cross, there was nothing better. Even if you'd been dead reckoning in the middle of a storm, or if overnight the Gulf Stream had taken you a hundred miles off course. If you had done your calculations properly, there would be a moment when you found that the star you were looking for was exactly where it should be on the horizon. In that instant the universe made sense, and you knew that no matter what else happened in the world, the stars would always tell you where you were, and when they did, you would always be able to find your way home.

The group was quiet on the way back to Salem. Some of them were writing in their logbooks, some just watching the stars as the sky grew darker and the constellations moved higher in the sky.

When he pulled into his slip, some of the crew were there to meet them. His friend Josh tied them up, and another crew member handed him a six-pack of beer he'd brought along.

"You can open the wine now," Hawk told the ladies.

"Really?" They seemed surprised.

"Sure," he said. "You earned it."

Josh handed Hawk a beer. Hawk looked at his watch. It was almost eleven. He definitely wasn't going to get to Zee's railing tonight.

★ *24* ★

Z EE ATTENDED THE CAREGIVER-SUPPORT meeting
at Salem Hospital. The room was surprisingly crowded. There
were coffee and pastries in the back. It was rather more like a twelve-
step program than she had expected. One by one, the people got up and
told their stories.

A low level of depression seemed to run through the group, or maybe
it was exhaustion. Certainly there was disillusionment and resentment,
tales of siblings who didn't help enough or of parental demands that
put such a strain on the caregivers that for the most part they seemed
to have given up their lives. One woman, who had teenagers at home,
talked about the stresses of trying to care for an ailing parent and deal
with teenagers and menopause at the same time. Several other members
of the group commiserated or nodded approval.

"Aren't you a little young to be here?" one of the women asked Zee.

"My father is in his late sixties," Zee said. "And he has Parkinson's."

"I'm sorry," the woman said.

Though Zee got some good and practical tips for Finch's care, for
the most part this group was depressing. She couldn't help but wonder
if Mattei had known it would be. Perhaps this was a cautionary tale.

"Caring for an ailing parent is a lot like caring for a baby," the group's moderator said. "Except with a baby, you get to look forward to the results."

THAT ZEE WAS ALREADY A bit depressed seemed evident to Jessina, who kept making excuses to stay a little later each day and to try to engage her in conversation, often talking about her son, whom she clearly adored. Tonight she told Zee that Danny wasn't home and that she'd been wanting to bake a cake for Finch. She didn't have a proper mixer or the right pans at her apartment, she said. Zee knew it was an excuse, because Jessina had just recently baked Finch a cake at home. So far that cake was only half eaten. Jessina hovered around her and kept asking if there was anything she needed. She didn't need anything, Zee said, but she appreciated the offer.

At seven forty-five, Jessina finally went home, leaving a spice cake with white frosting in the refrigerator for Finch. At eight o'clock, someone knocked on the front door. At first Zee thought that Jessina had forgotten something, but no, she always came in the kitchen door at the other end of the house, and she had a key. Zee found herself holding her breath, hoping it wasn't Michael.

In the events of the last few days, she'd almost forgotten about Hawk and the handrails, but she found herself relieved to see him standing here now. He was wearing jeans and a T-shirt and was carrying a tool bag.

"I have to take some measurements for the railing," he said, as if thinking Zee might have forgotten why he was there. "Sorry it took me so long to get here."

She led him to the hallway.

"Is this an okay time to do this?" he asked, seeing her expression. "I can come back tomorrow if you want."

"No," she said. "Now is fine."

She showed him where the OT had said the railing should go, about thirty inches off the floor.

"Usually they're thirty-four."

"The OT gave me the height," she said. "She wants it to match the height of my father's walker."

"Makes sense," he said. He looked inside the tool bag, cursed, then went out to the blue van for a tape measure.

When he came back, she was still standing in the hallway. He made her hold one end of the tape while he measured the wall once and then again.

"I've got to run up to Home Depot to get the stock," he said.

She nodded. "You want some money?"

He shook his head. "Just pay me when I finish the job."

WHEN HE RETURNED THE NEXT night, Hawk started trying to guess where he knew her from. Over the course of the evening, it had become a joke between them—a game, really—and the only conversation they made.

"The yacht club," he'd say.

"Not likely."

"What about Maddie's?"

"In Marblehead?" she asked.

He nodded.

"Nope. Sorry. Never been there," she said.

Zee tried to keep things light. But she wished he would give up the game. It made her nervous. The last thing she wanted to do was to explain her relationship with Lilly to Hawk. Patient confidentiality prohibited any discussion of Lilly's case, any explanation of why, as Lilly's psychotherapist, Zee had been unable to save her. Not that she had any explanation that would satisfy anyone anyway. The truth was, she hadn't seen it coming. She had failed.

★ ★ ★

HAWK CAME BACK THE FOLLOWING night at six, and the night after that, and by the fourth night he had completed the handrail. It was a nice job, rather more finish carpentry than Zee had expected. He had sanded and varnished it so that it was smooth and splinter-free.

"It looks like a ship's rail," she said, running her hand across the sanded surface.

He smiled. "At least I didn't make it out of rope," he said, and she laughed.

She could see him notice the spot on her finger where the engagement ring used to be, the patch of paler skin that highlighted its absence. She quickly let her hand drop from the railing.

"Really, it's nice," she said. "It should work well for him. Thank you."

"I'll come back Thursday night to do the grab bars," he said.

"Thursday's good."

He looked at her again.

"What?" she asked.

"I know where I saw you," he said. "We met at the fund-raiser for the Home for Aged Women."

"Excuse me?"

He pointed in the general direction of Derby Street.

"Oh." She laughed, remembering the building from childhood, though they had changed the name on it over the years. "No, I wasn't invited to that one."

"I'm not giving up," he said. "I never forget a face."

ON THURSDAY NIGHT, JUST BEFORE it was time for him to arrive, she was surprised to find herself peeking in the mirror to check her hair. She realized it had been a while since she'd even bothered to look. But tonight she found herself putting on a little makeup as well, just some mascara and lip gloss, but she noted it, and it surprised her.

Hawk was an attractive guy, dark-haired and good-looking by anyone's standards. He had a winning smile and a fading scar that ran down the right side of his face, just enough imperfection to make him interesting. But he wasn't her type. Not that she even knew what her type was. Her mind went to Michael. This was ridiculous, she thought. It was too soon. And there was Lilly.

She put the makeup away and frowned at herself in the bathroom mirror.

INSTEAD OF WAITING AROUND TO see him, Zee took a walk. She wandered down by the Willows and played a game of skee ball, then walked over and got herself some popcorn and sat on a bench listening to music and feeding the gulls. In the cove a class of first-time kayakers practiced rolling over and righting themselves.

When she got back, Hawk was standing in the kitchen, his tools packed away. "The job is finished. You want to see it?" he asked, already leading her down the hall toward the bathroom.

She moved past him in the small space, stepping toward the tub, then turning to face him. "Good work," she said.

"Didn't require a lot of skill." He looked at his work. "I hope the height is okay. This was the only place I could put them that had wall studs."

"It's fine," she said. "Thank you."

He grinned at her. "So what's next?"

"I guess we're done, and I should pay you."

He laughed. "Okay."

"Let me get my checkbook."

It was a small bathroom, and as he moved back to let her pass, she brushed by him. He tried to step out of her way, but she miscalculated and went in the same direction, bringing them chest to chest in the tiny space.

"Sorry," she said.

"Not a problem." He didn't move out of the way immediately but stood there looking into her eyes for an extra moment before he stepped back. "After you," he said finally, acting out as much of a chivalrous bow as the small space permitted.

He smells like the ocean, she thought as she moved past him.

SHE LOOKED EVERYWHERE FOR HER checkbook, but it was nowhere to be found. "I'm sorry," she said. "This is ridiculous. I had it this morning." She thought about it. "I can drop off a check to you to-morrow when Jessina comes," she said.

"That's okay," he said. "I'll stop by and pick it up tomorrow night after work."

"Are you sure?"

"No trouble," he said.

She walked him to the door. "It gives me one more day to figure out where I've seen you," he said. "Or you could just tell me."

"What?" she said.

"I could tell that you recognized me that first day on the wharves." It wasn't a confrontation, more a statement of fact. "So I figure you can just tell me so we can stop this dumb game we've been playing and maybe move on to something more interesting."

He smiled at her, and she felt herself flush. *Damned Irish skin,* she thought.

Not giving her a chance to answer, he turned quickly, and before she could say anything, he was gone.

★   ★   ★

ZEE HAD TROUBLE SLEEPING THAT night. She kept think-
ing about Lilly Braedon and the funeral and whether or not she should
tell Hawk where he had seen her. She didn't mind him knowing, but
she didn't want him to ask a lot of questions. As Lilly's therapist she had
confidentiality issues, to be sure. But it was more than that. Whether or
not he was attracted to her, Zee knew that the minute she admitted it,
she would be judged. Therapist of a suicide? He would judge her the
same way she'd been judging herself.

She finally fell into a fitful sleep at about three in the morning. She
didn't wake up until almost eleven. She was alarmed as she looked at
the clock. Jessina was supposed to leave at ten-thirty, but she wouldn't
leave Finch alone.

Zee pulled on her cutoffs and a clean tee. For the last several nights,
she had been sleeping in Maureen's room, where it was quieter and the
one place that Finch wouldn't wander.

Jessina and Finch were sitting in the kitchen. He was wearing a
canary yellow shirt with red pants and eating a piece of cake accompanied by a big glass of milk. Zee couldn't help but smile.

"I'm so sorry," she said to both of them. "I really overslept."

Finch, as if just realizing where she'd been sleeping, looked up the
stairway but said nothing. He had long ago closed off Maureen's room.
Zee could tell he didn't like the idea of its being opened again.

"You look better," Jessina said.

Zee realized that she felt better.

"You want some cake?" Jessina offered.

"For breakfast?" Zee laughed. "No thanks. I might have a piece
after lunch, though."

Jessina looked satisfied. She removed the apron she'd been wearing
and draped it onto the hook. "How do you like your father's new look?"

"Colorful," Zee said.

Finch groaned.

"You look younger," Jessina said, patting him on the head as she passed. "Younger is never a bad thing for a man. You get out, you see. The ladies will fall on you."

Finch looked at Zee in horror.

"I think she means the ladies will fall all over you."

"Yes," Jessina agreed. "That's what I said."

Finch's expression of horror was no less pronounced.

"How's Danny?" Zee asked, trying to change the subject.

"He's fine. He's going to day camp to learn to swim." Jessina pointed up-harbor toward Children's Island.

"That's great," Zee said.

"I'm just cleaning up before I go," Jessina said. "Anything else you need me to do?"

"I think we're all set," Zee said. Jessina came in twice a day, once in the morning to feed and bathe Finch, then later to give him dinner and get him ready for bed.

"I'll see you at dinner," Jessina said to Finch. "Fish tonight."

He smiled weakly as she left.

"I don't think she realized the nature of your relationship with Melville," Zee said, pouring herself a cup of Dominican coffee that Jessina had brewed.

She was trying to engage him in conversation about it, as she had promised Melville she would. But Finch wasn't biting. Instead he turned and looked up the stairs. "Why are you sleeping up there?" he said. "You have a perfectly good room down here."

She didn't want to tell him the reason; she was afraid it would hurt his feelings. The real reason was that she couldn't take his sundowning. It scared her to wake up and find Finch in her room. He was simply checking on her, the way he had when she was a child, but it kept her from sleep. Ever since the freezing episode when she'd awakened to the fearful look in his eyes, she hadn't been able to sleep downstairs.

She knew that she wasn't required to answer, that the question was rhetorical. Finch was simply expressing his disapproval at the door, which, having been locked for so long, now stood open and leading up the stairway to the room where they'd found her mother.

Zee kept herself busy cleaning all day. But she couldn't stop thinking about what she was going to say to Hawk. Finally she realized that the only logical thing to do was to tell him that they'd seen each other at Lilly's funeral and stop the game. She had a certain curiosity about what had made him attend the funeral in the first place, though it was not that uncommon among witnesses. But she knew she wouldn't ask him that. And she couldn't discuss anything about Lilly. She would tell him that she'd seen him there and hope that ended it. She was pretty certain it would, along with any attraction that he either did or did not feel for her.

Zee tried to keep busy and not think too much more about what she was going to say. But as the day wore on, she found herself growing more and more agitated.

At five-thirty she opened a bottle of wine. She sat on the deck drinking and watching the boats.

At six o'clock Jessina brought her out some cheese and crackers to go with the wine. "You shouldn't drink that with no food in the stomach," she said.

Zee thanked her and was about to invite her to join her for some wine when the doorbell rang. Jessina hurried to answer it.

Zee watched as Jessina led Hawk to the deck.

"Nice view," he said.

"Pretty much the same as yours," she said, looking back toward the *Friendship*.

"Yeah, but you own yours," he said.

She smiled. "I don't, my father does."

She got her checkbook and started to write. Then she looked in her wallet and realized she had money she hadn't used to reimburse Jessina for groceries. "Would you rather have cash?"

"Always," he said.

She was a little altered from the wine. She saw him notice the bottle. "Would you like a glass?"

"I'm not much of a wine drinker," he said.

"How about a cracker?" she asked. "The cheese is pretty good."

He took a cracker, but he didn't sit down.

If she was going to say anything, it had to be now. "Please," she said. "Sit."

He took a seat opposite her at the table.

There was no way to say it but straight out. Emboldened by the wine, she went ahead. "I'm going to tell you where we saw each other," she said.

He looked at her.

"It was at Lilly Braedon's funeral."

"What?" He couldn't have looked more surprised.

"You were the eyewitness on the bridge," she said.

He was quiet for a long time. "Were you a friend of Lilly's?" he finally asked.

"In a manner of speaking," she said.

"What does that mean?"

She had resolved not to tell him more, but she found herself explaining. "I was her therapist."

It was worse than she'd thought it would be. She should never have said anything. If she hadn't been a little buzzed, she never would have opened her mouth. She could feel his eyes on her, judging her. *I couldn't save her,* she wanted to say, but instead she just sat there waiting for him to say something.

It took a long time for him to speak.

"Damn," he finally said.

PART 3:

July 2008

Even with the advent of modern navigational tools, it is still prudent to verify one's course by the taking of daily sun and star sights: one at noon and then again in the twilights of both dawn and dusk in those brief moments when the stars and horizon are both still visible, just before the horizon merges with the darkness or the stars are consumed by the light of day.

THE REENACTORS WERE ON the benches outside Ann's store again, and this time they were drunk. Not all of them. None of the pirates (not even the ones who sang the sea chanteys) seemed to be drinking, and they drank most of the time. No, this time it was the Revolutionary War reenactors who were sitting on the benches, sipping out of flasks or bottles concealed in paper bags. The redcoats and patriots sat on opposing sides hurling Colonial-era locker-room insults at each other.

This was too much, Ann thought. They were probably very good at what they did—they were certainly staying in character— but they were taking the whole Fourth of July thing way too seriously. Ann thought she noticed a bit more bravado than they'd shown in previous years, probably a result of the HBO *John Adams* miniseries, which had just come out. They seemed to have picked up a little more historical accuracy as well: the clip-on ponytails they sported better matched their hair colors, and several carried powder horns or wore hobnail shoes that fastened with large rectangular metal buckles.

Some of the patriots broke into a song meant to further taunt the redcoats:

Why come ye hither, Redcoats,
Your mind what madness fills?
In our valley there is danger,
And there's danger on our hills.
Oh, hear ye not the singing of the bugle wild and free?
And soon you'll know the ringing of the rifle from the tree.

At the end of the song, one of the patriots lifted his rifle and fired it into the air.

"Enough!" Ann said.

Long famous for its witches and even for pirates, Salem had never been known for having Revolutionary War reenactors. Though the first blood of the Revolution was actually spilled in Salem, the reenactments always took place in towns like Concord and Lexington. So it was particularly irksome to Ann to see the Revolutionary soldiers on the bench outside her store today. Why couldn't they stay on their own turf to party? Why did they always have to come to Mickey's?

Ann frowned at them from her doorway. "Could you gentlemen please move along? You're scaring my customers," she said.

"*We're* scaring *them*?" a redcoat with a perfect Sussex accent said to her. The thought seemed terrifically funny to the soldiers. In honor of the holiday, Ann was dressed in her full witch regalia. Last night she had tinted her almost-waist-length red hair with black henna, and the result was a color that seemed to morph as she moved, creating a vaguely iridescent, hallucinogenic effect. "*You're* scaring the hell out of *us*."

"I can manage to scare you a whole lot more if you don't move along," she offered.

"It's a free country," the one costumed as Paul Revere said. "It's the Fourth of July, for God's sake."

The Fourth of July was one of the busiest days of the year for Ann.

Not only did people like to buy souvenirs on Independence Day, but for some reason they seemed to like to have their fortunes told as well. She had appointments booked throughout the day, but the big traffic would be the walk-ins. Her girls would all be busy today. On the holiday Ann brought in almost double what she made on a regular weekend—that is, if people would actually come into the store, and she was sure as hell not going to let these guys intimidate her clientele.

She was contemplating how best to scare them. She could pretty much count on their scattering the minute she started to chant, but that might drive away some of the potential customers who were lingering at the wharf taking in the water views or waiting to get into one of the waterfront restaurants. She needed something subtler. She had all but decided to sprinkle some fairy dust on them. It wouldn't teach them to fly, but it smelled pervasively of heliotrope, a very feminine scent that spread quick and wide. It occurred to her then that she could just as easily call her friend Rafferty and have them cited for public drunkenness, but Rafferty wasn't a beat cop, or even a detective anymore. He was chief of police and probably too busy to bother with something so petty. Besides, Ann didn't have anything against drunkenness, public or otherwise—she just didn't want it interfering with business. No, she wouldn't call Rafferty. Instead she picked a package out of one of the bins in the front of the store, something meant to repel rodents, a horrid herbal blend she had created by accident one day when she was mixing potions. She and her girls had nicknamed it "stink-bomb herb." She stood in the doorway, checking out the wind direction before she let it loose, when Mickey Doherty suddenly appeared on the sidewalk dressed in his pirate costume, complete with eye patch and three-cornered hat and with a capuchin monkey on his shoulder.

Clearly here to rescue her from the soldiers, Mickey had a way of anticipating Ann's needs that she'd always found a bit disconcerting. She was aware that he had a crush on her. He'd been threatening to take her on for years, telling her he had magic powers of his own that could rival hers and inviting her to check them out. She'd never taken him up on it, though she had to admit she'd been tempted a few times. Annoying as he could be, Mickey Doherty was a carelessly attractive man.

Mickey was like the old-school movie heroes he'd obviously watched and emulated. He looked like Errol Flynn, though his attempts at flirtation were more like Groucho Marx. She wondered who he really was, thought she'd heard somewhere about some dark past—but no, that was a brother maybe. She couldn't remember. All in all, the Dohertys were an interesting family. But dark. Quite dark.

Mickey had gone into a rage when his sister died, had turned against Finch and more particularly Melville, though no one could really blame him for that one. Mickey could be a bit of a brawler. She remembered, more than once, hearing on her scanner that the police had been called to break up some kind of disturbance at Mickey's shop.

Ann's one vice was a serious addiction to her police scanner. She had one in the shop and one by her bedside at home. Her habit had started when she'd first become a witch. In those days there were not a lot of witches in Salem, just Ann and Laurie Cabot and a few others who had not yet come out of the proverbial broom closet. In an act of paranoid practicality, Ann had purchased her first scanner in order to make sure she had a head start out of town if Salem's famed witch-hunting ever started up again. In reality she had nothing to worry about. Sensing an opportunity for tourist revenue that the town sorely needed, Salem had for the most part embraced its new witches. But by now she was addicted to the chatter of the scanner.

"Come on, gentlemen," Mickey said as he rounded up the soldiers. He gestured toward his shop with his sword. "I've got grog."

The soldiers picked themselves up off the benches and followed him across the wharf to his store. When the last of them had filed in, Mickey removed his three-cornered hat and bowed to Ann.

She rolled her eyes and went back inside.

The sea-chantey singers had arrived and were setting up outside Mickey's shop. On the wharf, people walked their dogs, and someone was assembling a booth for face painting. Ann thought she'd heard that the *Friendship* was sailing today, but she wasn't sure. Already there was a line waiting to tour it where it sat at the wharves. Though the *Friendship* did sail on occasion, she was not allowed public passengers, just crew and, rarely, some special guests. Ann had heard that they were trying to change that status, to have the ship commissioned to sail with groups of tourists aboard, but so far nothing had come of it.

If they were taking the *Friendship* out sailing today, they'd better do it soon, Ann thought. It was going to storm later, and it was going to be a doozy. She didn't know how she could tell this—she hadn't heard a forecast—but Ann always knew about a day ahead exactly what the weather was going to do and when. If she hadn't been a witch, she could easily have been a meteorologist.

She sighed at the thought of the day that lay ahead. Her first reading was already waiting inside, a twenty-something girl who'd been to the shop for readings several times in the last few months. She hoped to marry her live-in boyfriend, but he was holding back. With so many readings to do, Ann had almost forgotten that Zee was coming. She'd called and asked if she could come by, and Ann had offered lunch, completely forgetting that today was the Fourth. She had thought about rescheduling, but she hadn't seen Zee much since she got back, and she knew that things must be tough for the girl. Finch had never been an easy man to deal with, though Ann had always liked him. Even when Maureen was having such a hard time of it, Ann had never blamed Finch. Though Maureen had been one of Ann's best friends, it wasn't difficult to see how sick she was.

What Maureen had seen in Finch in the first place was anybody's guess. Still, it seemed that she'd loved him and longed for him in the same way that poets long for the romantic ideal, the merging with the beloved. Yet it didn't take her psychic powers for Ann to tell that some of the stories Maureen related about their passion were clearly fictional. Maureen was, after all, a writer of fairy tales. But over the years Ann had come to suspect that the stories Maureen told weren't about Finch at all, or if they were, then it was more wishful thinking on Maureen's part than reality.

After her mother's suicide, Zee had taken to hanging around Ann's shop.

"Do you believe in reincarnation?" she had asked one day.

"I don't know, sweetie," Ann said. "Why do you ask?" Of course she had known exactly why she would ask, but she wanted Zee to talk. In the days since Maureen's death, Zee had been far too silent.

"My mother believed in past lives," Zee said.

Ann nodded. "Yes, she did."

"I was thinking that she might come back as someone like Juliet."

"You mean, as in Romeo and Juliet?"

"Yes, I know she wasn't real, but someone like her. One of the great star-crossed lovers."

Ann considered.

"Or maybe," Zee said, "she might come back as a radish."

"As in the root vegetable?"

"Why not?" Zee said. "Why do we have to come back as people at all?"

"Why indeed?" Ann said.

"My mother used to grow radishes."

"Did she?" Ann asked. "That's one thing I didn't know about your mother."

"There's a lot you didn't know about my mother," Zee said.

Ann thought that was probably true. Zee had always known far more than any child her age should have to know.

"She really did love radishes," Zee said. "She ate them all the time. Finch told her if she ate any more of them, she was going to turn into a radish."

It brought a smile to Ann's lips. She was really fond of this kid. Didn't seem much like her mother at all, or her father either, for that matter. She was definitely her own person.

"I have some books on reincarnation," Ann said. "If you want to read them."

"No," Zee said. "I just wanted to know if you believed in it."

"I'm not sure what I believe about it," Ann said.

ANN FIRST MET MAUREEN THE year before Zee was born, when Maureen enrolled in one of Ann's herbal-remedy classes, one that was meant for practicing witches but was open to the public as well.

It was a decidedly manic period of Maureen's life. She was spending Finch's money with abandon and signing up for everything in town. It would have been annoying if she weren't so charming. Seldom had Ann seen anyone as beautiful as Maureen. When she walked into the class— late, of course—the energy of the entire room changed. Heads turned.

Maureen's purpose for taking the class, she said, was that she was afraid she couldn't conceive. She was desperate, had tried all the regular methods, and wanted to try an herbal remedy. She announced this to the class as they went around the room, each person stating her particular areas of interest in herbalism. Most wanted spells, or child-safe remedies, or to learn to make perfume by brewing essential oils.

"What kind of traditional methods have you tried?" Ann asked Maureen at the break. No matter how New Age Ann might be, she was still a New Englander, and she didn't believe Maureen should share such private information with the whole class.

"We tried different positions, of course, with me remaining prone with my legs in the air for hours. We've tried different times of the month. We've even tried a turkey baster."

"Why would you try that?"

"The problem is really more with Finch," Maureen said. "His libido, if you must know."

Ann didn't need to know—in fact, she would have preferred never to know. But she was afraid that if she didn't address this new bit of information right away, Maureen might be tempted to share it with the whole class. "Talk to me after this is over," Ann said. "Maybe I can brew something up for you."

Maureen looked so grateful that Ann feared she might turn to the class and make another announcement, but she didn't.

After class was over, Ann did brew something up—several things, in fact. Though it was long before Viagra, Ann had pretty good luck with raising people's libidos, sometimes to the point of being less a gift and more of a curse. "It's a tea," Ann said. "Steep it for at least five minutes, and make sure he drinks it hot." It was one of Ann's most powerful potions, and it was popular among Salem's male population. Even so, she doubted that her potion would work for Finch and Maureen. Ann had known Finch for years. She had been surprised when she heard he'd gotten married.

Maureen completed Ann's introductory class in herbology. And then she took another, more advanced class. And somewhere along the line, Ann and Maureen became friends.

All that spring, Maureen fed Ann's tea to Finch.

"So is it working?" Ann asked her one day after class.

"It is," Maureen said. "Though I've taken to putting it in his wine instead of brewing tea."

"I'm not sure about that," Ann said. "You're supposed to drink it hot."

"Well, it seems to be working," Maureen said. "Plus, I added a little something."

"What kind of little something?" Ann asked.

"Just something I read about that enhances pleasure."

Ann looked at her strangely. In the last month, Maureen had purchased every book on herbs and plants that Ann sold. If there was something in there that enhanced pleasure, chances were that Ann had already added it to the mix.

Maureen picked up on Ann's concern. "Don't worry about it," she said.

"Hey," Ann said. "If you found something that got Finch going, you ought to give me the recipe. We can package it and make a fortune."

"Thanks so much," Maureen said.

Ann didn't realize quite how it sounded. "I didn't mean it like that," she said.

"Sure you did," Maureen said.

It was the first time Ann realized that Maureen wasn't in denial.

"I don't get it," Ann said. "Why do you stay?"

"Hey, it's working," Maureen said. "And we really want to have a baby." Maureen's eyes filled up with tears. "Finch would make such a good father," she said.

Ann had already overstepped, and she knew it. "I wish you many blessings," she said.

THAT SUMMER MAUREEN AND FINCH went their separate ways, Finch to Amherst and Maureen to Baker's Island. It had been Mickey, and not Maureen, who'd told Ann about the split. So when they showed up at the store together, Ann was surprised.

"We have something to tell you," Maureen said. "We're pregnant." For someone who had just gotten everything she said she wanted, Maureen didn't look quite as happy as one might expect.

Finch, on the other hand, seemed ecstatic.

"Congratulations!" Ann said. "This is the best news!"

The pregnancy kept them together, as Maureen had hoped when she originally asked Ann for potions. The father-to-be was so attentive that Maureen couldn't help but be happy during the duration of the pregnancy. Still, something was clearly bothering her. When Ann finally decided to ask, Maureen quoted Oscar Wilde: *When the gods wish to punish us they answer our prayers.*

ANN DID FOUR MORE READINGS before Zee showed up. She was beginning to doubt that Zee was coming at all when she suddenly appeared at the door.

Ann got one of her girls to take over her station, then led Zee through the back rooms past beakers, bottles, wands, crystals, jugs of distilled water and stacks of handmade soap, candles, and rows of books on magick and the healing arts.

Ann had recently replaced her Indian-print door curtain with a beaded one and her futon with a brass daybed she'd bought from an old witch she'd met at the Farmington midsummer festival who was retiring and moving to Florida.

Zee hadn't been in Ann's private room in years. Looking around, she thought it seemed more brothel than witch's lair.

"Too *McCabe and Mrs. Miller?*" Ann asked.

"No, I like it," Zee said, heading straight for the bed and sitting cross-legged as if they were about to do Transcendental Meditation, as they had in the old days when her mother brought her along. Zee had been the most devout little student, keeping her eyes closed and holding the lotus position for longer than anyone else and with such an expression of sheer determination that Ann and Maureen couldn't help but laugh.

Ann had made sandwiches with sprouts and early tomatoes on the multigrain bread she bought at A & J King. "Thank the goddess for that bakery," Ann said.

"I've been meaning to stop there," Zee said. "The place right next to Cornerstone Books, right?"

"The other side of the building," Ann said, turning on the electric kettle. "Would you like a cup of herbal tea?"

"Sprouts, herbal tea, the world has moved on, you know."

"You're wrong about that," Ann said. "The world is moving backward. Yoga is back. And everyone's vegan."

"Not everyone," Zee said. "I'm sure as hell not."

"Everyone in my circle," Ann said.

Zee laughed and took a bite of the sandwich. "Actually, it's really good," she said, thinking she should get some of this bread for Finch's sandwiches.

Zee looked at Ann's bookshelves. "You still stock books on reincarnation?" she asked.

"A few," Ann said. "What are you looking for?"

"I don't know," Zee said. "I just thought I'd read something about it."

"You still think your mother's coming back as a radish?"

"A what?"

Zee had clearly forgotten her earlier speculation. Ann waved her hand to clear the words. She went to her bookcase and pulled out a book by Edgar Cayce that one of her students had given her.

"Cayce is a good place to start," she said.

Zee put the paperback in her bag.

"Have you started to believe in reincarnation?" Ann had to ask.

"No. Maybe. . . . I don't know," Zee said. "What about you?"

"Pretty much. I believe more in simultaneous incarnations. Though I do agree with what Eleanor Roosevelt said about reincarnation."

"What was that?"

"I'm paraphrasing here, but it was something to the effect of, 'I don't think the idea of my being here in a past life is any more surreal than the idea of my being here now.' Something like that."

"I always liked Eleanor Roosevelt," Zee said. Then, thinking about it, she went on, "I'm considering giving up my practice."

"Interesting segue," Ann said.

Zee shrugged.

"Why would you do that?"

"I'm just not sure I'm any good at it," Zee said.

"I would imagine that you're very good at it."

"Don't bet on it," Zee said.

"Has something happened?"

"A lot of things have happened," Zee said.

"Like what?" Ann asked.

"Like, I'm not sure why I got into it in the first place."

"That's not too difficult to figure out," Ann said. "After what happened to your mother."

"That doesn't mean it was the right choice, does it?"

"Not necessarily," Ann said. "But I'm still surprised. You worked so hard to get there. Is there something else you'd rather be doing?"

"I don't know," Zee said.

Ann thought about it for a minute. "So you're giving up your practice and your engagement all within a month," Ann said.

"I'm just thinking about giving up my practice. I haven't made any decisions."

"Interesting," Ann said.

"Which means?"

"Interesting," Ann said again. She thought about it some more. "Don't become a full-time caregiver," Ann said.

"Why not?"

"Because I've seen what it does to people. To Melville, for one."

"Poor Melville," Zee said.

"What the hell happened between those two?" Ann asked. She knew it was something big, could feel the weight of it, but she had no clue as to its origins.

"I wish I knew," Zee said.

Some kids were setting off firecrackers on the wharf. A cat scooted under the bed.

"What was that?" Zee saw it flash past.

"That's Persephone. She's a Katrina cat," Ann said. "They shipped a lot of them up here. I got her at the shelter."

The three masts of the *Friendship* moved by Ann's window. She was headed out for a Fourth of July sail. Ann noticed Zee watching it. She thought about the weather. There was no sign of a storm on the horizon as yet, so they should have smooth sailing for an hour or so.

Maybe it was the reenactors, maybe it was the *Friendship* itself—the three masts of the tall ship and its rigging made Ann think of Salem's past days of shipping, the bustle of the busy wharves, the excitement of Salem as a world port. She pictured the powerful shipping families, the man they called King Derby who owned the next wharf and the Pickerings who owned this one. At any time there might be a hundred ships like the *Friendship* in port, loading and unloading their bounty. The tunnels that ran under Derby Wharf and up to the houses owned by the shipping families were a perfect place for hiding their taxable goods. Ann lived in one of the historic houses up on Orange Street. In the middle of her kitchen floor was a trapdoor that led to the old Derby tunnel. It was a place that Persephone loved to hide, and Ann had taken to blocking it off at night, so the cat wouldn't end up lost in the tunnel somewhere under the wharves and more frightened than ever.

One of the *Friendship*'s sails was set, and the huge ship moved solely on wind power as she left the harbor now. Hawk was high in the rigging, helping set the foresail.

Ann observed Zee watching the ship and handed her a pair of binoculars she kept on her desk.

"Binoculars. A police scanner. Have you started working for the CIA?"

"Just nosy by nature," Ann said.

Zee held up the binoculars and looked at the ship.

Ann watched as Hawk moved quickly down one mast and up another. "I'm surprised he doesn't fall," she said.

"He moves really well," Zee said.

Something about the way she said it took Ann by surprise.

The people on the wharf began to cheer and clap as the *Friendship* hoisted her second sail.

Zee didn't stop looking and was still watching Hawk as the ship reached the mouth of the harbor.

Oh, my God, Ann thought. *She's sleeping with him.* The thought came to her in words, and she was relieved to find that she hadn't uttered those words aloud.

And just as quickly another thought came to her, and before she had a chance to censor herself, this time the words *did* come out of her mouth. "Be careful of that one," Ann said to Zee. "He's not who you think he is."

"What?" Zee asked, surprised to have her thoughts so clearly invaded.

Ann knew that Zee didn't believe in any of this stuff. But she also observed a blush starting on Zee's face that quickly spread all the way down her neck.

LIGHTNING HIT THE MAST of a moored Hunter 31 that had sailed north to the tip of Cape Ann and into Rockport Harbor even before the storm appeared on the horizon. Luckily there was no one on board at the time. The charge traveled down the aluminum mast, and, not finding a path to ground, it side-flashed, blowing out the boat's hull.

"Shit," someone said. "That boat just exploded."

Hawk flew down the rigging of the *Friendship* as if he were on a slide.

"Lightning," he said.

No one agreed. The sun, so strong just minutes ago, was now behind a cloud. But the sky was still bright blue. The general opinion was that it was probably a leaky propane tank, but Hawk had seen the strike from his post high in the rigging.

The captain listened to Hawk and put into Sandy Bay, just outside Rockport Harbor. "Better safe harbor than sorry sailor," he said. The plan had been to reach Newburyport in time for the fireworks, but the wooden mast on the *Friendship* had been hit once before, and the captain didn't want to risk it again. Though Gloucester Harbor would have been a much better choice, there was no time to get there. Within five minutes the sky had blackened and lightning flashed overhead like natural fireworks.

The *Friendship* dropped anchor.

"Everybody below deck," the captain ordered. "And don't touch anything metal."

As a general rule, Hawk liked thunderstorms. He especially liked them on the water, where they came up fast and you could see the thunderheads forming and pushing upward in the sky. But this one seemed to have come out of nowhere, a phenomenon he'd heard about but had never yet seen. There were people struck by lightning as much as thirty minutes before a storm arrived. It wasn't that uncommon. The charge could travel.

But today he'd been on the rigging when the strike hit. It was close enough that he felt the elation from it before he saw the burst. The hair on his neck and arms stood up as the errant bolt passed. By all rights it should have hit the *Friendship,* which was by far the tallest ship around, but instead it moved on, striking the Hunter. He knew it wasn't random—lightning followed the rules of electricity—but it seemed personal somehow. The *Friendship* would have survived the strike, but Hawk, on the rigging, would most likely have been its casualty. He couldn't help feeling he'd been spared.

He didn't share his story; he knew these guys too well. They'd had enough trouble believing that there'd been a strike at all, though they certainly believed it now. The ocean had come up, and the ship rolled as it took the swells sideways. Even Rockport's breakwater did nothing to stop the surge.

The sailors sat down below, listening to the crack and boom. As the sky lit up, the town of Rockport froze in silhouette, leaving a burned, stuttering image of terrified tourists huddled in doorways on Bearskin Neck.

Normally a rowdy group, the men were unusually quiet as they watched the Hunter 31 burn and sink.

"I thought aluminum masts didn't conduct electricity," one of the sailors said.

"Sure they do," Hawk said. "The problem must have been in the grounding."

"Shit," one of the other guys said.

"Double shit," another said. "We're the highest mast in the harbor, and wet wood is a conductor."

"We'll be okay," Hawk said. "We have lightning rods, and we're grounded with copper."

Everyone was silent, hoping that he was right.

When it finally ended, the crew made their way back on deck. One of the lines was singed, probably the result of a side flash from the Hunter 31.

Someone pointed to the mouth of the harbor. A rolling fog was moving in slowly from open ocean. It was an odd occurrence, more suited to the Pacific than this part of the Atlantic. Usually the New England fog fell in patches rather than rolled.

"Jesus," one of the crew said.

By 6:00 P.M. THE WHOLE of Cape Ann was fogged in. There would be no making it to Newburyport tonight.

They all walked into town. Until recently Rockport had been a dry town. Even now the only place you could get a drink was at one of the local inns, and so that's where the crew headed. When they got to the top of High Street, Hawk broke from the group.

"Where do you think you're going?" his friend Josh asked.

"I'm going to Salem," Hawk said. "I'll be back here in the morning."

"How're you gonna get there? Fly?" someone else asked.

"Yeah," he said. "I'm gonna sprout little wings."

"I wouldn't doubt it," one of the other guys said. The group had been in awe of his climbing skills, and of the idea that anyone actually liked being up in the air so high.

★ ★ ★

HAWK DECIDED TO HITCH A ride to the Rockport train station. The first two cars passed him, but the third one, a car full of college girls, pulled over and opened the door.

They were headed to Newburyport to a party, and they wanted him to come along.

"I don't think so," Hawk said, shaking his head. "I know trouble when I see it."

"Oh, come on," one of them said with a smile. "It'll be fun."

He waited at the station for the Salem train. There was almost no one riding tonight. Hawk sat alone in the last car.

The train pushed through the fog in Beverly. He could see people lining the wharves waiting for the fireworks: families on blankets, tailgaters.

When he got off the train in Salem, the streets were dry. He walked down Washington Street through groups of partying tourists and then cut down Front Street to Derby. He didn't stop at the wharf, didn't even stop at his boat to change. People crowded the grass at the end of Turner Street and sat in the gardens at the Gables. There was no moon tonight, so it would be a good show. He took a quick look to make sure no one was watching him, glad that the streetlight near the old house was burned out. Then he climbed the vines to the room on the second floor and let himself in through Zee's open window.

★ 27 ★

ZEE COULD HEAR JESSINA downstairs, the sound of silverware clanking as she cleaned up. Breakfast was over, and she was baking something.

Zee noticed the scratch marks she had left on Hawk's back. She felt bad about it, hoped he wouldn't take off his shirt at work today. But watching him half dressed and sitting on the edge of the bed, something stirred in her again, and she wanted to reach out to him.

"Do you have to go?" she said to him, and he laughed and turned to face her.

"I've got to get back to Rockport," Hawk said.

She reached out and pulled him onto the bed, unzipped his pants and went down on him. He groaned.

"Shh," she said, hearing Finch's walker below, heading toward the kitchen.

"I'm not the one who needs shushing, am I?" He grinned as he moved slowly on top of her. And when he was close and when she started to moan, he clamped his hand over her mouth and pressed hard. She arched her back and rolled onto him and bit down hard on his hand, and he didn't pull it away. And she didn't care anymore if Jessina heard them or even if Finch did, because she was no longer here.

★ ★ ★

THEY'D BEEN SLEEPING TOGETHER FOR almost a month. Zee knew that Mattei would tell her it was obsessive, especially so soon after Michael. Mattei would tell her that Hawk was her drug of choice. But she didn't want to think about Mattei or about Michael or Finch downstairs with Jessina still hand-feeding him his meals and Zee letting it slide. Zee knew she shouldn't let her do it, because he needed to be able to feed himself, to hold on to that skill. She had been here for six weeks now, and things with Finch were clearly slipping. She couldn't help but let them slip, because there were so many of those things, too many details to manage. Everyday tasks the rest of us take for granted, from buttoning a shirt to getting up from a chair, had to be watched and aided. So when Zee could escape for a while into another world with Hawk, she did so gratefully.

If Hawk was her drug of choice, then he was her only vice. She couldn't get enough of him. She lived in two worlds, or so it seemed. Her days were filled with the business of caregiving and all the things that went along: ordering food from Peapod, diapers and lotion so Finch's skin wouldn't break down, a soft washcloth to bathe him, prunes for constipation, Oreos for treats. When Finch wandered, which he did whenever he got to the tail end of a dose, she followed him, making sure he didn't fall with each unsteady step.

She couldn't get him to use the railings that Hawk had installed. It wasn't that he wouldn't use them, more that he couldn't seem to figure out how, or couldn't make his hand grasp the rails that would steady him. Instead Zee kept placing his walker in front of him, reminding him softly each time he moved to "use the walker."

Most of the time, she felt as if she were talking to a child, though she knew full well that he understood her words. This was her father, yet it wasn't. It was a duality she had stopped trying to resolve. Finch was now both child and father. She realized that her need for a father was profound. But with so much unresolved between them, theirs had often been an uneasy relationship. Still, he had always been there when she needed him. And now he was the one who needed her.

The tender feelings she had for Finch, when they came to her, seemed to come from that vulnerable place she recognized in him, a place that may have always been there but that was now the more prevalent part of his otherwise thorny personality. Finch had always used his intellect to distance himself. When things became too much for him, he had often spoken in quotes or riddles, a quality that seemed to amuse Melville but one that Zee had found frustrating. And now, once the new drug had left his system, the one that caused the hallucinations, he had stopped speaking as Hawthorne, but he had pretty much stopped talking altogether, though she could tell that he still understood her. When he spoke, his speech was perfect, but he chose to do so less and less, and he uttered not much more than single syllables if possible when Jessina was in the house, though Zee could tell that Finch liked her.

"You don't need to talk down to him," Zee said. "He may not be talking much, but he can understand you well enough."

"I'm not talking down to him," Jessina insisted. "I would never do that."

Jessina bathed Finch and dressed him in the mornings, then came back again to feed him dinner and put him to bed. In the long hours in between, Zee read books to him, something she knew that Melville had done, though Melville had had better success with it than Zee. Mostly, when his meds were at their peak, Finch dozed. She would get up, prop a pillow under whichever side his head flopped to, and sit back down again, reading more quietly now so as not to disturb his sleep but not altogether stopping in case her words might drift to someplace in his subconscious that might still be vibrant, a place she could not often reach when Finch was awake.

She did not presume to read Hawthorne to Finch. The book she picked from Finch's shelf was Proust's *Remembrance of Things Past,* partly because she had never made her way past the first volume and partly because she thought the words might jar Finch's involuntary or Proustian memory. She wondered whether she could get Jessina to make madeleines, if Zee could find a recipe.

When she found herself unable to read any longer, Zee would put on the soft music she knew that Finch favored: Tchaikovsky's *Swan Lake,* or sometimes Puccini.

When his meds wore off, Finch grew agitated and felt compelled to walk, though it was the worst possible time to do so. He had fallen twice already. Luckily, neither fall had hurt him, but falling was a serious threat to the elderly in general and to Parkinson's patients in particular. Though Finch was only in his late sixties, and far too young to be experiencing the extreme effects of aging, the Parkinson's seemed to be moving much faster than Zee had expected.

And so Zee followed him as he walked through the house, accompanying him everywhere—to the kitchen, to the bedroom, to the bath—trying to afford him some privacy but being careful that he didn't get up and wander, leaving the door partly open so she could hear him if he needed her. "Leave me," he would often say.

"I'm sorry," she answered. "I know how much you hate this."

She tried to explain what the VNA nurses who came once a week had told her: "It's important to keep him clean. It's important that he get dressed every day." She understood the first but wasn't altogether certain she agreed with the last. It was just too difficult sometimes, she thought. He didn't want to do it. He would have preferred to remain in his robe and pajamas, which would have seemed fine to Zee.

But every morning Jessina happily picked outfits for him, dressing him like a little doll, in vibrant color combinations Finch would never have chosen for himself. Jessina seemed to have a genuine affection for him.

Zee rarely left Finch alone, not unless she prearranged it with Jessina, who was glad to oblige when she could. But Jessina was the single mother of a teenage boy, and she didn't feel good about leaving her son alone for too long. She could almost see her house from Turner Street, but the neighborhoods were vastly different, and there was all sorts of trouble Danny could get into if left unsupervised.

And so most of the time it was just Finch and Zee. He didn't want to go out anymore, didn't even want to go for rides in the car. As bad as his reaction to his meds had been, Zee sometimes thought she preferred his Hawthorne hallucinations to the quiet depression he seemed to be experiencing now.

For her own mental health, Zee had to get out of the house every day and used the two sessions when Jessina was with Finch to escape. Salem was a great walking city. Sometimes she walked down to the harbor or over to the Willows for a game of skee ball at the arcade, a game she had loved as a child. Sometimes she met Melville for coffee or walked over to the gardens at the Ropes Mansion. This was her city more than Boston had ever been. Its diversity of person and place suited every mood she was having that summer. There was part of her that simply felt better here.

On the occasions when she could hire Jessina for more than a few hours, she would escape for longer periods, usually to the beach or to Winter Island, often coming back to find Jessina and Finch sitting in the den watching the Lifetime Channel. It was out of character for her father to watch television at all, let alone such estrogen-based dramas. Still, they seemed to be among the only things that captured his interest, and he sat, eyes glued to the set, his reactions intense and perfectly timed to the story, as if the whole drama were unfolding not on a small screen at all but right here in his den.

ZEE HAD BEGUN TO SLEEP in Maureen's room even before she started seeing Hawk. Finch's sundowning was getting worse, he'd begun to have the hallucinations so common to Alzheimer's patients that was a sign of the crossover the doctor had been telling her to watch out for. After the sun went down, Finch grew more and more agitated and confused. He often wandered, waking her, and she could never get back to sleep.

It didn't happen when she stayed upstairs. Finch couldn't climb the stairs anymore, and he wouldn't try, but still she would worry about him waking up, so she checked on him every few hours. As a result she was still often exhausted and grouchy from lack of sleep. For a while she raised the side rails on the hospital bed the OT had ordered, but then the VNA nurse talked her out of it.

"The problem is, they try to get out anyway," the nurse said. "I've seen more hospitalizations because one of my dementia patients tried to climb over the bedside and got himself tangled and ended up breaking a bone."

It was Jessina who suggested the alarm. "They use them at the nursing home," she said.

The next time Jessina came in, she brought one of the alarms with her. It clipped to Finch's bedclothes and to the bed. When the connection broke, the alarm went off. Finch clearly hated it, but it served its purpose. Zee began to sleep through the night, waking only when she heard the buzzing.

ZEE OFTEN TALKED TO MELVILLE either in person or on the phone about what was happening to Finch. And she consulted with several doctors who basically told her what she already knew, that there was nothing much that could be done.

Mattei left messages on her cell. She returned the calls when she could bear to do so, which was less and less often as time went on. She didn't want to talk about Finch or about Michael and how the whole situation made her feel. She remembered something one of her patients had replied when she asked him how he felt about the illness of a parent: *How do you think I feel about it? I feel fucking awful.* By the end of each day, Zee could feel an inescapable heaviness descending on her. It was about Finch, of course, but it was about Lilly, too, and about Michael and her career and basically about all the choices she'd made in her life so far that were either not well enough thought out or just altogether wrong.

Now, for the first time she could remember, there were no choices to be made. Instead of trying to fix things or plan her life, she only needed to be present for her father, something she found easier than she might have expected. She couldn't remember ever spending this much time with Finch.

And so every night when Jessina put Finch to bed, Zee would give him his first sleeping pill and take her evening walk. When she got home again, she would give him the second pill, telling him what was new in town, talking about what she'd seen. She would kiss him good night, lingering for a minute with her hand upon his shoulder. Then, after Jessina had gone for the night, Zee would go upstairs to her other life, drawing herself a long bath and waiting for Hawk. Though a simple set of stairs connected the two worlds, they could not have been more different.

EVER SINCE EARLY JUNE, WHEN she'd told Hawk who she was, Zee had been having dreams about Lilly: Lilly on the bridge. Lilly being chased by Adam. So when she started having her recurring dream about Maureen's story again, she was almost relieved. The night she started up with Hawk had been several weeks ago, back on June 10, the first really warm night of the season.

Zee had been too tired to sleep. She was so exhausted, and it was far too hot upstairs. Every time she settled down, her legs would jump her awake again. Desperate, she'd taken one of the sleeping pills Mattei had prescribed.

And then she'd had a dream about the *Friendship,* a dream she'd had off and on for years. Zee dreamed about the lower level of the ship, as Maureen had once imagined and described it, with very specific details: the hold, the bunks, a lantern that hung from a chain.

When she woke up, Zee became obsessed by the idea of seeing the *Friendship* for herself and finding out how accurate Maureen's description had been. The fact that she didn't want to wait until morning, when she could pay her admission and go aboard the historic vessel, should have been her first clue that the obsession was a reaction to the sleeping pill. Everyone had heard stories of people who'd done odd or unusual things while under the influence. But the drug was still in Zee's system, and so her compulsion to immediately see the *Friendship* seemed logical.

Her mother had never set eyes on the *Friendship,* or rather on the replica of the 1797 merchant ship that the City of Salem re-created in the 1990s. Maureen had died back in the 1980s, long before the plans for building the ship were even drawn up, though money was beginning to be raised for the project. Tonight, for some reason, Zee was obsessed with discovering how accurate her mother's detailed description had been.

And so she quickly dressed and snuck out of the house, tiptoeing down the stairs, stretching over the squeaky one near the bottom, and letting herself out through the kitchen door, careful to close the outside screen door slowly so that the spring didn't slam it shut and wake Finch. Once outside, she cut across the backyards and alleys until she reached Derby Wharf, where the *Friendship* was tied up. The night was clear, the stars seemed bright and close.

The ranger's station was deserted, as was the rigging shed. When she got to the *Friendship,* the ship was dark and there was a chain across the gangplank. But the moonlight was strong, and she easily ducked under the chain, removing her shoes so that she wouldn't make a sound on the ramp. When she got to the ship's deck, she looked around. She knew there was security, knew Hawk to be part of the team who took shifts making sure the *Friendship* was safe, mostly from kids who might sneak aboard and vandalize it. The Park Service rangers were really the ones in charge, but the men who worked on the ship also volunteered on occasion, taking turns keeping watch.

Zee found the stairs and descended to the cabin below. Her heart was racing. It was so dark that she could barely see a few feet in front of her. Though she was still drugged, she was beginning to realize that this had been a stupid idea. She should have waited until tomorrow and taken the tour with the tourists.

Ever so slowly her eyes began to adjust to the darkness. The moonlight merged with the streetlight, and the beam from the tiny lighthouse at the end of the wharf provided just enough illumination that she began to make her way around. She could see only traces of things. She moved as if blind, feeling for the structure of objects as Maureen had described them and the positions where she knew those objects to be. Here was the hold, the bunk, there the hanging lantern. Each confirmation filled her with awe, but it also scared her a little. The sea was calm and the ship tied securely, but she could feel it rolling, feel the floor shifting beneath her feet as if it weren't here in port at all but in the middle of a stormy sea. It must be the sleeping pill, she thought, and then it occurred to her that she might be only dreaming now, dreaming that she'd left Finch in his bed and made her way down here on such a determined mission. She began to hope she was dreaming.

A beam of light swept toward her, and she froze.

"What's going on?" Hawk's voice filled the empty space. Then he stopped in recognition as the beam from his flashlight lit her face. "What are you doing here?"

She might have passed out. Or maybe it was the effect of the drug. But the next thing she knew, she was sitting on his boat. He was making her tea or coffee or something hot. And she was coming back. He didn't ask again what she was doing on the boat. He didn't ask anything, just waited for her to explain, which she didn't do. She'd heard about this kind of thing. Sleeping pills affected people in a variety of ways. Some had blackouts where they didn't remember driving. The prescription came with warnings: *Don't drink, don't operate heavy machinery, blackouts may occur.* This wasn't a blackout, not in any traditional sense. But sitting here, embarrassed and confused, she made a mental note never to take another sleeping pill. There was something too intimate about being here on his boat, with his personal things scattered about. She wasn't sure what she was feeling exactly, except that she wanted to erase this night.

When she was okay again, Hawk offered to walk her home. As they walked down Derby Street, she started to shiver, and he gave her his jacket. They walked in silence.

At the door she realized she had locked herself out. She'd left the interior door unlocked, but the screen door had clicked shut and locked behind her, an extra precaution she had set up to stop Finch's wandering. Hawk tried one of the side windows, but they were also locked. Then, looking up, he spotted the vine that led to the open window in Maureen's room. Zee stood watching as he climbed the vine in the same easy way he'd climbed the rigging that first day she'd seen him, and for just a moment she saw him as the young sailor in her mother's story.

When Hawk let her in the kitchen door, Finch's alarm was going off. He stood at the far end of the tilting hallway, staring at Hawk.

"It's okay," Zee said. "You remember Hawk. I locked myself out, and he let me back in."

Finch didn't answer but just stood staring at them both. "Let me get you back to bed," Zee said.

By the time she got him settled and calmed him down, Hawk was gone.

THE NEXT NIGHT ZEE ASKED Jessina to stay late.

She walked down to the *Friendship* and then to Hawk's boat, moored at one of the slips on Pickering Wharf. He wasn't there. She found him at Capt.'s, sitting at the bar with the rest of the crew. All heads turned as she entered.

Hawk stood and came over. "Two nights in a row," he said. "Lucky me."

She realized she could take the remark two different ways.

"I wanted to thank you," she said.

"For what?" he asked.

"For walking me home. For your jacket. For not having me arrested."

He laughed.

She handed him the jacket. He put it on and went outside with her, holding the door as they exited.

They walked down the wharf, past the *Friendship* and the dog walkers and the granite benches to the tiny lighthouse almost half a mile out into the harbor. They sat on the bench.

She had expected to have to offer him an explanation, had been working on what she would say for most of the afternoon, but everything she could think of sounded lame.

But he didn't ask her. Instead he sat looking out across the harbor.

"What are you looking at?" she asked.

"The house I grew up in," he said, pointing to the Marblehead side of the harbor.

"Which one?" She could see two houses, both with wharves.

He pointed to a blue house.

Her face went red. "You didn't have a cuddy-cabin cruiser, did you?"

"Our neighbors had the cuddy," he said.

It was the boat she had stolen, the crime for which she'd been arrested and Melville had posted bail.

"Why?"

"No reason," she said.

He looked at her curiously. "You're an odd woman, Dr. Finch."

"You have no idea," she said.

He laughed, his smile catching her by surprise. It was that smile, she decided, that's what the attraction was. It had been a long time since she'd been attracted to anyone but Michael, and there had not been a lot of smiling lately.

It was more grin than smile, she thought, still trying to analyze what was happening to her when he leaned over and kissed her.

That first kiss and the feeling of electricity that passed between them took her by surprise. He was watching her now, to see how she felt about it.

He didn't have to wait long for her answer. The kiss had effectively stalled any objective analysis she'd been trying to perform. She kissed him back.

She didn't get home until after midnight. They had gone back to his boat, and afterward, when she looked at the time, she had rushed to get dressed and hurried away, embarrassed, not really certain how everything had moved so quickly and yet happy about it, giddy even.

Standing there later in front of Jessina, she'd felt like a teenager about to be caught. She had dressed hastily, and she hoped like hell she hadn't put her shirt on backward or, God forbid, inside out.

I N THE WEEKS THAT followed, they talked about a lot of things. He had gone to school in England, Hawk told her, to study celestial navigation, a field for which there wasn't much demand, especially in the United States these days. "Which is why I'm a carpenter," he said.

"You're not a carpenter, you're a rigger," she said, quoting the remark he'd made the first day they met.

Zee told Hawk about Finch and Melville and about Maureen and the way she'd died. Later, to lighten the mood a bit, she told him that she was the girl who had stolen his neighbor's cuddy-cabin cruiser.

"I remember when that happened," he said.

"I was a wild child," she said.

He laughed. "You're a fairly wild adult."

She smiled to think how most people she knew these days would disagree. Certainly Michael had never had such a thought about her.

"Seriously, didn't you go to jail for that?"

"What?"

"My mother told me that the cuddy thief was doing time."

"Probation," she said. "And a lot of community service."

"I was relieved when they caught you," he said. "Before that, I was certain our neighbor suspected me," Hawk added, kissing her playfully.

They were lying in bed looking up at the ceiling and the sliver of moonlight coming through what appeared to be a skylight.

"What's up there?" he asked.

"It was the widow's walk."

He thought for a minute and then said, "I never noticed a widow's walk from the outside."

"We don't have it anymore, a previous owner cut it down. Way back in the early 1800s."

"Mind if I take a look?" he asked.

"Be my guest."

He got out of bed and walked to the center of the room, drawing over the chair from Maureen's writing desk. He reached up and opened the hatch. Then he pulled himself up. "Great view," he said, looking back down at her. "You want to come up?"

She had never particularly wanted to go up there. It was too much a part of her mother's story. Plus, Finch always told her it was dangerous. But tonight her curiosity got the best of her. She stood on the chair, and he reached down with both hands and pulled her up through the opening. They stood together on a small perch mid-roof. There was no platform anymore; the captain, in his fit of rage, had chopped it away, leaving only the sharp shards of splintered frame to hint at its existence. Hawk examined the gashes from the captain's ax that were still visible on the hatch frame.

"It leaks sometimes," she said. "If we get a really heavy rain."

"I could fix that," he said. "It wouldn't be difficult." Then, tracing what was left of the frame, he added, "I could rebuild the entire widow's walk if you wanted me to. I couldn't do it until October, though."

"It's not my house," she said.

"Just a thought," he said, then added, grinning, "It would be nice to make love up on the widow's walk."

It was a little too close to her mother's story, and it bothered her.

"Not in October, it wouldn't," she said, wrapping her arms around herself.

Hawk looked at her strangely.

"It's cold up here," she said.

They stood looking at each other for a long moment.

"Did I say something that offended you?"

"October," she said.

"What?"

"You said the word 'October,'" she lied. There was no way she was going to tell him that this was about a fairy tale.

"I'll remove the word permanently from my vocabulary."

She laughed.

Talking about restoring the widow's walk had been too close to Maureen's story for Zee. Not that she believed in reincarnation or anything. She had thought about it a while back, even read some books, but in the end the theory just didn't resonate with her the way it had with Maureen. Her objection was much more practical than that. Restoring the widow's walk would be something Mattei would see as an attempt to fulfill the mother's dream. Just the thought of it made Zee uncomfortable.

"Let's go back inside," she said. "I'm cold."

HAWK BROUGHT UP THE SUBJECT of Lilly Braedon on a number of occasions. It was always tentative, a testing of the waters that Zee recognized from her practice. Sometimes it was an offhand remark or even a question that hung at the edges of the confidentiality issue but didn't exactly breach it. *How long had Zee been treating Lilly? Had she ever met her children?*

"I can't talk about Lilly Braedon with you," she said. "I can't even talk about her with her own family."

It's not that Zee didn't want to talk about Lilly. In one way he would have been the perfect person to talk with. He'd been an eyewitness, and, as was typical in such cases, he felt a certain connection to Lilly and her fate. She knew he would always wonder if he could have saved her. He'd told her as much. But Zee knew that if she started talking about Lilly with Hawk, it would be difficult to stop. Lilly was in her thoughts more and more these days. Zee ran the risk not only of crossing the lines of confidentiality but of using the relationship as a substitute for the therapy she obviously needed, something that she was aware she might already be doing, though in a different way. She genuinely liked Hawk, she didn't want to use him in *any* way. She was well aware that she needed therapy concerning the death of her patient, but she wasn't ready, not yet.

By the third week of July, she was as ready as she would ever be, and so she booked a session with Mattei and drove to Boston.

Mattei looked surprisingly different—she was quite tanned and dressed in a skirt that looked like it was out of the early sixties.

"I don't think I've ever seen you in a skirt," Zee said.

"I don't think I've ever worn one," Mattei said with a laugh. "I'm practicing for the wedding." She walked across the room to demonstrate. "I'm feeling very Betty Draper."

Zee took a seat. "So how are things going here?"

"Not too bad. Michelle has taken two of your patients, and Greta has the rest of them. They all want you back, but for the most part everyone's doing pretty well. I had to increase Mr. Goodhue's meds."

"We knew that was coming," Zee said.

"I've been sending anyone new over to Greta. There's one guy who keeps asking for you and saying he'll wait."

"What guy?"

"He says his name is Reynaldo. He's evidently a referral."

Zee knew the name. She had heard it before. But she couldn't remember where. "A referral from whom?"

"I'm not sure. I can find out."

"No," Zee said. "It's not important."

"So what do you want to talk about today?" Mattei asked. "I'm sure you didn't come all the way in here to chat about the office."

"I want to talk about Lilly," Zee said.

"I was expecting that you might," Mattei said.

Zee sat for a minute but didn't say anything. Finally, and with difficulty, she spoke up. "I still don't think her death was a suicide," Zee said.

"All evidence to the contrary."

"She didn't leave a note."

"Not all suicides do."

"Maybe."

"Your own mother didn't leave a note."

Zee stopped. "Why did you mention my mother?"

"Why do you think?"

"I don't know how it happened. Lilly was doing better."

"As is often the case."

"No, this was different." Zee could feel her face getting red.

"You're angry," Mattei said.

Zee nodded.

"At whom?"

"Right now at you," Zee said.

"Who else?"

"At myself."

"Why are you angry at yourself?" Mattei said.

"Because I could have stopped it."

"How?" Mattei asked. "How could you have stopped it if you couldn't see it coming?"

"I could have stopped him," Zee said.

"Adam?"

"Yes, Adam. Who do you think I'm talking about?"

"How could you have stopped him?" Mattei asked.

"I could have insisted that the police do something," Zee said.

"I think you have to let yourself off the hook for that. You did everything that could possibly be done. More, actually."

"You think I crossed a line," Zee said.

"Is that what *you* think?"

Many lines, Zee thought. She had attended the funeral. She had treated Lilly at home. She had given unasked-for advice.

Zee had also let the line blur between Lilly and Maureen, so much so that she wondered every day if she'd been objective enough, or if her wish to make this case turn out differently from her mother's had made her too involved with Lilly's case and that that involvement had somehow blinded her. The day she told Lilly that she had to leave Adam had been the turning point, the day Zee crossed the first big line. And the worst part of it was that she knew she would do it again. You were supposed to let the patient find her own course of action. But if it happened now, Zee would have tried to do *more* to stop it, not less. Which was another reason she had recently begun to question her choice of career.

"I crossed more lines with Lilly than you know," Zee said.

Mattei looked at her, waiting.

"I don't want to talk about it," Zee said.

They sat silently for a while. When it was clear that Zee was not going to explain, Mattei spoke. "Losing your first patient is very difficult."

"Are you telling me there will be more?"

"Probably," Mattei said.

"How many have you lost?"

"A few," Mattei said.

"How many?"

"Is that important to you?"

"Yes," Zee said.

"Why?"

Zee didn't answer. She knew that it was an attempt to make Mattei cross the same kinds of lines she had been crossing, and she knew that Mattei was wise to her tactics.

Mattei considered for a long time before answering. "Three."

Zee felt immediately sorry. But at the same time, she was grateful.

"How do you live with that?" It was a sincere question.

"Day by day," Mattei said.

"I don't think I'm cut out for this," Zee said.

"You're absolutely cut out for this," Mattei said. "I wouldn't have hired you if you weren't."

She looked at her computer, scribbled down a name and number on a piece of paper, and slid it across the table to Zee.

"What's this?"

"The shrink's shrink," she said. "He's very good. I go to him myself on occasion. You need to talk to someone about this, and it can no longer be me."

"Thanks," Zee said, meaning it. The line they'd crossed had been blurring for years, and a new one had now taken its place. At this moment they were no longer doctor and patient, or even employer and employee. They were friends.

ZEE MADE AN APPOINTMENT FOR the following week with the new therapist. It went as well as could be expected, considering that it would take a while for him to get to know her. But at least she was talking to someone, she thought. After that first appointment, she stopped by the office to pick up some of her things as well as turn over some files to the people who were covering her patients.

It was a day for cleaning things out. Once she'd finished at the office, she headed over to Michael's condo on Beacon Hill to clean out the rest of her things. She had arranged to do it on a day he would be out of town, so there'd be no chance of running into him. Zee had hoped to be done by rush hour, but she'd gotten a late start. By the time she had emptied her closet and made three trips down to the Volvo, it was five-thirty.

Finally finished cleaning out the closet, she walked through the house, looking around, surprised by how few things in the place were actually hers. There were a few CDs that she'd picked up in college, a few more books, and the cowboy coffeepot that Melville had given her. Everything else in the house belonged to Michael. It hadn't seemed odd to her when she lived here, particularly since she had moved into his house. Still, it seemed strange now, as if she'd never really been anything but a visitor and, on some level, had never intended to stay.

Zee left her engagement ring in Michael's top drawer. She had planned to leave a note with it, but she couldn't find any words that didn't sound wrong. She let herself out through the back door, leaving her set of keys on the kitchen counter so he would see them as soon as he walked in.

ZEE DIDN'T NOTICE THE RED truck behind her as she pulled out of the driveway, just as she hadn't noticed it follow her out of her office parking lot, where it had been parked every late afternoon for the last two weeks. She turned from Joy Street onto Pinckney. When she got to Charles Street, she stepped hard on the gas to avoid a cross light. The engine sputtered as she floored it, and she made a mental note to have it tuned. The Volvo was the last car across as the sign changed to WALK, and Zee was looking ahead toward Storrow Drive. She had wanted to head north before the rush-hour traffic got too bad, but now she found herself in the thick of it. The light turned just as she cleared the intersection, and the red truck sat stuck halfway into the crosswalk, as pedestrians crossed both in front of it and behind.

$\star$ *29* $\star$

I T WAS SCRABBLE NIGHT at the Salem Athenaeum, the historic membership library where Melville had worked for the last
several years. Though he wasn't playing tonight, he had volunteered
to stay. After they finished, as Melville was locking the front door, he
ran into Ann Chase. She was coming from the public library across the
street.

"What are you doing on my side of town?" he called out.

"Slumming," she replied, and since the McIntyre was probably the prettiest historic district in town, they both laughed at
her joke.

"Where are you living?" Ann asked. She knew about the split, but
she didn't know the details.

Melville pointed toward Federal Street.

"I love that street," Ann said. While most of the McIntyre district
had Federal period housing, Federal Street ironically had some of the
earlier period homes.

"It's actually the street behind Federal," Melville said. "You want to
come up for coffee?"

"I don't drink coffee," she said. "But I'd love to see your place."

He explained that it wasn't really his place, that he was house-sitting. As they climbed the stairs, Bowditch snarled and barked and threw himself against the door.

"What the hell have you got in there?" Ann asked, having second thoughts.

"Wait till you see." Melville smiled.

The minute he opened the door, Bowditch jumped on him and wagged his tail. Then he waddled over to Ann and sniffed her.

"Good puppy," she said, laughing. "You're a big faker."

Melville walked her to the kitchen.

Old photos were spread out on the table, several of Finch and Zee in better times. An empty wine bottle sat upended in the sink.

"Yesterday was not one of my better days," he said.

"I'm so sorry," Ann said, meaning it. It sounded as if someone had died. It was almost as sad.

"Whose place is this?" she asked, trying to change the subject.

"Someone I know at the Peabody Essex. He's gone to China for the better part of the year.

"And you inherited Cujo here?"

"Bowditch," he said.

"As in Salem's famous navigator?"

"Nathaniel Bowditch. The very same."

Bowditch raised his head as if he were being summoned.

"Sorry," Melville said to the dog, who had started to stand up. "Stay."

Bowditch sighed and put his head back down.

"He's a good fellow," Ann said.

"That he is."

Melville went through the cabinets. "Good thing you didn't want coffee," he said. "I don't have any."

She laughed.

"Would you like some wine?"

"No thanks," she said. "Water would be great, though."

He poured them two glasses of water and sat down.

Ann was looking through the photos. "These are great," she said. There were several black-and-whites that Finch had taken of Melville and Zee with his eight-by-ten camera and another, much earlier one from the same camera of Maureen and Zee. "Where did you get this one?" she asked, turning it over and noting the inscription on the back: *Christmas 1986.* Ann thought it was a bit odd that he would have a photo of Maureen, even if Zee was in it, too.

"I stole it from Finch," he said.

"You really are in a bad place, aren't you?" she said, wondering why he would want such a reminder.

"Let me put it this way," Melville said. "It's probably a good thing I ran into you tonight."

ANN STAYED UNTIL ALMOST MIDNIGHT. As he walked her to her car, she turned to him. "You know what I always do when I break up with someone?"

"I'm sorry to admit I have no idea."

"I do all the things I couldn't do when we were together," she said. "It might not seem like much, but it helps you remember who you used to be."

He hugged her, and she got into the car.

"Didn't you once own a boat?" she asked.

"I still do," he said. "It's been sitting in Finch's driveway for the last six years."

"Maybe it's time you put it back in the water," she suggested, squeezing his arm good-bye.

★   ★   ★

IT WAS A GOOD IDEA, Melville thought as he walked back to the house. Tomorrow he would call the boatyard and have them pick it up. It would probably need a lot of work, but he could do most of it himself. He didn't know how long it would take to get the boat in shape, but it was something to do. And she was right, it would remind him of who he used to be.

★ *30* ★

AFTER THEY MADE LOVE for the second time that night, Hawk asked Zee out on a date.

"Why?" she asked.

"Why?" He was clearly amused. "You're kidding me, right? You know, in some cultures, it's customary for people to actually go on a date or two *before* they have sex."

"Not in ours," Zee said. "Not these days."

"So that's a no?"

"It's difficult for me to get out," she said. "Because of Finch. Jessina can't often stay late in the evenings."

"So let's make it on a night she *can* stay."

Zee didn't answer.

"Okay," he said. "Now you're starting to piss me off. Maybe I'll just go climb into the window of someone who actually wants to be seen with me."

She laughed. "It's not that. It's that I just broke up with Michael, and . . ."

"And you don't want to be seen with me." He grinned at her.

She had to laugh. "I don't want to run into Mickey," she said. "I haven't told him yet."

"What if I take you to dinner out of town?"

"Okay," she said.

"Okay when?"

"Okay, as soon as I can set it up with Jessina."

Finch's alarm bell went off. Zee got up and pulled on her robe. "Don't go anywhere," she said.

He put his hands behind his head, looking up through the skylight at a patch of starry sky. He sighed. "Where would I go?" he said under his breath. But he was smiling.

★ *31* ★

Melville and Zee met for coffee at Jaho. He told her that he was having the boat picked up and was going to try to get it back in the water.

"That's a great idea," Zee said.

"It's something," he said. "Maybe we can take it out together sometime."

"I'd like that," she said.

He paused for a moment, then asked the same question he always asked: "How's Finch?"

Zee wished she had a better answer to give him. "About the same," she said.

"You look a little tired," he said.

"I'm fine."

"I think you need some more help."

"I'm handling things," she said.

"There's a lot to handle."

"He thought I was Maureen this morning," she said. "He thinks that a lot."

Melville considered. "It's an honest mistake," he said. "You look like your mother."

"Not that much, I don't," she said.

"So what are you doing for you?"

She wanted to tell him about Hawk but thought better of it. She already knew what he would say. It was too soon.

"Enough," she said.

"Name one thing."

"I play skee ball." She smiled.

He laughed. "God, that brings back a memory."

In the summers when Melville had first lived with them, Zee had a habit of disappearing. Melville often hunted her down at the Willows playing skee ball. Sometimes, if it wasn't too late and Finch wasn't worried about her, Melville would play.

"I've developed the perfect bank shot," she said.

He looked at her.

"I'm really all right," she said again. "Good, in fact."

MELVILLE DIDN'T WANT TO INTERFERE, but he was worried about Zee. He thought this was all too much for her. She wasn't herself. He was worried about Finch, too, if the truth be known. He still spoke with Jessina once in a while, still paid her weekly salary, though Zee had told him not to. It was the least he could do, he said. Meaning it was something.

He wanted to stop by the shop to talk to Mickey about it. He was aware that Mickey hadn't forgiven him for Maureen, probably would never forgive him for breaking up her marriage, but it didn't matter. This was about Finch, and it was about Zee, and some things were more important.

He walked down Derby Wharf, past the rigging shed, looking up at the *Friendship* as he went by. He remembered when they were building her, had donated money for it, in fact. He'd been there the day that lightning had struck the main mast, and they'd had to raise more money to replace it. She was an amazing ship, if you thought about it, though he found he couldn't think about it without thinking about Maureen and the story she'd been writing when she died.

Seeing Mickey was like looking at Maureen. Their eyes were the same. But as soon as Mickey spoke, the illusion shattered.

"Hi, Melville. What can I do you for?"

It was an old New England expression, but the twist was implicit.

"Funny," Melville said.

"I want to talk to you about your niece," Melville said. "I'm worried about her."

Mickey listened without interrupting to insert his usual sarcasm. In the end he promised to help out. To take Finch out once in a while, just to give Zee some relief.

"You were friends once," Melville said by way of justifying his request. He knew it was a mistake as soon as he said it. Mickey had already agreed.

"Age-old rule," Mickey said. "Stop selling when you get to yes."

"Thank you," Melville said. He started toward the door.

"Hey," Mickey said, calling him back.

"What?" Melville said.

"I may never like you," Mickey said. "But that doesn't mean I don't appreciate what you do for my niece."

TODAY ANN WAS READING lace. She'd been doing this more and more in the last few years, ever since her friend Towner Whitney had given her all of her late Aunt Eva's pieces. Ann thought of the lace as another reader might think of a crystal ball, something that you gazed into to help you see images. She'd done two readings before lunch and was now turning and crumpling a piece of black antique lace in an effort to gain more perspective about her regular customer, the one who wanted so badly to get married.

What she got was more of the same, a bad relationship that was getting worse by the moment. Ann thought it was time to tell the girl everything, and she was just trying to find the words when an image began to form in the lace. It looked like a vine, and it was moving. Ann watched as the vine turned to feathers and one of the longer feathers turned into a woman's neck. Ann realized that what she was looking at was a swan. And then she saw something in the lace that she'd never seen before, but something she'd heard her friend Eva describe from her own lace reading. The swan began to move, and it turned to a man, and she recognized Melville.

The hopeful bride looked strangely at Ann, who had been staring, trancelike, into the lace for a very long time. The breeze from the ocean cooled the room, breaking the spell. Ann turned toward the open door in time to see Melville walking away from Mickey's shop and across the parking lot toward town.

She excused herself, hurried to the door, and called to him. He turned around. She could see that he was upset. He waved to her, but he didn't stop.

Z EE PAID JESSINA TO stay until morning. Her son was on an overnight at Children's Island Camp, and she was free.

They took Hawk's boat to Clark Landing in Marblehead and walked over to the Barnacle for dinner. She could see Children's Island from here and thought about Jessina's son, who had helped her clean out some of Finch's things just the week before.

They sat on the porch and watched as dogs played on the patch of beach below. They skipped dessert in favor of getting ice cream on the way back. After dinner they walked up to Fort Sewall and sat on a bench looking out to sea. All of the border islands were visible from here: Children's, the Miseries, and Baker's Island with its lighthouse off to the north. In the middle distance, she could see Yellow Dog Island, the shelter for abused women and children. Zee thought about May Whitney, who ran the shelter, and the great work she was doing out there. Zee wished that she had been able to do as much for Lilly.

But she didn't want to think about Lilly tonight, didn't want the thought to come between them. Instead she concentrated on the beautiful view. It was Race Week in Marblehead, and sailors from all over the world had come to compete. A long line of spinnakered J/24s moved along the horizon.

"Mickey says you could make your way across the ocean just by looking at the stars."

"It's a little more complicated than that." Hawk laughed. "The Park Service is running a class in celestial navigation, if you're interested."

"Didn't you teach that class?" She thought she remembered him saying something about teaching such a class.

"Just a few classes," he said. "I'm not a teacher."

"Not a carpenter, not a teacher. It must be nice to know what you're not," she said.

"Are you having doubts about your career?" It was a real question.

"Let's change the subject," she said.

"I understand that we can't talk about Lilly, but now we can't talk about your career either?"

"The two are hopelessly intertwined, I'm afraid."

He sat silently for a minute.

"I think *I* need to talk about it," he said.

"About your career?"

"About Lilly Braedon," he said.

"I understand why that might be true," she said.

"That's just it, I don't think you do."

"Nevertheless," she said.

It was meant to politely end the conversation, but it had the opposite effect on Hawk.

"What the hell does that mean?"

"I'm sorry," she said sincerely. "If you're having trouble reconciling your feelings about her death, and you need someone to talk to, I can give you some names. It just can't be me."

He was clearly annoyed.

"I'm sorry," she said again. "I understand that you might be angry at me."

"I'm not angry," he said. "Let's drop it."

★ ★ ★

THEY WALKED BACK TOWARD THE car in silence. At sunset the cannons from the yacht clubs fired, the blasts echoing around the harbor.

She assumed that the date was over. But she noticed Hawk's mood lifting as they reached Coffey's ice-cream shop. The line was out the door.

"Do you still want ice cream?" he asked.

"Sure," she said. "I mean, if you do."

"Yeah," he said. "We have to do something to save the evening."

He held the door for her, and she walked inside. "Do you know what you'd like?" Hawk asked, still formal but softening a bit.

"Not really," she said, looking at the display case. She'd bought ice cream for Finch, always coffee. Michael had been a Häagen-Dazs guy, either that or gelato. She honestly couldn't remember the last time she'd ordered ice cream for herself. It was ridiculous to be flustered by such a small thing, but there it was. He was waiting for her choice, and she didn't have one. She felt suddenly the way a little kid might feel. The decision seemed monumental. Her mind raced. She thought back to what she would have ordered as a kid. "Moose Track and Bubble Gum with gummi bears," she said.

"You're kidding," he said. "I was going to order that, too."

"Funny," she said.

THEY SAT ON ANOTHER BENCH down by the landing eating their ice cream. In the harbor, sailors blasted signals for the launches. The owner of the ice-cream store locked up and walked to his car, nodding to them as he passed.

"Show me how to navigate by the stars," she said.

He looked at her strangely but didn't respond.

"I'd really like to learn."

"There are too many lights here," he said. "You can't see the stars well enough for a lesson. Plus, you have to take your readings at dawn or dusk when you can still see the horizon."

"Too bad," she said.

"Maybe another time," he said, meaning it.

THEY SAT FOR A WHILE longer. "What do you want to do now?" she asked. "I hired Jessina for the whole night."

He thought about it. "I have a place up the street," he said, "though it's pretty much a dump."

She didn't have to be back until morning, so going to his place would be the easiest thing to do. But she wanted to offer something more, something of herself she couldn't explain to him in words, so she made a counterproposal. "I might have a better place," she said.

"Where?" he asked.

"Someplace dark enough to see the stars."

"Let's go," he said.

HE LET HER PILOT THE boat. She checked the fuel level automatically, then laughed at herself. She hadn't been at the wheel of one of these boats since she had stolen them when she was a kid. There was something freeing about it.

She maneuvered slowly through the crowded moorings of Marblehead Harbor, and when they passed the red nun and the end of the 5 mph limit, she opened up the engine and headed for Baker's Island.

★ *34* ★

J ESSINA DECIDED TO BAKE cookies for Finch. It was hot, and she had the kitchen windows open to the offshore breeze. She rifled though the baking cabinet, pulling down red and green sugar, more Christmas than July colors. Though it was past July Fourth, she'd been hoping for red, white, and blue. Still, she made stars with the colors she had, shaking powdered sugar over the red and green.

Finch loved her cookies, which she made soft enough for him to eat. Each afternoon he ate two with a large glass of milk, not the 2 percent kind Zee ordered from Peapod but the full old-fashioned stuff Jessina bought at one of the *colmados* on Lafayette Street. Finch needed to put some weight on—he was wasting away.

WHEN THE PIRATE FIRST APPEARED at the window in his tricorn hat and eye patch, Jessina thought she was seeing things. Then, when he spoke, she recognized Mickey's voice. She'd heard him do local radio spots, seen him marketing his tourist traps on Salem Access TV. A lot of the kids who lived in the Point worked summer jobs for Mickey, which made him a good guy at least in that respect. He did use mostly college kids from Salem State, but he also gave the Dominican high-school kids a chance. She was hoping that next year, when he was too old for day camp, Danny might get a job working for Mickey.

Mickey asked for Zee first, and then, when Jessina informed him that Zee wasn't there, he reluctantly asked for Finch.

Jessina walked him down the hall to where Finch sat in his new recliner watching a soap opera. Finch looked up in surprise when he saw the pirate, huge in this small space, his hat just inches away from the ceiling beam.

"Hello, Finch," Mickey said to him.

Finch looked at Mickey and then at Jessina. It was clear that he had no idea who Mickey was. He kept looking as if he were waiting for either an explanation or a punch line.

"How are you?" Mickey asked.

Finch seemed surprised by the question. "Fine, thank you," he said. "And you?"

"Pretty good for an old man," Mickey said.

"An old pirate, you mean," Finch said.

"That, too," Mickey said.

Picking up on Finch's obvious confusion and wanting to defuse the tension Mickey must be feeling, Jessina turned to Finch. "Perhaps we should offer Mr. Doherty one of our cookies."

Finch looked baffled by the thought.

"Would you like a cookie, Mr. Doherty?" Jessina said.

"No thank you, no," Mickey said.

"I'm tired," Finch said to Jessina.

"Yes, Papi, I know you're tired, but Mr. Doherty has come to visit you."

"It's okay," Mickey said. "I was just stopping by for a minute." He had come in the kitchen door, but now he walked toward the front door, which was closer to the den. He couldn't get away fast enough. "Just tell Zee I stopped by," he said.

He could hear Finch chuckling softly to himself as he walked out. "We just had a pirate in our den, didn't we?" He looked at Jessina for confirmation.

"We certainly did," she said.

★ *35* ★

ZEE POINTED THE FLASHLIGHT along the path leading to the cottage.

She reached into the window box, fishing for the key. Skeletons of old plants and flowers, annuals planted when Maureen was still alive, crumbled under her fingers, but the key was still there. The screen was ripped and its frame twisted out of alignment. The last time she was here, she obviously hadn't bothered to pull the door shut, and the winter damp had warped the wood. But the inside wooden door, though swollen, was still intact. She had to push hard to open it.

"Whose place is this?" Hawk asked.

"It's mine," she said. "But I haven't been here for a long time."

The kerosene lamp sat on the table in the middle of the room. Zee walked to the kitchen drawer and pulled out an old box of safety matches. They were damp and a bit moldy, but on the fifth try she managed to get one lit.

A circle of warm light radiated outward, illuminating the couch and the tiny kitchen with its soapstone sink and hand pump, the oak icebox. Zee walked to the sink and opened the interior shutters and the French windows beyond. The stars and moon reflected off black water. She walked window to window, opening them and letting the salt air erase the musty smell.

"This place is amazing," Hawk said.

"You think?"

It occurred to her that Michael had never seen the place, had never seemed interested. Like Finch, Michael wasn't a water person. Still, she wondered why she hadn't insisted on showing it to him.

Hawk looked at the pump. "Is that salt or fresh water?"

"Salt," she said. "There's a well down that way for fresh." She saw him pick up the bucket. "I don't think the pump works," she said.

"Let's give it a try," he said. He carried the bucket down to the tiny beach in front of the cottage and filled it.

It took many tries, but he got the pump going. Then he laughed at himself. "I'm not sure why I did that," he said.

"Thanks," she said.

She smiled. She pumped some water just to see it. When she was little, she had done their dishes in salt water, she'd had to stand on a stepstool to reach. It was a good memory of Zee and her mother, one of the only good ones, and she was grateful to Hawk for giving it back to her. Any good memories she had of her mother were from this place: Maureen reading her stories aloud while Zee sat on the braided rug sketching dragonflies and gulls, the summer they picked beach plums and made jam, hauling both the sugar and water from the mainland. There were a lot of scraps and flashes of memory that came to her now, and she was grateful for each of them.

They sat at the table and played gin rummy with an old deck of cards Zee found in the drawer with the matches. He won all but one hand. "So what do you want to do now?" he asked.

"How about an overnight?" she asked.

"Like at camp?"

"Yeah," she said. "Just like that."

"You got any marshmallows?"

"If I do, they've got to be twenty years old."

"What about scary stories. Do you know any?"

"I know some," she said, thinking suddenly of Lilly Braedon. *We both know one,* she thought. Then she thought about the other story she knew, the one her mother had written. She wasn't about to tell him either story. Not tonight. She'd have to think of something else.

"Okay," he said. "I'm game."

Hawk blew up the old canvas air mattress while she rolled out the rug and got the blankets down from a shelf.

The cottage was situated in such a way that the views were almost 360 degrees. They lay down together, looking up through the huge doors that lined the west-facing wall. With the doors open, they had a clear view of the stars. They could hear the waves crashing on the rocks below.

First he pointed out the constellations, the easy ones she already knew, and the signs of the zodiac: Aries and Libra. Then he tried to point out some of the fifty-seven stars used in celestial navigation.

"I had an easier time with the zodiac," she said.

"No, look, there's the Big Dipper. Polaris is there."

"The North Star."

"Yes. Polaris is always within one degree of the North Pole. You can pick up your latitude by looking at Polaris."

"I see the North Star, but I don't see the other one you were pointing at," she said. He moved her head into position and extended his pointing arm from over her shoulder, adjusting for her sight line. "Still don't see it," she said.

He laughed.

"Well, you see the moon. We use the moon a lot, and the horizon," he said. "So you have three points of reference. You can only take readings at dawn and dusk, because when it gets this dark, the horizon disappears. But at twilight, for just a little while, the stars are still visible." He pointed again, this time to a spot low on the western horizon.

"Look, there's Spica, in Virgo, one of the brightest stars in the sky. Spica is a blue giant, and it's not really one star but two stars that revolve around each other so closely that they appear as one."

"That's either very romantic or hopelessly codependent," Zee said, looking where he was pointing.

He laughed. "See it?"

She shook her head. He pointed again. "Do you see the Big Dipper?"

"Yes," she said. "That I can find."

"Okay, follow the handle of the Big Dipper." He lay behind her, placing himself at her eye level and raising her arm with his until it traced the handle. "That bright star there is Arcturus. Now, if you keep tracing the straight line about the same distance, you'll find Spica. Right there. See?"

She squinted her eye.

"Spica is key if you're ever navigating at the equator."

"Good to know," she said.

"In another month you'll hardly be able to see her in the night sky at all," he said. "She won't be back until next summer."

"She?"

"Spica is definitely female. See her?"

"Sorry," she said.

"Right there," he said, tracing the line again.

"It's sad when Spica disappears below the horizon," he said. "But she has her heliacal rising right around Halloween."

"Her what?"

"At morning twilight in the middle of October, Spica will be visible again on the horizon for just a few days. It's like a tiny sunrise. It's always good to see her again when she shows up."

"I think you have a thing for this star."

He laughed. "I just love bright, beautiful Virgos, what can I say?"

She laughed.

He traced the line one more time, pulling her closer to him, lifting her arm with his. "Right there. See? She's the brightest star in Virgo."

"I've never seen Virgo, and I don't see her now."

"I think that's sad. You *are* a Virgo," he said, laughing again. "Actually, you can only see part of Virgo right now. She's mostly below the horizon this time of night."

"Spica. Virgo. This is how you navigate across the ocean?"

"Yes."

"Don't you believe in maps?" she asked.

"No way. Ocean maps are incredibly inaccurate."

"What about GPS?"

"I do believe in GPS," he laughed. "I just believe in the stars more."

"More than GPS?"

"GPS is electronic. It can malfunction. If you put your faith in the stars, you can always find your way home."

"Unless it's a cloudy night," she said.

"Yeah," he agreed. "On a cloudy night, I believe very strongly in GPS." He stopped talking then. "Listen," he said.

"To the stars?"

"No." A soft hissing sound was barely audible. "I think this air mattress has a leak," he said.

She laughed. "I wouldn't be at all surprised."

THE AIR COOLED DOWN QUICKLY. Zee got some more blankets from the drawer. "We really need a campfire," she said.

He wrapped the blanket around her shoulders. "You promised me a scary story," he said.

"I have a better idea," she said, kissing his neck.

"I thought we were supposed to be at camp," he said.

"We are."

She pulled off his T-shirt and ran her hands over his chest.

"Obviously, my mother sent me to the wrong camp," he said.

ZEE ROLLED OVER, TRYING TO get comfortable. The air mattress had completely deflated during the night, and she woke to find herself sleeping on the cold floor. The sky was beginning to lighten. Hawk was across the room by the open window, setting up the brass sextant.

"What's that?" she asked.

"Come here and I'll show you," he said. "If I were taking sights today, this would be the time. In fifteen minutes, when the horizon line is more clearly defined, you'll no longer be able to see those stars."

He showed her the star he was plotting. "That's Procyon," he said.

She leaned over and looked through the sextant.

"It's there, just above the horizon," he said.

"I see it." She smiled. "It's beautiful." She looked at the star for a long time. "You take sights at both dawn and dusk?"

"Morning and evening twilight," he said.

"And from this you can find your way home from anywhere in the world?"

"Pretty much," he said. "As long as I have a good quartz watch and an almanac."

"Amazing," she said.

"Not really," he said. "You could learn to do it, if you wanted."

"I can't even find Spica," she said.

Hawk laughed. "True enough." He kissed her good morning. "I need coffee."

She pulled the blanket tighter around her. "God, it's cold," she said.

He pulled her to him and hugged her. Looking over her shoulder, he spotted the closed door. "Is that another room?"

"It's the bedroom," she said.

"We slept on a cold, hard floor when we had a bedroom?" He was across the room and had the door open before she had a chance to stop him.

She followed him inside, watched as he discovered the bed with its fading green chenille.

"I don't get it," he said.

"It was my parents' marriage bed," she said.

"And?"

"And, as a result, we always just sleep in the living room."

"I still don't get it, but I get the idea that I'm supposed to drop the subject," he said.

"You do get it," she said with a laugh.

★ *36* ★

WHEN ZEE GOT BACK to the house, Jessina was whipping egg whites into a white mountain of frosting for the chocolate cake she was making. Worried, she related to Zee the story of Mickey's visit.

"Finch didn't recognize Mr. Doherty," Jessina said.

Zee was surprised, though she tried to rationalize it away, telling herself that the two men hadn't seen each other for a long time. Still, it was difficult not to recognize Mickey Doherty. It could have been something with Finch's medication. Lately he had started to spit out his pills. She checked in between his chair cushions and on the surrounding floor. He seemed all right today, if somewhat drowsy.

At dinner Finch mistook her for Maureen again.

Zee called the doctor and left a message.

She called again in the morning and asked that the doctor fit them in.

IT WAS CLEAR FROM THE office visit that things were deteriorating fast. The last time they'd been there, Finch had been able to walk the straight line, albeit shakily, that the doctor had taped to the floor.

This time he couldn't do it without his walker, and even then he was so tired he could only make it a few feet before he reached out for Zee's arm, and she rushed to help him.

The doctor suggested some physical therapy. He offered to set it up so that they could come to the house two times a week to walk with Finch.

"I walk with him," she said, somewhat defensively.

"You have enough to do," he said, and had his nurse make the call.

Finch's speech seemed somewhat garbled, his voice shaky and very hoarse.

"Is there any chance that he's just sick?" Zee asked hopefully. She hadn't thought of it until this very minute.

The doctor took his temperature. "He doesn't have a fever," he said. "What time did he take his last pill?"

"He's almost due," Zee said.

The doctor asked him basic questions from the AMTS. *What is your age? What is the year? Who is president?* Finch answered the third question correctly but hesitated on the first and second. When he was asked what year World War II began, he answered without hesitation. He also scored well on the facial-recognition tests, knowing the doctor and others who worked in the office, though he was unable to say what their positions were. When asked to count backward from twenty, Finch looked at her helplessly. And when asked to remember an address he was given at the beginning of the questioning, he didn't even remember hearing it.

There was a second test, this one meant for Zee to answer, which measured the rate and changes in Finch's mental decline. They were all questions about memory, and Zee was asked to comment on each, stating whether things had stayed the same or changed. She found she could answer very few of them, having been there for only a short time and having come to realize just how much Melville and Finch had been hiding from her. "I'll have to fax this back to you," Zee said to the doctor. She had to talk to Melville.

The doctor spoke with Finch for a while, a very conversational chatter that didn't fool Finch for a minute. He might not know the answers to some of the questions, but Zee could tell from Finch's eyes that he knew very well what they were here to determine. He looked both frightened and angry.

When the doctor was finished with his final line of questioning, he spoke to both of them.

"I'd say we're pretty deep into the Alzheimer's crossover," he said. "It's almost inevitable in Parkinson's patients. At some point in the progression of this disease, it begins to act more like Alzheimer's. The same is true for advanced Alzheimer's—those patients begin to develop the movements common to Parkinson's."

She'd heard it before, but it had always seemed to be some vague possibility that might occur a long time from now. She took Finch's hand. She had wanted to talk with the doctor privately about this. She understood the ethics involved. The patient had a right to know. But she could see from the look on Finch's face that he understood too well, and it scared him.

"How long has it been since he was diagnosed?"

She was appalled that the doctor didn't know. "About ten years," she said.

The doctor was quiet for a moment and then said in a serious but far too casual tone. "Ten years is a good long run for Parkinson's."

She looked at Finch to see if he had understood the doctor's meaning. His masked face was difficult to read. Zee could feel the anger rising up in her. She wanted to tell the doctor what she thought of him. She wanted to call him a son of a bitch. How dare he talk to a patient like this? Disclosure was one thing. Zee believed in the right to know. But to dismiss a life so casually was beyond cruel.

However, anything she could have said on the spot would only make things worse. She hoped that Finch had missed the doctor's meaning. She remembered the words Mattei often used to describe neurologists: *The geeks of the doctor world. No bedside manner. Little princes.* She wanted to kill him. To literally rip his smug face off.

Instead she helped Finch from the office, his steps agonizingly slow as he tried to maneuver the walker out of the office and down the hall.

The warm air in the parking lot calmed her slightly. Maybe Finch hadn't heard what the doctor said, or hadn't caught his meaning.

She unlocked the car door and helped Finch in. He was stiff, the pill overdue. She put the walker in the trunk. Then she got into the driver's side of the car, reaching into her purse for the water and the box of pills labeled with the times of day. She pulled out his three-o'clock dose, undid the water bottle, and passed it to him. He swallowed the pill dutifully. Then she reached across and buckled his seat belt, which she had forgotten to do. As she pulled her hand back, she lingered on Finch's arm. "I love you," she said. He smiled weakly.

As she pulled the Volvo out of the parking lot, Finch finally spoke, his voice so weak from needing the meds that it was barely audible. "So what he was saying is that I'm going to die soon."

She pulled the car over on Mass Avenue.

"That doctor is a son of a bitch," she said. She was about to tell him they would never go back, that neurologists were a dime a dozen in Boston, and that she'd have a new one for him by morning. But Finch spoke before she could form the words.

"It's all right," he said. "I want to die."

★ *37* ★

Zᴇᴇ ᴄᴀʟʟᴇᴅ Mᴇʟᴠɪʟʟᴇ ᴀɴᴅ left a message. Then she called Mattei.

"I'm really worried," she said. "He's clearly depressed."

"You want me to prescribe something?"

"I know he needs something, but I don't want to interfere with the meds he's already on," Zee said.

"I can come out there if you like," Mattei offered.

It wasn't something Zee would have asked of Mattei, but she felt relief at the prospect of seeing her and getting her opinion. "I'd really appreciate it."

"I can't come tomorrow, but I can be there on Saturday," Mattei said.

"Thanks," Zee said.

She doled out Finch's meds to Jessina, then took the pill bottles upstairs, locking the door when she came back down. She could tell that Jessina was curious, but she didn't offer any explanation.

Sʜᴇ ꜰɪɴᴀʟʟʏ ꜰᴏᴜɴᴅ Mᴇʟᴠɪʟʟᴇ ᴀᴛ the Athenaeum. He seemed happily surprised to see her there, but the expression on her face told him this wasn't a social visit.

"What's going on?"

"Is there someplace we can talk for a minute?"

He led her into the stacks of the membership library and down a flight of metal stairs to the basement. It was close quarters, but it was quiet. The stacks extended three floors deep. Today there were no visiting scholars, no one asking to see the voyage and travel collections or the books that Hawthorne read in the days he had spent at the Athenaeum. For the moment they could be alone here to talk. Someone entering on any of the three skeletal floors would be clearly visible.

Melville led her to a small table where he'd been cataloging some old maps and travelogues.

Zee handed him the survey she'd gotten from the doctor. "I know what's been going on in the last month," Zee said. "But I couldn't fill in the progression of his disease."

Melville looked at the paper. There were sixteen questions, all having to do with Finch's memory and how it had changed in the last ten years. The answers ranged from "much improved" to "much worse." It was an easy questionnaire to fill in, though he knew that there would be nothing encouraging in his answers. He went through the questions carefully, aware that Zee was watching him. When he was finished, he slid the paper back across the table to her.

Zee read it over, looking at the answers Melville had circled. Most were labeled "much worse" or "a bit worse." Nothing indicated any improvement.

"I don't understand how you were keeping this from me," Zee said.

"We've had this conversation before," Melville said. "It's what he wanted."

"The doctor basically told Finch he was going to die," she said, shaking her head.

Melville looked at her.

"And Finch said that's what he wants."

Melville reached across the table and took her hand. "I'm sorry," he said.

"But not surprised," she said.

He thought about lying, but there was no point now. "No."

"God," she said. "This is terrible."

"Yes," he said. "It is."

"I'm afraid he might be suicidal," she said.

He understood. He knew that Finch didn't want to live with the progression of the disease. But in all their conversations about the future, they had both been keenly aware of the effect any such disclosure might have on Zee.

Melville's lack of surprise shocked her. "You're not okay with it?"

"Of course I'm not okay with it. But we've talked about the eventuality. He doesn't want to live with end-stage Parkinson's," Melville said to her. "He doesn't want to wind up in a nursing home in the fetal position for the next ten years."

Zee sat silently for a few minutes. "Well, he's not going to kill himself," she said finally. "Not on my watch."

⋆ *38* ⋆

ZEE HAD CALLED EARLIER and told Hawk she couldn't see him today. It was his day off, and they had planned to take his boat out to Baker's Island.

"There's something going on with Finch," she said. "I have to stick around."

"You still want me to come by tonight?" he asked.

"Maybe not this time," she said.

He didn't know what to say, so he didn't say anything.

"I'll call you tomorrow," she said.

HAWK WASN'T IN THE BEST of moods. He'd been looking forward to spending time with Zee. Not knowing what else to do with himself, he drove the van to his place in Marblehead to pick up his mail. As he climbed the steps, a police cruiser that had been circling pulled up.

"Been away on vacation?" the cop asked.

"No."

"Your mail and papers have been piling up."

Hawk retrieved the mail, thinking the cop's question strange.

"So where have you been?" the cop asked.

"Working," Hawk said.

"Not in town."

"In Salem."

"You working for one of the construction crews over there?"

Hawk knew the officer, though not well enough to call him by name. He had often seen him on his beat. Though his tone was friendly, the cop wasn't as a general rule someone known to stop and make small talk.

"Do you have a real question you'd like to ask me, or are we just shooting the shit here?"

"Only trying to be friendly," the officer said.

"I'm working on the *Friendship*."

The cop looked at him blankly, clearly having no idea what Hawk meant by his last remark.

"It's a boat," Hawk said. "In Salem Harbor."

It had always amazed Hawk that the towns of Marblehead and Salem shared not only a border but a harbor, yet few people he met knew what was going on from one town to the next.

"You shouldn't leave your mail out like that," the cop said. "It's a written invitation." He turned and walked back to the cruiser.

Hawk watched as it pulled away. "Weird," he said under his breath as he let himself in.

Y OU NEED TO CALM down," Mattei said to Zee. Mattei had
talked with Finch for over an hour.

"What do you think?"

"I think he's depressed," Mattei said. "Who wouldn't be?"

Zee had to agree.

"This isn't suicidal thinking," Mattei said. "This is a logical thought
progression in the course of a devastating illness."

"He's not exactly logical. He doesn't even recognize people he's
known for years."

"He's not Maureen," Mattei said.

"I know that."

"Or Lilly."

"I know it's not the same thing," Zee said. "But I don't think I can
live with another suicide."

"I understand," Mattei said.

"I don't want to make this about me."

"You're entitled to your feelings," Mattei said.

"Which is probably why Finch and Melville have been keeping
things from me."

"Have you made another appointment with the therapist I told you
about?"

"Not yet," she said.

"Now might be a good time to do that."

"Just let me get Finch stabilized first."

Mattei's look revealed her doubts. Instead of discussing it further, she got on the phone and called the neurologist. When she hung up, she pulled out her prescription pad. "I think we should add Effexor to the mix," she said. "It seems to work well with Parkinson's, and it won't interfere with his other meds." She wrote the prescription. "This should help his mood a bit," Mattei said. "You have to do some thinking about what's next."

"What do you mean?"

"He should be in a long-term-care facility," Mattei said. "You know that as well as I do."

"The whole point here is that he would rather die than end up in a nursing home," Zee said.

"He needs physical therapy, and he needs counseling. He needs a good nutritionist and a nurse administering his meds."

Zee wanted to say, *Nevertheless,* but she kept quiet. She knew that Mattei was right.

"Let's give these new pills a chance to work. Then we can see what we're dealing with," Mattei said.

They sat at the table for several moments, neither of them saying anything. Then, from the bedroom, Finch's alarm began to ring.

"I'll be right back," Zee said, and headed toward his room.

Mattei spotted the unopened wedding invitation on the lazy Susan and picked it up. She was still holding it when Zee came back into the room.

"Is he okay?" Mattei asked.

"He's fine. He just got a little tangled in his sheets." Zee saw the envelope in Mattei's hands.

"I've been meaning to send back the RSVP," Zee apologized. The wedding was not until Labor Day weekend. "I'll be there."

Mattei hesitated before speaking. "I'll understand if you don't want to," she finally said. "I hear that Michael's bringing someone."

Zee stared at her. "Well, that was fast."

"I'd say his ego is a bit bruised," Mattei said. "Again, I'll understand if you don't want to come. Though both Rhonda and I will be disappointed."

"I'll be there," Zee said.

★ *40* ★

M ELVILLE STILL REMEMBERED THE date that same-sex marriage had become legal in Massachusetts. It was May 17, 2004. On May 20 of that same year, on the anniversary of the day that Melville and Finch first met, he had proposed to Finch.

It wasn't as if they'd never talked about marriage before. They'd been talking about it for years before the law passed, discussing every aspect of what it might mean for them: long-term care of each other, custody of Zee if anything should happen to Finch. When Finch was diagnosed with Parkinson's, it became even more important to him for a while, though by that time Zee was in college and the custody issue didn't much matter anymore. Still, there were reasons that Finch and Melville along with the rest of the gay and lesbian communities in Massachusetts had lobbied for same-sex marriage, and when civil unions became legal in Vermont, they had briefly contemplated a move to that state, but then they'd rejected it and campaigned harder than ever to get a real marriage bill passed in their home state.

By the time it happened, Finch had stopped talking about it. His disease had taken such a toll that it was all he could do to make his way through each day, let alone fight for the changes that he'd once found so important.

But Melville wanted to marry Finch more than ever, and for a number of very practical reasons. He didn't care about inheritance—Finch had long ago set up his trusts providing generously for both Zee and Melville. But Melville had not been able to get Finch to sign a health-care proxy appointing him to make decisions in the event that Finch was no longer capable of caring for himself. The reason was simple: Finch wasn't certain that Melville had ever agreed with his wishes.

For the last few years, Finch had been hoarding his medications. Anytime he took a fall and a doctor provided a painkiller, Finch filled all the prescriptions. When his primary-care physician did his annual checkup, Finch complained to him that he wasn't sleeping, then hoarded the sleeping pills the doctor prescribed. When Melville called him on it, Finch got angry, claiming that Melville wouldn't help him when the time came.

"I never said I wouldn't help you," Melville said.

"You never said you would."

"We have years before that becomes an issue," Melville said, persuading Finch to let him flush the pills, telling him that they would have long since expired by the time Finch got sick enough to want to use them.

They hadn't talked about it since. But the previous summer, in 2003, they'd been up in Wolfeboro, New Hampshire, staying at a favorite bed-and-breakfast and doing a bit of antiquing in an old barn, when Finch found a small brown bottle among a collection of vintage bottles in the loft. He'd been looking at it, rolling around the little silver balls inside the amber glass, when Melville came up behind him.

"What's that?" Melville asked.

Finch thought about it for a minute before answering.

"Strychnine," Finch said. "They used to prescribe it as medicine."

Melville was horrified. He knew well how Maureen had died. It had been a horrible death, unbearably painful, the kind of thing you wouldn't wish on your worst enemy. He stared at the silver balls that Finch held in front of him.

"You're not thinking of using that," Melville said.

"It worked for my wife," Finch said.

"I'll help you," Melville said, never wanting Finch to suffer.

Finch stood looking at him.

"Put that back," Melville said, taking the bottle and setting it among the others. "Or better yet, tell the man to get rid of it. They shouldn't leave such things around."

The shopkeeper was approaching. Melville couldn't stand it. He was close to crying. He walked outside and stood in the sun, willing himself to breathe.

MELVILLE WASN'T THERE TO SEE Finch slip the amber bottle into his pocket. It wasn't that he didn't believe Melville. He did. But he knew just how hard things were going to get, and he knew that Melville, when faced with it, might not be able to keep his hasty promise. The strychnine was Finch's insurance policy.

ON MAY 20, 2004, MELVILLE took Finch back to the same bed-and-breakfast. Finch could no longer climb the stairs, so they had taken a first-floor room with a view of Lake Winnipesaukee. For the last few weeks, Finch had seemed confused. He'd forgotten several appointments and was having trouble finding things in the house. Melville had wondered if Finch was fighting something off; they'd had this problem before since he'd been diagnosed. Usually it flared up when he was about to get sick.

Melville wondered if he should postpone the weekend. He wanted the night he proposed to Finch to be perfect.

By Friday, Finch had not come down with anything. Though he still seemed confused, he was looking forward to the weekend, so Melville didn't cancel the reservation.

They had dinner at Mise en Place, a favorite local bistro, then walked down to Lake Winnipesaukee to get some coffee. Unsteady on the way back, Finch took his arm. Melville watched as some looks came their way. Perhaps he should have picked Provincetown, Melville thought, or at least someplace in Massachusetts. But no, Finch had always loved Wolfeboro.

When they got back to the B and B, Finch took his pills. Melville had bought champagne, and he poured each of them a small glass, just enough for a toast.

"What's this?" Finch asked, taking a seat next to Melville on the balcony.

From the bandstand an orchestra played "When I Fall in Love," its sound echoing over the water. It couldn't have been more perfect.

Melville didn't get down on his knees. That was a different tradition. Instead he turned and said quietly to Finch. "Will you marry me?"

Finch looked at him sadly. Though everyone had been talking about the landmark legislation that had just happened in Massachusetts, Finch seemed to have removed himself from the importance of this historic event.

"It's far too late for all that," he said.

★ *41* ★

WHILE JESSINA WAS FEEDING Finch his breakfast, Zee walked down to Walgreens to fill his new prescription.

When she came back, the kitchen was in shambles, there was broken glass on the floor, and Jessina was carefully picking it up. Everything had been dumped on the counters—even the canisters had been emptied.

"What happened?" Zee asked.

"Finch did this," Jessina said. "I went to check the laundry, and when I came back, he had trashed the place. He claims he was looking for something."

He's looking for his pills. The thought alarmed Zee, but she knew she was right. Though she usually kept the pills on the lazy Susan, she had begun to lock them in the upstairs room. She wasn't about to tell Jessina, but she had been expecting this. "Where is he now?"

"He's asleep in the den. I tried to clean the flour off of him, but I couldn't get it all." Jessina was clearly shaken.

"It's okay," Zee said.

She helped Jessina clean up the mess, then opened the new prescription that Mattei had written and woke Finch to give him the first dose of the antidepressant. She hoped to God that it would work.

★ *4 2* ★

ZEE DIDN'T CALL HAWK on Saturday, and she didn't call him all day Sunday. By Sunday night he had decided that if she didn't call him by the time he finished work, he'd walk over to see her. It was after 9:00 P.M. when he found himself at her door. He saw the light on in her upstairs window, but he no longer felt comfortable climbing the ivy. Instead he knocked on the kitchen door.

She unlocked the dead bolt and let him in.

"I'm sorry I didn't call," she said. "I meant to."

Hawk eased the door shut behind him, not wanting to let it slam and wake Finch.

"My father is having trouble," she said.

"What kind of trouble?"

"Severe depression."

Hawk could certainly understand. "I'm sorry," he said. "Is there anything I can do?"

"No," she said. "But thanks for asking."

There was a long silence.

"I'm glad you came by," she said. "We need to talk."

She motioned him to the kitchen table, then took a seat across from him.

He bumped the table as he sat, setting the lazy Susan in motion. He reached out and stilled it. "You look as if you haven't been sleeping much," he said.

"I'm a mess," she said, suddenly self-conscious about her appearance.

"You look beautiful," he said. "Just a little tired."

"Weary," she said.

"Good word."

They sat in silence for a minute.

"I came back here to take care of my father," she said.

"Yes."

"And I'm not doing a very good job."

"Because of me." He already knew it was where the conversation was going.

"No," she said quickly. "Because I've been having far too much fun with you."

"We've only been on the one date," he said, trying to lighten the mood.

"Finch needs to be watched every minute," she said. "Especially right now."

He didn't say anything.

"This isn't going to work out," she said.

"What isn't going to work out?" he asked.

"This . . . Us."

"Because of Finch?"

"I'm afraid he might try to hurt himself."

Hawk understood only too well what that must be doing to her. "I'm sorry," he said.

"I have to watch him every minute," she said again.

"I understand," he said.

"I just can't do anything else right now."

"What about Jessina?"

"Jessina is great, but she's only here for five hours a day."

"I'm here, too," he said. "I can help."

"That's a really sweet offer," she said. "But it's too early in our relationship for you to take on that kind of responsibility."

"So instead you're going to break us up?"

She didn't answer.

"It doesn't seem very logical to me," he said.

"It probably doesn't," she said.

"Is it what you want?"

"I don't know what I want," she said, her eyes filling up with tears. "I'm too tired to know what I want. All I want right now is sleep."

"You should go to bed," he said, touching the side of her face.

She looked toward the bedroom.

"I'll go," he said, standing up, starting toward the door.

"No," she said. "Don't."

Finch dreamed of the python, the earth dragon of Delphi, which was tightening around his thighs and stomach. He was aware that he was sweating and hoped the sweat would make it easier for him to slide out of its death grip. Just as the pressure became unbearable, a sound from upstairs woke him, and he struggled to place himself. He was in his home, his bed. But even now, in his wakened state, the snake was tightening its hold, and it took him a moment to realize that this was not a snake at all, but his top sheet in which he had become tangled. His struggle to free himself from the twisted sheet had succeeded only in making its snakelike grip tighter.

Panic seized him now, and it took everything he had to keep from crying out. His limited range of motion was no match for the monster who held him so tightly. With no Apollo to slay the beast, he had to rely on the logic that had once come so easily to him. He was trapped in a tourniquet that was cutting off his blood supply until he could no longer feel his right leg at all or catch the air to breathe. The more he pulled against it, the tighter it snaked around and gripped him.

He fought for calm, forcing himself to think strategically, breaking down the steps he needed to take to save himself. "Surrender" was the word that came to mind. Surrender was counter to his body's natural response, but it was what was needed here. With all his will, he stopped pulling away and moved toward the beast until, feeling his surrender, it loosened his grip on him and his sweat-covered body slipped free. As soon as he was out of its killing grip, he heaved the beast onto the floor, and in its flight it resumed the ghostly form of the top sheet it was and floated innocently to the floor as if it had no idea what it had been to him only moments before.

He wanted to call out for his wife, for Maureen. He could hear that she was home, in the room upstairs. But they hardly spoke now. He could feel his heart slamming his chest wall, could feel it in his leg as the blood rushed back to the appendage. The bottom sheet was wet, and for a moment he wondered if he had wet the bed himself, as a helpless child might do, and he felt the shame of it, but no, it was his sweat that had pooled on the base sheet in an effort to cool his burning body. He had never been so hot. It was unbearable.

The window was open. He could smell the sea air from the harbor. Across Turner Street he could see Chanticleer, the rooster, near the gates of the Gables, having escaped the enclosure that old Hepzibah had built to keep him inside. His eyes filled with tears, grateful that the rooster had been able to escape his shackles, so much did he identify with the wiry old bird of Hawthorne's story that he failed to realize for a moment that it was not the fictional rooster of his imaginings at all but Dusty the cat.

By the time the realization hit him, Finch had climbed out of his bed and was making his way down the hall toward the kitchen and his escape. Behind him the alarm began to sound. Not stopping for his walker, for the first time he used the railing that had so recently been installed. His shaky hands groped their way laboriously not to the front door—which was much closer to his room—for it wasn't the street he sought, or even the Gables, but something else. Slowly, methodically, he moved down the long hall toward the kitchen with its back entrance that was so much closer to the cool ocean below.

The sound of the alarm faded behind him with every step down the tilted hallway until he could no longer hear it, the rhythmical sound of the gentle harbor waves, real or imagined, muting its incessant whine. He didn't think of the pain in his legs or of his skin that burned with every brush against rail or wall, but only of the seawater that had the properties to cool and heal, water as salty as blood, a replacement perhaps for his own blood, which betrayed him with every searing step.

He crossed the high threshold to the kitchen. Seven more steps and his hand was on the door. With all the strength he had, he turned the handle, expecting to have to pop the dead bolt, knowing the difficulty of the task. He had tried before, but his fingers worked their own will and not his these days, and he had failed. Tonight, to his good fortune, he realized that the dead bolt was not set, that the only lock was the flimsy one on the door handle. The door opened easily. In one freeing step his bare foot found the deck.

With no rail to grip for support, he crossed the deck painstakingly, finding first a chair, then a table on which to lean, moving from one piece of furniture to another, a zigzag path of navigation to the three stairs that held him above the earth and sea. It might as easily have been a hundred. For a moment he almost turned back, but the sea, which had never called him before, was calling to him now. The harbor spread its cool darkness beyond the small patch of earth below. He could see the jeweled lights around its perimeter. With his last reserve of strength, he gripped the handrail and lowered himself ever so slowly to the earth below.

The beach reeds burned his bare legs. The rocks cut his feet. He could feel their sting, but he could also feel the cool of the sand, and he moved deeper into its coolness until the water found his ankles, his

calves. With each step he took, the phosphorescence sparkled and glimmered its healing miracle around him, creating a Masaccio-like halo
around him as he moved.

He could feel the water, the cold release of it, as the silt from the
mudflats surrounded his feet, holding him steady while the gentle ocean
swell moved higher on his bare legs, first to his thighs and then upward
to his waist. He sighed at the blessed coolness of its caress.

$\star$ *44* $\star$

THE SOUND OF FINCH'S alarm woke Hawk first, then Zee. She grabbed her robe and ran downstairs to Finch's bedroom, but he was not there, nor was he in the den, or even in Zee's childhood room. She glanced immediately at the front door, which was very close to his room, but it was secure. She told herself to relax, that she'd find him. Then she felt the cross breeze blowing up from the harbor at the rear of the house. Dread filling her, she turned and ran down the hall toward the kitchen. The back door was open.

"He's outside!" Zee yelled at Hawk.

"What?"

"Finch is outside!" She motioned to the kitchen door.

THEY LOOKED FOR HIM ON the street. Then, because Zee determined it would be the first place Finch would go, Hawk scaled the fence to the House of the Seven Gables and looked around the grounds.

When he wasn't at the Gables, Hawk ran down Derby Street, looking in every doorway and alley, though he doubted that Finch could make it very far, being so unsteady on his feet. Hawk was dialing the Salem police on his cell when he heard Zee yelling to him.

He found her at the water's edge, wading in to where Finch was stuck, his feet planted in the mudflats, the harbor water soaking his thin pajama top.

They pulled him out together, bundled him in blankets, and drove him to the emergency room at Salem hospital. He wasn't hurt, not even slightly hypothermic—he hadn't been in the water that long. But the hospital wanted to keep him overnight, just to make sure.

HOURS PAST MIDNIGHT HAWK DROVE Zee back to the house. When they pulled into the driveway, she started to cry. Her sobs were huge and wrenching, and he held her for a long time, telling her over and over that everything was going to be all right.

He said it once more after she was calm enough to speak. "It's going to be all right," he said.

She turned to him, her face puffy and red from crying.

"That's just it," she said. "It isn't."

They sat in silence for a long time.

"I can't do this anymore," she finally said.

For a brief moment, he thought she meant taking care of Finch. He hoped that was what she meant, both for her sake and for his own. But he knew from the way she looked at him that he was kidding himself. It was over. She had told him just tonight that she wasn't ready, that this wasn't the right time for any kind of relationship between them. As much as it hurt him, he knew he was going to have to let her go.

⋆ *45* ⋆

WITHOUT ZEE IT WAS too hard for Hawk to be in Salem. He gave his notice to the Park Service. He had committed to one more sail with the *Friendship,* on Labor Day weekend, and they couldn't find a replacement. He had paid for his boat slip for the whole season, so he told his friend Josh that he could stay there for the next few weeks. Hawk would go back to his apartment in Marblehead. He didn't want to run into Zee.

It all happened so quickly, and though he had known it was a bad idea (rebound relationships were never a good idea, were they?) he had fallen hard. He couldn't explain it; nothing like this had ever happened to him before. It wasn't just the sex. It was something else. The moment he met her, it seemed as if they'd always known each other.

He'd tried several times to tell her about Lilly, but she blocked him at every turn. She couldn't even talk about the case with Lilly's own family, she'd said.

He didn't know Lilly's husband, though he had met her children when he'd done carpentry work at their house. They were great kids. Lilly had talked about them all the time, and about her fears that she was a bad mother. Pretty much the same stuff she'd talked about in therapy, if Lilly was to be believed.

If you're having trouble reconciling your feelings about her death, and you need someone to talk to, Zee had said, *I can give you some names. It just can't be me.*

Well, he *was* having trouble reconciling his feelings, more trouble really than he wanted to admit. He'd been depressed about it, actually. Before he met Zee, he'd been really down. Mostly he was upset that he hadn't been able to save Lilly. He imagined that it was pretty much the same thing Zee must be feeling, so it was too bad they couldn't talk about it together. At least that was how he felt on one level. On another he was relieved that she hadn't allowed him to speak about Lilly. Though he was a pretty honest guy, he realized that one more broaching of the subject of Lilly might drive Zee away, and more than anything he hadn't wanted that to happen. Ironic that he'd lost her anyway. By all signs, including how horrible he felt right now, he figured he was pretty much in love with Hepzibah T. Finch. For all the good it was going to do him.

He cursed himself for getting involved in the first place. He should have seen this coming.

Hawk grabbed the rest of his clothes and some other things he would need from his boat. Then he scribbled his Marblehead address on a piece of paper and left it for Josh, who had promised to forward his paycheck the minute it arrived.

★ *46* ★

MATTEI CALLED AND ASKED Zee to meet her for lunch at Kelly's in Revere.

"I can come in to Boston," Zee said.

"I'll meet you halfway," Mattei said.

THEY SAT IN THE PAVILION and looked out at the ocean.

"Want some?" Mattei asked, offering a bite of her roast-beef sandwich. Zee had ordered fried clams and was waiting for the order to be called.

"I know you love Kelly's, but what's the real reason you wanted to meet me here?" Zee asked.

"We had a visit from Adam the other day," Mattei said.

Zee stared at her. "Adam was at the office?"

"He didn't come in when I was there, but he evidently gave our new receptionist a scare, saying you'd have to answer for what you'd done to Lilly. I've alerted both the Marblehead and the Boston police."

Zee stared at her.

"I don't think he'll bother us again," Mattei said. "But I think it would be better if you stayed away from the office for a while."

"And here I was afraid you were about to fire me for being away for so long." Zee was trying to keep her tone light, but she was having a hard time of it.

"No such luck," Mattei said. "So how's Finch doing on the new meds?" she asked.

"Besides trying to drown himself in the harbor, you mean?" Zee replied.

"How's he doing now that he's been on them for two full weeks?" Mattei asked.

"Actually, he seems a little bit better," Zee said.

"And what about you, my friend?"

"I'm fine."

"Yeah," Mattei said. "You look fine."

Zee tried to smile.

"Are you going to tell me what else is bothering you, or do I have to ask you pointed questions? You know I'll get it out of you eventually. I'm even more pushy as a friend than as a therapist."

Mattei listened while Zee told her the story of Hawk, the whole story: from the dream to her walk to the *Friendship,* to the night on the island, to pulling Finch out of Salem Harbor and their breakup.

"Interesting," Mattei said.

"Textbook," Zee said.

"In what way?"

"Isn't it obvious?"

"Enlighten me," Mattei said.

"The unfulfilled dreams of the mother. I'm acting out my mother's story," Zee said.

"Her story, maybe. I don't know if it was her unfulfilled dream."

"Of course it was," Zee said.

"It's a pretty dark story," Mattei said. "Not the part you've been acting out, but the rest of it." Mattei thought about it for a minute. "I would have thought that your mother's unfulfilled dream was rescue. First by a man, and later, when it was clear that it wasn't going to work out, by you."

Zee just stared at her.

"Any chance you just really like this guy?"

Zee sat silent.

"It's okay if you do," she said. "I never thought you were right for Michael."

"You were the one who fixed me up with Michael," Zee said.

"That was before I knew you very well."

Zee was frustrated. "Were you ever going to tell me that?"

"Of course not. And remember, you and Michael were speeding down the track to marital bliss. I wasn't going to derail that based on a vague hunch. But now that you've split up, I'd urge you to consider the opposite."

"What are you saying?" Zee asked.

"I'm asking you to consider what *you* want for a change. You have a pattern of doing what is expected of you, what other people want you to do. It's not an unusual pattern for women, but it's more extreme in your case, first with your parents, then Michael, and even with me, with this job. You go along and go along, but then you begin to act out. Stealing boats, sabotaging your wedding plans, not telling me everything about Lilly Braedon. All little acts of rebellion that lead to big consequences you blame yourself for. But I would argue that the acting-out part might just be a natural aspect of you that needs expression. You were a pretty willful kid, from the stories you told me. You did what you wanted until events in the family changed the situation. Then you stopped choosing things for yourself and just did what you thought other people wanted you to do. Until now. This time you mutually initiated the relationship. That might not mean it's the right relationship for you, but it does indicate a change."

"Doesn't it occur to you that maybe I didn't choose, that I was just acting out my mother's story?" Zee said, frustrated.

"I don't think so," Mattei said.

"It matches."

"It seems to match by coincidence. You didn't *ask* Hawk to climb up the side of the building, or to let you into a house you'd locked yourself out of."

"I knew he could climb."

"You didn't go to the *Friendship* that first time looking for him. You went to Mickey looking for a carpenter. Again coincidence."

"On some level I must be playing out the story. The one my mother wrote and that the psychic told her belonged to me," Zee said.

"Is that how you feel?" Mattei asked.

"It's what I sometimes think."

"I'm not talking about thinking, I'm talking about feeling," Mattei said.

"I don't know what I feel," Zee said.

"Sure you do."

"I feel that there's something wrong with this whole scenario, but I don't know what it is," Zee said.

"Stick with that."

"My Aunt Ann told me to watch out for Hawk, that he's not who I think he is," Zee said.

"Ann the witch?" Mattei made a face. "Psychics, witches . . ."

"Good point."

Zee went back to her original statement. "I *feel* that there's something wrong here, but I don't know what it is."

"It's uncomfortable for you," Mattei said.

"Yes."

"Why do you think it's uncomfortable?" Mattei asked.

"Because I can't figure out who he is," Zee said.

"What do you mean by who he is?"

"I can't figure out what he wants. I mean, besides the obvious," Zee said.

"And can you usually figure out what people want?"

"Probably not," Zee said. "I'm not sure anymore."

Mattei nodded. She paused for a moment before continuing. "I think what's uncomfortable for you is not this guy. Let's set him aside for a minute. I think what's getting to you is not that you can't figure out Hawk's motivation, but that you can't figure out your own. You just broke off an engagement. You're faced with caring for an ailing father. You started something up with someone new. In every scenario you have to think about what you want, and it makes you very uncomfortable. Because you don't *know* what you want. How could you? For a long time you've been doing what other people wanted. So when you actually wanted Hawk, it was a first. It doesn't really matter how authentic the relationship is, or where it goes. What matters is that you went after something that *you* wanted, and then you couldn't handle it."

Zee sat for a very long time. "You're right. 'Simple, simple, case closed,'" she said, quoting Mattei.

"You, my friend, are far from simple." Mattei smiled.

Zee tried to smile.

"Of course there's another possibility we've neglected to talk about," Mattei said.

Zee was surprised. Mattei had so clearly nailed it that there didn't seem to be any other possibility. "What's that?"

"There's the possibility that the psychic your mother dragged you to was right, that the story Maureen wrote was really your destiny. That you and Hawk were the young lovers in the story."

Zee stared at her. Never in all her time with Mattei had she heard anything so out of character. "You don't believe that for a minute," Zee said.

Mattei threw her a "gotcha" smile. "Of course I don't."

47

ZEE DIDN'T KNOW HOW she felt about her lunch with Mattei. She was tense and confused. Still, she knew that something had changed. She felt the way people often feel immediately after a break-through in treatment, more at odds and more vulnerable than ever.

And, if the truth were known, all she could think about was Hawk.

It took several days before she decided to do something about it. She was hoping the urge to see him would go away. Or that he would call. When neither of those things happened, she decided she had go to him.

She was nervous boarding his boat. What was she going to say to him? That she'd made a mistake? She wasn't altogether sure that she had. But the fact was, she wanted to see him again.

She let herself onto the boat and started down the steps when she came face-to-face with Hawk's friend Josh. She recognized him from the *Friendship*.

"Is Hawk here?" she asked.

"No," Josh said. "He quit. He rented me his boat for the rest of the season."

"Do you have any idea where he is?"

"I know," Josh said. "But I'm not so sure he wants me to tell you."

"Please," she said. "I really need to talk to him." She took a breath and tried to compose herself. "I made a mistake."

He thought about it. He looked around and found the address. Still skeptical, he copied it down and handed it to her.

"Thank you," she said.

AS SHE DROVE TO MARBLEHEAD, she tried to figure out what to say. He had every right to hate her, but she hoped he didn't. Maybe she would say that, she thought. She tried to figure out what she wanted from the relationship, but it was too early to know. If he asked her, she'd have to admit she had no idea. All she knew was that she couldn't stand the prospect of never seeing him again.

His apartment was on a busy part of Pleasant Street. She couldn't find a parking space on the right side of the street, so she turned around in the bank's parking lot and parked in front of the Spirit of '76 Bookstore. She waited for the light, then crossed in front of the Rip Tide and walked down a few houses until she found the number Josh had written on the paper. There was a seamstress shop on the first floor of the building and an outside staircase leading to an apartment on the second floor. Hawk's van was in the driveway. The upstairs windows were open. He was home.

She told herself to calm down as she climbed the stairs and rang the bell. The name on the mailbox read MOHAWK.

She couldn't tell if the doorbell had rung—she couldn't hear it. She waited. When no one came to the door, she decided to knock. Her heart was pounding.

Hawk opened the door and stared at her. "What are you doing here?"

"May I come in?"

He held the door open, and she walked into the room.

"I went to your boat. . . . You weren't there." It was probably the stupidest thing she had ever said.

He looked at her. He said nothing.

"I'll go, if you want."

"No," he said. "Just give me a minute." He walked to the other room and finished a phone call. "Have a seat," he said, gesturing to a plush green couch against the back wall.

She took a seat. The couch was more comfortable than it looked. She sank into it. She sat there, looking around the room, surprised by how familiar it seemed to her, how it made her feel. Though she was nervous about what she was going to say to him, she felt something different here. Safe, she thought.

A few minutes later, he came back and took a seat across from her in a straight chair that looked anything but comfortable.

"I wanted to apologize," she said.

"You don't need to," he said, shrugging it off.

"Yes, I do," she said.

He looked at her.

"I'm really sorry," she said.

"Okay," he said.

She had no idea what to say next. She looked around the room. "I feel as if I've been here before," she said. Then she searched for something else to say. "I thought you lived on the Salem Harbor side of town."

"I grew up there. My mother lives there now."

She nodded. "I have the weirdest feeling I've been here before."

"So you came all the way over here just to tell me you've been here before?"

"I came to apologize."

"No need," he said again.

"You want me to leave?"

"I don't know what I want," he said.

"I don't know what I want either," she said.

They sat for a long time. "I'm lying," she said. "I do know."

"And what is that?"

"I want to see you again."

"You sure about that?"

"I'm not sure about anything," she said. "I'm just trying to go with my feelings here. Forgive me, it's all rather new."

A sound from outside interrupted the conversation: something slamming, metal on metal followed by the sound of breaking glass. Hawk rushed to the window. "Damn," he said, running to the door. "What the hell are you doing?" he yelled down the stairs.

"Stay here!" he yelled back at Zee as he rushed down the front stairs.

By the time Zee got to the doorway, Hawk had someone pinned against the van. His passenger-side window was smashed, and his tools were scattered in the driveway. A crowd from the Rip Tide was gathering to watch.

Her heart began to pound, and she had to hold on to the doorframe to fight the dizzy feeling that was overtaking her.

The soothing music from the ballet school across the street was the wrong sound track for what was happening in the driveway.

Hawk released the man he had pinned against the car.

The man cursed. "You owe me a fucking hammer," he said, swiping one out of Hawk's tool kit and starting down the driveway.

"Nice," Hawk said. "Very civilized."

As the man left the driveway, he paused and looked up at Zee.

It was Adam.

He spotted her before she had a chance to step back into the shadows. He stared up at her, then looked at Hawk. Then he started to laugh. "That fucking figures," he said, slamming the hammer against the side of Hawk's van as hard as he could, leaving a huge dent in the door. He looked up at Zee one more time and pointed the hammer at her to make sure she had understood the threat. Before Hawk had a chance to get to him again, he was out of the driveway.

Hawk rushed up the stairs. "Are you okay?"

Zee nodded, stunned.

"He knows you," he said.

"He came to my office and made some threats," she said. "His name is Adam."

Hawk looked at her strangely. "His name is Roy," he said.

She looked at him. "What?"

"*My* name is Adam."

THE GREEN COUCH. THE SIGN in the window. The music from the ballet school across the street. The safe feeling she'd had a few minutes ago, the one she realized now had been the feeling of safety that Lilly had described when she talked about this room, had completely disappeared. Safe was the last thing she was feeling now.

48

THAT AFTERNOON THEY HAD closed the job site early. It was the Thursday before the long weekend, and Roy was leaving for Weirs Beach the next day and needed to cash his paycheck. He had asked Lilly to go with him, but she couldn't get away. He couldn't get over the feeling that she was messing with him, trying to fuck him up. She was clearly trying to end things—she had told him that—but there was no way. If anyone was going to end things it would be him, and he would be the one to say how and when. Not that it was such a bad thing. Lately she'd been crying a lot. And guilty about what she'd been doing to her kids and to the man she had started to call "Sweet William," which bugged the shit out of Roy. Sweet William was just some rich fuck who'd been lucky enough to snag one of the prettiest girls in town and now couldn't keep her in his bed.

Roy's construction crew had done some work at her house. Well, not his crew, really—it was owned by a general contractor, another rich fuck, but a working guy, so he wasn't so bad. And he let Roy run the show, stopping by only to do the bids and pick up the checks. When they worked on the Braedon house, they never saw the husband. They just dealt with Lilly, and she did things like make lemonade for the crew if it was a really hot day, or maybe some cookies, even. All the crew got a little crazy when she walked through the house, though Hawk hadn't been part of the crew then, but the other guys just went wild for her. When Roy had finally nailed her, they'd made him talk about it for a week, and they were coming in their pants just hearing him tell how wild she got the first time out, taking her clothes off in his truck in broad daylight down by the Marblehead Lobster Company and doing him right there.

"Psycho Pussy" was the best. He'd heard someone say that once. They were right, too, at least at first. For a while he thought she was the best time he'd ever had. It wasn't so good lately, though. And it definitely wasn't good since she'd started to give her husband the name Sweet William and talk about her kids all the time. Talk about losing wood.

All year he'd been seeing a new woman in New Hampshire. Lilly didn't know it, and nobody had better tell her either. It wasn't serious, just some biker chick he'd met last June. A bleached blonde with stand-up tits bought for her by the guy on the bike she rode in on. She'd had a catfight right there on the boardwalk with some girl who'd been flirting with the biker. Roy hadn't seen it, but everyone was talking. From what he heard, she left the other girl with four stitches across her right cheek, and he didn't mean her face cheek either. She walked out on the biker after that, and when Roy met her, she was in the bar at the end of the boardwalk, and she was looking to make the guy jealous, so she took up with him. Left the guy there, too, taking off in Roy's truck—or really the company truck, a good one, though, top of the line, a Ford F-350 with four-wheel drive and an extended cab.

The next time he came up, she told him to make sure he brought drugs with him, the good kind that came in on the boats, not the kind that left you with a headache and a bloody nose, which was pretty much all you could get around here, especially now that she'd left her biker, who was her only good connection. She was class in that department, didn't do crank the way he'd heard some of the biker chicks did. She didn't want to rot her teeth, she said. And she didn't smoke crack either, just liked the good stuff the old-fashioned way. Anything smooth, that you can snort through a straw, was what she told him when he asked what she liked. She wore a twenty-four-karat cross around her neck that hung low into her best assets and had a straw built into its stem. When he told her how clever he thought it was, disguising the coke straw that way, she got mad and told him she was a Christian, too, and never to assume otherwise. Then she sat on his lap and undid his fly and hopped onto him right there in the truck, which was a little too much like what had happened with Lilly, though he wasn't complaining, not at all. He just hoped he hadn't picked another psycho.

It made him really angry when he thought about Lilly, even angrier when he heard about Lilly and Hawk.

It had happened the afternoon he'd gone to get the check cashed. She'd come into the Rip Tide, looking for Roy. She'd been wearing a T-shirt, one of the guys on the crew got some great pleasure telling him, and it was wet because of the rain, and you could see everything. And she didn't even seem to notice. But the rest of the crew noticed. Especially Hawk.

Hawk bought her steak tips. He didn't know why the guy told him that part, except to lead to the next. That Lilly had left with him. The guy had gone out to have a smoke, and he saw her go into Hawk's apartment with him. Stupid shit.

He already had an issue with the guy. Adam Mohawk. What kind of name was that? That he called himself "Hawk" pissed Roy off. He hated these college types who worked construction. They weren't good at it, and they were always complaining.

They'd had a lot of trouble that summer with crews. Hawk was hired by Roy's boss and sent over to do some finish carpentry at the Braedons'. Roy hated him on sight. Not because of anything he did—

his work was good enough—but because Lilly had taken a liking to him. She wouldn't admit it to Roy, but everyone could see it. Roy had recently had to fire a couple of people and was dangerously close to being understaffed, or he would have found a way to get rid of Hawk. When Roy's hammer disappeared on the job site, he had accused Hawk of stealing it. Actually, it wasn't Hawk, it was another guy, someone Roy had already let go, but he needed someone to blame. As payback, Roy took Hawk's hammer, which was a twin to his.

"You should write your name on your tools," he heard one of the other guys say to Hawk.

"This isn't the first time," another said.

The next day the hammer was gone from Roy's box. He went over and grabbed it from Hawk, who pointed to his name and phone number scratched on the side.

Stupid shit.

ROY HAD BEEN WAITING FOR Hawk that Sunday night after he heard about Lilly. Sitting in the alleyway in the truck, lights off, just waiting. Hit him in the side of the head with one of those hammer staplers he'd stolen from the job site. College boy deserved what he got. Hawk never even saw it coming. Wasn't back on the job site for almost a week. And when he came back, he had a line of stitches down his right cheek, and this time it *was* the face cheek he was talking about.

★ 49 ★

H AWK HAD DRIVEN ZEE'S Volvo the back way out of
town, heading up Elm Street and cutting down Green Street to
West Shore Drive. Even if Roy was following them, Hawk had managed to lose him.

"I don't mean to scare you," he said. "But Roy is a pretty dangerous
guy."

"I'm aware of that," she said.

"Plus, one of my buddies told me they're laying off some of the
crews. After the job he's working on is finished, Roy will be out of work.
So his anger level is pretty high."

"He doesn't know that I'm in Salem," she said.

"Who does know?"

"Just Mattei. And Michael."

"You need to call them. I'd tell you to get a restraining order, but
then he'd find out where you are. Not to mention that they don't always
work."

Before Hawk's mother had moved back home to Marblehead, to
the house on Salem Harbor where she'd grown up, there had been several restraining orders. Not only had they not helped, but they seemed
to simply challenge the man she was living with after her divorce, a

man who was not Hawk's father. Thank God that Hawk's grandfather had taken them in when he did. In Hawk's opinion restraining orders weren't worth the paper they were written on.

"Make sure you stay out of Marblehead for a while. The good news is that I hear he's planning to move to New Hampshire," Hawk said.

"Why is he so angry with *you?*" Zee asked.

Hawk didn't answer at first. He was trying to figure out how to tell her the story he'd been attempting to tell her all along, and now he didn't know where to start.

As they passed Waterside Cemetery, where Lilly was buried, she stopped him. "You were sleeping with her." She'd heard Lilly's stories about Adam in almost as much detail as she'd heard Maureen's stories. Now it made her sick to think about what Lilly had described.

"We were friends," he said. "I can't tell you I didn't think about it. When I first met her . . . But no. I never slept with her."

They drove in silence for a moment.

Then she remembered contacting the police. "Mattei and I called the police in Marblehead to file a report. Because Lilly told me that a man named Adam had threatened her."

Hawk finally understood why the police kept driving by his house, why the cop had acted so strangely the last time he was in town. After Roy had jumped him that day, Hawk had beaten him up. They were on the job site when it happened. Everyone on the crew thought it was payback for Roy's attack, but it wasn't. It was about Lilly. The cops talked to both of them, then talked to some of the other guys on the crew. They decided that it had been a jealousy thing and let it go. But the police had started watching him after that, which was one of the reasons he left when he did. "What did the cops tell you about me?"

"Only that you had left town. And that you weren't the only guy that Lilly was involved with."

He'd seen what Roy had done to Lilly when he got her to run away with him and then dumped her back on her doorstep three days later. The whole crew was talking about it.

"Next time you want to hit somebody," Hawk told him right before he threw the first punch, "don't pick on a woman."

The guys had just watched as he hit Roy. No one helped. No one came to Roy's defense or to Hawk's either, though he didn't really need it. It wasn't a long fight. But it was brutal. And it went all the way back to childhood. Every punch he'd wanted to deliver then on his mother's boyfriend, he delivered that day on Roy.

Hawk left his job after that. Roy had been there for years and was the foreman, though no one liked him very much. And hell, Hawk was glad to get away. Lilly had taken to sitting on his doorstep sometimes when he got home. It wasn't safe. He didn't mean not safe for him. He meant for her.

The truth was, he was angry at Lilly. Though he'd never met her husband, he'd gotten to know her kids while working at their house, and they were great. He didn't understand why she would risk every-thing, especially for someone like Roy. It was too close to what he'd seen growing up.

But he could also see how frightened she was. There wasn't anyone else she could talk to about this, she said. She felt safe only when she was with him. "I'm afraid he's going to do something terrible," she said.

"Has he threatened you?"

He couldn't tell if she was lying when she said no, or if she was just backing away because she knew he would take it to the next level, either to Roy himself or to the police.

In the end, feeling bad for her, Hawk gave her his cell number. He promised he'd come get her if she got into trouble, but he told her to go back to her husband and children, not to go near Roy again.

"You think I *want* to go near him?" She was crying.

The last time he saw her, she was in his apartment. He wasn't certain, even now, how she had broken in. He was living on his boat, and the place was empty. He'd come home one afternoon to find her there. She was wearing one of his T-shirts, and her hair was wet as if she'd just gotten out of the shower. From the look of things, she'd been there for a while.

"What's going on?" he said.

"I'm leaving William," she said. "I want to live with you."

Hawk was taken by surprise. He'd known for a while that something had shifted, that she had somehow transferred any feelings she'd had for Roy to him, but he didn't want that. Not that he didn't have feelings for her, too. Hawk had always been a sucker for a woman in trouble, especially a beautiful woman like Lilly. But he wasn't about to break up a family. He'd had too much experience with that as a kid. And he'd also begun to realize just how much was wrong with her. He was happy after that when she called and told him she was seeing her therapist again, and she called him a lot. Too much, really, because the guys on the *Friendship* had started to tease him about the number of calls and texts he got from her.

"I'm sorry if I gave you the wrong idea," he'd said. "That was never what I intended."

"I'm afraid," she'd said.

"Go home to your husband," Hawk said. "Tell him what happened between you and Roy. Then go to the police."

"I can't do that," she said.

THE LAST DAY SHE CALLED, when she told him she was going to jump, he'd gone after her. Tried to talk her out of it, to get her to meet him somewhere, but she was already headed to the bridge. He'd gotten her to pull over for a while, into the McDonald's parking lot on the Lynnway. He'd told her to wait for him there, that he was on his way.

She tearfully agreed. But then she got scared. Said she couldn't wait. Someone was after her, she said. There was nothing anyone could do.

He drove so fast. He would have called the cops, but he didn't want to get off the phone with her.

When she jumped, he was only six cars behind her.

"I can see you," he said. "Pull over and I'll pick you up."

She did pull over, but she didn't look back. When she went up and over the side, he was still on the phone with her. He could see the phone fly out of her hands as she went down. It all happened so fast.

He wondered every day what he could have done differently. He went over it and over it in his mind. It bothered him so much he had considered seeing someone to talk it through. But then he met Zee, and everything seemed different. The fact that she felt as guilty as he did about Lilly's death had actually helped him feel a bit better. She hadn't *told* him how she felt, of course—she was far too professional for that. But he knew.

HAWK TOLD ZEE THE WHOLE story. At the end of it, she told him what she'd told the Marblehead police.

Hawk's blood chilled. He didn't move. Lilly had been troubled, he'd always known that. But her jump up and over the railing had begun to make sense to him in a way it hadn't before. He knew that Roy was a dangerous guy, an abusive guy, and he also knew that the most dangerous time for a victim is when she tries to break up with her abuser. He'd read an article about it in the Salem paper just last week, something that the local shelter had put out, or maybe it was that woman on Yellow Dog Island, May Whitney. He couldn't remember.

Hawk sat very still. He looked directly at Zee in a way that made sure she wouldn't look away. He didn't reach out to her, just said as calmly as he could, "I never slept with Lilly Braedon. . . . And I sure as hell never threatened her. I was trying to do the same thing you were," he said. "I was trying to save her."

He's not who you think he is. Ann Chase's words came quickly back to Zee.

THEY DROVE THE REST OF the way to Salem in silence. Hawk pulled Zee's Volvo into Finch's driveway and shut off the engine. He turned to her. "I need you to believe me."

No one spoke for a long time.

"I do believe you," she finally said. "But I can't see you anymore."

PART 4:

August 2008

Only when one learns to determine his true location by looking at the stars will he be able to chart an accurate course to his final destination. The tools needed are simple enough: the chronometer, the sextant, the almanac, the charts, and some relatively simple method of mathematical calculation.

★ *50* ★

THE INVITATION TO MATTEI and Rhonda's wedding still sat on the lazy Susan where Zee had left it. She had told Mattei she was coming, but she called the office now, just to confirm that she would not be bringing anyone. At some point Zee would have to go to town to get a wedding present, but not today.

It was cold for the end of August. Channel Five had promised a warming trend by Friday, which would be good for Rhonda, since the ceremony was outside on Sunday night. The reception was at the Boston Harbor Hotel, something Zee would not have predicted. Though everything about this wedding seemed to be much more traditional than she expected, the hotel was a great location for Zee, who could just catch the ferry from Salem and walk across from Long Wharf to Rowes. It also gave her an excuse to escape early. The last ferry of the night left for Salem at ten.

The office would be closed all month, but she knew that Mattei would be checking messages. She hadn't told her what had happened, that she'd stopped seeing Hawk, or even that Hawk was really Adam. The story was too complicated and coincidental to be believed, much less understood. Mattei was already worried that Zee was preoccupied with Lilly Braedon. If she told Mattei that Hawk was Adam, she was afraid that Mattei's alarm bells would go off and she would believe that this was something Zee had known all along, something she'd pursued. Zee would tell Mattei eventually—she would have to—but not yet. Not until she figured out how to frame it. She was glad the office was closed for the traditional month of August. She didn't want to talk.

What Zee did instead was to look into nursing homes. During the last few weeks, Finch had lost a lot of ground. More often than not these days, he called her Maureen, something he'd done on occasion since she arrived but that he was now doing with alarming regularity. Zee knew it was time. She wanted to be proactive, to pick a good place, a facility that treated both Parkinson's and the Alzheimer's crossover he was experiencing more and more lately. She interviewed and rejected at least six places before she found one that she actually thought Finch might tolerate. It was a combination of assisted living and nursing home, with a special unit dedicated to early dementia. Finch had taken two falls in the last few weeks. It was clear he needed more care than he could get at home. Unfortunately, the place she liked had a long waiting list. Even full-paying patients like Finch could expect to wait almost a year.

In one sense she was relieved. She knew that it was the right thing to do, but it still made her sad to think of Finch in a home. Zee added his name to the waiting list, but then she took another tack, hiring Jessina full-time and augmenting Finch's daily care with more help on nights and weekends. Though she was still having doubts about her choice of career, Zee knew she had to get back to work. This new plan would allow her to commute back and forth to Boston.

She'd met Melville for dinner a few times since her breakup, at Nathaniel's and at 62 on Wharf or at the Lyceum or the Regatta Pub. Melville was still a foodie at heart, and she was glad to join him for a delicious meal when invited. The night Finch fell for the third time, they had been together at the Grapevine, sitting in the outdoor garden and eating their famous chowder when Jessina called Zee's cell.

By the time they got back to the house, the EMTs were already there. Jessina was crying, and Finch was lying flat on the floor in the hallway, his walker upended. His breathing was irregular, and he was in and out of consciousness.

The EMT suspected a broken rib, maybe a punctured lung.

Zee rode in the ambulance, and Melville followed behind. It took eight hours before they admitted Finch into a room, and Melville waited in the lobby all night.

Finch had two broken ribs. He looked as if he'd been beaten. He had a bump on his right temple.

"He has a scalp hematoma on his right temple, and they were worried about hemorrhage," Zee said when she finally came out to send Melville home. "He seems confused. But now they're convinced that his confusion is from the dementia, so they can give him the painkillers he needs."

Melville went home, but he returned the next morning. He didn't come into the room but hung back in the hall, waiting for Zee to see him and come out.

"You look terrible," he told her. "Why don't you go home for a while and get some sleep."

"What if he wakes up?" Zee said.

"When did he get his last shot?" Melville asked.

"About an hour ago."

"I'll sit with him. If he starts to wake up, I'll get out of the room quickly and give you a call."

She wasn't sure.

"Go," he said.

She did go home, and she did sleep.

And though Finch didn't wake up, Melville sat with him for the rest of the day.

★   ★   ★

IN THE DAYS THAT FOLLOWED, Finch was allowed a few visitors. Mickey came by. He brought Finch a chop-suey sandwich from the Willows and Zee a bag of the popcorn he knew she liked. Finch didn't wake up enough to eat, and Mickey ended up consuming the sandwich.

Finch slept most of the time, and when he did wake up, he seemed more confused than usual, as much a product of the continuing painkillers as the dementia. Ann came to visit every afternoon, bringing tea and novels from Cornerstone Books for Zee to read. She loaded her iPod with music she knew Zee would like and loaned it to her.

Melville came by every day after work, though he always sat in a chair by the door and didn't speak much while he was there. Whenever Finch's eyes blinked awake, Melville would slip out the door so quietly it was almost as if he'd never been there at all.

THE LABOR DAY SAIL was scheduled to leave the wharf at 6:00 P.M. on Friday. Hawk got to the *Friendship* just as they were casting off.

"I figured you weren't coming," Josh said. "Thought maybe you'd run off with Zee and gotten yourself married."

"No such luck," Hawk said. If there was any way he could have gotten out of this commitment, he would have done it. He didn't want to be anyplace near Salem. But he'd given his word. They were heading north to the Isles of Shoals for the weekend, stopping for an event on Star Island. Many of the historic tall ships were making the trip, which was essentially a benefit to raise money for the National Park Foundation. There would be pirates and privateers and people singing sea chanteys and telling maritime ghost stories. Same old same old, Hawk thought. The weekend was advertised as "Labor Day Fun for the Whole Family." There was nothing Hawk wanted to do less. At least they weren't staying for the Monday holiday. They would be home late Sunday night.

ANN CHASE WALKED ACROSS PICKERING Wharf and back toward her store. Mickey Doherty was being even more ridiculous today than usual. She'd come over to complain about his monkey. Mini

Mick had jumped on her cat, Persephone, from the top of the window box where Ann grew her herbs. When he tried to ride the cat, she went wild and dug scratches into the monkey's face.

Ann was an animal person, and she certainly felt bad about the monkey's injuries, but maybe this time Mini Mick would learn a lesson.

"Sounds like my boy got what he deserved," Mickey said, putting the monkey into the cage he'd fashioned out of an old supply closet, its door removed and replaced with chicken wire. As the cage doors closed, Mini Mick began to masturbate enthusiastically.

Mickey chose that moment to ask Ann out to dinner.

It was unfortunate timing, and she frowned in response.

"Is that your answer?"

For a long time, Mickey had been telling Ann she should ditch the guys she usually favored and go out with him.

"Come on, time to give up the crunchy granolas and the weird warlocks and give me a go," he said. "I've been asking you out for the last three years."

"More like five," she said.

"Okay, five. I'm clearly quite persistent."

She turned back to face him. "Oh, for God's sake," she said. "Will you leave me alone if I say yes?"

"Maybe," he said. "That depends on how it goes."

"Forget it," Ann said, heading for the door.

"Okay, okay, just one date and I'll leave you alone." He crossed his heart.

"Saturday at five. Finz," Ann said, naming a local restaurant she favored.

"Five? What are we, senior citizens?"

"Take it or leave it," she said.

"Okay, okay, Finz at five."

"And leave the damned monkey at home," she said.

★ *5 2* ★

ON SATURDAY MORNING ZEE moved Finch to rehabilita-
tive care at one of the nursing homes she had interviewed and
rejected.

If Finch minded, he didn't say so. His bruises had started to yellow,
and his breathing was easier. But his injuries had left him unable to
stand. He would need a lot of physical therapy before he could walk
again.

Zee checked him in, then sat while they tested him. That he recognized Zee's face was a relief to her, though he couldn't seem to recall her
name. He failed his cognitive-skills test.

"That could be the drugs," the nurse said. "He's still on a low dose
of oxycodone."

The nursing home told her they would quickly wean him off the
drug.

"Won't he need something for the pain when they start physical
therapy?"

"Yes, but probably something milder."

She didn't want Finch here. But for now it was the only choice. He
couldn't be cared for at home as yet, that much was clear.

She followed the administrator to the office to fill out more paper-
work.

"Does he have a health-care proxy?" the admitting nurse asked.

"I don't think so," Zee said.

"Does he have a wife?"

"She's deceased."

"Any other children?"

"Just me," she said.

"What about a DNR?"

"A Do Not Resuscitate form?" Zee asked.

The nurse nodded.

"I don't know."

"If he doesn't have a health-care proxy, he probably doesn't have a DNR."

She thought about Finch's skills as organizer. He had a tendency to let things slide.

"Probably not," she said.

"It's a good thing to have," the nurse said. "In cases like this. You can't do anything until the doctor declares him mentally incompetent, though. After that you can probably sign a DNR for him."

Zee thought about the AMTS test they had just taken. Finch had been able to pass about a third of it before. This time he hadn't been able to answer a single question.

"I plan to bring him home when he's better," Zee said.

The nurse looked doubtful but didn't comment.

ZEE DECIDED TO KEEP JESSINA on even after Finch left the house. Sometimes she asked her to go to the nursing home so that Finch would have more company, and sometimes she had her work on the house, cleaning out and sorting the years of papers Finch had collected.

Over the last months, Zee had become friends with Jessina and Danny, whom she sometimes brought to work with her if they needed help cleaning or moving things around. Jessina kept baking, taking Finch cookies or cupcakes every time she went to visit, sharing the extras with the nursing staff. These days the old house on Turner Street always smelled like a bakery, which provided a comforting feeling that Zee appreciated a lot. In a way it was too bad they weren't selling the house, Zee thought. The aroma of baking alone would have brought bidders to the table.

One day when they were cleaning out, Danny found a pile of eight-by-ten black-and-white photos under some old school papers Finch had saved. He was showing them to Jessina when Zee came into the room.

"These are beautiful," Jessina said. "Why did he not hang them up?"

Zee looked over their shoulders at the photos. "Finch took those," she said. There were several pictures of Zee and of Melville and many more of the House of the Seven Gables taken from the street, all with dates and descriptions. Zee couldn't answer Jessina's question. For some reason Finch had never displayed any of his photos.

"Look at this one," Jessina said, holding up a picture of Maureen. "That's your mother, yes?"

Maureen was young in the photo, early twenties if she was that. She was dressed in a stylish suit, and around her was a halo of mist. Her smile seemed so innocent and full of promise that it startled Zee.

Jessina turned the photo over. The label on the back read simply *Honeymoon. Niagara Falls.*

"This should definitely be in a frame and put out for everyone to see." Jessina held it up to a shelf to indicate a possible display location.

"No," Zee said, taking the photo.

She stared at it. Though she had always known that Maureen's stories were embellished, it shocked her to think that her mother had lied about her honeymoon. Maureen had looked so happy in the photograph that it seemed odd she would have bothered to create a whole fantasy around Baker's Island. Had Finch been telling the truth when he said he'd never been there? Zee had dismissed his statement as part of his dementia, but now she was inclined to believe him.

In a flash, Zee realized the real reason she kept getting Maureen and Lilly mixed up. It wasn't that they were both bipolar. It wasn't even that they had both committed suicide. It was something else that they had in common, and it had nothing to do with their illnesses. Mattei's old adage came to Zee's mind now: *Everybody lies.* Maureen and Lilly had both lied to Zee. That was no big surprise. But it was more than that, she realized now. The lies or stories that Maureen and Lilly told were not lies they were telling Zee, they were the mythology they were creating for themselves. When they were no longer able to believe their own fairy tales, they lost all hope.

It was a huge revelation, and it explained a lot.

THAT NIGHT JESSINA AND DANNY stayed around until they were certain that Zee was all right. It surprised Zee to find that she was not only all right but that she was better than she'd been for a long while. She was understandably sad about everything that had happened that summer. But something had changed inside her when she saw the happy picture of Maureen. Something had lifted.

"I'm okay," she said to Jessina. "I really am."

MATTEI AND RHONDA WERE GETTING married on the Sunday of the long Labor Day weekend. As fate would have it, Sunday was both the last day of August and Zee's birthday, and somehow she had let this slip to Jessina, who was busy at work making her a birthday cake when Zee had to leave to meet Melville.

"I'll put it on the table when I go," Jessina said. "It's chocolate with white vanilla frosting," she said. "Your favorite."

"Sounds delicious," Zee said. "Thank you."

Zee had to leave earlier than Jessina had planned. Melville made her promise to meet him for an early birthday dinner at Finz before she caught the ferry into Boston for the wedding. Though there would be dinner at the wedding, she agreed to meet. She needed to talk to him about Finch's advance directives.

STAR ISLAND WAS CROWDED with spectators. Many had come in their own boats to watch the tall ships sail in, and even more had come by ferry for the festivities on the island.

After the *Friendship* was anchored and her sails finally lowered, Hawk went onto the island with the rest of the crew.

He followed Josh through the crowds, past the encampment where the pirates had spent the last three days without breaking character. A wench in a low-cut top smiled at Hawk and asked if he'd like some grog. He smiled a weak smile and kept walking.

"Oh, man," Josh said. "You've got it bad. That wench was a fox."

They grabbed two beers at the concession stand.

"Come on," Josh said, spotting a tent at the far end of a line of buildings. "This is the one I was looking for."

The tent was hot and crowded. Inside, people sat cross-legged on the grass as a tag team of sailor storytellers engaged in a game of one-upmanship. Right now they were trading sailing superstitions.

"Never sail on a Friday," one of the sailors offered.

"Hey, we all sailed up here on Friday," Josh said aloud as he and Hawk sat down.

"A very bad omen," the host said, and the crowd laughed.

"Never bring a woman on board," another sailor declared.

"For any number of reasons," someone else said.

"Never allow a preacher on board," the first sailor said.

"I would have thought a preacher would be good luck," the host said.

There was a loud chorus of noes.

"It annoys the devil."

"You don't want to do anything to get him too riled."

"The preacher or the devil?" the host asked, to more laughter.

"The preacher if you're on land, the devil out at sea."

One of the sailors stood up and took off his shirt to reveal a cross tattooed on each arm. "This'll keep you safe," he said. "But only if you have it on all four limbs." He started to drop his pants.

Howls of protest rose from the audience. "For God's sake!" one of the mothers yelled. "There are children present."

The sailor shrugged and sat back down.

"I take sand on the ship with me," another sailor said. "To throw at the devil. Like Ahab did."

"Which worked so well for him," the host said.

"You can't say the word 'pig' once you're on board the ship," another sailor offered. "It's very bad luck."

"But if you tattoo a pig on your knee before you get on the ship, it's good luck."

The host looked at his watch. "It's four o'clock," he said. "We should switch to the storytelling competition, since the ferry's coming at six."

"That's what I came to hear," Josh said to Hawk.

Two of the more talkative sailors in the group spoke first, recounting stories about the wrecks that had taken place in these waters. The first was the story of a ship called the *City of Columbus,* which had run aground on a reef off Martha's Vineyard aptly named the Devil's Bridge. The ship carried an interesting group of passengers, mostly invalids trying to head south in an effort to escape the harsh winter of 1884. The captain's attempt to free his ship from the reef only put the craft in more peril, and a rogue wave swept most of the women and children from the deck into the ice-filled waters, where they died almost immediately. The rescue of the remaining passengers was performed by a group of Wampanoag Indians. Unable to get close enough to the ship, they urged the passengers to jump into the frigid waters, and the Indians picked up what survivors they could.

The second story was a more local one that had happened very close by, where the wreck of a Spanish ship had become an early grave for fourteen unfortunate sailors. That wreck took place in the group of islands they were on now, between the two isles of Malaga and Smuttynose.

The minute that Smuttynose was mentioned, another storyteller was on deck waiting to tell the story about the famous ax murders that had happened there back in the late 1800s. Two women were murdered on the island while a third escaped into the rocks, where she hid until morning. The event had inspired a number of books, including Anita Shreve's *The Weight of Water*. Today the grisly details of the murders elicited a shudder among the crowd and another warning that there were children present. The storyteller then switched to describing the worn thole pins found in a stolen dory, which became part of the evidence that convicted the killer.

"What are thole pins?" someone in the crowd asked.

"Oarlocks," the host said.

"More or less," the storyteller said. "They were usually wooden in some of the older ships."

"Oarlocks," the host said again.

"Yes, but made of wood," the storyteller said. "Kind of like two dowels," he said. "The man who owned the dory that the killer stole had just replaced them. The fact that they were worn out was evidence that someone had rowed a very long distance."

One story led into another, and soon a member of the crew of the *Friendship* was next up. "I have a story about thole pins, or oarlocks or whatever you want to call them, and mine happened earlier than the one on Smuttynose, but worn thole pins were the primary evidence in that case, too."

Hawk listened as the sailor told the story of the house on Turner Street and of Zylphia and her sailor, a story he'd never heard before.

"That's your ex-girlfriend's house he's talking about," Josh whispered.

When the sailor detailed the part about the young sailor climbing the side of the house on Turner Street to make love to Zylphia on the widow's walk, Hawk stood up.

"You okay?" Josh asked.

Hawk didn't speak, but he listened to the rest of the story, about the beatings from the captain and how it was believed that Zylphia and her Haitian housekeeper had poisoned him, how Zylphia had made her escape, the worn oarlocks on the stolen dory found on the Miseries becoming the evidence that she'd gotten away. The lovers had simply and very mysteriously vanished, leaving behind only the dory with its worn thole pins.

The women in the front row loved the story, which led to teasing from the sailors. "It's so romantic," one of the women said, putting a hand to her heart.

"Remind me not to go out with you," the host said.

"You can go out with her," her friend said. "Just don't marry her."

"Fair enough."

Hawk was standing now, a nervous feeling overtaking him. He didn't find the story romantic—he found it brutal and horrifying. His mind wandered to Roy and what he'd done to Lilly. And how there hadn't been anything he could do to stop it. And then he thought about Zee, had been thinking about her all along, really.

Roy had recently moved to New Hampshire. Not to this part of New Hampshire, but a couple of hours from here on the other side of the state. Hawk had made sure Roy was long gone before he left town. He couldn't do much for Zee, but he could do that.

Still, he didn't feel better. He was very agitated. It was hot in here. He needed to get some air.

Josh caught up with him outside. "I thought everyone knew that story," he said.

"I didn't," Hawk said.

★ *54* ★

S IGN THE DNR IF they let you," Melville said to her. "But I'm not certain that a doctor can declare him incompetent. I think you might have to go to court to do that."

"It sounds as if you've looked into this," she said.

"I thought it might come to this, yes."

Zee kicked herself for bringing it up. "I don't want to sign a DNR."

"But it's what he would want."

"If he wants it so much, why didn't you have him appoint you as his health-care proxy?" she said.

"Probably for the same reason that we didn't make marriage plans," Melville said. "We always thought we had time."

"I'm sorry," Zee said. "I wish you had gotten married." She thought about the wedding she was going to tonight, and how lucky Mattei and Rhonda were by comparison.

"Let's change the subject," Melville said finally. "Happy birthday." He held up his glass and toasted her. She smiled.

"Virgo," he said. "Very neat and organized. Great at detail work. Observant. Picky. You can think a thing to death. The phrase 'analysis paralysis' comes to mind."

"You're quite the little astrologer," she said.

"Happy birthday," he said again. "To better things in the year to come."

She looked up in time to see Mickey and Ann walk into the bar. Mickey held a chair for Ann, and she sat down. Melville and Zee exchanged looks.

"Is that a date?" Zee was amazed.

"It sure as hell looks like one," Melville said.

"I don't believe it."

JESSINA SEARCHED THE CABINETS FOR cake decorations. She had used most of the colored sugar on the Fourth of July cookies. Now she found some green shamrocks, which she rejected, and some heart confetti, which would be perfect to scatter lightly about. But she needed something more. Climbing up on a kitchen chair, she looked deep into the baking cabinet and spotted the amber bottle with the silver dragées. The little silver balls would be perfect, she thought.

She placed them around the perimeter of the cake, spaced every inch or so. Then, with enough left, she spelled out HAPPY BIRTHDAY ZEE in the middle. When she was finished, she covered her creation in plastic wrap, using toothpicks to hold the wrap away from the frosting.

She cleared everything off the lazy Susan and placed the cake in the middle, spinning it just enough so that the birthday message would be clear to Zee the minute she walked into the kitchen.

ZEE LOOKED AT HER WATCH while Melville signed the check.

"Thank you for dinner," she said.

"Are you going to be okay at that wedding all by yourself?" he asked. "I could go with you if you have time for me to run back and change into a suit."

"I'll be fine," she said. "But thanks."

They stopped by the bar on the way out to say hello to Ann and Mickey.

The bar was packed with diners waiting for tables and a preppy-looking group of sailing types. Some guys turned to check out Zee as she passed.

"So what are you two up to?" Zee asked Ann and Mickey.

"Don't ask," Ann said.

Mickey smiled widely and stood to offer Zee his seat.

"We're just heading out," Melville said.

"Mattei and Rhonda are getting married tonight," Zee said.

"Oh, I forgot about that," Ann said. "Should be fun."

"My boss," Zee said to Mickey by way of explanation. Then, knowing Mickey's feelings on the subject, she added. "And her girlfriend."

Everyone waited for Mickey's reaction. "Hey, if that's what the good citizens of Massachusetts want, who am I to protest? I'm a progressive guy."

Ann rolled her eyes. "Sure you are," she said.

Two seats at the bar opened up, and a young man who had been eyeing Zee found the courage to walk over.

"Hey, we've got seats," the guy said. "If you and your father want to join us for a drink."

Zee smiled and declined.

"You and your father," Mickey said to Melville. "That idiot. How did he know you weren't her date?"

He was being genuine, but it didn't come off that way. "Older man, younger woman, it happens all the time." He smiled at Ann.

It was funny, Ann thought, regarding Zee and Melville, how much alike they looked. Ann was surprised she had never noticed it before. They could easily have been mistaken for father and daughter. In many ways Zee looked just like her mother. But if you examined the cheekbones, the eyes . . .

"I'll bring the car around," Melville said, leaving them.

"I thought you seemed a little too dressed up for this place," Mickey said. "Happy birthday," he added, kissing her cheek.

"Happy birthday, Hepzibah," Ann said.

"Don't stay out too late," Mickey said.

Zee laughed. She kissed them both and walked to the curb.

"What?" Mickey said, noticing Ann looking at the car as Melville pulled up.

"Nothing," Ann said.

A big plate of Stoli oysters that Mickey ordered arrived. Ann started to laugh. "Oysters?" she said. "What part of vegan don't you understand?"

"Hey, you're the one who picked Finz."

"And I'm planning to order their vegan dinner," she said. "To say nothing of that ridiculous cliché. Oysters? Are you kidding me?"

"I took a shot."

ANN WATCHED THROUGH THE WINDOW as Melville pulled the car up to the curb. She watched as he got out and walked around to the passenger's side to open the door for Zee. Ann was lost in thought as the car drove off. It took her a moment to realize that Mickey had been trying to tell her something. "I'm sorry. What?"

Mickey gestured toward the frustrated hostess who was waiting to take them from the bar to the restaurant. "I said, our table is ready."

ELVILLE DROPPED ZEE OFF at the ferry.

"Call me if you need a ride back," he said.

"I'll be fine," she said. "It's just a few blocks, and it won't be that late."

"Happy birthday," he said again. She kissed him on the cheek.

He sat in the parking lot until the ferry pulled out. Then he sat longer, looking at the harbor and out toward Baker's Island. He opened the glove compartment and pulled out the book of Yeats.

He'd thought about giving it to Zee as a birthday present. He'd even gone so far as to get a card to go with it and inscribed it with her full name before he decided the whole thing was a very bad idea.

He sat for a long while, just looking at the title. Then he opened to the middle of the book and took out a folded piece of paper.

The paper was what he and Finch had fought about that day when Finch had literally thrown the book at him, the afternoon that had ended their relationship.

Zee had always believed that Maureen hadn't left a suicide note, and it had been important to Finch that she keep believing that. But it wasn't true. Maureen had known what she was doing. She hadn't left the note on the bed where Zee was as likely to find it as Finch. Instead she'd left it in Finch's study, for his eyes only.

Dear Finch,

*By the time you read this note, I will be gone. It is best
for all.*

*Secrets are often carried to the grave, but this is one I will
not take with me. Do with it what you will.*

*The child I bore for you to father is not yours. It belongs
to the man you betrayed me with. It happened only once, in a
moment out of place and time.*

The fates are cruel, they make fools of us all. . . .

Maureen

At the bottom of her suicide note was a message that was meant for
Melville, completing the inscription he'd left for her so long ago:

Come away, O human child!
To the waters and the wild.
With a faery, hand in hand.
For the world's more full of weeping than you can understand.

★ *56* ★

IT HAD HAPPENED BEFORE he met Finch, back when Melville was writing the article on the Greenpeace splinter group. He was coming back from Gloucester on his boat when his engine died. He knew what was wrong immediately and cursed himself for not having gotten around to fixing it. He also knew he'd never make it all the way back to Salem, so he put in at Baker's Island, hoping to use a phone or, barring that, to borrow a skiff and go to Manchester Harbor to pick up the part he needed at the marine supply.

It was June. Few of the summer people had yet arrived. The little store was closed, and Melville had to walk to the far end of the island before he found an unshuttered cottage.

He stopped at the door to ask if he could use the phone.

She'd been hesitant to open the door. In retrospect he wasn't certain why she had.

She stood in the doorway looking at him. Her red hair was tied back, and she had a pencil stuck through it, holding it in place. Her eyes were piercing blue. He stood outside the door just looking at her. It was a long moment before he remembered to ask about the phone.

She told him she didn't have a phone. When she heard his story, she offered to lend him her boat. He took it into Manchester Harbor and picked up the part he needed at the marine shop.

By the time he got back with the part, it was early evening. It wasn't a hard fix, but it was in a bad place, and he had to pull up the deck and several of the floorboards to get at it. He'd shorted out his running lights in the process. When he finished the job, it was after dark. He figured he'd sleep on the boat and head out again at first light.

That she appeared on the wharf surprised him. It was chilly, and her house was all the way at the far end of the island.

"I've made dinner," she said. "If you're hungry."

His inclination was to say no. He had some food on board, nothing any good, but enough to get him through until morning. However, when he turned to answer, she was already back at the top of the dock, motioning for him to follow. He called after her, but the wind was against him, and she couldn't hear. He watched her disappear onto the blackening path.

Melville took his flashlight along with him to her house. He could see her lone light ahead, but the path was narrow and hadn't yet been mowed for the summer. A false step in any direction could sprain an ankle, especially in this darkness.

She was waiting there for him, framed by the doorway. He'd meant to tell her no, that he was fine on the boat, but then he saw the table set for two. The oil lanterns that lit the room cast him back to another place and time, and he suddenly noticed her lace dress. She was beautiful. Her red hair hung wild and curling halfway down her back. Without saying anything he had planned to say, he found himself walking through the doorway to the table. She poured the wine.

Later he would remember thinking it had been as if he were awakening to something possible, something he'd never before considered. He noticed the ring on her finger; she didn't hide it. Something about his senses heightened, and every movement of her hands seemed like flight. Her neck was pale and long, a swan's neck, he thought. His thoughts ran to poetry and art, imagery of Leda and the swan,

Leonardo's sensual sketch and the lost Michelangelo. She was beauty of form and movement. The feminine ideal. And he found himself speaking aloud the poetry that came to him:

> *A sudden blow: the great wings beating still*
> *Above the staggering girl, her thighs caressed*
> *By the dark webs, her nape caught in his bill,*
> *He holds her helpless breast upon his breast.*

She came to him. He lifted her hair away from her neck and kissed her. And more poetry came to his lips, all the Yeats he'd learned and forgotten came back to him, and he spoke the words in chant as they made love. And when the verses he hadn't known he remembered ended, all the magical words of "The Harp of Aengus," they slept soundly in each other's arms with the innocence of children.

HE LEFT THE NEXT MORNING, not entirely certain what had happened. It wasn't that he didn't like women. At one time he'd considered himself not gay but bisexual, but that had been so long ago he'd almost forgotten that early period of his life. He laughed to himself now, thinking he had been seduced by a siren. It was all so strange and dreamlike that he wasn't truly certain it had ever happened.

For the next several weeks, he wanted to go back to the island. Instead he went to Gloucester and booked on one of the sword boats, then a bigger boat that was going out for several months. He slept with every man he could, in every port, dangerous and nameless sex meant to remind him of who he really was.

But he couldn't get her out of him. He heard her poetry on the sound of the wind and the tides. He left the ship in Newburyport and hitched back to Manchester. He stopped in the bookstore and bought the white volume of William Butler Yeats. And he inscribed the book to her and scrawled a quote meant for her across the title page: *Come away, O human child! To the waters and the wild. . . .*

He took his boat to Baker's Island and walked to the cottage. But he found it boarded up for the season.

Feeling both disappointment and relief, he placed the book between the two doors, hoping it would last through the winter, through the rains and snows that were to come, and that one day, if she existed at all, she would find it.

MELVILLE LEFT SALEM FOR THE second time the night Finch and Zee brought Maureen home from the hospital. As they helped her into the house, Maureen stopped and slowly turned around to see Melville standing across the road looking at the house. She saw his face just for an instant before he recognized her, and in that moment she understood. Their eyes met, and held. They stood in the moment frozen like statues until Zee and Finch turned to see what Maureen was looking at. Guiltily, Finch hurried Maureen into the house.

Melville had left that same night, this time for California and later north to the Aleutians. He hadn't come back home to Salem until almost a year after Maureen died.

When he eventually returned, he took the job at the Athenaeum and settled into a quiet life, keeping to his side of town.

When Finch finally found him, he brought the suicide note. "Come back to me," he demanded.

"I can't," Melville said. "It could never work. Not after what happened with Maureen."

"Don't you see?" Finch said. "This relationship has to succeed, not in spite of what happened with Maureen but because of it."

★ ★ ★

MELVILLE MOVED INTO THE OLD house on Turner Street with Finch and Zee.

Though they were never able to forgive themselves for Maureen's death, they found it in their hearts to forgive each other.

They loved their daughter, delighted in her in a way that surprised them both. Finch had always wanted to be a father, but Melville had never considered the possibility. Still, he embraced it and was fulfilled by it.

Together they took the book and the note that Maureen had left and placed them where Zee would never find them.

The years had not been easy, but real love rarely is. They learned to put the past behind them. At least it seemed so until the progression of Finch's disease and his crossover into dementia brought the past back to them as if it had happened not years ago but only yesterday. And the betrayal, once experienced anew, had become real enough for Finch to feel its sting in such a strong way that his anger was able to unravel all the years they had woven together as family.

★ *57* ★

MELVILLE WAS UNAWARE THAT he'd been crying until he saw the teenagers staring at him as they walked across the ferry parking lot. He recognized one of them from Mickey's store. Melville looked away.

TONIGHT MELVILLE HAD ALMOST MADE a huge mistake. He had almost told Zee that she was really his daughter. Though he would never have given her the suicide note, he had almost given her the book. He had even gone so far as to label the birthday card he'd intended to give her with her full name, Hepzibah Thompson Finch.

He knew he had to talk to Finch, and that it had to be tonight.

MELVILLE CARRIED THE BOOK AND Maureen's letter into the nursing home. He signed the visitors' log at seven forty-five.

"Charles Thompson?" the receptionist asked.

He nodded.

"Are you family?"

"Yes," Melville lied.

"Visiting hours are over at eight," the receptionist told him.

"I'll be just a few minutes."

Melville walked down the long hallway toward Finch's room. When he got to the door, he paused. If Finch was asleep, Melville would have to wake him.

Feeling himself being watched, Finch opened his eyes.

"Who's there?" he asked.

"It's Melville," he said. "I came to talk to you."

Finch didn't move. Then, finally, when his eyes focused, he looked at Melville.

"Could you please put my bed up first?" Finch asked. "I can't breathe with it so low."

Heart pounding, Melville walked over to the bed. His fingers found the control buttons, he pushed the "up" arrow, and the head of the bed began to slowly rise, bringing Finch to a sitting position and the two men eye to eye.

"Is that good?" Melville asked.

"Wonderful," Finch said, and sighed. He looked at Melville for a long time. "This is the weekend, right?" he said, trying to remember.

"It's Labor Day weekend," Melville said. "It's early this year. This is Sunday night, Zee's birthday. Tomorrow is the first day of September."

They had done this before. It had become a ritual in the last few years they'd spent together.

"Yes," Finch said. "September."

Melville braced himself, waiting for Finch's rage to surface. When it did, Melville would explain in a way that would make him understand everything that had happened. He'd explain well enough, and he'd ask for forgiveness. Finch would forgive him again, just as he had so many years ago. And if Finch's rage came back tomorrow, he would explain again. And then, maybe one day, Melville would be able to convince Finch that they should explain the whole thing to Zee.

Finch returned his stare. But the anger wasn't there.

It's over, Melville thought, thanking God. This must be the next stage the doctor talked about, when they become less angry and for a while things seem almost normal again. Melville's neurologist friend had told him about this. The honeymoon period, he had called it. The period before late-stage Alzheimer's crossover.

"Are you comfortable now?" Melville asked, reaching over to fluff Finch's pillows.

Finch nodded. Still looking at Melville as if he was trying to figure something out, he finally smiled. "I haven't seen you working here before," he said. "You must be new."

58

THE *FRIENDSHIP* STOPPED IN Newburyport on its way
south. The battery on Hawk's cell phone was dead, and for some
reason he couldn't get reception using anyone else's. When they got to
town, he walked up to State Street looking for a pay phone.

He hadn't called Zee the first week after their talk about Lilly. The
second week he'd driven over to the house on Turner Street on two different occasions, finding the courage to ring the bell, then losing it just
as quickly, as he sat in front of the house. She didn't want to see him.
The connection with Lilly made it too much for her. He could understand that. But at the same time, there were things he needed to say to
her and questions he needed to ask. He knew he wasn't going to let her
go without those things being said.

Tonight Hawk wasn't going to say any of those things. He just
wanted to make sure she was all right. The story of Zylphia had done
something to him, worried him in a way he couldn't explain. True, the
similarities were strange. But Hawk wasn't someone who believed in
ghost stories or even sea lore. No, this was different. He was worried
about her in some exceedingly practical way, yet there was nothing practical he could put his finger on.

There's a disturbance in the Force, he thought as he dialed.

It was Jessina who answered. She was cautious at first, not wanting to reveal too much.

"Is she there?" Hawk asked.

"Not at the moment," Jessina said.

"Can you just tell me if she's all right?" Hawk asked.

Jessina thought about it before answering. She liked Hawk a lot; she hadn't really understood what had gone wrong between them.

"She's fine," Jessina said. "She's at a wedding in Boston."

"Right," he said, remembering the invitation on the lazy Susan in the kitchen. Then he remembered that Zee had told him that the wedding was on her birthday.

Maybe the reason for his agitation was as simple as that. She would be seeing her ex-fiancé at the wedding. Hawk felt jealous just thinking about it, though he knew he had no right to feel that way. Maybe it was the wedding that was making him feel so tense.

Not knowing what else to do, he decided to leave a message. "Just tell her happy birthday."

THE CREW HAD GONE TO dinner at the Black Cow and sat outside on the deck. The sailors were rowdier tonight than usual—he could hear them from around the corner as he approached. They were all good guys. He was going to miss working with them.

When Hawk sat down, they were talking about the application that the *Friendship* had recently filed to officially commission the ship. It was a great idea. If the ship was to be officially commissioned, they could take groups out sailing. And classes full of kids.

Too bad he wouldn't be around for it, Hawk thought. He would have loved to be part of that.

59

ANN AND MICKEY CLOSED down the restaurant. It was surprising how much they had to talk about when they actually began to speak to each other. Mostly they talked about Zee and Maureen. And Mickey talked some about Ireland and about his brother Liam, the one who had died. They talked so much that they lost track of how late it was and were genuinely surprised when the waitress came over to tell them she was going home and would they please pay the check?

Ann excused herself and went to the ladies' room. As she washed her hands, she looked into the mirror for a long time, trying to see something in her face, something that had changed.

Mickey paid the check and caught up with her at the door. They walked past the wharf and toward Ann's shop.

"You want to come in?" she asked.

"Into your store?" he said.

"Yes," she said. "I'll make you some tea."

He looked at her. "What kind of tea?" he asked, thinking about the kind she was famous for.

She smiled at him.

"You sure?" he said.

"I'm not at all sure," she said. "But I'm feeling adventurous tonight."

"Okay," he said, following her into the store, waiting as she locked the door behind them and led him through the beaded curtain to the back room. "But I won't be needing any tea."

"We'll see," she said.

★ *60* ★

ZEE MISSED THE LAST boat home. It was ten-thirty. She'd stayed until the very end, through the traditional first dance, the cutting of the cake, and the tossing of the bouquet.

She walked back from the wharf to the front of the hotel and the taxi stand where Michael stood with his date waiting for the valet. She nodded to him as she passed.

He excused himself and followed.

"Zee?" he said.

She turned around. They had managed to stay away from each other all night. Mattei and Rhonda had seated them at opposite sides of the room, Zee with her colleagues and Michael with his.

"Happy birthday," he said.

"Thanks."

"I was going to ask you to dance," he said. "But I got cold feet."

"It's probably better that you didn't," Zee said, looking toward his date.

Michael shrugged. "You're more daring than I am. I didn't want to come here alone tonight."

She smiled.

"How's Finch?"

"Not very well," she said.

"Mattei told me he took a fall," he said.

"He's in a nursing home," she said.

"I'm sorry," he said.

"Thanks."

"I'm also sorry about the way I ended things," he said.

"It was pretty brutal," she said.

"And cowardly," he added.

"Maybe."

"I'm sorry," he said again.

"Apology accepted."

"I was pushing you into something you clearly weren't ready for," he said.

"I don't think what I was or not ready for was clear in any way," she said. "Least of all to me."

"And is it clear now?"

It was an odd question to ask, particularly with his new date standing only a few yards away. Still, she knew he deserved an answer and that she had never given him one.

"It is," she said.

"And?"

"Good-bye, Michael," she said.

ROY SAT AT THE kitchen table counting his money. Four hundred and fifty dollars. Plus the money he'd taken off the girl. He hadn't counted it yet, really had only taken it to make things look like a robbery. The thought of Hawk behind bars made him laugh out loud. He'd left the hammer with Adam's name on it right next to the body where they would be sure to find it. Roy knew they'd figure things out eventually, but by the time they did, he'd be long gone.

He spun the lazy Susan around and looked at the cake. HAPPY BIRTHDAY ZEE, it said. The letters were crooked and sloping.

Roy was hungry. He wanted to eat the cake, but he needed something more. He'd already drunk almost two bottles of the wine he'd found in the rack. He wasn't fond of wine, but it was all he could find. He peered into the refrigerator for some food, but there were only two very old-looking sandwiches that he wasn't about to touch. Didn't anyone shop for groceries anymore? Roy found some American cheese in the vegetable bin, individually wrapped slices. He checked the date on the side of the package and unwrapped a piece.

He couldn't believe they'd laid him off. He'd been foreman at Cassella Construction for almost twelve years. They'd said it was cutbacks, but you don't fire your foreman for cutbacks. You do that and your whole crew goes to hell, taking long lunches or not showing up to work on time. Stupid fuck didn't know what the hell he was doing.

Besides the paycheck, the worst part was losing the company truck. He'd had to buy an old, beat-up Chevy with his last paycheck, and the damned thing burned oil like a motherfucker. He'd ditch it as soon as he got out of state, if it even made it that far. The thought of the Chevy as a getaway car made him laugh, and he realized he was drunk. He took out the coke he had bought with the last of his money and drew some lines on the table, sucking them up through the gold-cross straw he'd taken from her neck. Christian, right, he thought. So Christian that he'd walked in on her with another guy. He'd been planning to surprise her, bought the drugs she liked with money he should have been saving. Well, he'd surprised her all right, in the end. As soon as the other guy left the house, he'd surprised the hell out of her.

The coke woke him up. Where the fuck was the shrink? He wasn't a guy who liked to wait, and for a minute he thought it wasn't worth it, but then he thought of Lilly and what she had done to her, and his rage flared. How dare she tell Lilly to stay away from him? It was Hawk she should have told her to stay away from, not him. He loved Lilly.

He had loved her on Halloween night when he'd gone to her house to take her with him, though he couldn't make her believe him. He had taken the gun just in case anyone tried to stop him. He hadn't meant to threaten her family. He'd only done that because she'd told him she wouldn't come with him. The cat was something else. He'd always hated that cat. But he wouldn't have hurt her family. She had to know that. He confessed his undying love for her, something he'd never done before for any woman. He even told her he'd kill himself if she didn't come, and still she'd refused him. And then something just snapped in him, and he heard himself threatening to kill them all. He only said it so she would believe him, so she'd know how much he loved her. She had to know he didn't mean it.

In the days that followed, he didn't mean to hit her either, but she just wouldn't stop crying, telling him she wanted to go home. Roy didn't blame Lilly for that. He blamed the shrink.

Roy pounded his fist on the table, and the cocaine dusted upward, then settled back down again in a wide arc, leaving a film on the surface of the old oak table.

He'd been following Hawk for the last week, waiting for the right time. But that time hadn't come. When he'd followed him here, Roy knew he'd hit the jackpot. Hawk just sat in his van, looking at the house. Drove right by Roy when he left, never even seeing him. A minute later her Volvo pulled into the driveway, and Dr. Finch got out and went into the house. Roy couldn't believe his good fortune. He'd been trying to get to her all summer, ever since Lilly died, maybe even before.

Roy counted his money one more time and wondered how long he could make it last. He'd already rifled through all the drawers in this house, upturning some of them, making it look like a real robbery. He was searching for money—he was going to need it. But there was nothing here, just books and a few prescriptions in the medicine cabinet upstairs, which he pocketed. There was no cash and nothing decent that he could pawn.

Roy pulled the plastic wrap off the cake and carefully removed the toothpicks that were holding it away from the frosting. When she got here, he would light the candles. Then they would celebrate her birthday, just the two of them. He'd already checked out the house. He thought the upstairs bedroom, her room, was the perfect place for a birthday party.

He took the rest of the bottle of wine up the stairs. He took the cake, too. He was about to go back for the rest of the cheese when he heard her come in.

★ ★ ★

SHE ENTERED THROUGH THE MAIN door on the Turner Street side. She didn't stop in the kitchen or in the rest of the house. If she had, she would have seen the broken window, the overturned drawers in Finch's study, their contents dumped on the floor.

But she was tired. She knew that Jessina had left a cake for her in the kitchen, but she couldn't face it tonight. The week had been tough, and seeing Michael again had taken its toll. Instead of stopping she walked straight upstairs to the bedroom. She saw the glow from the birthday candles but thought at first that someone had reported the broken streetlight and it had been repaired. Or maybe they had a new light across the street at the House of the Seven Gables.

Roy was quick. He gagged her first, coming up behind her as she stared at the cake. Then he pushed her down on the bed and tied her there. She struggled hard, but he was double her size. When he had her where he wanted, he sang "Happy Birthday," then went over to get them each a piece of cake. He laughed at the thought, because she couldn't share the birthday cake with a gag on. She couldn't even blow out the candles.

He ate the cake slowly, taunting her and seeing the fear in her eyes. He watched her struggle against the ropes he had used to tie her. He'd been careful to use the constrictor knot, one he used for almost everything and one that Hawk would recognize as Roy's signature, if Hawk was the one who found her.

★ *62* ★

John Rafferty, Salem's chief of police, was waiting on the wharf as the *Friendship* tied up.

"I need to talk with you," he said to Hawk. "You want to take a walk with me?"

Hawk seemed surprised. He stopped what he was doing and walked down the ramp with Rafferty.

"Where were you Saturday night?"

"On the ship."

"All night?" Rafferty asked.

"We were at Star Island first. Then we had dinner in Newburyport."

"Can anyone vouch for you?"

"Sure, they can all vouch for me. Except for about ten minutes when I was making a phone call."

"I tried your cell," Rafferty said. "You didn't answer."

"The battery's dead," Hawk said. "What's going on?"

"The Marblehead police are looking for you. They got a call from Weirs Beach."

"About me?" Hawk was surprised. He hadn't been anywhere near Weirs Beach.

"About a hammer with your name and phone number scratched into the handle."

Now Hawk was interested.

Rafferty watched him.

"What did he do?" Hawk asked.

"Who?"

"His name is Roy Brown. He stole my hammer a couple of weeks ago. Said it was payback for one I took of his at my old job site. Which was a total lie."

"Did anyone see him take the hammer?" Rafferty asked.

"Yeah," Hawk said. "A lot of people." He thought about it. "Zee Finch was there."

"Let's go talk with Zee," Rafferty said.

"I was just going to do that," Hawk said. "Let me get my gear."

"Leave your gear," Rafferty said.

Rafferty called the Marblehead police as they walked to his car and told them to pick up Roy at his last known address.

"What did he do?" Hawk asked again as they got into the car.

"He killed a woman at Weirs Beach," Rafferty said.

★ *63* ★

ROY SAT AT THE table in her room watching her struggle. He finished both pieces of cake before he got undressed and came to the bed. He wanted to take his time. He was tired, but he was up for this. He folded his clothes neatly and then ripped the strap of her dress. It fell away, revealing her breast.

A shock like lightning went through him. Maybe it was the coke, maybe it was just knowing what he was going to do and how he was going to do it that made him so excited, but the thrill of it shot through him like electricity, up his arms and all the way down his spine.

Zee stared, terrified, as Roy moved closer.

★ *64* ★

Hawk spotted the broken kitchen window as Rafferty pulled in. His eyes scanned the street for the red truck. He might have felt relief at not seeing it, but he didn't. He was out of the car before Rafferty had a chance to pull over.

Hawk ran into the kitchen, saw the cross and the coke still on the table.

"Upstairs!" he yelled back at Rafferty, taking the stairs two at a time.

Rafferty got to the top of the stairs as Hawk pulled Roy off of Zee. Hawk threw him with such force that Roy immediately went into spasm, his back arching wildly, bending him backward until his head almost touched the ground as the first wave of the strychnine hit him.

There were eight spasms in all before he died. In between he collapsed limply while his body gathered energy for the next spasm.

Rafferty called for both backup and an ambulance. Beyond that, there was nothing anyone could do but watch.

PART 5:

September—October 2008

*The North Star is one of the truest stars in
the sky, its location the most constant. But it
is often not bright enough to be counted on.
One's bearings must be taken from other stars
that sit lower in the sky, stars that rise and set
along the horizon.*

65

MELVILLE PULLED THE OLD lobster boat up to the wharf
on Turner Street and helped Zee aboard, taking her duffel bag
and a few other things she had brought along and stowing them in the
cabin for her.

"Careful," he said, holding her arm as she jumped in. "It's slippery."

At the end of the season, Melville had finally gotten his boat back
into the water after it sat dry-docked in Finch's driveway for as long as
he could remember. There were a few repairs he'd had to make, but all
in all it was in surprisingly good shape.

Bowditch lay in the stern, sunning and snoring. When Zee jumped
aboard, he lifted his head and wagged his tail, though he didn't get up.

Melville had talked her into this. She hadn't wanted to come today.

"You know what I always did when things got to be too much for
me?" he'd said.

"You ran?" she answered, remembering how he had disappeared.

"I went to sea," he said. "Until things cleared up."

"How long did that usually take?" she asked.

"One time it took four months, and the next time it took two years."

"I haven't got two years," she said. "Or four months, for that matter."

"I could argue that point with you," he said. "Instead I'm going to
suggest a week or two."

"Where would we go?" she asked.

"Does it matter?"

"Not really," she said.

"South," he said.

"Okay."

THEY HEADED DOWN TOWARD CAPE Cod, cutting through the canal and out the other side and then on over open ocean to the Vineyard. Melville picked up a mooring from the Edgartown harbormaster, and they stayed on the boat. Though there were plenty of bunks below, Melville would often awaken to find Zee sleeping on the bench in the stern of the boat, as she had done as a child in the years after Maureen died. Bowditch snored loudly, asleep next to her on the deck.

Melville called once a day to see how things were going at home. Sometimes he talked to Ann or Mickey, who were taking shifts visiting Finch, but mostly he spoke with Jessina.

"He's well," she told him. "What I mean to say, in other words, is he's not worse. No falls, no new developments. He's eating a lot of my cookies."

The fact that Jessina considered the cookies a positive sign might have alarmed Melville even a few weeks ago. Now he was grateful that Finch had an appetite and wasn't showing signs of depression at Zee's absence.

"I'm doing what you would want me to do for our girl," he said aloud. Lately he'd been talking to Finch as if he were here, hoping that whatever earthly rules and constraints we come to accept as normal no longer applied in whatever mental realm Finch now inhabited. It was clearly an act of faith, something new for Melville.

There were phone and text messages from Hawk and from Michael. He answered the ones from Mattei.

"How is she?" Mattei asked.

"It's hard to tell," Melville said. "She doesn't want to talk."

"I can understand that," she said.

"I'm worried about her."

Mattei considered. "She's got a good head on her shoulders. She'll talk to you when she's ready."

Melville's sense of time seemed to be shifting. Summer was slipping into fall. September turned to October. The maple leaves were turning yellow and red.

When it was too cold to stay on the boat, Melville rented them adjoining rooms at an inn in town, a place that would allow pets. She took her duffel bag and he took his. Then he went back to the boat to get another load. He handed her some other items she'd brought along, some books, a jacket, and a mahogany case he didn't remember seeing before.

"That's not mine," she said when he put it in her room.

"It's not mine either," he said.

He opened it up and saw the brass sextant.

"That belongs to Hawk," she said. "How did you get it?"

"I don't know. I thought you brought it."

"I didn't," she said.

He handed her a paper, thinking it was a note.

"You read it," she said.

He opened the paper and looked at it curiously. "It's not a note," he said. "It's a chart of the constellations."

"You didn't know about this?" she said to him.

"I swear I didn't," he said. "I can put it in my room if it bothers you."

"No," she said. "Leave it."

He closed the mahogany case and left it on her bureau.

THE NEXT TWO WEEKS WERE bad. The weather was gloomy, and they both missed being on the boat. At night he left the door open between their two rooms so he could wake her from her recurring nightmares. Bowditch planted himself in the doorway between them.

THE THIRD WEEK OF OCTOBER, the weather cleared and Zee went outside. She walked to town in the mornings. At night, if she couldn't sleep, she would sometimes walk to the beach. He worried about it, and told her so.

"What could happen to me that hasn't already happened?" she said.

He could think of a million things. Things he'd had in his mind since she was a kid, a parent's worst nightmares. He offered to walk with her, but she wanted to be alone. Sometimes he would follow her to the beach, where he watched her looking up at the stars as if searching for something.

He was pretty sure she knew he was following her, but she never said so. A few times she looked back in his direction, but she didn't acknowledge his presence, and he kept his distance, often planting himself on a nearby dune and looking up at the sky in an effort to see what it was she was looking at.

One cold night in mid-October, she stood up and brushed the sand from her jeans. Then she walked over to him and sat down.

"Did you find what you were looking for?"

"Some of it," she said. She pointed up at the sky. "There's Gemini," she said. "There's Cassiopeia. Virgo has completely disappeared."

"Where has she gone?" he asked.

"South for the winter, I'd say."

"Smart lady," he said.

They walked back to the room together. Bowditch, who had been pacing and whimpering, met them at the door. When he saw her, he dragged himself over and leaned against her leg. She reached down to pat him. He collapsed at her feet and sighed.

66

Z ee awakened just before dawn. Her nose was cold.
She could hear the sound of the radiators creaking and groan-
ing, coming on for the first time since spring. The smell brought back a
sense memory of the house on Turner Street when she was little. Tears
came to her eyes, but they didn't fall. It wasn't a sad memory, rather one
of security, but she couldn't place it. While Maureen was alive, maybe?
But no, she'd been older than that. She stayed with it for a moment,
hoping to pull it forward, but it dissipated like harbor fog. Still, she
found herself grateful for that image and not the one of Roy she'd been
waking to for the last month and a half, an image she'd had to work
hard to push from her consciousness every morning.

From her bed she watched as the horizon line started to appear. A
few stars were visible, but she couldn't identify which ones. She wondered how many navigators were taking sights at this moment, jotting
down notes, cross-referencing them as backup to the elaborate systems
the ships carried now, ones that weren't ever supposed to fail but sometimes did, leaving the navigator forever more to take sights every dawn
and dusk until he reached his final destination.

She watched the stars along the horizon. Then, remembering something Hawk had told her, she opened the mahogany case and pulled out

the sextant. She looked at the star chart. She didn't have an almanac and wouldn't really have known how to use it if she had, but she'd been looking at Virgo for so long now that she knew its path across the sky. She moved the bureau in front of the window and set the sextant on top of it, pointing it at the spot in the sky where Virgo should be if she were visible. Then she waited.

Spica's rising was not as dramatic as the sunrise a few minutes later. It appeared on the horizon as a sparkling dot, stayed there for just a few minutes, before its light was consumed by the illumination of the rising sun. But for those few minutes, it was brighter in the sky than any other star on the horizon, and Zee knew without a doubt what it was she was seeing and how fortunate she was that today was clear and that she just happened to be awake and just happened to unpack the sextant and take a look. Spica would disappear now until next year, when Virgo would again be visible in the northern night sky, but she had seen it, found it for the first time, and for now that was enough.

She watched for a very long time, until the stars disappeared and the sunlight through the wavy glass of the window grew bright and strong. She wondered what time it was. In the doorway between the rooms, Bowditch snored loudly, the rhythm regular on the intake and the exhale, like an old clock or a slow and steady heart. Beyond him she could see Melville, still asleep, with just his blond hair sticking out above the covers. She stood in the window, letting the sun warm her.

There were already a few people on the street below. "It's Wednesday," she said aloud, surprised that she knew and surprised again that she hadn't seemed to know what day it was for a long time.

She pulled on her jeans and Melville's old sweater that he'd been letting her borrow, then took the back stairs to the street.

When had it turned from summer to fall?

There were pumpkins everywhere. She thought of Salem and Halloween, and she felt a twinge of homesickness. She stood in line at the coffee roasters, bought herself a macchiato, and took it to one of the outside tables. She looked on as the woman opened the bookstore and put a sandwich sign outside.

She watched as people came in to get their coffee, then left again. She wondered about their lives. Mothers walking kids to school, people rushing to work, life as usual, as if nothing alarming were happening, had happened. She wondered about the unfulfilled dreams of the young mother who sat across from her, then realized she hadn't wondered about anyone for a while. She thought about Finch, and a twinge of something went through her. It took a moment for her to realize what the feeling was. Longing, she thought. It was longing.

When she finished her coffee, Zee went back inside and asked if she could use the phone to make a collect call. She dialed Mattei's office number and left a message. Then she bought Melville a pumpkin latte and Bowditch a coffee-flavored scone and walked back to the inn.

Bowditch was in Melville's room.

"Our boy was worried about you," he said. Both Melville and Bowditch looked relieved to see her.

"Sorry," she said. Then, hoping to make it better, "I brought coffee." She handed the latte to Melville and put the scone in Bowditch's bowl.

Bowditch did as much of a dance as a thirteen-year-old basset hound can manage.

She could see Melville watching her. Something had definitely changed.

"How are you doing?" he asked.

"Okay," she said.

They sat sipping their coffee and watching the sunlight play off the water in the harbor. From here you could see Melville's boat, still at the mooring where they'd left it.

"It's almost Halloween," she said.

"That it is," he said.

"Salem is the place to be on Halloween," she said.

"Very true," he said.

They sat silently for a few more minutes.

"Let's go home," she said.

EPILOGUE:

MAY 2009,

MEMORIAL DAY

WEEKEND

*If one knows the latitude of home port and can locate the
North Star and keep it at a constant angle, it is possible
simply to sail down the latitudes to find the way home.*

T HE HOUSE ON BAKER'S Island had just been opened for
the season. Zee had packed away her mother's chenille bedspread
in the old cedar trunk. She would want to see it again one day, but not
now. Today she was having a party on the island.

She'd spent most of the year in Boston, back working again, but
only part-time. On weekends she'd been volunteering on Yellow Dog
Island, counseling some of the women and children who had been so
badly abused. She was good at it. She'd just received an offer of full-
time employment from May Whitney, who ran the shelter out there,
and she was seriously considering it.

Zee made herself a list of things she'd forgotten to pick up for the party and headed into town, leaving the door open for any guests who arrived early and a welcoming note on the table.

She and Melville were going to see Finch. There was a Memorial Day party at the nursing home today, an event that was doubling as a going-away party for Finch, who would be coming home next week. He didn't know her name anymore. Didn't know Melville either. He thought that Melville was someone who worked at the nursing home, someone who came to read to him every afternoon, almost always from Hawthorne, though lately he'd begun to favor Emerson and the other Transcendentalists, who seemed more cheerful to Finch than Hawthorne and seemed to make him happier.

When Melville suggested to them both, as he was visiting one afternoon, that Finch could probably go home if Zee would hire Melville as a full-time caregiver, Finch jumped at the chance. He wasn't sure where home was, not anymore, but he was certain it was somewhere he'd like to go, and especially if his caregiver was coming along. He remembered something about a big house with a gabled roof and a cat named Dusty. And he seemed to remember a rooster as well.

That he clearly loved his new caregiver was apparent to anyone who watched him light up in Melville's presence. The staff at the nursing home had been happily surprised by Finch's improvement under Melville's care. Though they knew it wasn't the best practical decision, there had been no one who disagreed with the decision to take him home as long as he would be cared for by such an attentive home health aide.

The plan was for Melville to move back into the house, pretending he was a hired caregiver, with Jessina as daytime help so that Melville could keep his job, which he did only at Zee's insistence.

Finch hadn't been able to use his walker again; he was in a wheelchair permanently now. Zee knew only too well what a toll the role of full-time caregiver could take, and she wasn't about to let Melville do it alone. That was the deal, take it or leave it, she said. "You're as much a father to me as Finch is," she said. "I need you to be around."

Melville took the deal.

Today they said prayers for the veterans of World War II, many of whom were residents of the nursing home, and for Vietnam and Gulf War vets as well as for the soldiers now fighting in Iraq and Afghanistan. They sang "God Bless America" and drank ginger ale and ate cake that was decorated with red, white, and blue sugar. Zee drank the ginger ale but passed on the cake.

When Finch fell asleep, they wheeled him back to his room and helped him into bed. They kissed his forehead and walked out together. He opened his eyes and smiled at Melville.

Zee picked up a few last things for the party. Since Mickey's boat was too small for more than two people, Melville had loaned him the lobster boat. This way Mickey could transport most of the guests out to Zee's party on Baker's Island. Zee and Melville planned to take the water shuttle out to the island when Finch's event was over.

They waited for the water shuttle for almost an hour. When she couldn't stand it any longer, Zee turned to Melville. "Come on," she said.

She drove back to Derby Wharf and parked in Mickey's space. Then she went to the slip where the dory was kept.

"Please tell me we're not taking the dory," Melville said.

"Why not?" Zee said. She'd taken the dory many times.

"Because it's a heap of junk, to say nothing of Mickey's elaborate security system." Melville pointed to the wires and ropes and padlocks.

"Piece of cake," Zee said.

She had the boat unlocked in less than a minute. Then she shorted the wires to start the engine.

"Get in," she said to Melville.

"I don't believe this," he said. "You're back to stealing boats." But he was smiling.

★ ★ ★

MELVILLE WATCHED ZEE AT THE controls, guiding the dory out over calm waters. About two-thirds of the way out, the motor coughed and died.

She choked the engine, tried several times to restart it, but it was dead.

"Damn," he said. "He never did take decent care of this thing."

He was looking around for someone to flag down when Zee started to row.

"You don't need to do that," he said.

"It's okay," she said, liking the idea. "It'll be fun."

He started to protest, but she was so into the idea that he just let it go. "Let me know when you want me to spell you," he said.

It took her more than an hour and a half, but she never asked him to take over. Melville put his head back and closed his eyes, enjoying the sun.

When they finally got to the wharf, Mickey and Ann were waiting.

"You stole my goddamned boat!" Mickey said. "I didn't tell you that you could take my boat."

"Why were you rowing?" Ann asked.

"Your goddamned boat's engine broke down," Melville said.

"No way," Mickey said, climbing in to see for himself.

"The water taxi didn't show up," Zee said to Ann. "So we borrowed Mickey's dory."

Ann nodded, amused.

"Where is he?" Zee asked, looking up at the house.

"He's working the grill," Ann said. "We ate already, but he saw the boat coming and started cooking again for you two."

Zee and Melville walked up the ramp toward the island. At the top of the wharf, she turned right toward the cottage. Melville stood looking down the cliffs and into the ocean below.

"Are you coming?" she asked.

"You go ahead," he said. "I'll catch up in a bit."

Zee nodded and hurried her pace. When she got close to the house, she laughed. Hawk was at the grill, wearing a chef's apron and the old straw hat with a big hole in the top where the mice had stolen the silk flower.

"Nice look," she said.

Mattei and Rhonda stood next to Hawk. Jessina and Danny sat at the picnic table, trying to figure out how to make the coffee.

Hawk grinned. "Come here," he said, kissing her for a long time. "I've got the burgers going, but we need either you or Melville to make cowboy coffee."

He'd already brought out the pot and the egg. She took it and handed it to Danny. "Throw it into the pot as hard as you can," she said.

"You're kidding me, right?" the boy said.

"Nope." Zee held the pot while Danny wound up and threw.

"I'd say you've got a future Red Sox pitcher there," Mattei said to Jessina.

Zee stirred the egg and some water into a paste as Jessina watched carefully. Then she filled the pot with water and put it on the grill.

"ARE YOU GOING TO PLAY mechanic all day, or are you going to join the party?" Ann asked, starting back up the ramp.

"I'm coming, I'm coming," Mickey said, grumbling something about Zee and Melville wrecking the engine. He took the oars out of the oarlocks, where Zee had left them, and placed them back where they belonged.

"Look at this," he said to Ann, pointing to the oarlocks, which were worn down almost to bare wood.

"Look at what?" Ann said.

"She wore out my thole pins," he said.

"Your what?"

Mickey gestured to the wooden pins next to the oars. "These are antiques. She may be my niece, but she's going to have to pay for them."

"What are you complaining about now?"

Mickey pointed at the wooden dowels that served as oarlocks. Ann thought of the story, "The Once," about Maureen and the story of Zylphia and her young sailor. It wasn't the Miseries—she could see the Miseries just slightly to the northwest—but it was an island. "I'll be damned," she said, looking up at the house, where she could see Zee and Hawk standing arm in arm.

"She's going to have to either pay me or replace them," Mickey said again.

Still grumbling, he caught up with Ann, and they walked to the cottage.

MELVILLE HIKED TO THE LIGHTHOUSE at the far end of the island. He stood on the cliff, looking out toward Manchester, and thought about the day so long ago when another boat had broken down, and how he had stopped here and what that day had meant. Then he opened the bag he'd brought along and took out the book of Yeats's poetry. He opened to the title page and to the dedication. He saw Maureen's suicide note still tucked into the pages of the book, and just as Finch had thrown the book that day, he threw it now.

It seemed as if he'd been sorry forever, but he found he couldn't be sorry any longer. As he watched the book fall into the blue ocean below, disappearing into the foam, he said the only kind of prayer he knew now, not one asking forgiveness, not anymore, but a prayer of gratitude: for Maureen, and Finch, and Zee, and Jessina, and Danny, for Mattei for helping Zee through, and Rhonda, Ann, Bowditch, and even Mickey, and for this new man Hawk who had come into their lives, and for Michael who had left them. He said a prayer of gratitude for the days he had left with Finch, and one asking for the wisdom he knew he would need as those days went on. Then he said a final prayer of thanks for all that had happened in their strange and surprising lives. And for all that was yet to come.

ACKNOWLEDGMENTS

First to Gary, for so many things, and for not letting go of the dream even when I thought it impossible. For research and for the phrases: "How can I help?" and "Whatever makes you happy."

To Rebecca Oliver, for making it all possible and for her time in Austin and endless reading and rereading. To Laurie Chittenden, who is not only a great editor but who understands and respects the artistic process. To the whole team at William Morrow who have helped every step of the way, and in particular to: Liate Stehlik, Ben Bruton, Tavia Kowalchuk, Andrea Molitor, and Mac Mackie.

To Hilary Emerson Lay at Spirit of '76 who read two early drafts and to Emily Bradford who read and read. To Sarah Anne Ditkoff for all of her help.

To the city of Salem, my chosen home. To Kate Fox and Stacia Cooper at Destination Salem. To all my friends at the House of the Seven Gables and in particular to Anita Blackaby and Amy Waywell, thank you for letting me write in your beautiful gardens. To the National Parks Service and the *Friendship*: Colleen Bruce, Jeremy Bumagin, John Newman, Martin J. Fucio, and Ryan McMahon. To Jean Marie Procious and Elaine von Bruns at the Salem Athenaeum. To Teri Kalgren and the staff at Artemesia Botanicals. To Laurie Cabot. To William Hanger at Winter Island. To Beth Simpson and everyone at Cornerstone Books. To HAWC. And finally to Dusty the cat and his family.

To the great town of Marblehead, the town where I and seven generations of my family grew up. To the Marblehead harbormaster, Charlie Dalferro. To Fraffie Welch. To Cathy Kobialka at Waterside Cemetery. To the Marblehead Garden Center and the Spirit of '76 Bookstore.

To my writing group, the Warren Street Writers: Jacqueline Franklin and Ginni Spencer, who cheered me on through the first book and remained patient and dedicated through the second.

To Alexandra Seros for her friendship and for great notes and for making that first magic phone call.

To Fravenny Pol for her help with all things D.R.

To my early readers: Jeannine Zwoboda, who read and commented twice. Mark W. Barry and Mark J. Barry, who turned reading into a father/son competition. To Mandee Barry, Whitney Barry, and Sherry Zwoboda, who read on the raft at the summer house when they could have been doing other things. To Cayla Thompson. To my wonderful friend Susan Marchand, who read section by section. To Ken Harris and Debra Glabeau for expertise on pirates and Melville and for making us laugh far too much.

To the Greater Boston medical and psychiatric communities for patiently answering every question (there were so many). Thanks to Dr. Peter Bevins. And thanks to Lucy Zahray, "The Poison Lady," for her lecture at Crime Bake and for her very interesting set of tapes.

To Hawthorne and Melville. And, of course, to Yeats.

And a bow and a prayer to my friends who didn't live long enough to realize the happily-ever-after: Tommy, Chuckie, Robbie, Shirley, and Jay.

AUTHOR'S DISCLAIMER

Liberties taken. The weather. The houses. With the exception of the House of the Seven Gables, not one of the homes in this book is real. They are for the most part imaginary places set where real houses now stand. Don't go looking for them, they do not exist. The same is true for the homes on Baker's Island, which is a private island on which many generations of families have summered quietly. The only way we can visit Baker's is by having a friend (or family member) who owns one of the cottages. I hope to get a second invitation one day. I have taken liberties of time with the factory in Lynn where Maureen worked when she met Finch. The factory was a real one, Hoague Sprague, and was owned in partnership by my great grandfather, Morton Hoague. It closed in the late 1950s, so Maureen could not have worked there.

I read many books in my research for *The Map of True Places*. For a suggested reading list as well as book club questions, please visit mapoftrueplaces.com.